William Salter Price

My Third Campaign in East Africa

A Story of Missionary Life in Troublous Times

William Salter Price

My Third Campaign in East Africa

A Story of Missionary Life in Troublous Times

ISBN/EAN: 9783743387225

Manufactured in Europe, USA, Canada, Australia, Japa

Cover: Foto ©Raphael Reischuk / pixelio.de

Manufactured and distributed by brebook publishing software (www.brebook.com)

William Salter Price

My Third Campaign in East Africa

MY THIRD CAMPAIGN.

MY THIRD CAMPAIGN.

FRERE TOWN AS SEEN FROM THE HARBOUR.

MY THIRD CAMPAIGN

IN

EAST AFRICA

A STORY OF MISSIONARY LIFE IN TROUBLOUS TIMES

BY

W. SALTER PRICE, F.R.G.S.

FOUNDER OF FRERE TOWN, AND LATE DIRECTOR OF THE CHURCH
MISSIONARY SOCIETY'S MISSIONS IN EASTERN EQUATORIAL
AFRICA

" A great door and effectual is opened unto me, and
there are many adversaries."—1 Cor. xvi. 9

SECOND EDITION
POPULAR ISSUE

LONDON
CHAS. J. THYNNE
"WYCLIFFE HOUSE," 6, GREAT QUEEN STREET
LINCOLN'S INN FIELDS, W.C.
1898

PREFACE.

"My *Third* Campaign" implies a *First* and a *Second*. My first was from 1874 to 1876, when I was specially charged by the Committee of the Church Missionary Society to establish a Settlement on the coast for the reception of freed slaves. The result was FRERE TOWN, now a flourishing colony, and the base of all the Society's operations in Eastern Equatorial Africa. It was so named in honour of the late revered Sir H. Bartle-Frere, to whom my own connexion with the work in East Africa was largely due, and who was himself one of the truest friends of the sorely oppressed races of that unhappy country. My Second Campaign was in 1881 and 1882, when I was sent out as "Special Commissioner" to investigate and report on certain matters and make some re-arrangements which time and circumstances rendered necessary.

It has been intensely interesting to me on each successive visit to witness the development of a work in the inception of which I had had some share.

East Africa has now become a great centre of attraction to the civilized world. It is no longer the "Lost," though, alas! for more reasons than one, it may still be called the "*Dark* Continent".

Twenty years ago – it is not too much to say—the

average educated Englishman knew nothing and cared nothing about East Africa. To all save a few experts it was a *terra incognita;* and many places, the names of which are now as familiar to us as household words, and which figure conspicuously on our maps, had then never been heard of. Verily, the lost has been found! a nation has been born in a day! We are living in a wonderful age, and, to my mind, one of the greatest wonders of the age in which we live is the Providential opening up of this hitherto hidden-away portion of the habitable world to the blessed influences of Gospel light and civilization.

The indications of this are very striking to one who, like myself, has been an eye-witness of the changes that have taken place, and is in a position, from personal observation, to contrast the present with the past.

Fourteen years ago an English steamer entering Mombasa harbour was a rare sight, which put us all in a flutter of excitement—*now* it is a matter of daily occurrence, and sometimes as many as six or eight fine vessels are seen at one time riding at anchor on its quiet waters.

Then we were cut off from the rest of the world, and seldom saw a white face except those of our own party. *Now* there is a continuous inflow of Europeans of many nationalities—chiefly English—who penetrate the country in every direction. There are men of science who are delighted to find here "pastures new" in which to carry on their loved pursuits—men of trade and commerce, who are keenly on the look-out for fresh markets for their manufactures—mighty hunters whose ambition is to kill elephants, buffaloes, and other big game which abound in some parts of the interior; and to these must be added not a few adventurers who, with no definite object in view—and often with little or no money in their pockets—come out simply to take their chance, concluding, not altogether unreasonably, that in a country just bursting forth into new life something may " turn up " to their advantage.

But the most notable event of the last two years has doubtless been the assumption by the IMPERIAL BRITISH EAST AFRICAN COMPANY of the protectorate—or rather rule—over almost unlimited territory, peopled by many different races. Mombasa—their chosen base of operations—must soon become the most important town and trading port on the coast, as it will also be the starting point of the new route to the Lake region. Under the auspices of this enterprising Company we may confidently expect to see, within a few years, wondrous improvement in the condition both of the country and people.

The new era has already commenced—good roads, one of the first conditions of civilized life, are being constructed—the electric cable connects Mombasa, *viâ* Zanzibar, with Europe—the first sod has been turned of a Railway which, when completed, will bring Uganda, now a dreadful journey of four or five months, within two or three days of Mombasa!—the natural resources of the country are being developed—and, best of all, a death-blow has been given to the accursed traffic in human beings, with all its abominations.

It is a grand undertaking, and every true friend of

Africa will bid " God speed " the I. B. E. African Company, and pray that, ever true to the motto inscribed on its flag, it may carry the blessings of " Light and Liberty " into all places under its sway—from the Indian ocean to the shores of the Victoria and the banks of the Nile.

And how have these wonderful changes come about ? Mainly, if not entirely, as far as human agency is concerned, they are traceable to the quiet, persevering, self-denying labours of three men—three Missionaries ! David Livingstone—Lewis Krapf—and John Rebmann.

These were the men who opened the eyes of the world to the frightful havoc caused by the man-stealer, and to the cold-blooded cruelties connected with his abominable traffic—it was they who lifted the veil, and revealed to us, not a desolate uninhabitable region of interminable deserts and pestilential swamps, but a country of lofty mountains, and mighty rivers, and fruitful plains, and inland seas—a country possessing every variety of climate, and in which untold treasures are stored up, awaiting only enterprise and skill to bring them to light, and turn them to account, for the benefit of the world—moreover, and more important than all, a country peopled by many strange tribes of the great human family, who, in spite of their isolation, and centuries of cruel oppression, instead of degenerating into abject barbarism, as might have been expected, have retained many noble qualities, which, when developed under happier conditions than they have hitherto enjoyed, will entitle them to an honourable place in the brotherhood of the civilized world.

It is too soon to write the history of "the Dark Continent regenerated," but, when the time comes, it must not be forgotten that it was the three men whose names I have mentioned who turned the key, and unlocked the door into this new world, and made possible the marvellous events we are witnessing to-day. All honour to the memory of these brave men, and not less to that of their devoted wives, each of whom found a grave in her adopted country.

They were all animated—possessed—by one desire —to win Africa for Christ. Said Krapf in conversation with a Native Chief: "We are not traders, but Preachers of God's Word, who desire to spread the Gospel throughout the whole of Africa". Noble Ambition! Wonderful Faith! On another occasion, when keenly feeling the loss of his wife, and enfeebled by attacks of fever, he writes:—" Meanwhile, I often prayed fervently for the preservation of my life in Africa, at least until one soul should be saved; for I was certain that if once a single stone of the spiritual temple were laid in any country, the Lord would bless the work, and continue the structure, by the conversion of those who were now sitting in darkness and the shadow of death, and to whom our missionary labours were but as the dawn of the day-star from on High".

We want to go back to these days—45 years ago— in order to realize " what God hath wrought," and how in one of the darkest of the dark places of the earth " He has opened the door of Faith unto the Gentiles ".

Many Books have, of late years, been published on East Africa. They are for the most part the work of enterprising travellers, and treat largely of the natural features of the Country ; of the manners and customs of its many races ; of its fauna and flora ; of the difficulties of travel, and so on. I need scarcely say that these matters, deeply interesting as they are, are not in my line. Though constantly on the move from Station to Station, I had no opportunity of making long journeys into the interior, and consequently had no sensational or blood-curdling stories to relate of encounters with wild beasts or savage men. My simple object in the following pages has been to give an honest account of Missionary work, carried on at a very critical time and under peculiarly trying circumstances, in the hope that, with God's blessing, it may arouse some to a deeper interest in the welfare of Africa ; and enable others—not a few I gladly believe —who are already longing and praying for the spread of Christ's Kingdom in that Country, to realize more fully what God has done with us ; what a grand opportunity He is presenting to us ; and what a solemn call there is to all true-hearted servants of the Lord, to be up and doing, taking their part—whether here or there—in earnest loving endeavour to reclaim the millions of Africa from their long night of sorrow, and to bring to them " the light of the glorious Gospel of Christ ".

Here and there the reader will meet with some record of little intrinsic importance, and only so far relevant to my object, as being a link in the chain of our daily life. My wish has been to furnish, as far as possible, a connected story of the stirring events through which we passed, in so far as they affected us and our work.

In a personal narrative such as this, I have had to rely mainly on my Journals. I have also made free use of my own letters; because these, as a rule, give a more vivid picture of the state of things—of the life we lived—than could be gathered from any other source.

Where Native words or expressions occur, I have allowed them to remain, only marking them by inverted commas, and of these I have given a Glossary at the end of the Book. This will, I hope, be helpful not only to my readers, but to those also who read other books of African travel, as well as Missionary Periodicals, where such words too often occur without any explanation.

WINGFIELD VICARAGE, *October*, 1890.

CONTENTS.

CHAPTER VI.

CHAPTER VII.

CHAPTER VIII.

CHAPTER IX.

CHAPTER X.

CHAPTER

CHAPTER XII.

CHAPTER XIII.

MY THIRD CAMPAIGN IN EAST AFRICA.

CHAPTER I.

HOW IT CAME ABOUT.—NOTES BY THE WAY.

AFTER my return from my second visit to East Africa in 1882, I was often asked, "When are you going back?" to which inquiry I could only say "I really cannot tell; humanly speaking there is no prospect of my going out again, but I consider myself on the reserve list, and if the call comes I am ready". The fact is, the East African Mission had such a hold upon me, had so become a part of my very self, that I never could divest myself of the thought that sooner or later the time would come for me to take down my staff and sally forth again to take active part in a work in which my soul delighted. It came at last, as such things often do come, when least expected. One morning, in December, 1887, I received a letter from one of the secretaries at Salisbury Square giving me a somewhat gloomy account of the state of things in the East African Mission. Bishop Parker was away some hundreds of miles in the interior, and could not be back for several months—the two senior missionaries had broken down

in health, and had been invalided home—and so the
Mission, at a very critical juncture, owing to a variety
of circumstances, was left practically without a head.
The letter ended with the simple question, "Can you
help us?" Having read and re-read the letter, I rather
startled my wife by saying, "Here's a call for me to go
out again to East Africa". For what could I say to
that question? How could I possibly help in such an
emergency? I could think of only one way; so after
carefully thinking the matter over I replied :—" .   .   .
You ask 'Can you help us?' Well, I know only one
man who possesses some qualifications for the work
and who would at the same time be really willing to
respond to a distinct call to undertake the task. He
is just turned 62 years of age, has, humanly speaking,
several years of good active work in him, and his heart
has long been in East Africa. The man I refer to seeks
no distinctions, is just willing to be a servant of servants.
so he may be in any way an instrument in forwarding
the Lord's cause in Africa. I need say no more—I
dare not—for it is with the Holy Spirit to separate
whom He will."

On January 20th, 1888, I heard again from the Committee. Whilst expressing themselves deeply grateful
for my offer of help, they felt a difficulty in availing
themselves of it. As founder of Frere Town, and
quondam director of the Mission, I had had a free hand,
which under the altered circumstances of the Mission,
they could not now offer me. The Bishop was now
director of the Mission, and he would be back in a few
months. What was now wanted was a man to " hold

the Fort," and keep things going till his return, and they thought that this was scarcely such a dignified position as they could ask me to accept! If I had entertained any feelings of this kind, there would have been an end of the matter; but as nothing was further from my thoughts, I replied as follows :—

"I quite see your difficulty and appreciate it. If I *did* go out under present circumstances, my *rôle* would no doubt be very different from what it was on former occasions; I quite understand that. I should not indeed dream of such a thing, if I did not feel that I could loyally carry on the work, on the lines laid down. This would be all the easier to me, inasmuch as, to the best of my knowledge, there have been no violent new departures; and it has been a source of no little gratification to me to find, that the changes, such as they are, are for the most part only such as might naturally be expected to result from the development of plans and suggestions which I submitted to the Committee some five years ago; even the Shimba Mission which I feared had fallen through, is, I am glad to see, being taken up in earnest.

"I have said perhaps all that I ought to say on the subject. I wish, however, the Committee clearly to understand that my offer of service is not made lightly, or without counting the cost. I have got beyond the age of romance, but my interest in the East African Mission will last to my dying day, and if I can be of any use in connexion with it, you know where to find me; and, better still, He who rules all things according to His will, and for the good of His own cause, as well as of each of his servants, knows also. There I desire to leave it."

It will enable friends of the C. M. S. to see how difficult questions are dealt with at Salisbury Square, if I give here an extract from the letter I received in reply: " Many thanks for your very kind note of the 23rd. We warmly appreciate its spirit. We considered the whole question carefully yesterday in Group sub-Committee, and agreed to recommend the Committee to avail themselves of your kindly expressed readiness to go for a limited time to take charge of the Mission. This recommendation will not be before the Committee till their next meeting on February 7th.

" There are certain considerations which need attention at once, however, in view of your possibly undertaking the responsibility. The next steamer sails three weeks to-morrow—the next after that at a further interval of four weeks. From the last mail's letter I fear that Mr. Binns, who is nobly holding on, may have to leave at any moment, and that probably the sooner he is relieved the better and the kinder it will be. Then, when the Bishop will be down again, who can tell? Suppose Mr. Stanley's arrival at Wadelai, and consequent events render Uganda open, the Bishop will probably wish to see the place, and possibly to confer priest's orders on Gordon. It seems almost impossible to forecast the future in this matter. We should not propose to you any arrangement which would involve the resigning of your Living ; the length of the visit you could pay would depend therefore on the Bishop (of Norwich). We could probably supply your place by a missionary at home for as long as the Bishop would spare you. These questions of the *date* of departure—the limit of your stay—and the Bishop's leave should perhaps be at once considered, though no definite arrangement can be made till after February 7th. . . . "

I don't think I was over-anxious as to the result ; but a fortnight's suspense in a matter of such vital importance seemed rather a long time. I only requested that the earliest intimation might be given me of the Committee's decision. Accordingly on the Evening of Feb. 7, I received a Telegram : "The Com. thankfully accept your offer". I was at the time at St. Leonard's, giving addresses in connection with a Missionary Loan Exhibition. I had, of course, to cut short my engagement, and hasten to Town by the earliest train next day. That Telegram had changed the whole current of my life ! A fortnight hence I must be on my way to East Africa, and between now and then how much has to be done ! I have to be examined and passed by the Medical Board—I must obtain *first*, " permission " of the Archbishop of Canterbury ; and *then*, " leave of absence " from the Bishop of Norwich—I have to make provision for my Parish—to hand it over to my *locum tenens*—to pack up—to say a parting word to my people —and a hundred matters to arrange before I can slip cable and be off.

Happily everything worked smoothly, difficulties were one after another overcome, and on the 21st I was at Salisbury Square by the invitation of the Committee, to have my farewell interview with them. I expected a very quiet affair, as I saw on the Agenda Paper—" Take leave of the Rev. W. Salter Price, proceeding to East Africa "—one little item in a long list of important matters, which were to occupy the attention of the Committee.   I was accompanied by my wife and we were little prepared for what awaited us.   There seemed to be an unusually good attendance of members —the large room was nearly full ; and on our entry, they all stood up and received us with acclamation.   I was overwhelmed at such an unexpected reception.   We were seated together in front of the chair, which was occupied by Mr. Morris ; and the " Instructions " were read by Rev. R. Lang.   They were couched in the kindest and most flattering terms, and read in a clear voice and not without evident emotion.   Next came dear good Bishop Perry with a few words, full of love and encouragement, and then the Chairman.   They all expressed the gratitude of the Committee for my readiness, on such short notice, to go again to the front, at a critical conjuncture in the Mission.   We were then most appropriately and touchingly commended to God in prayer by Mr. Whiting and Mr. Sharpe ; after which came a cordial hand-shaking all round, with many expressions of regard and goodwill on the part of individual members of Committee.

Was it all a dream?   No, it was real enough ; though a few weeks ago it would have seemed almost impossible. Here am I at 62, going forth once more to my old post at Frere Town, owing to the breakdown in health of the only two missionaries, whose experience might have enabled them to take the direction of affairs in the absence of the Bishop. It was one of those crises in one's life which can only rarely occur; and the solemn event of to-day with all the circumstances connected with it, and the whole scene in the Committee Room, left an impression on my mind, which cannot soon be effaced. My own words were altogether inadequate to the occasion. How could it be otherwise? I was so taken by surprise; so completely overwhelmed by the kindness and sympathy so warmly expressed by all. Of course it was highly gratifying to receive such assurances of the Committee's confidence, and to have once more the great honour and privilege of being called to active service in the Mission field, but more than all I felt humbled to the dust, when I thought how utterly unworthy I was of it all. I can only hope that God will, of His great mercy, pardon my unworthiness, and that He will enable me by His grace faithfully and wisely to fulfil the task entrusted to me.

The next day was spent quietly at Canterbury, and with the following morning (February 23rd) came the inevitable partings—the last prayer! the last loving word! the last look! These are things which can only be understood by those who have gone through them. My dear wife was to have gone with me to Dover, but it was out of the question: I left her in bed, suffering from a severe cold. It seemed cruel, parting so; but perhaps after all it was best. It was a bitterly cold morning, with a high wind—snow and sleet—and we had a rough passage from Dover to Calais. Most of my fellow-passengers were in a bad way, and the saloon was soon converted into an hospital; so being left to myself, I had time to meditate on the important step I had taken, and to try to realize my new position. After all, I go forth not knowing the things that shall befall me there ; except that trials and difficulties of one kind or another I shall be sure to meet with. Feeling however that I am in the path of duty, I have no misgivings :

> " I do not ask to see
> The distant scene : one step enough for me ".

A journey by land and sea of some 6000 miles, must needs furnish many incidents worth telling, but it would not be germane to my present object to tell them. I will only say that by dint of rapid travelling through France and Italy, I passed, in two days, out of the depth of winter, into genial spring. We left Brindisi early on Monday morning, Feb. 27, in the P. and O.'s fine steamer, the " Pekin," and had splendid weather all the way. The only disagreeable affair that we met with was a sand-storm which overtook us in the Suez Canal. It came on quite suddenly ; there was first a dry hot wind which brought up clouds of fine sand from the desert, turning day into night, and which not only made us all very miserable by getting into eyes, nose and mouth, but also delayed us several hours on our journey. As a pleasant set-off to this, that same night Col. Euan Smith, who was on his way to Zanzibar as H. M. Consul-General, came on board at Ismailia, and I had his company for the rest of the voyage, and opportunities which I greatly valued, of conversing with him on many topics of interest to both of us. At Aden we had to exchange the " Pekin " with its splendid accommodation, for the B. I. S. N. Co.'s boat, the " Baghdad ". It *was* a change indeed ; but perhaps as great improvements in this service are inevitable before long, the less said about it the better. It must be recorded however that the Captain did his best to get speed out of the old ship, and so brought us into Port two or three days before we were expected ! We anchored in Mombasa harbour at 9 a.m. on March 14, having made the trip from Aden in *seven* days, and from Dover in *twenty !*

It was, for obvious reasons, most desirable to open up communications with Bishop Parker, with as little delay as possible, and with this object, I addressed to him the following letter, to be forwarded on arrival.

March 9th, 1888,
" On board the ' Baghdad '.

" My Dear Bishop Parker,—

"You will be surprised when you get this, to learn that I am again at Frere Town. As, with this, you will be sure to receive letters from the Committee giving you all information as to the reasons for my coming, I need not enter into that.

" I saw Shaw in England, and learnt from him all I could as to the present condition of things in the Mission. There has been trouble at Teita. According to the Report shown to me at home, Wray and Morris were attacked by a lot of hostile natives. By the accidental discharge of a gun, one of the assailants was shot, and the Missionaries had to pay a considerable sum by way of compensation. Whatever may be the merits of the case, it seems clear that the relations between our Brethren and some of the natives are very strained.

The Committee contemplated the possible necessity of withdrawing the Mission, at least for a season. In a few days I hope to know more of the exact state of affairs, and will write you fully by the first opportunity. Meanwhile you may depend upon my doing my best to carry on the Mission on the lines laid down.

"We are just rounding Cape Guardafui, and hope to be at Mombasa five days hence, so I shall keep this open, in order to report my arrival and give you the latest items of intelligence. I shall do all I can to persuade Binns, if he has not already left, to stay on, at least till your return, should the state of his health admit of it.

"Col. and Mrs. Euan Smith are my fellow-passengers. He asks me to give their very kind regards and to say, that he received your letter of Sept. 5, 1887, at Aden, but not Mackay's Journals, which you speak of as forwarded same time.

"I shall be very anxious to get a letter from you, and hope to hear that God has opened you a way out of your difficulties, and made your enemies to be at peace with you. We shall have you in constant remembrance in our prayers, as we trust you also will us. I hope you will write to me freely and fully as to any matters you wish attended to. Please forget that I have ever been Director of the Mission; think of me simply as an old Missionary, who is only too glad and thankful to be permitted to render a little more service in the Master's cause, and that in a part of the vineyard endeared to him by many associations of the past.

"With kindest Christian regards to yourself, Ashe,

Walker, the brave Mackay, and all the Brethren, and earnestly praying you may be preserved, and abundantly prospered in all your plans and labours.

"I remain,

"Yours very faithfully,

"W. SALTER PRICE."

It painfully brings home to us the uncertainties of life in East Africa to note that the day this letter was despatched (March 14) was the very day on which Bishop Parker wrote his letter to the Committee, giving a touching account of the last days and death of dear Blackburn, and that, just a fortnight later, the good Bishop himself after a few hours illness entered into his rest. Of course neither this letter, nor one I wrote to him a month later ever came to his hand, and he passed away without any knowledge of my temporary appointment.

CHAPTER II.

ARRIVAL AT FRERE TOWN.—GETTING INTO HARNESS.

FEW things in this world are more inspiriting than
getting into port. This morning (March 14) soon after
dawn, the welcome news spread through the ship that
land was in sight, and that in a few hours we should
be at our anchorage. It set everything in commotion—
the crew were "about ship" laying out cables, opening
hatches, getting up cargo, and doing a hundred things
which have to be done on such occasions ; whilst the
passengers in every variety of dress and undress, and
with binoculars in hand, were crowding the deck, and
straining their eyes westward to take in the view. At
first there was nothing to be seen except the long
stretch of coast, which, in the mist and glare of early
morning, was not very distinct ; but presently, as we
drew nearer to the land, and the sun rose higher in the
heavens, the peculiar features of the coast came, one
after another, into sight, and we make out clearly where
we are. First of all, the " Corona," a cluster of three
conical hills, about five miles inland—the true landmark
of Mombasa ; then about twenty miles to the south, the
Shimba heights, a range of hills of singular conforma-
tion, running parallel with the coast ; then the Sultan's
red flag flying over the old Portuguese Fort of Mombasa ; then the Fort itself, and the Town, which, sink

of corruption though it be, looks picturesque enough in the distance ; and lastly, right in front of us—most gladsome sight of all to me—the Mission Settlement of Frere Town. The view as you approach it from the sea is singularly beautiful ; a pleasurable surprise to those who look on it for the first time. For one thing it occupies a splendid site—the best, I believe, on the whole East African coast. In the foreground lies a long stretch of shelving sandy beach, in the form of a crescent, behind which, rising abruptly some seventy feet stands Frere Town, presenting the appearance of a huge natural amphitheatre. Conspicuous to the view are " topes " of giant Mangoe trees, with their massive dark foliage ;—and hundreds of graceful Palms, towering high above them, with their waving crowns and clusters of fruit—numbers of " Gold-mohurs," which I imported from Bombay twelve years ago, now grown into stately trees, and covered with gorgeous flowers ;—and many other specimens of tree and bush which delight in the moist heat of this tropical region ; whilst, here and there, the houses and other Mission buildings, peeping out from amongst all this exuberance of verdure, give a touch of life to the scene, and add finish to a picture, which, although exquisitely charming to the eye, is not easy to describe in words.

How different the feelings with which I look on it to-day, from those with which I saw it last, nearly six years ago : all the difference between putting off one's armour, and buckling it on ! Then I had come out entrusted with a special commission, connected with matters seriously affecting the welfare of the Mission, and requir-

ing very delicate handling. I had been only six months
in the country—the limit of leave kindly granted to me
by my Bishop—but they were six months crowded with
stirring events, and varied experiences. On the one
hand I was twice laid low, almost at death's door, with
African fever— I had had to encounter the secret
hostility and base treachery of the Wali of Mombasa :
an Arab of the Arabs, who, whilst professing " eternal
friendship " for me, was plotting against me and the
Mission—and I had narrowly escaped falling into the
hands of the rebel outlaw, Mbaruk. In regard to these
and many other difficult matters, I had good reason to
acknowledge " the good hand of God upon me ". And
on the other hand, I had been enabled to accomplish
to the satisfaction of the Committee, the difficult task
entrusted to me, and to give the Mission a fresh start.
I had succeeded, after much tedious negotiation, in
obtaining a footing for a Mission Station on the Shimba
heights, which may become a sanatorium, and an evangelizing centre for the hitherto neglected Wadigo people :
a step urgently pressed upon me by my dear old friend
Dr. Krapf, the father of the East African Mission—I had
been permitted once more to see " my children," and to
have much happy intercourse with them, and with my
Missionary brethren, some of whom I came to know
now for the first time—and lastly, I had enjoyed bound-
less hospitality and kindness at the hands of Col. Miles,
H.M. acting Consul-General, Capt. Luxmore, commanding H.M.S. " London," Dr. Robb, and many
others, which can never be forgotten. No wonder it
was with very mixed feelings I turned my back on

East Africa, and my face homeward on that occasion! What those feelings were may be gathered from the following extract from my journal written at the time: "And is it so? Can it be that I have seen Frere Town for the last time? that my work there is finished? that I shall no more go in and out among those whom I have known and loved so long? and that henceforth I have nothing to do with plans for carrying out the grand idea of extending a chain of Christian Missions across the Dark Continent? It is hard to realize all this; but the future is in His hands, who knows what is best for His own glory—what is best for the Mission—and what is best for His poor unworthy servant; and there I will try to leave it, and learn to say, 'Thy will be done'."

My soul is stirred with other thoughts to-day. God in His good providence has opened the way for my return to the scene of former labours; and I am full of hope that He has a work for me to do, and that He will give me strength and grace to do it. I am not weighted, as on a former occasion, with any distasteful and troublesome business, to make my visit unwelcome to anyone; I may find some causes for disappointment, but at the same time I shall no doubt see many signs of progress to refresh and cheer me. I am looking forward to a happy meeting with many dear old friends, to whom my coming will be a glad surprise; and to add zest to my undertaking, events and changes are impending, which cannot fail seriously to affect, for better or worse, the welfare of the East African Mission. It is a most critical time!

Whilst these thoughts were rapidly passing through my mind, the "Baghdad" had threaded her way through the narrow channel—the gun had been fired announcing the arrival of H. M. mails—and we were quietly anchored in the beautiful harbour of Mombasa, just under the old Mission House, and about a mile from Frere Town. Not a soul at Frere Town knew of my coming, so when the news was carried on shore, the people could scarcely believe it. It was as if I had suddenly dropped out of the clouds. As soon as they *did* realize it, they flocked to the beach, and as their old "Papa" stepped out of his boat a chorus of "yambos" greeted him—their joy knew no bounds—they were beside themselves. I was completely taken by storm—all being eager to shake hands, or to get some token of recognition ; at last one sturdy fellow pushed through the crowd and stooping down took me on his broad back, and carried me off in triumph up the steep path to the Mission bungalow. Mr. Ehlers, a German gentleman and fellow-passenger, was with me, and never having seen an African welcome before, was greatly amused and delighted.

Apart from this warm reception my experiences of that first day and night were the opposite of charming. In the first place, as I was unexpected, I found nothing ready. The Bishop's house, in which I was located, had been shut up, and left to rats and bats. It was in a filthy condition, and the stench was poisonous. To sleep inside was out of the question, so I got an old bed rigged up in the verandah. Then as I had come out on such short notice, and for only a few months, I had not brought with me either provisions or cooking pots ; I had been assured that I should find everything of this kind in the Mission—as a matter of fact I found next to nothing. I am quite sure the Brethren would gladly have supplied my wants, but they very naturally supposed that I was independent of their help, and the result was that I was wholly destitute and rather miserable. It had been a very trying day ; what with the excitement of the morning, and two or three trips in an open boat, under a blazing sun, to the steamer and back, I was completely knocked up. I went early to bed, but not to sleep. About 11 p.m. I was startled by a sudden glare as of the noonday sun. At first it seemed as if the house was on fire ; it was satisfactory to find it was nothing more than a flash of the " Mariner's " electric light.

Next morning, in spite of a sleepless night, I was up with the sun, feeling considerably refreshed. Everything had put on a brighter look. I had had a fit of lonesomeness, not much to be wondered at under the circumstances, of which I now felt more than half ashamed. I was thankful it had passed away, and that I was able to take a more reasonable view of my position and prospects. I had not come to East Africa with any idea of a pleasure trip. I had counted the cost, and knew pretty well, what I had to expect ; and it would be silly now, to mope and fret and get home-sick, because I don't find myself in " a bed of roses ". No, I have a work before me, which will demand all my thoughts and time and energies, and my wisest course is, looking to the

Strong One for strength, to get into harness and buckle to without delay.

The " Baghdad " left to-day for Zanzibar carrying with her my good friends and fellow-voyagers. A parting present was brought to me from Mrs. Euan Smith, in the shape of a hamper packed with all sorts of good things, which not only set me up in housekeeping requisites, but landed me in the lap of luxury. I was thankful for the things—they were most timely and acceptable—but a hundred times more, I valued the kind "good Samaritan" spirit, which prompted the sending of them.

A small party of Englishmen from one of the ships paid a visit to Frere Town this afternoon. Meeting one of our young men, one of these gentlemen asked sneeringly " Are *you* a Christian ? " The youth replied, " Are *you*, Sir ? " " No," he answered, " I'm a devil." It is very sad, but God's work has to be carried on in spite of such stumbling blocks.

March 17. Having arranged with Captain Arbuthnot to pay a visit to Rabai, we set out in the " Mariner's " launch at 7 a.m.—an hour too late ! The distance is 15 miles, of which the first 10 are by water up a creek, and the remainder by land—rather an up-hill walk. We had not gone far before we missed our way, and got entangled among mangrove trees, and only just escaped having to spend the day in the dismal swamp. As it was we lost a good hour, and did not reach the "banderini" till nine, and then, for want of a small boat, we had difficulty in landing. By this time the sun was out in full force and we had a fatiguing walk to Rabai, which we did not reach till nearly 11 o'clock. A number of men, some 300 or 400, were awaiting us at the "banderini," and from there to the Mission Station I was greeted with the wildest demonstrations of welcome—guns went off on every side—the men danced, leapt, shouted and sang, and every now and then came the *refrain* in which all seemed to join, "Bwana wetu amekuja," (our Master is come). Captain Arbuthnot, who had never seen anything of the kind before, was greatly interested; but the heat and excitement were almost too much for us. In the large open square between the Church and the Mission house, all the people were assembled—between one and two thousand, in their Sunday best—for the final welcome. There were a good many old faces, which I recognised at once, and of course a good many new ones; but old or new, they were animated by one intent; and here, it was evident, the grand reception was to take place; but by this time we were both completely done up, and had to beat a hasty retreat to the shelter of the Mission house, and get a cold douche on our heads. I was really sorry to balk the good people of their design of doing me honour, and showing their regard, so I asked Mr. Jones (Native Pastor) to apologize and explain, promising to pay them another visit shortly and make amends for my seeming rudeness.

What a contrast between Rabai when I first visited it thirteen years ago and as it is now! Then, I found there dear old Rebmann in his blindness, and, at the most, half a dozen native Christians. Now, there is a well laid out town with a population of nearly 2000 people.

Some of them are freed slaves, but the greater number are pure Wa-nika, from the surrounding country. They are all either Christians, or such as have "joined the Book," *i.e.* have given up their heathen customs, and are under regular instruction in the Christian Faith. The community is entirely self-supporting, and for the most part they maintain themselves by the cultivation of the land.

The new Church, opened nearly two years ago, is a conspicuous object. It is a plain but substantial building, with accommodation for about 800 people, and is generally, both at week-day and Sunday services, well filled. I hope the kind friends who, in response to my appeal some twelve years ago, exerted themselves to collect the funds, as well as those who contributed, will take note that, notwithstanding many difficulties and disappointments, the good work has been completed, and a Christian Temple now crowns the heights of Rabai " whither the tribes go up" to offer prayers and praises to the living God, and to listen to His life-giving word. In so short a time, and tired as I was, it was not possible to enquire much into details of the work, which at present is entirely carried on by the Native Pastor, my old friend, William Jones. The thought which more than any other forces itself on one's mind is "the harvest," how great! "the labourers," how few! Here is an almost unlimited field, a wide and open door. A superintendent Missionary, three or four devoted English ladies, and a good Schoolmaster, would be a barely sufficient staff to grapple with the work ready to hand; whilst at present all is on the shoulders of the

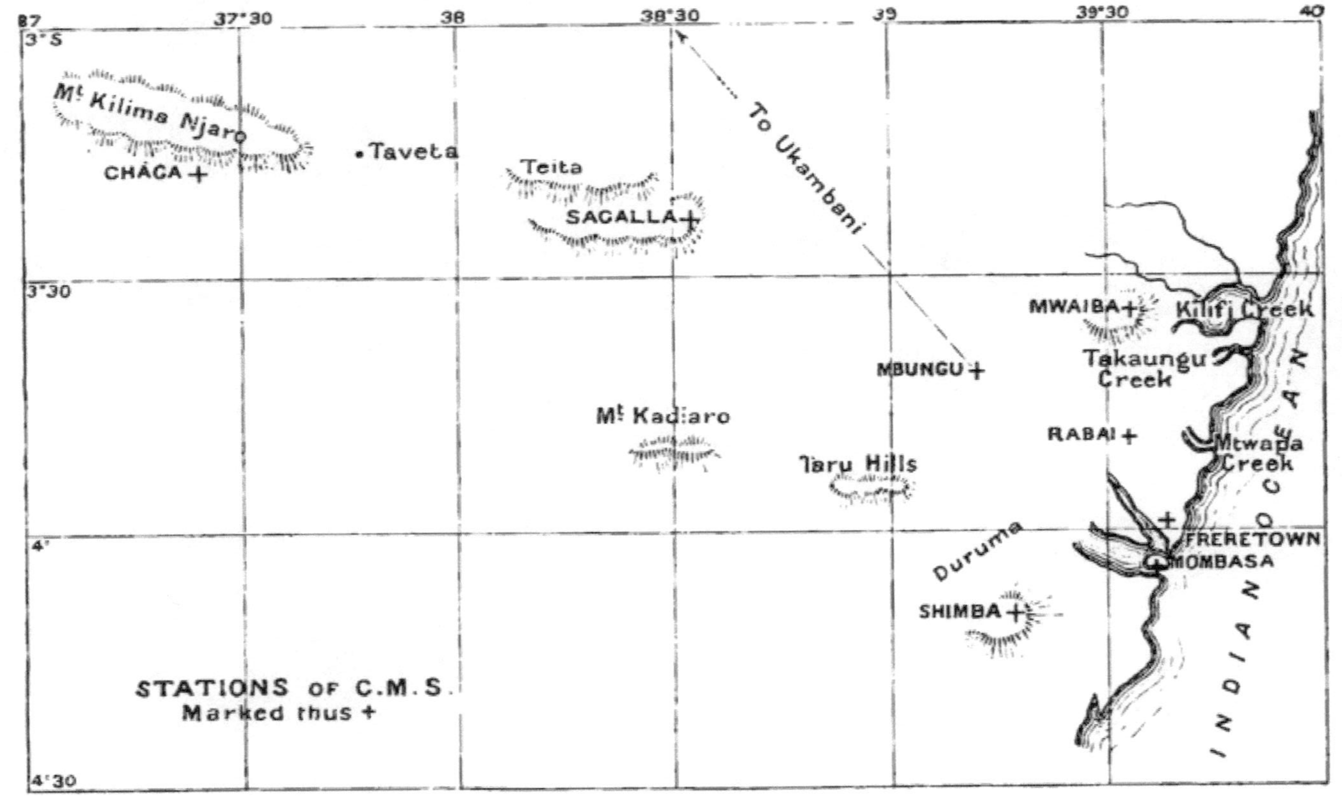

Mt Kilima Njaro
CHAGA
Taveta
Teita
SAGALLA
To Ukambani
MWAIBA
Kilifi Creek
Takaungu Creek
MBUNGU
Mt Kadiaro
RABAI
Mtwapa Creek
Taru Hills
Duruma
FRERETOWN
MOMBASA
SHIMBA
INDIAN OCEAN
STATIONS of C.M.S.
Marked thus +

Native Pastor. We did not get to the "banderini" till after sun-set, but as we had the blessing of a bright moon and were steered by a native Christian pilot thoroughly acquainted with the ins and outs of the creek, we reached Frere Town without any mishap about 8 p.m.

Lord's Day, March 18. At Capt. Arbuthnot's request, conducted Divine Service on board the "Mariner". It was a great treat to me and the English brethren—a quiet English service on board a British man-of-war, with a congregation composed entirely of our own countrymen. Mr. Smith read prayers, the Captain the lessons, and I preached from "What does it profit, etc." It goes without saying that the sailors were very orderly and well-behaved: more than that they were most attentive, and joined heartily in the service.

In the afternoon I attended the Native Service. The temporary Church was well filled with a strangely mixed congregation. The majority, adults and children, are freed slaves of many African tribes, presenting a great variety of feature. They are all, as at Rabai, either baptized Christians, or catechumens under instruction. In their case we see how God "has made the wrath of men to praise Him," and "turned the curse into a blessing". Humanly speaking, had they not fallen into the clutches of the cruel man-stealer, they would never have come under the sound of the Gospel.

It was with very grateful feelings I looked round on that congregation, as I called to mind what they were when they first came to us. They were as ignorant as the brutes that perish, with not a glimmering of the great God who made them, or of the blessed Saviour who came into the world to save them. Much patient labour has been bestowed on them, and it has not been in vain; certainly a wonderful change for the better has come over them, and it has been brought about in a wonderful way. This is true of all, whilst of not a few it may be said they are living decent Christian lives, and giving us every reason to hope that "they have not received the grace of God in vain". To-day I see them "clothed and in their right minds," sitting in God's house listening with attention to the eloquent and earnest utterances of a young man, one of themselves, who came to me a poor slave boy some twelve years ago. Then, too, the behaviour of these poor people strikes one much after what, alas! we are so accustomed to see in so many churches at home. None of them think of taking their seats without first going on their knees. Whilst waiting for Service to begin, you might almost hear a pin drop, no talking or noise; and the Service itself is heart-stirring, all, old and young, joining in the singing and responses. I could not help thinking if some of our young men in Suffolk could witness what I have witnessed to-day, they would feel just a little ashamed of themselves.

There are many people, I know, who do not believe in African Christians. I am not surprised at that; for undoubtedly the races of Africa with whom we have come into contact have been so miserably low, intellectually and morally, in the scale of humanity, apparently so dull and unimpressionable, that to persons who take no account of the regenerating power of the Holy Spirit it must seem a thing incredible that any of them should become intelligent Christians. That they can and do become such, is beyond all question to those who, from personal observation, have the opportunity of forming an opinion; that in some cases indeed their conversion is intensely real is evidenced by the heroic conduct of the Uganda Martyrs. The only account that can be given of it is, that " with God all things are possible," and that it often pleases Him " to hide these things from the wise and prudent, and to reveal them unto babes ".

It would be unreasonable to expect from them— from such at least as come to us as adults—a high standard of spiritual attainments. They have never studied the Evidences, and never heard of Paley and Butler, or other great champions of the Faith. They have simply heard the Gospel: " line upon line "—their hearts have been opened to receive it—they have found in it something which meets their souls' needs—and is it nothing? Nay, is it a small thing if they can say, as many of them can, " whereas I was blind, now I see "?

Thursday, March 22. A tornado came on in the night. It was a deluge, accompanied with terrific lightning and thunder; the wind nearly blew me out of bed. It is just a month to-day since I left home, and I have been here a week. I am beginning to settle down and form plans for future work. Preliminary to this I have been carefully reading up the Minutes of the Finance Committee, correspondence, etc., so as to make myself thoroughly acquainted with the actual state of affairs in the Mission. I have to remember that my work now is not to *organize*, but to carry things on upon lines already laid down. The accompanying chart, kindly furnished me by my friend and colleague, the Rev. W. E. Taylor, will show at a glance the Stations for the supervision of which I am responsible. They have all, with the exception of Rabai, come into existence during the last ten or twelve years; and each Station is a centre for evangelistic work among a distinct tribe, having its own language, customs and superstitions.

I have now made the acquaintance of all my fellow-labourers. They are all, with one exception, new comers, and have of course much to learn, and something to unlearn; but as far as I have seen of them, they are men and women of the right " stuff," whose hearts are in their work, and I have no doubt we shall get on happily together. To avoid repetition I may here say that we have a noon-day Prayer Meeting every day, and a weekly Bible-reading on every Monday evening, at which all the workers—European and Native—come together.

Miss Fitch reminds me that it is just a year to-day, since she and I met at Brighton. How little we thought then, we should ever meet in East Africa! All my old Nasik * friends are, of course, greatly delighted to see me amongst them once more, and they make very particular enquiries after " Mama " and the " Baba lôk". One of them, Cephas, has been cooking for me, and when I told him that my eldest son, whom he only

* Africans trained by me in India.

remembered as a child, was married and had a daughter, he almost went into fits. Poor Cephas now and then gets a fit of another kind, otherwise he is not at all a bad cook, and is very willing and attentive to me.

Monday, March 26. Paid a visit to the Wali of Mombasa, Salim bin Halfan, and found him very civil and obliging; rather more gushing than I like, but then he is an Arab and I a cold-blooded Englishman! I spoke to him about the "watoro" said to be in our Rabai Station, and told him plainly that we had no wish to harbour any of these people, and that if he heard any complaints, and would let me know, I would do everything in my power to satisfy the just claims of the Arab and Suaheli owners. He replied that there was no need for hurry in the matter, adding, "Wise men act slowly".

After arranging with him some other matters of business he with much satisfaction showed me a travelling clock, which our Society, through Mr. Shaw, had presented him with; and a nicely bound Arabic Bible, which was carefully kept in a silk case. In answer to my question, he said he was reading it, and I urged him to do so the more as it was God's "Word of Life".

Have had several men and women employed on the ceiling of the Bishop's house; removing accumulated filth of bats and other vermin—a horrible business! I hope the Bishop will be grateful to me for making the place decently habitable. "Missionaries live in palaces," say some. Alas! it is quite true and this is a good specimen.

Wednesday, March 28. A caravan went on to-day

to Teita and Chaga, which gave me my first opportunity of communicating with our Brethren at these two outlying Stations. How isolated they are! and what a claim they have on our sympathy and prayers! Messrs. Morris and Wray, at Teita, are surrounded by hostile natives, and in daily and hourly jeopardy; whilst Br. Fitch has bravely held on single-handed, and is still holding on, in the face of opposition and difficulty, waiting for the opportunity of proclaiming the "glad tidings" to the poor dark heathen of Chaga.

Saturday, March 31. Mr. England, schoolmaster of Frere Town, has paid a visit to Rabai, and reports very unfavourably of the state of the school there. And no wonder, when we consider how badly off we are for Teachers. We ought by this time to have had a goodly staff of well-trained young men to draw upon, for this and other work. That we have not is much to be regretted.

Arranged with Taylor for him to go to Shimba for a week or so on Monday next. He can ill be spared from here, but I have no one else to send, and the Station has been already too long without a head.

We have had a Prayer-Meeting every night this week, reading Dr. Vaughan's *Lessons from the Cross and Passion.* They have been well attended by members of the Mission, and I trust not without profit.

News reaches us of the death of Said Bargash, and of the appointment of his brother Said Khalifa as his successor. I hope there may be no disturbance, but things are in a very unsettled state, and it is impossible to forecast what may take place any day.

Easter Day, April 1. Holy Communion at 7 a.m. The whole Service was in Kisuaheli, and I took the Priest's part. As I had very carefully prepared, I felt quite at home, and got through without a hitch. The communicants were seven English, and about fifty Africans, and among the latter I was very thankful to see the faces of some—male and female—of my old Nasik children. The Morning Service was at 11 a.m., when the little church was well filled. Taylor preached, and how I envied him his fluency in the language!

Dr. Ardagh who is living in Mombasa has been suffering the last few days from fever, diarrhœa, etc., and feels it necessary to have a change for a week or two. This is just a case which shows how desirable it is to have a decently comfortable place on the Shimba hills: a house of refuge for the sick and weary. I have no doubt it would often be the means of saving precious lives; and so, even in a pecuniary point of view, a great gain to the Society. At present there is no proper accommodation there for an invalid.

Monday, April 2. Two weddings came off this morning. The bridegrooms are two steady young fellows, who have learned trades, and saved money enough to build their own cottages and start housekeeping; and the brides are young women who have been brought up in the school, and of whom Miss Fitch gives a good account. A wedding here is not the tame affair it so often is in England—every man, woman and child is interested in it. On coming out of Church, each couple walked arm in arm through the Settlement, calling in at the houses of the Missionaries and others, accompanied by a crowd of their friends in the highest state of excitement. The climax was reached by one of the bridegrooms carrying an umbrella very gingerly over his spouse, to shield her from the sun!

This evening we had a Magic Lantern exhibition which attracted a room full of people, but just as I was going to begin, it was discovered that there was no chimney to the lantern. What was to be done? Happily Reid, who is a capital fellow at a pinch, set to work and in ten minutes produced a *pro tem.* chimney which answered every purpose. The slides were from my own Photos taken in E. Africa, and as one after another they were thrown on the screen and recognised, there were shouts of applause ; but when Ishmael, the Native Pastor, and his family—and Khamis bin Saad, a leading Arab of Mombasa, stood out, almost life size, on the canvas, the spectators were almost frantic with delight. It was fearfully hot work, but our poor people, old and young, enjoyed it immensely.

Thursday, April 5. The monsoon is just setting in. We have had heavy rain to-day, which has produced a sudden fall in the temperature, and brought out flannel coats. We are all feeling chilly and more or less "out of sorts". Sent Ishmael to the Wali to complain of thieves at the Mombasa Mission house. He sent a polite message back, and promised to place an "askari" on the look-out.

This evening the Chaga Mail comes in, bringing letters from Fitch, and from Morris at Teita. The latter reports himself far from well—weak and prostrate, and kept prisoner in the house by the hostility of the natives. Arranged with Dr. Ardagh to send up medicines to-morrow, and a party of men to bring him down here for a change.

Friday, April 6. Another stormy night—torrents of rain with strong gusts of wind. I had had my bed brought in from the verandah, but as doors and windows were wide open, I had been almost better outside. I dared not get up, so covered myself well up in my rug. Rain has continued throughout the day, and the tanks are all full, which is a blessing. Had a " Shauri " with Adamji and the " Dhobi," both of whom need to be sharply looked after. Hard at work with letters for the English Mail, and for the Brethren up-country.

Sunday, April 8. After afternoon Service set out with Ishmael on a house to house visitation. The Settlement has grown considerably since my last visit in 1882. More freed slaves have been received, and many who were then boys and girls have become men and women, and are married and settled. The cottages of these latter are, as a rule, better built, and more trimly kept than the others. The freed slaves are of several different tribes, and each tribe has its own quarter of the Colony. This, I venture to think, is a mistake, as it will tend to foster a clannish—if not a caste-feeling—amongst them, which is very undesirable. and may lead some day to unpleasant consequences, Each cottage has its own bit of land or allotment, on which mahindi, muhogo, and a few other vegetables are grown for home use ; and I noticed that the contrast between the good and the poor farmers was just as apparent here as it is in Suffolk. This is just the busy time for getting in seed. Very pleasant it was to go among them once more, to say a kind word here and there, and to hear and see for myself what God hath wrought for these poor people.

Monday, April 9. At our weekly Meeting to-night commenced the Pastoral Epistles. After a short introduction the subject is left open for remarks or discussion. As this was the first occasion, only two or three joined in, but once they get accustomed to it, the Brethren will feel more freedom, and these Monday evening gatherings will become more interesting and profitable. They afford a good opportunity for all the Mission workers— Native and European—to come together on equal terms for Prayer and Scripture Reading.

Tuesday, April 10. Hard at work finishing off letters for Home, etc. This is my wedding day, and how little I dreamt a few months ago of spending it here ! All blessings on the dear wife, wherever she may be— my loving companion " for better, for worse," these 39 years. They have not been uneventful years. We have had more perhaps than fall to the lot of most, of the " ups and downs "—of the joys and sorrows of life ; yet looking back on all God's dealings with us, I feel sure we shall unite to-day in a " Te Deum "— " surely goodness and mercy have followed us "—nay, may we not in humble confidence adopt the future and say " *shall* follow us all the days of our life ".

Having been here now four weeks, and made myself pretty well acquainted with the situation, I take this, the earliest opportunity, of writing to Bishop Parker, and of giving him full information as to what is going on in this part of his Diocese. The following letter is invested with a melancholy interest from the circumstance that a fortnight before it was sent off the Bishop had " finished his course," and found his grave on the southern shore of the Victoria Nyanza. As it was written at the time and on the spot, it will give my readers a better idea of the condition of things in the Mission than I could otherwise furnish.

To Bishop Parker, Usambiro.

Frere Town, *April* 10, 1888.

" My Dear Bishop,—

"You will have received my short letter of March 15, announcing my arrival, and giving you one or two items of intelligence. I have now been here a month, and in spite of some things changed, everything seems so natural to me, I can scarcely realize that it is nearly six years since I was here last. The greatest change is in the *personnel* of the Mission. Dear Taylor is the only one of my old fellow-workers ; all the rest are new hands. What I have seen of them I like much. They all appear to be earnest, conscientious workers, though of course they have a good deal to learn. You will be glad to hear we are a united party.

" My coming was a great surprise to all my old African friends, and you can better imagine, than I describe, how they gave expression to their feelings. No doubt it was a great pleasure to me to see many of them again ; and I earnestly pray God to bless my visit to them.

" It is just a little difficult for me to write to you as freely as I could wish, because till I hear from you we are scarcely in touch. However, I have done my best to post myself up in all that has taken place in the Mission during the last three or four months, and have carefully read your letters and directions to Binns, Shaw, etc.

" 1. I am thankful to be able to report, on the whole, a clean bill of health as regards the English staff. Dr. Ardagh is the only exception ; he gets fever every few days, not severe attacks, but sufficient to lay him aside from work. I hope a change to Rabai or Shimba for a week or so may set him up ; though I doubt if he is to be reckoned upon for any long stay in this climate. The last three weeks have been very trying to us all, but the S.-E. Monsoon will soon be here.

" 2. Taylor will give you full information as to his Translation work.   He appears to be at a stand just now, waiting to hear from the Universities' Mission. As no one else could be spared, I have asked him to go to Shimba for a week or two, to look up the Native brethren there, and to report on the work.

" 2. I have had R. Keating (Native Catechist) down from Mwaiba. He has spent a few days with his wife and children—had a little pleasant intercourse with his Christian brethren—given us an account of his Mission—and to-day he returns, refreshed and encouraged, to his work among the Wa-Giriama. It is three months since he was last here, which, on every account, is too long an interval. He is not, as you know, a man of much power ; but as far as one can gather, he is doing his best to let his little light shine in that dark place and we may hope God will bless him.

" 4. Mr. and Mrs. Burness are expected by the next Mail, and I am having the iron house, in which Miss Fitch did live, made ready for them, at anyrate as a temporary residence till we can hear from you as to their destination. It is the only place. Can the Committee at home have any idea how very limited the house accommodation is at Frere Town? As regards Mr. B.'s location and employment, much of course will depend on his 'Instructions' which I have not yet received. All we know at present is, that he is by trade a Builder, in which capacity he has done good service as an Agent of the Society in West Africa; but that he now comes out as a *spiritual* agent—a full lay Missionary— and that his desire is to be employed in spiritual work.

" 5. For want of an accountant Mr. Smith is, I am sorry to say, still tied down to the desk and cannot possibly find time to apply himself to the language, or to prepare for Priest's Orders. I doubt if our friends at Home are at all aware what a big concern this Office has become, and what an amount of attention to details—of book-keeping and correspondence, there is in connexion with it. It is the central agency for the whole of the E. Equatorial African Mission. If it were in London, there would be at the head of it a well qualified man of business, with book-keeping at his finger ends; and one or two smart clerks under him as assistants; and how this growing work is to be carried on efficiently as regards the various Missions, and without loss to the

Society, unless some such provision is made here, I cannot imagine. This is a matter for very serious consideration.

" 6. R. when not away in the ' H. W.' * is very fully and usefully employed on shore as Overseer of Public Works. He is in many ways a capital man for this post, and with a little wise and kindly supervision, will do good work.

" 7. England, as you know, is looking for his furlough at the close of the year. He is pretty well again just now, but he has a very washed-out look, and I am sure it would be good policy to relieve him as early as possible ; and then a duplicate of E. is sorely needed for Rabai, where three or four hundred children are running about wild. What you want, I venture to think, is, a good elementary school at Rabai in which all the children could be disciplined and taught the three Rs, and from which you could from time to time draft off the brighter and more promising ones, for higher training at Frere Town. It is a fine field for a good English schoolmaster—plenty of raw material to work upon. Other helpers are also needed for Rabai, especially two or three ladies, for work among the women and girls. It almost makes one weep to go there and see fields so ready to the harvest, and alas ! no reapers. May the Lord quickly raise them up, and send them forth. The one thing which strikes me more than anything else on revisiting the Mission after an interval of six years is—in the face of increased and ever increasing opportunities—how fearfully it is under-manned !

* " Henry Wright."

"8. I note what you say about the Steam-launch, and entirely agree with you. I have been saying the same thing for I can't tell how many years. What the Mission really wants is a fairly commodious Steam-launch or pinnace, which at the outside, fitted with everything necessary, would not cost more than four hundred pounds—a boat in short that would bring all the Coast stations within easy reach of head-quarters. A vessel costing a thousand pounds or so would be too big for this work, and practically useless.

"9. Miss F. naturally felt rather lonely when Miss H. left, but she is so thoroughly in her work that she finds no time for moping. The presence of such an earnest devoted lady is of itself a blessing to the Mission.

"10. For the present I am occupying part of your house ; I had almost to fight my way in, against a host of bats and rats. The former were in greater force, and we have killed them off by scores—as Taylor says, ' we have had a regular *battue*'. I shall do my best to exterminate them, and one or two other nuisances, so that when you return, you shall find the ' Palace '—save the mark—none the worse for my occupancy.

"11. I have a cheery letter from Fitch. Paul at his request is going every Sunday to Mandara, to read to him the Bible. The situation at Chaga has decidedly improved, and it would seem as if dear Fitch was about to realize the promise, ' In due time ye shall reap if ye faint not '.

"12. I hear from Morris that he has been quite laid up for the last six weeks, and is getting worse. The Dr. finds it difficult to prescribe for him in the dark, so I am sending up a party of men to bring him down to the coast. He can then be properly treated, and we shall be able to get information as to the actual state of things in the Teita Mission.

" 13. I shall keep my letter open to the last moment to add in P.S. anything of importance that may turn up by the Mail. I will now only say that we are anxiously looking for news of yourself and of your movements. We shall be glad of particulars, to stimulate us in our prayers, and that we may enter as much as possible into your position. As regards myself I begin to feel that time is slipping away. I should be very sorry to return without meeting you ; but unless anything serious occurs to prevent it, I must be homeward bound by the beginning of August, as I have only six months' leave from my Bishop. I should like very much to pay at least a flying visit to our Brethren in Teita and Chaga, but that can only be by your being here about the middle of June. Be it as God shall order. With kindest regards to yourself and all the dear Brethren with you,

" I remain, etc., etc."

CHAPTER III.

VISIT ZANZIBAR.—HEAVY TIDINGS.

Wednesday, April 11. The " Baghdad " came in
at 7 a.m. and took off our English mail ; what a relief!
Mr. Wise from Msalala was a passenger, on his way
home.   He came over to breakfast, but I could get little
out of him about the Lake brethren or the work.   A
young man also came bringing me a letter from Archdeacon Hodgson.   He seems to be an adventurer, who
has found his way from England to Zanzibar without a
penny in his pocket.   He has some of the manners of a
gentleman, but there is a mystery about him—he worked
his way from the Cape as butcher's mate.   His idea is,
to get to Hooper at Nasa, and he seems to think it
would be an easy matter for me to fit out a caravan to
convey him up-country.   I can of course do nothing for
him, but return him to Zanzibar.   Going into our little
Chapel he was shocked to find we had no candles on
" the Altar " ; and gave it as his opinion that it would
be better to conduct Divine Service in Latin, rather than
in Kisuaheli !   He would certainly be " a fish out of
water here " ; but he may possibly find some temporary employment in the Universities' Mission.   I met
Major Macdonald late Acting Consul Gen. on board,
and heard from him an interesting account of his visit
to Rabai.

H. M. S. S. " Mariner " came in this afternoon and Capt. Arbuthnot kindly offers me a passage to Zanzibar which for several reasons I most gladly accept.

Thursday, April 12. Washing day! I have put it off as long as I could, and am come to my last shirt. Jaeger's clothing is delightful wear, and I have nothing else, but it has this serious drawback, that you must— here at least—do your own washing. I have tried my hand at many things, but this is altogether a new line; we must however go on learning. I followed the directions as nearly as I could, with the help of my cook, and the result so far promises to be a success. My verandah is quite gay with a long line of shirts, drawers, etc., hung up to dry. It is rather humiliating that, after all, I must call in the aid of a professional " Dhobi" to do the ironing ; but this requires tools and skill, neither of which I possess. A heavy downpour of rain for several hours to-day, which has set all the houses leaking. Capt. A. came over in the evening and we had a long pleasant ramble over the Settlement.

Saturday, April 14. Started last night in the " Mariner " and sighted Pemba about 8 a.m. but owing to a strong adverse current did not get to our anchorage till noon. We entered, through the Uvingie channel, a large harbour, bounded on one side by the island of Pemba proper, the hills of which are profusely covered with vegetation—forests of Palms, Mangoes, Acacias, etc., with here and there a grassy glade, having a lawn-like appearance ; whilst on the other side, are a series of small rocky islands—once probably joined together and stretching for several miles parallel with the island, but

now broken here and there by narrow gaps, through which vessels can generally find a good deep passage.

In the afternoon Capt. Arbuthnot and I paid a visit, in the steam launch, to a small town on the island, about 5 miles distant, named Weti. Had rather a rough passage, and did not get there till about 5·15. A walk of a mile through plantations of cloves, the strong odour of which impregnated the air, and was very oppressive, brought us to the centre of the town, where a market was in full swing, and a motley, noisy crowd assembled. There were different kinds of fish, with tobacco, supari, paraffin oil, and a lot of other things, exposed for sale; and besides, a sort of general store, kept by an enterprising Hindi " Whiteley ". The people generally had a surly look, and sometimes did not even return our " Yambo "; we were not sorry to get away before night.

Three boats of the " Mariner," which are employed cruising about, and watching the gaps for slave dhows, come in for provisions; they take a fifteen days' supply. These men must have a dreadfully hard time of it at this season.

Sunday, April 15. Had a quiet night, but this morning was squally, with now and then heavy rain. Held Divine Service in the men's quarters, on the lower deck. We were closely packed, and it was very hot and stuffy, but we had a hearty Service. Most, if not all the men have had the benefit of early training, and can read and write. Some of them are intelligent fellows, and all, more or less, the better for discipline.

We left anchorage at 1 p.m. and threaded our way very gingerly through the little islands and reefs, to the

open sea, making for Chag-chag, the fine open bay of
which we entered at 5 p.m.   After letting go the anchor,
the Capt. discovered that the place was not safe, so all
had to be gone over again—soundings were taken, and
after much anxious examination of charts we finally
settled down in a snug berth with plenty of water.
And this is Pemba! a very gem of the ocean; an earthly
Paradise as to appearance, " Where every prospect
pleases, and only man is vile"; yet alas! possessing a
deadly climate, and chiefly notorious as the charnel
house of the slave, many thousands of whom—kidnapped
in the interior of the continent—are annually imported,
to drag out a wretched existence, and die an early death.

Monday, April 16.   Left anchorage at 6 a.m. with
a heavy sea and in torrents of rain.   In the channel between Pemba and Zanzibar, a boat was lowered, which
boarded and overhauled two dhows, but no slaves were
discovered.   Very rough work this for the sailors, in a
small boat and in such weather.   Made Zanzibar about
4 p.m. and found a cordial welcome awaiting me at the
Agency.   They have made, and are making, wonderful
alterations in the house; when completed, it will be an
Oriental Palace.   Sorry to find the Colonel seedy from
overwork; but his bright wife having had a turn of fever
seems all right again.

Tuesday, April 17.   Busy in the town—very hot and
steamy.   In the afternoon paid a visit with Mrs. Euan
Smith to Kiungani and Mbweni, two Stations of the
Universities' Mission.   We had a delightful drive
through the groves and " shambas".   At the former
met Miss Thackeray, Mr. Goodyear and Mr. Watson;

and at the latter, Archdeacon and Mrs. Hodgson, Miss Woodward and Miss Bartley.

Wednesday, April 18.   Walked over to the other Station of the Mission, situate in the heart of the town, on or near the old slave market, and here I met Archdeacon Farler, Messrs. Clarke and Highton, and Miss Mills. On my way back I called on Polly Nyondo.   She is sadly changed from the neat, modest-looking woman she used to be.   I had a serious talk with her, and at last she burst into tears and asked what she should do? I gave her my best advice, and she promised to think over it, and write to me.   I should be thankful indeed if I might be instrumental in leading this poor erring woman to return to a better life.   I thought of what my old churchwarden said to me when I took leave of him : "If your going to Africa be a means of bringing one poor soul to the Saviour, it will be worth while".

Thursday, April 19.   In the night I was startled out of sleep by a strange noise : a rotten beam in the ceiling got loose and came down with a crash—only just missing my bed ; but thank God, it *did* miss ! Then a cold wind was blowing over me, which gave me a chill, so to-day I am in bed with fever, accompanied by diarrhœa and sickness.   Mrs. Euan Smith, all kindness, called in Dr. Corcorran of the " Mariner ".

Sunday, April 22.   It is not by choice I am spending the Lord's day here instead of at Frere Town.   After a few days' rest and good nursing, with God's blessing upon all, I am coming round ; but I am still weak, and so by advice of the Dr. I have deferred my return.   Attended Service this morning on board the " Mariner ".

In the afternoon I sent round notice to the Bombay African Christians, that I would see them at the Agency, and at 5 p.m. fathers, mothers and children, all—with one or two exceptions—turned up, to the number of 40 or more. Had a quiet talk with each in turn, and learnt from them their history, etc. In most cases they had been driven from Frere Town for some fault or other; and without much attempt "To restore them in the spirit of meekness," they had been turned adrift amongst all the temptations and pollutions of this sink of iniquity and just left to their fate. What a delight it was to them to see me, to have a kind word spoken to them, and to find that their old "Papa" had not forgotten them! Some of them have, I fear, fallen a prey to the evil influences surrounding them, yet on the whole they have been wonderfully preserved. None of them as far as I could ascertain have thrown off their Christian profession. Most of them attend the Services at the Mission Church, although they do not feel at home there, and are not much looked after or cared for, unless they happen to be able to make themselves useful in one way or another in the Mission. After conversing with each separately, I spoke to them collectively, and then, all kneeling, I offered prayer, concluding with the Lord's Prayer, in which all joined. I was very glad of the opportunity of meeting these poor outcasts, and saying a word to them in love, which may God bless! They would all gladly return to Frere Town, and if I were going to remain, I would heartily welcome them back, and give them another chance. As it is, I could only promise to consider the case of one and all—each on its own merits—and let them know the result. If Bishop Parker comes back in time for me to see him, I shall lay the whole matter before him, and hope he will take a kind interest in them. In most cases they were anxious about their children, who are growing up in ignorance, and surrounded by the polluting influences of this godless place. I would not have missed this meeting for anything, and if nothing else comes of my visit to East Africa I shall still thank God that it has not been in vain. May He of His great mercy watch over these few scattered sheep, and keep them from the power of the enemy, and bring them at last to His kingdom !

There is no chance now of my seeing the Sultan this time. On the day first arranged for my interview, I was down with fever, and when the second day came, which His Highness had kindly fixed, the Consul-General was himself too ill to accompany me, so this part of my programme fell through, and ended in complimentary messages between us. Still my journey to Zanzibar has served a useful purpose. I have had an opportunity of enlightening Col. Euan Smith on some matters affecting the Mission, and of taking his advice on others. And now I am eager to be back at my post; for though nothing could exceed the bounteous hospitality of this house, and I can never forget the kindness I have received, yet the life altogether is out of my line, my friends and I move in different grooves, our aims and aspirations are too far asunder to admit of full sympathy between us. Where we do find a common interest it is most pleasant.

Of Zanzibar itself I can give but an ill report. It has often been described, and all that *can* be said in its praise has been said over and over again. Viewing it from the deck of a steamer, we may agree with Stanley when he says, "One of the fruitfullest islands of the Indian Ocean is Zanzibar"; but no sooner do you set foot on shore than the fair scene vanishes from view, and sights, sounds and smells assail the senses, which put to flight all thoughts of the beauties of nature. The lot of the European community, now a very numerous and an ever increasing body, is by no means an enviable one. For the most part they do not live—they exist—there is no *home* life.

But it is chiefly when seen in its moral aspect that the worst features of the place stand out in sickening relief. If any one wishes to know what Mohammedanism is as a civilizing and renovating power, let him pay a visit to Zanzibar. Here, at any rate, it has had full scope, and everything in its favour. The Arabs have had it all their own way for generations, and tens of thousands of slaves have passed through their hands, coming under their power and influence. What have they done to improve their condition—to raise them in the scale of humanity? absolutely nothing; the place at this day is a very Sodom—a city of abominations—one of the darkest of "the dark places of the earth". It is much to be deplored that the Christianity of the European population, made up of various nationalities, is, as a rule, of a low type, in too many cases "the salt has lost its savour".

My detention here, much as I chafed at it, has not

been all loss; it has given me an opportunity for correspondence with dear friends far away, which I shall not easily find, when again in harness. One or two extracts from letters written at this time may not be without interest to some of my readers. They are side lights, which bring out details in the picture of Missionary life which would otherwise be wanting.

To my son in Sierra Leone.

" DEAREST MAC,

" I had a good many letters by last Mail, but among them only one I valued more than yours, dated from Teneriffe, March 3rd. It is all the more welcome because it comes just when I need a little comfort, being on my back with fever at the British Agency, Zanzibar. I was very well my first month in F. Town, but since coming here a week ago, the climate has got hold of me and " I am as other men," under similar circumstances. Of course I am here in the lap of luxury; my host and hostess are most bountifully kind, and I can have anything I want for the asking; but I long to get back to my home and work nevertheless. I should not have come to Zanzibar but as a matter of duty. For one thing as representing the C. M. S. it was desirable to call and pay my respects to Said Khalifa, the new Sultan; and for another there were important matters concerning which I had to confer with the Consul-General.

" I am glad to hear of the kind appreciation of your ministry on the part of the good folk of Las Palmas, and also, at the same time, of your being able to return to Sierra Leone. I confess I am doubtful of your being fitted for that climate, and I hope if you again break down, they will pack you off at once, and not allow you to run down as before.

.   .   .   .

"I do not, of course, know what may be God's will in leading me a third time to East Africa, but I am thankful I came, and have seen enough already to encourage the hope that my coming will not be in vain. Give my kind regards to the Bishop, and explain why I have not replied to his very kind letter, which I got before leaving England. Remember me also very warmly to Nevill and his good sister, whom I thank for her kindness to you. I hope this may find you in good health, and happily engaged in your interesting and important work. It is indeed strange that you should be at *Free* Town and I at *Frere* Town: on opposite sides of this 'dark continent,' and both engaged in the same work: the setting forth of Him, whose alone it is to make 'free indeed'. We cannot reckon on the future, but if it should please God to spare us both, what a joy it will be to gather once more with your dear mother and sister and brothers and A.—a united family, under the dear old roof at Wingfield. For the present, looking to the Lord for needful strength and grace, let us seek to acquit ourselves as good soldiers of Jesus Christ. God bless you, my dear boy, and prosper you in soul and body, for Christ's sake.

"Your loving Father."

To my man, John Barber, Wingfield.

" DEAR JOHN,

" It is 9 p.m., my door and windows wide open. I am very lightly clothed, yet the perspiration is rolling off me from head to foot, and my whole body is covered with prickly-heat, which makes me look as if I had the measles. Wouldn't you like to be here ? No, John, you are better where you are. This dreadful heat would kill you in a fortnight. Though I am not altogether new to it, I feel that it is fearfully taking it out of me. Then perhaps you will say ' Why did you go ? ' Well, if any one had offered me £10,000, I would have said, ' No '. But it seemed to be a clear call from God, and I hoped He had something for me to do here, and that is just all about it. Nothing else would have induced me to come. It is very hard for an Englishman to live here. There is the climate, and there is the food ! What would I give for a crust of one of Ann's loaves ! But after all what does it matter if we are in the path that God has marked out for us ? I feel the deepest interest in you, your dear wife and children. I should be glad to hear that Ted had come out boldly on the Lord's side ; he might be such a blessing to other young men in the Parish. I quite hope he will be given to his good mother's prayers.

" Shall we ever meet again in the flesh—and have our cold drives, and quiet talks, to Eye and Diss and Harleston—and our pleasant times in the garden, sowing and planting and gathering in the fruit ? Well, God only knows. Anyway let us only follow Christ with all our hearts, and then if not here, yet *there*, in the land of everlasting rest, we shall meet and rejoice together. I will ask you to give my Christian love to your dear wife, etc., etc."

Tuesday, April 24. The fine weather is at an end. The ?S.-E. Monsoon is fairly setting in, and all the morning the rain has come down in torrents; but storm or sunshine I must away. Lunched with Capt. Arbuthnot on board the " Mariner "; and after taking leave of my kind friends at the Agency, set out at 3 p.m. in the " Henry Wright," for Mombasa, right glad this time to turn my back on Zanzibar and all its charms. My fellow-passengers are, my old friend Mr. Buchanan, of the I. B. E. A. Co., and two Missionaries of the Bavarian Mission, going to Jimbo.

Wednesday, April 25. After a very fair passage, for which we had the blessing of a bright and nearly full moon, anchored in Mombasa harbour at 6.30 a.m. I have never made the passage more comfortably. Found the Mission party all well; and received from all a hearty welcome back. Mr. and Mrs. Burness have arrived in my absence, and are settling down. I am most thankful for this addition to our working staff, and trust we may regard them as the vanguard of a goodly band of devoted men and women, who will soon be coming out, to fill up our much thinned ranks.

Friday, April 27. Two very busy days; arrears to be cleared off and many things to be attended to; the more so, as I am anxious not longer to delay paying a quiet visit to Rabai.

To Rabai.

Monday, April 30. Favoured by wind and tide accomplished the 10 miles of water to the " banderini " in less than two hours. Called in at Jomvu, and spent an hour with Mr. Carthew of the Methodist Free Church Mission. I was carried in my new " zoli " part of the road, by way of testing its qualities, and found it answered capitally. Even up the steep Buni hill it was quite easy, and the men did not seem distressed. It will be a great convenience for ladies and invalids.

Tuesday, May 1. I find the Mission compound a wild jungle—everywhere rank vegetation, cutting off the houses from light and fresh sea breezes, and completely hiding from view the palm-clad hills, which, divided here and there by deep craggy gorges, sombre with dense foliage, stretch right away for several miles towards the sea, and present a charming picture, with which the eye never tires. Set men to work clearing off grass, and cutting down superfluous trees. I don't blame anybody; if a place here be kept ever so nice and trim it only needs to be unoccupied for a month or two to be turned into a wilderness.

Walked over the Settlement under Jones's guidance. It took us two hours, and even then we left some parts unvisited. Jones has hit upon a novel plan of obtaining a fairly correct census of the population. There are eleven distinct Districts, and taking one District at a time, he will require each house-holder to bring to him as many grains of Indian corn as there are persons in his house. I should think, at a rough guess, they will not fall much short of 2000 souls !

Friday, May 4. Have greatly enjoyed my few days' visit to Rabai. W. Jones is in sole charge as Native Pastor, and appears to be admirably fitted for the post; he is always at it, " in season and out of season," dili-

Rev. W. H. JONES AND FAMILY.

gently tending his flock, and at the same time exercising a beneficial influence upon the surrounding Wa-Nika, the Elders of whom have come to look up to him as their best friend. May he long be spared, and greatly blessed of God, in his good work!

The more I see of this Mission, the more I am impressed with it, as a remarkable instance of the way in which God by His providence is working with us, over-ruling events for the spread of the Kingdom, and "making the wrath of men to praise Him". There is a grand opening here for every branch of Missionary work. If I were ten years younger, I would gladly give up everything in England, to spend the rest of my days in this deeply interesting Field. May God put it into the hearts of many devoted men and women to come and take advantage of this open door.

Return to Frere Town. A great Sorrow!

Saturday, May 5. After a few pleasant and busy days at Rabai, returned this morning to Frere Town. I had scarcely landed, when a packet was put into my hand containing letters from the Brethren in the interior; and one from Col. Euan Smith, conveying the terrible tidings of the death of Bishop Parker and Blackburn. There was also a telegram from Mr. Wigram to the Consul-General—"Tell Price to assume full powers". A tremendous responsibility is thus suddenly cast upon me. God, be Thou my Help!

The following extracts from letters written at the time will perhaps best explain the new and painful circumstances in which we were placed by the lamented death of our good Bishop:

To the Secretary of the C. M. S.

"May 5. I returned from Rabai to-day in order to

be here to administer the Lord's Supper to-morrow. On landing I received a packet from the Consul-General, conveying, among other things, the overwhelming intelligence of the death of Mr. Blackburn and of the Bishop. It is a dreadful blow to us all, as I am sure it has been to the Committee. We cannot tell what it means. It is almost too solemn an event to speak about; for an explanation we must wait. Just now all we can say is, 'It is the Lord'. 'Precious in the sight of the Lord is the death of His beloved.'

"The Consul-General forwarded me Mr. Wigram's telegram. I can only say that I will do my best, with God's help, to direct the affairs of the Mission according to the expressed wishes (which I know) of the late dear Bishop. As far as the Coast Stations are concerned, there is no immediate cause for anxiety. On the whole, things are going on satisfactorily. I am just a little concerned about Miss. F. I learn that she is off her food, and she is looking thin and jaded. If we had a decent place at Shimba, which I hope we shall have ere long, I would get her there for a change. She is worth her weight in gold, and more.

"How these sad events may affect my plans I do not know, and the incoming Mail cannot bring me any specific directions from the Committee. All I can say is, in your consultations just bear in mind, that as far as it rests with me, I am quite at your disposal. Make any use of me you think fit. If, however, it should seem desirable for me to stay on, I must ask you to make all straight with the Bishop of Norwich. My dear wife too must have her voice in the matter. She will not stand in the way, whatever it may cost her, where there seems a plain indication of God's will. This I know, for she is a God-fearing woman and a true Missionary. But as I was coming out only for six months, and could not foresee the present changed condition of affairs, I did not even sound her as to her willingness to come out again to E. Africa. If in the providence of God the way should be made plain for me to remain, she might elect to come, and need I say what a comfort and support it would be to me to have her once more at my side? And if only she could bring her 'Benjamin' with her, it would be a joy indeed, and, I venture to think, not a small gain to this Mission. But I am writing quite in the dark. It may be that you have some man of experience ready to come out and take up the work. It will be five weeks before I can hear from you or know anything of your plans, and between now and then what may happen? Nothing that our heavenly Father does not see to be wise and good. Any way I wish the Committee to know that, failing any better arrangement, they may depend on me to do my very best to carry on, as long as it pleases God to give me health and strength. I am inviting al the Brethren to join, on Friday next, in a Special Service of humiliation and prayer; and, amongst other things, we shall remember the Committee, seeking that they may, at this juncture, be endued with heavenly wisdom in their dispositions for this Mission.

"Give my Christian regards to General Hutchinson, and tell him Burness and I have been prospecting, and I think there is every probability of our getting good stone—not coral-rag—for the Church, which will now be in memory, not of one, but of two bishops."

To Col. Euan Smith.

" FRERE TOWN, *May* 8, 1888.

" DEAR COLONEL,—

" Your letter with the heavy tidings from the Nyanza was put into my hand on Saturday just as I returned from Rabai where I had been for a few days, and just as the steamer which brought it was moving out of the harbour. We were all overwhelmed by the sad and startling news. Poor Parker! cut off almost at the beginning of his Episcopate; and Blackburn, who had left his young wife at home, and come out from a sense of duty. He was expecting her out shortly. She may be even now on her way, unless, as I hope, your telegram has been in time to stop her. Should she come *via* the Cape, she had better perhaps come on here and rest for a month or so, where she will meet with some friends of her late husband, and with some who also know her, unless she wishes to go back at once.

" Thank you for sending me the telegrams, which I return. I shall of course do my best to carry on the work, although it will be another month or more before I can get any detailed instructions from the Committee. It is no little help and comfort to me, that I have the full sympathy and good-will of all the Missionary party here. I am writing to the Committee to put myself entirely in their hands, if it should seem to them for the good of the Mission that I should prolong my stay.

I only bargain that, in that case, they should send out my wife, if she elects to come.

"I had a packet containing letters from the late Bishop to several members of the Mission, some of them written only a day or two before his death, and one giving a very detailed account of the illness and death of Blackburn.

"I am so glad to hear you had a cruise with dear Capt. A. and that it has done you good. For work in E. Africa a man wants a *mens sana in corpore sano.*

"I thank His Highness for his letter to the Wali. The latter gentleman and I are on the best of terms. He is going to Zanzibar by the Mail to see the Sultan. I hope he is sincere; but his predecessor was quite as polite, and turned out a traitor.

"On Saturday last one of our women and her boy (about 13 years) were pounced upon by three *Suahelis*, gagged, carried away to Mombasa, and confined in a house. Through the cleverness of the lad (who is half-witted), they made their escape. I have sent the case over to the Wali; but if the Vice-Consul were here, he might have something to say to it.

"Fitch of Chaga informs me that two of the Germans there have purchased women from Mandara and some of the natives are casting it in his teeth, 'See, you wa-zungu also buy slaves!' I am seriously thinking of taking on myself the responsibility of inviting Fitch to the Coast. He is a noble fellow, and for nearly four years he has held on, in spite of the bullying of Mandara. It is quite time, for his own sake, he had a change. My difficulty is to supply his place *pro tem.* We have obtained a footing there and, 'German influence' notwithstanding, are not inclined to give it up.

"I want when the V.-C. is here to invite the Wali and 'wazee' to a 'shauri,' to explain to them our position in regard to the 'watoro,' and to come to a good understanding with them on the subject,

"I remain, etc., etc."

To the Rev. H. Walker, Usambiro.

"*May* 13, 1888.

"Dear Mr. Walker,—

"The news of the removal by death of Br. Blackburn, so soon followed by that of Bishop Parker, has come upon us all as a great shock, and filled our hearts with sorrow and sadness. Very dark and mysterious to us are these things; but it is our comfort to know that it is the Lord, and that He makes no mistakes. Verily death seems very near to us all; God help us to make 'full proof of our ministry,' 'to work whilst it is day,' and so to live that when our call shall come, we may be able to say, 'It is better to depart and be with Christ'.

"Our sympathy has been much drawn out towards you and the other dear Brethren of your party. We could do nothing but pray for you, and earnestly do we hope that all grace has been given you according to your need.

"The sad event has of course disturbed many plans and arrangements, and how it may effect my own movements, I cannot tell. Had the Bishop returned, as we were expecting, I should have left by the August mail. For the present Mr. Wigram telegraphs me to assume charge of the Mission; but I can get no particulars as to the further wishes of the Committee till next Mail, a month hence.

"You and the other Brethren are fully cognizant of the late dear Bishop's plans and intentions as regards the Lake Mission, and will no doubt do your best to carry them out. I will only ask you kindly to keep us well-informed, and always to let me know if there is any way in which I can be of service to you. For myself I earnestly ask your prayers that I may be divinely enabled to discharge the heavy responsibilities, which have been so unexpectedly thrown upon me.

"I am in doubt where this will find you. Dr. Pruen, in a letter dated April 23, writes: 'Mr. Walker was leaving for Uganda when the last mail left'. If this is so, may the Lord be with you and Mr. Gordon and 'save you from the lion's mouth'. Ashe, I regret to hear, has resigned his connexion with the Society; so I write to you as the only one of the Missionary brethren, whom I personally know. It must have been you who drove me in on one occasion from Yarmouth station to your father's house. I was again at Bradwell last year for C. M. S.

"Accept for yourself and all the Brethren my Christian love, and believe me, etc., etc."

Sunday, May 6. The Church was completely filled to-day. All hearts were bowed by a common grief, as they realized that not the Church only, but each individual member had sustained a heavy loss. After

Morning Service administered the Lord's Supper to fifty communicants.

Wednesday, May 9. Disappointed at the non-arrival of the homeward Mail steamer from Zanzibar, in preparation for which I have been hard at work the last two days. Probably the Consul-General has detained her for some cause. The delay however afforded me an opportunity of packing, with the help of Smith and Morris, four boxes of the late Bishop's things, to send home by the mail. They contained chiefly his robes and wearing apparel, with some private papers, and a few small articles of jewelry.   It was a melancholy task, but it had to be done.

Morris came over in the evening, and I had a long quiet talk with him about Teita Mission affairs. How little people at home realize what some Missionaries have to go through ! Our brethren at Teita, for instance, live in what is little better than a wigwam, their living room being about 10 ft. square. As to food, they get no fresh meat, and have to depend mainly on tinned meats which the stomach learns to loathe. Even fresh water they can come at only by stealth under the darkness of night.   For many weeks they have been virtually prisoners, not daring to venture beyond their own compound, owing to the hostility of the surrounding natives. And yet, in the face of all this, Morris is anxious to get back, and Wray is by no means disposed to give in ! I feel that by comparison with these good men, we are in pleasant pastures ; although for the last two hours I have been doing battle with hosts of loathsome insects, which get into my beard, crawl down my neck, find their way into my ears, and even meander over my "specs". I have fought them till I am tired out and running down with perspiration. I have killed battalions, but still they come to torment me, and remain in possession of the field. Will our good friends at home, who put their "mites" into the Missionary collection, try to take this in? And yet, I say again, by comparison with Fitch at Chaga, and Wray and Morris at Teita, *we* are in clover.

Friday, May 11. The "Oriental" came in yesterday and took off our English Mail; so to-day we are free to unite, as arranged, in a solemn Service of humiliation and prayer, in connexion with recent unhappy events in our Mission. The Kisuaheli Service in the morning was well attended. Jones preached from Phil. i. 21 a powerful sermon and to the point, in which he touchingly alluded to the deaths of Bishops Hannington and Parker.

At 4.30 p.m., we had a special Service in English attended only by the European Mission party and our two ordained Native brethren—W. Jones and Ishmael Semler. The "Penguin" arrived from Zanzibar, and the good Captain at once came on shore, and with some of his officers dropped in towards the close of our Service. It is a great pleasure and refreshment to us Missionaries to come in contact with so many men wearing H. M. uniform, who are at the same time earnest followers of Christ, and in full sympathy with us in our work. Such men are themselves Missionaries of a high order.

CHAPTER IV.

TEITA TROUBLES.—TRIP TO SHIMBA.

Saturday, May 12.   The English Mail is over-due. We are straining our eyes for the signal of its approach.

Had a talk with Taylor on affairs of the Mission. He generously volunteers to go to Chaga for three months, to set Fitch free to come to the coast for a change.   I am much inclined to accept his offer, but it has to be thought out.

Had a visit to-day from the son of Mbaruk, the late rebel chief; and another from the acting Wali of Mombasa.   Each comes with a retinue of Arabs and slaves who fill up my room and overflow into the verandah.   I accommodate the grandees with chairs as far as they will go, the rest squat picturesquely on the floor. These visits are rather irksome, and take up too much time; but Arabs think nothing of that.   Taylor is my " master of the ceremonies" on these occasions, and is just in his element.

Sunday, May 13.   English Mail arrived, and sadly marred our enjoyment of the Day of Rest.   As she stays only a few hours, our boat has to ply to and fro to bring off letters and packages, and all is hurry-skurry, to the last moment.   Much as we were longing for our home letters, we would gladly have waited for them another day, rather than have our Sabbath so disturbed.

Monday, May 14. Capt. King-Hall kindly invited us

to take all our children, about 200, on board the "Penguin". He made arrangements for them to be taken round in batches with some of the Officers to point out and explain to them all the wonders of an English man-of-war. The children had a happy time of it, and so also had the "blue-jackets". The latter generously feasted their guests with their own biscuits and some gallons of tea, and it was difficult to say which had the greater pleasure, the givers or receivers.

Tuesday, May 15. Capt. King-Hall, accompanied by Smith and W. Jones, paid a visit to Rabai. As I was busy preparing for the Chaga Mail, I was unable to go with them. The Captain, I hear, was greatly delighted. At his request Jones summoned the people by ringing the Church bell, from their fields and "shambas," and when they were assembled, the good Captain—whose heart was touched at the sight of so many poor Africans, once dark heathen, but now, at any rate, humble followers of Christ—gave them a short Gospel address, with Jones as interpreter. Despatched the "Henry Wright" to Zanzibar with letters, etc., for the Lake brethren.

Had a meeting of the Brethren at which it was finally resolved to accept Mr. Taylor's offer to go to Chaga for three months. Wrote to Fitch to that effect. The following extract from my letter will explain :—

To the Rev. E. A. Fitch, Chaga.

"*May* 16. 1890.

" MY DEAR FITCH,—

"I am enclosing two letters which, I take it, are from the Bishop, and you will be as grieved to hear as I to tell, that the writer of them is no more . . . . but you will doubtless hear from your dear sister full details about these sad events.

" I must now briefly refer to one or two points in your interesting letter of April 24. We all felt very much for you in your trouble in connexion with the illness and death of poor Patrick M. The disease 'Kilimi' is well known here, and the remedy. It does not appear to be infectious, but you acted wisely in burning the clothes, etc. I am sorry there is no available *iron* bed in store, but we are sending you up a small 'Kitanda,' which will perhaps serve you for the present.

" I do not wonder at your being annoyed by H.'s letter ; but I have had so much experience of this sort of thing in my time, that I should care much less about it now than I used to do. We have to go on, dear Br., trying to do the Lord's work ' thro' evil report and good report'.

" What you say about the goings on of the Germans is very sad. This is another way in which the devil is trying to keep God's light out of the ' Dark Continent': —' it must needs be that offences come, etc.'

" What I am now going to say will perhaps take you by surprise. I have long felt that it is highly desirable, from every point of view, that you should have a change to the coast. I should have urged it on the Bishop had he lived ; so now being more free to act on my own responsibility, I have no hesitation (with the full concurrence of all the Brethren here) in inviting you, unless you see any serious objection to it, to make arrangements to come down at once, or at least as soon as you can be relieved. My only difficulty has been removed by Taylor kindly offering to go and take your place for three months. So all being well, he will be with you about a month hence; the middle of June. He brings with him a 'Mwalimu' to assist him in his translations. He is hoping to get what he may want in the way of stores from you—all except flour, which he brings.

"You know all about the Teita anxiety. I am asking Taylor to stay a day or two there on his way up, to enquire into and report on the state of the Mission; and I shall be very glad if you will do the same on your way down. Two independent Reports will greatly assist us in deciding what is best to be done there. You will have time after receiving this to make your preparations to set out as soon as possible after Taylor's arrival: say two or three days. It will be good for Mandara to have a strange 'mzungu' to deal with for a time. He will probably miss you, and be ready to welcome you back, with open arms, as an old friend.

"I need not tell you what a delight it will be to your dear good sister to see you; and indeed I can assure you of a warm welcome from all the Brethren here. May the Lord prosper your way.

"Believe me, etc., etc."

Whitsunday, May 20. Held an English Service this evening and preached from John xvi. 16-22. The Brethren all attended, and were glad of the opportunity, but I feel it is rather too much of a tax upon them, after two full Kisuaheli Services, and two Sunday schools, in this climate!

Tuesday, May 22. Just now I am sorely bothered with house-keeping. My cook has been on his back for more than a week, with fever and inflammation, and I am at the mercy of a dirty boy, who came in this morning coolly to tell me there was no breakfast ! so I had to content myself with three small biscuits ; a repetition of my supper of last night.

I am sure that a good deal of the sickness—fever, etc., of European Missionaries, which is usually set down to climate, is more frequently caused by improper food. I found for instance only one baker in the place, and him a man not only dirty in his person, but suffering from virulent ulcers in both legs ! The sight of the man was enough to turn one's stomach, whilst his bread was cloggy and unfit for human food. Then too there is a scarcity of fresh meat, especially of mutton and poultry. Beef can be obtained in Mombasa but it is generally poor and tough, and there is always the suspicion that the poor beast "has been killed to save its life". Some of our friends fall back on tinned meats, including salmon and lobster! most unwholesome substitutes, which soon tell on the appetite and health of those who indulge in them. Now that there is such an increase in the number of Missionaries, and especially of ladies, something should be done to place this matter of food supply on a better footing. Wholesome food, clean and properly cooked, has more to do with one's health in E. Africa, than many seem to be aware of. My remarks refer to those engaged in School or other Station work, and who are settled down. Of course there are times —on the march for instance—when a Missionary must not be too dainty, but be content to take what he can get, asking no questions.

Thursday, May 24. A heavy day's work. Final arrangements with Taylor and Morris about Chaga and Teita affairs. Held a special Service this evening to take leave of these Brethren, and to commend them in prayer to Almighty God.

Friday, May 25. Sent off porters to Rabai to get their Sunday's rest and be ready for the start on Monday. This afternoon a special messenger came in with an urgent letter from Wray. He is again in trouble with the people of Teita, and seems to think his life is in danger. This complicates matters and renders necessary some change in our arrangements. In the first place Morris was taking up a lot of stuff—provisions, etc. —a rather large supply. I advised him to take up only such things as would be absolutely necessary for the next month or six weeks, till we see what turn affairs may take. Then it occurred to me that, in the present crisis, it would be well that W. Jones should accompany the Brethren as far as Teita, and that he and Taylor should negotiate with the refractory Elders, and endeavour to place the relations between them and the Mission on a better footing. All agreed that, under the circumstances, this was the best course to pursue.

Saturday, May 26, " *To Rabai.*" As I did not feel quite sure how Jones would like being sent away on such short notice, I thought it best to accompany Messrs. Taylor and Morris to Rabai, so as to be able to explain the situation fully to him; and I am glad to find he willingly responds to the call. What I hope for, with God's blessing, from this, may best be gathered from the following letter to Mr. Wray :—

To Mr. J. A. Wray, Teita.

"RABAI, *May* 26, 1888.

" MY DEAR WRAY,—

" Not long after Morris's porters had left Frere Town for this place, came your letter, from which I am sorry to learn that your position at ' Sagalla ' is still one of difficulty, if not of actual danger.   It becomes a question for serious consideration, whether we should go on in spite of all the indifference and opposition on the part of these people ; or whether it may not be God's will that we should retire, for a time at least, and seek a more open door elsewhere.   Before coming to any decision, I have determined to ask W. Jones to go up with our two Brethren, who are leaving next Monday, to try what he can do to bring these poor silly people to reason.   As you are aware, he knows and is well known to many of them, and has especial claims on their gratitude.   He is a man of tact and possesses considerable powers of persuasion with all classes of natives.   Besides as a native himself, he can appeal to them from a different standpoint to ours, and can bring arguments to bear upon them which we cannot.   Give him a free hand, and I have hope that, by God's help, he may be able to bring about a better state of things, that so you may be able to carry on your work without fear or anxiety.   Failing that, there will be nothing left, I apprehend, but to withdraw.

" I will lay the whole matter, as you wish, before H.

M. Consul-General, on the first opportunity, though I very much doubt if he will feel himself authorized in interfering. The Wa-Teita will certainly be taught a severe lesson before long, unless they treat ' Wazungu ' better, but it should not be, and will not be, at the hand of the messengers of the Gospel!

" Till we see how things turn out, it would be unwise for Morris to bring up all his stuff, so he will leave the bulk here, to follow later on if the clouds pass away. Believe me, etc., etc."

Trinity Sunday, May 27. Very touching and impressive is the sight I have witnessed to-day. The Church was quite full some time before the time for Divine Service; the congregation being augmented by the Frere Town contingent of porters belonging to the caravan. It is refreshing to one's soul to join with these poor people in their hearty Service. This was the day for the monthly collection, which always takes place at the beginning of the Service, and occupies about fifteen minutes. The contributions are partly in money, but chiefly in kind. Half-a-dozen men go round the Church each with a large basket, into which the people empty the contents of their smaller baskets—consisting of maize or some other kinds of field or garden produce. As the baskets are filled, they are brought and emptied out in a small room, and then go the round again till all the congregation have made their offerings. I was much interested in this novel procedure. I believe every one in the Church—even the very poorest—gave something; certainly although I had a good view of the whole thing, I did not see any one putting off the collector with a nod! The collection to-day, which is, I am told, an average one, amounted to nearly Rs. 20. It is applied mainly to the support of a Native Missionary. When will our churches in England, which profess to *support* Foreign Missions, take a leaf out of this book, and have a Missionary collection, not once a year, but once a month?

Monday, May 28. No one who has not gone through it can form any idea of the miseries and anxieties connected with setting out on a long journey in this country, where practically there are no roads—no modes of conveyance—often for many miles no food or water—and where your money consists of heavy loads of cloth and beads, which must be carried on men's heads. We have been in the thick of this troublesome business from early morning. The first thing is to make up the loads, allowing about 60 lbs. per man. Then the men willing to engage as porters are mustered, and a selection made of the fittest, which is immediately followed by an amusing scramble for the lightest or most convenient loads; and then some stout calico is measured off, and cut up into eight cubic lengths, one of which is given to each man, wherewith he will purchase food for himself till he gets to Teita—a distance of about 100 miles or six days' journey. There were altogether seventy men, of whom ten were taking up stores for some Englishmen at Taveta. It was well for Taylor and Morris that W. Jones was their travelling companion, for he took on him the chief burden of the arrangements, and he is an old hand and a capital manager.

At 3 p.m. we met for a final word of prayer together

—it was under the circumstances a very solemn occasion —and then having seen the Brethren some distance on their way, we shook hands ; and then bidding them God speed, I turned my face towards Frere Town, which I reached at 7 p.m.

On my way I was met by Kunya, one of the oldest of the Wanika chiefs, who has been a warrior in his time, and who was badly wounded a few years ago in an encounter with Mbaruk. The old man expressed his delight at seeing me again, and spread out before me twenty-five newly-poisoned arrows, as a token of his readiness to fight for me, should I need his services !

GENERAL KUNYA.

Tuesday, May 29. Busy all day preparing for a trip to Shimba. Caroline David, one of our teachers, is very ill. The doctor was going to Rabai, but on my representing to him the seriousness of the case, he put off his journey. I visited her at midnight. The doctor had given her up, " it was only a question of a few hours," he said, and I was glad to find her not only resigned, but rejoicing in the near prospect of death. She said, " I am not afraid to die. I am going to my Lord, and to my dear old father, who was taken home four years ago." She re-

peated the 23rd Psalm, and other precious words of
Scripture, into the meaning of which she seemed fully
to enter. As I had to be off very early in the morning, I could not stay long with her but I felt it a privilege, and not a little encouragement to witness the
triumph of faith in this Christian young woman, a
daughter of Africa, and of my dear old friend of former
days, George David.

As I am about to give a short account of my visit to
Shimba, it may be well to preface it by a few words
about the place itself.

Shimba is the name given to a range of hills running
parallel with the coast line in a S. W. direction. The
particular hill on which our Mission Station is placed is
called " Kwali " by the natives, but we have dropped the
name out of use, and now always speak of the *Shimba*
Mission.   It is about 35 miles from Frere Town, of
which 20 are by water and the rest by land.   The
average height is 1400 ft. above sea level. It occupies
a splendid site, about 20 miles inland from the sea and
commanding a view of sea and coast for upwards of 60
miles to the N. E. and S. W.   Between it and the coast
lies a magnificent panorama of tropical scenery—lofty
well-wooded hills, which elsewhere would rank as mountains, separated by deep gorges and valleys of dense
jungle, wherein lions and other wild beasts have their
habitation.   Looking in a S. and S. Westerly direction
we see the Duruma range—a continuation of the Shimba
upheaval—and many a grand picture, which any one
may revel in, but which only a real artist may
attempt to describe.

The summit of our Hill is a plateau extending 4 miles N. by S., nearly level, and presenting all the appearance of an English park, with here and there " topes " of fine trees, which it is hard to believe have not been some time or other planted by the hand of man. From several points we get a view of the Teita mountains, distant some 100 miles. Altogether, in itself and in its surroundings it is a charming spot—an earthly paradise !

There is pasturage to any extent for cattle and sheep, and plenty of good ground for cultivation. With a little pains I have no doubt it might furnish our Missionaries at all the Coast Stations with a supply of English vegetables—an incalculable boon ! Good water may be obtained in any quantity ; and, better than all, the air is so pure and exhilarating that the change to one coming from the hot steamy plains is as life from the dead. It is just the place for a sanatorium for the E. African Mission ; and I feel persuaded that if only decent accommodation were provided for invalids and convalescents, many precious lives might be saved, and hundreds of pounds to the C. M. S. I hope the authorities at Salisbury Square will realize this.

My old friend, the late Dr. Krapf, urged upon me very strongly, on my first going out to E. Africa in 1874, the advantages of Shimba as a Mission centre ; but on that occasion my hands were too full with laying the foundation of the Freed Slave Settlement of Frere Town, and with other important matters, to leave me time for opening up new ground. On my second visit (1881-2) I was most anxious if possible to carry out this object, and for that purpose I made a tour in the Shimba country and selected what appeared to me the most eligible site for a Mission station. Having done this I fixed a day and invited the Wa-Digo elders—to the number of sixty—to a big feast. They came in from all parts, far and near, and we held a grand "shauri". I explained to them fully our objects and wishes, and after a good deal of consultation among themselves, and floods of oratory, which lasted till midnight, from the Ancients, I obtained permission to occupy "Kwali" as a Mission settlement, which permission was embodied in a document properly drawn, and duly attested by all whom it concerned. Alas! that was all I could do in the matter. I had to leave for England shortly after, and nothing further was done. The place was left unoccupied till in 1887 Bishop Parker paid it a visit, and having approved of the site selected five years before, arranged by way of experiment for some thirty of the biggest boys from Frere Town to settle there, under suitable supervision, for agricultural training. I should add that Shimba occupies a central position among the Wa-Digo—an unsophisticated race, similar in many respects to the Wa-Nika—for whom no missionary effort has been made. It is virgin soil; and indeed in 1882 I met many people who had never seen a white face before.

To Shimba.

Wednesday, May 30. Up early and got off at six. Mr. Burness is my companion. We were two hours too late, for tide being against us, we did not reach the

landing stage at Djimbo till ten. It was a grilling day—
not the vestige of a cloud. We spent a miserable four
hours in a dirty cattle shed, which afforded us little
protection from the heat ; so after a meal cooked under
difficulties, we set out at 2 p.m. for the march to Shimba.
We found the road in a wretched state, and if the place
is ever to be of use as a sanatorium, something must
be done to make it more easy of access. It is a trying
journey, scarcely possible for anyone not in robust
health. Tired out, we reached the top of the Hill at
night-fall—just four and a half hours—and as it was
something of a surprise visit, we thought it prudent to
send on a messenger to give notice of our approach.
In an incredibly short time, the residents extemporized
a reception. The whole settlement turned out to welcome us in the usual way—the men firing their guns,
and the women in their gayest dress, singing and
dancing before us.

Carus, one of my old Nasik boys—and also one of
Dr. Livingstone's " faithfuls "—who is in charge, was
greatly delighted to see me again. But we wanted rest,
and as it was too dark to put up our small tent, and
our beds had not come up, we were fain to shake down
in any way we could. I took the floor and my companion the table, and as the room we were in was only
slightly partitioned off from that of the thirty or more
African boys, we had more music and bed-fellows than
were conducive to a quiet night.

Thursday, May 31. After a rather troubled night
—up early and drinking in the delicious cool air. How
refreshing ! would we could bottle some of it up for our

friends at Frere Town! After breakfast, I got a nice quiet time for letter writing, and afterwards for enquiring into the state of the Mission. Burness went to work with his " fundis," putting up the little iron cottage we have brought up with us ; whilst all our spare porters were despatched to the wood, to cut down and bring in trees which are to serve as rafters. We all felt in good "form" and work of any kind was a real pleasure.

To my surprise I found Mr. Last here, in a small tent, engaged in his occupation of butterfly catching. He has netted some fine and rare specimens for which he hopes to get a good price.

Had a delightful walk in the afternoon with Burness some two miles along the ridge of the hill. I had a visit from Masideri, a M.-Digo, the very man who piloted me here six years ago. Having heard of my arrival, he came from his village bringing a present of "pojo". I was glad to see my old friend, and gave him a small present in return. I was both pleased and amused to find he remembered every detail of the circumstances connected with our first meeting.

Friday, June 1. I am glad to find things on the whole better than I had been led to expect. Carus is very good as far as he goes ; but there is much need of a wise and earnest Missionary at the head, who would throw his whole heart into the work. There is a splendid opening for an Evangelist; the Wa-Digo are coming and going all day long, and show a willingness to listen to the Gospel message which is not always met with. I believe if a true Missionary were established here—

one thoroughly conversant with the language—he would find abundant opportunities of proclaiming the " glad tidings " to these poor people, who have hitherto been uncared for.

Meanwhile, till some one can be spared for the post, the little cottage we have put up, when furnished with a few bare necessary articles, will make it possible for the Station to be visited more frequently by one or other of the Brethren, without the trouble and expense which such a visit now entails.

Return to Frere Town.

Saturday, June 2.   The hill was enveloped in clouds when we started at 7·30 a.m., and even on the plain the sun did not show his face, so we made good way and reached Djimbo at noon.   After half an hour's rest we got off, and had scarcely done so, when the storm which had been a-brewing all morning broke upon us in its fury ; our little boat was soon pitching and tossing as if we were in the open sea, instead of the land-locked harbour of Port Reitz, whilst the rain came down pitilessly, soon soaking us to the skin.   There was no refuge, and nothing for it but to sit and shiver in our wet clothes, and push along as best we could.   Happily we had the tide in our favour, and as our boatmen rowed with a will, we got in safely in just under three hours.   We were in sorry plight, but very glad and thankful to find ourselves at home once more.

Sunday, June 3. Have enjoyed a quiet day after our

toils of yesterday. Holy Communion. Burness is suffering from the cruel drenching we got on our way from Shimba. He has been in bed all day with fever; I hope there may be nothing serious the matter.

The Steamer will call in for our letters on Wednesday, so between now and then I have much to do. And then, a few days later, we shall be looking for the Mail from home. I am all uncertain what it may bring me. All is in God's hands, and I will try to "wait patiently". Have been much struck with the singular beauty and comprehensiveness of the collect for to-day: "O God, the strength of all that put their trust in Thee," etc.

My state of mind at this time may be gathered from the following extract from a letter to my wife :—

"As regards the future, you, if anyone, can enter into my feelings. I am in a strait betwixt two. I think of the dear home at Wingfield, with all its happy associations and long to be there; and yet it sometimes seems to me that I may perhaps be more fitted for the Master's service here, and I am very happy in this work —should be supremely so if you were at my side. And what a welcome you would get from many old friends if you ventured to come! But that is almost too much to hope for. I don't know what to say or think. I have committed it all to the Lord. May He in His mercy direct and order all things for us!"

A letter of sympathy to a dear friend may here fittingly be added :—

" RABAI, *Trinity Sunday*, 1888.

" MY DEAR C.,—

"I was greatly grieved to see in the "Record," notice of the death of your dear sister. How little expected was the event! I was quite prepared to miss some of my old friends should I return, or not to return and so be missed ; but your dear sister seemed strong and well, and was in the midst of her useful work ; and had we been asked, we would have said, ' Take this or that but not her; she can *not* be spared '. But ' the Lord's thoughts are not as our thoughts '. How little we know! We cannot doubt that she had done her work, and that the Master she loved and served so faithfully has taken her to Himself—to another 'room' in the Father's house. How soon she and her sainted mother are re-united in Paradise ! There is something solemn and sublime in the taking away of such a one. It seems to bring Heaven nearer to us. . . . .

"As regards myself I am sure you will be pleased to hear that God has so far prospered me, and given me strength according to my day. The lamented death of Bishop Parker has thrown a heavy responsibility on me and ' the care of all the churches '; but I am loyally supported by a band of willing helpers, and I praise God for the wonderful things I have seen. Why, this very day at Morning Service, there was a congregation of five hundred of whom ninety remained for Holy Communion. Their reverence, attention, and general behaviour, put me to shame as I thought of Suffolk. There was a collection for Missionary purposes, which is *monthly*, and which amounted to nearly twenty rupees. Twelve years ago there were only two or three native Christians in the place! So, be of good cheer, dear brother, God is working—His cause is prospering—the word of the Lord, in spite of many difficulties, is having free course and is glorified ; so go on pleading the good cause with Christians in England, assured that in God's good time it is bound to prevail over all enemies and every kind of opposition.

" Believe me, etc., etc."

CHAPTER V.

THE DAILY ROUND.

Wednesday, June 6. Sent off our letters for home by the " Java," and in two or three days we shall be on tip-toe looking out for the English Mail. It is a provoking arrangement—it would be far more to the purpose the other way about. As it is, the letters we are now expecting must remain unanswered for nearly a month!

Lord Hereford, who is making the tour of the world, came over with his two travelling companions, and inspected the Settlement.

Friday, June 7. The journey from Shimba was too much for Burness. He has been in bed with fever—a rather sharp attack—ever since ; and Dr. Ardagh is also, I regret to say, suffering.

A letter comes from Ishmael, who is in temporary charge at Rabái, to say that some porters have come in from Taveta and report that they were attacked by Wa-Masai and three of their number killed. It is, alas ! a too common occurrence, and the wonder is that these poor fellows are willing to run such risks, for a little extra pay. He also informs me that a man belonging to the German Mission at Jimba, 3 miles from Rabai, has been accidentally shot in the chest, and asks for the Doctor to go up and extract the bullet.

Sunday, June 10. Had a quiet service this morning with Burness who is still confined to his bed.

This afternoon H. M. Ship " Stork "—Capt. Pullen —came in from Zanzibar. Sitting in my verandah I saw, as she was fidgeting about for a snug berth, that she was running perilously near the rocks, just under my house.   She gave heed to my shoutings and frantic gestures and escaped by a very close shave.

Monday, June 11.   The " Baghdad " comes with our English Mail.   Praise God for good tidings of all dear ones at home.   I had kind and important letters from three of the Secretaries, but as there is no hint in them of any wish on the part of the Committee for me to prolong my stay, I must, I suppose, arrange to leave by the Steamer of August 1st.   For many reasons I shall be sorry to bid a final farewell to this Mission.   I would willingly give to it what remains to me of life and strength.   It has a hold upon me—a fascination—which I cannot describe.   I do hope the Committee will take care to have a good man—qualified by age and experience— to take the reins from my hands.   An interregnum just now might be disastrous   Perilous times are coming. So far I am thankful to feel that God has prospered me ; I have been enabled to set some things in order, and to sow seed which will one day bear fruit.

A party of three Englishmen and Scotchmen have come to Mombasa, intent, they say, on going up country to hunt and trade! They are a rough lot, and their move- ments are somewhat mysterious.

W. Jones returned from Teita this morning.   He sends a full Report of his mission, from which it appears that a better feeling between the Missionaries and the natives has been established.   I hope it may continue.

To Rabai.

Wednesday, June 13.   Anxious to learn from Jones more fully about Teita affairs, and also to get news from him of the two Brethren, I came here this morning.   It was well I did so, for poor Jones is laid up with fever. He came down by forced marches—overtaxed his strength—and has now to pay the penalty.   It's just the old story.

Friday, June 15.   Jones recovering.   Had an interesting conversation with him on Teita affairs.   The people are intensely superstitious.   If the weather goes wrong or crops fail, they put it down at once to Mr. Wray's magic, and wreak their vengeance upon him and his Brother Missionary, by all kinds of petty annoyances, and some which are anything but petty.   It needs a wonderful supply of grace to enable our Brethren, in face of all this, to hold on from month to month and from year to year, in the hope of living down opposition, and of winning these poor dark heathen to a better mind.

Friday, June 15.   *To my wife :—*

" It is 10 p.m. and I am sitting in Rebmann Lodge, after a rather hard day's work, pencilling my letter to you.   Some wild animal has just passed close by the door.   I called my boy Andrew to bring a light, and went forth gun in hand, but of course saw nothing more of the beast !   As a rule there are very few animals here now ; I never even hear our old friend, the hyæna.   The place is too populous for them.

"This afternoon I paid a visit to Kisimani—a large village about three miles from this.   When I was here last, I recommended its being occupied as an out-station

of Rabai.   This has been done ; Jonah and his wife are
settled there, and in a quiet way carrying on evangelistic work.   It is a purely Wa-Nika village, but we are
getting a footing in it.   Most of the people observe the
Lord's Day—some of them assemble daily for Prayers
and exhortation—whilst a few have gone so far as to
'join the Book,' being under regular Christian instruction, with a view to baptism.   Many of the children

KISIMANI.

attend school, and in addition to reading and writing
which they readily pick up, they all know the Creed,
the Lord's Prayer, and the ten Commandments.   It is
the day of small things, but ' in due time we shall reap
if we faint not '.   Yesterday I visited Fimboni, another
out-station, and a rather important centre, where a
similar work is being carried on by Lewis Bren (one of
our old Makua boys), whose wife is—or rather was—

WATERFALL IN THE DRY SEASON, ON THE WAY TO FIMBONI.

Florence Sharpe. This place is rather difficult of access, as it lies about two miles beyond the water-fall of Chororoni. It took it out of me, climbing those steeps to and fro; but I was amply repaid by what I saw.

"L. is here just now 'arning his living' by collecting butterflies and beetles! He dined with me to-night, and afterwards as we sat talking in the verandah, he said: 'How I wish I were with you in your work now'. Poor fellow! I am sorry in my heart for him. He has lost his opportunity, and all that now remains to him is to make a living as best he can. I shall be glad if I can in any way be helpful to him.

"It was a great pleasure to get dear Mac's letter, and I am thankful he is able to be back at his post. At the same time I cannot but feel it would be wise in the Committee, when Nevill returns, to transfer him to another Mission. He would be the very man for a second 'Fourah Bay' in E. Africa; which is just now the crying want of this Mission. We are greatly suffering from what I cannot but call the gross neglect of the young men."

Sunday, June 17. Thankful for a quiet and refreshing rest. The attendance at Church Services to-day not so good as usual. Many of the people have to be all day in their "shambas," scaring birds from the ripening crops.

Had a meeting in my house in the evening, attended by all the "fundis," my two boys, and a few others. We had several Hymns and Prayer, and a short address.

Monday, June 18. *Return to Frere Town.* Left at 9 a.m. Had a strong wind against us all the way. I have never seen the water so rough in the creek before. Got in about 2 p.m.

Tuesday, June 19.   *To my Wife :—*

"I am back at Frere Town, and should be off to Shimba to-morrow, but that I have too much on hand here.   The affairs of the late Bishop cause me a good deal of extra work.   How little we thought, when he and I sat talking over East African matters in our little Summer-house at Wingfield, that I should visit his Diocese, without even seeing him; and that I should have the melancholy task of packing up his things, and a chief part in winding up his affairs.   He appears to have been a man eminently fitted for the Office ; but, as you know, I always felt and still feel, that his going to the Lake— at any rate so soon—was a mistake.   I wonder who will succeed him; probably another Indian missionary.   May God guide the Committee in their choice !

"I shall be very busy between now and Mail time, so shall not be able to add much to this ; and as it must be posted before I get any further news from home, you may take it for granted, unless you hear to the contrary from Salisbury Square that I leave by the August Mail, due in London on the 21st, and I shall look for a letter from you at each of the Ports of call.

"I am anxiously expecting the 'Henry Wright' from Zanzibar.   She is over-due, and these two days it has been blowing a gale.   I was five hours coming from Rabai yesterday, and we were sorely tossed about in our little boat.

Wednesday, June 20.   "Rejoiced to see the 'H. W.' steaming into harbour this morning.   She had been de- tained in Zanzibar, and so escaped the rough weather.

She brings us a consignment of freed slaves—nineteen women, eleven men, and five children—all in a wretched condition ; also three of our old friends—Sophy, Rose Russell, and Harriet Dowman ; and an imploring letter from several others, who long to come back to F. Town, now that 'Papa' is there. Some of them have been hardly dealt with, and I shall do my best to make ready a place for them.

"My love to all the dear children. I'm afraid I shall not find time to write to any of them, and this is my last chance. Fully occupied as I have been, the days and weeks have glided away almost imperceptibly; and now I find it difficult to realize that this is my last letter to you from this side of the world ; and that the next following Mail, I shall not be sending a letter, but, if the Lord will, coming myself. If I can manage it, I shall perhaps take a run over to Jerusalem on my way home. I hear it can be done for £5 from Port Said, and within the week. I am writing to our old friend, John Robert Hall, for information. If I determine upon this, I will let you know, that you may tell when to expect me."

Thursday, June 21. Went to inspect the new comers, to see how they are housed, etc. I asked the women if they were comfortable, to which they replied, that only two things were wanted to make them happy, viz., "jembes" and husbands ! When asked if they would like to return to their own country, they burst into a loud laugh, which seemed to mean that the thing was ridiculous, or else that they were too well content with their present lot to wish to change it for the risks and dangers of their former life. This is very significant, and goes to show what a wretched condition they must have been in, in their old homes. They had no wish to return ; whatever may lie before them, it can't be worse than what they have left behind. God grant that their coming here may be the beginning of a new and better life, and that many may find the true liberty which Christ alone can give !

I have spent much time and thought this week in drawing up a scheme for the better accommodation of the girls' Dormitory—of the ladies in charge—and of a suitable Lecture Hall for a young men's Divinity Class. To-day I submitted it to the Finance Committee, and after some friendly discussion of details, it was passed *nem. con.* for recommendation to the Parent Committee.

A return furnished by Mr. Smith at my request, discloses the astounding fact that our cocoa-nut trees (between 2 and 3000), instead of bringing in a profit to the Mission of some £300 a year, which they ought to do, actually entail a loss. An intelligent layman—a good man of business—is sadly needed to look after this and many other things.

Sunday, June 24. Not feeling well the last few days —no fever or other particular ailment that I know of— but something which keeps one below par. I look to the Strong One for strength.

Held an English Service this evening in the room in my house, which it is proposed to convert into a Lecture hall. It answered the purpose admirably. There was a good attendance—all the English (ten) and twenty-five Natives. It was a bright hearty Service and we all enjoyed it.

To Rabai.

Tuesday, June 26.   Came here this afternoon in the hope of having three or four days quiet for writing, and to be on the spot to welcome Fitch, whom I was expecting from Chaga towards the end of the week. What was my surprise to meet Fitch and Jones on the road about a mile from the Station! He left Chaga only twelve days ago—of which nearly two were spent at Teita by the way—and by dint of forced marches arrived here this morning. What a picture he was! sunburnt and travel-stained and wondrously attired! My first thought on seeing him was, what a capital Deputation he would make at a Missionary meeting, just as he is! I praise God for his safe arrival, and for that of Taylor also at Chaga: a great relief to my mind. We spent a quiet, pleasant evening together ; he had much to tell of his work at Chaga—of Mandara—and of Teita affairs—much that was very interesting and important for me to hear. What a commotion there will be in Frere Town to-morrow!

Wednesday, June 27. Returned with Fitch to Frere Town. We got in quite unexpectedly, so there was no grand reception ; but it was pleasant to witness the delight with which dear Miss Fitch welcomed her brother, in his bronzed skin and his marvellous travelling turn-out. How strangely things are mixed up in this world! It is a time for joy and thanksgiving, and yet a matter comes before me this afternoon of a very painful nature, nothing less than a grievous falling out between two Brethren. Alas! it is an enemy that hath done this, and he is ever watching his opportunity.

Nothing would serve his purpose so well as to set us all at loggerheads.

Thursday, June 28. *Returned to Rabai.* And what a journey! It was raining when we started, and went on increasing all the way. I had only my thin white clothes on, and was soon wet through, and cold and clammy!   From the "banderini" the road was execrable.   It was as much as my poor "punda" could do to carry herself, so I was compelled to trudge it. Somehow or other I got in soon after 6 p.m.—had a cold bath—changed my "vestments," and hope I may be none the worse for it to-morrow, though I must confess to a feeling of "nimechoka".   To mend matters, my bright boy, Andrew, has mislaid my mosquito curtains. Three trips between Frere Town and Rabai in three days are no joke; but I have much writing to do for the Mail, and with the incessant calls upon one at the former, I should not be able to finish it in time.

Saturday, June 30.   Headache, and generally out of sorts; yet got through a fair amount of work for the Mail.   This evening the Chaga and Teita Mails arrived, bringing me two letters from Taylor, and his Report on the Teita Mission—also letters from Wray and Morris : plenty to think about and to do.

In some anxiety as to a matter referred to above, I wrote to a colleague :—

"If you should see anything going wrong between any of the Brethren, do your best to pour oil on the troubled waters.   We must do all in our power to defeat the tactics of *the* enemy, which are 'to stir up strife'. Everything depends on our preserving 'the unity of spirit, in the bond of peace'. We cannot all think and feel alike on every point, but we should at least remember that we are servants of the same Master, and that His command is 'that ye love one another'. I do not mention names because you can scarcely help knowing to what and to whom I refer. Do all that in you lies to make peace."

About another matter much upon my mind at this time I wrote to Mr. Fitch :—

"I feel it would be unreasonable to ask you to undertake any serious work till the next Mail has gone and come, yet I know you are anxious to be in harness. My time here may be short, and I am most anxious to see the Divinity Class fairly started before I leave. I shall be glad therefore if you can find time to confer with England (schoolmaster) and get from him the names of any youths, who may be eligible for such a class. We must be content with a small beginning. Once begun, it will grow ; and the hope of evangelizing the peoples of E. Africa, depends, under God, upon our having a well-trained and thoroughly spiritually minded band of Native Evangelists. To prepare such men is one of the highest and noblest works any man can engage in, etc., etc."

Sunday, July 1. A happy day of rest. Took part in administering Holy Communion—about a hundred partook. Meeting of "fundis" in my house in the evening for Praise and Prayer.

There are many trials and difficulties, but at the same time many encouragements, in connexion with the E. A. Mission. In spite of many sad things in the past, and many mistakes, the contrast between thirteen years ago and to-day, is simply marvellous. I do not believe there is in any part in the world a more " open door ". What is wanted is a body of men and women thoroughly consecrated in heart and life to the service of Christ—some to *sow* and some to *reap*. I never was more convinced that the time is coming when " Christ shall reign indeed ".

Spent a pleasant half-hour in writing to my dear Missionary son :—

" RABAI, *July* 1, 1888.

" MY DEAREST MAC,—

"Your welcome letter of April 9 found its way to me on June 10—just two months ! You might perhaps have done better *viâ* Marseilles, but I don't know. Anyway I was glad to get it, and to find that you were back at your post, and that in God's good providence we divide the Dark Continent between us, *i.e.* from a C. M. S. point of view—you being Acting Secretary for the West and I for the East. That at any rate is something unique.

" I am thankful to hear of your admission to Priest's orders, and although we did not know of it in time to think of you specially on that day, we shall certainly as you say, ' follow your life with our prayers '. May God the Holy Spirit fulfil you with all grace for the Holy Office, and make you a faithful minister : ' a workman that needeth not to be ashamed '.

" I can fully sympathize with you in your loneliness. I know now what it is to have the worry of house-keeping, and can feel grateful for the many years of freedom I have enjoyed from such complicated business. I am heart and soul in this work, which taxes all one's powers of mind and body to the utmost, and should be very happy in it, if only your dear mother were here to share it with me.

"I am amazed at what you tell me of the feeling on the part of some Native Christians in favour of polygamy. Whether we ought to refuse baptism to polygamous converts or not may be an open question ; but for one who is a baptized Christian to take more than one wife would be a sin and a shame and should never be allowed. . . .

"I have had a happy and I hope a useful time here ; and as to the future I leave all in God's hands. May He be with you, my dear boy, and prosper you in all your way for Christ's sake."

Tuesday, July 3. *Returned to Frere Town.* Among the many kind letters received by the last Mail were two that particularly cheered me—one from Mr. Wigram and one from Mr. Stock, to which I replied as follows :

To the Rev. F. E. Wigram.

"*July* 3, 1890.

"My dear Mr. Wigram,—

"I must thank you for your kind sympathizing letter of May 8—none the less grateful that it was unexpected. The news of the sudden removal of the late Bishop came of course as a severe shock to us all ; more especially to those who had personal acquaintance with him, and whose love and confidence he had gained in a remarkable degree, in so short a time. He seemed so eminently fitted by gifts and graces for the post of Bishop, that great hopes were entertained of happy results from his wise administration of the affairs of the Mission. For myself, I may say, it was a great disappointment not to have the pleasure of meeting him face to face, and of spending my last few weeks in happy intercourse and conference with him, on matters dear to us both. And when your telegram came I was at first almost overwhelmed as I realized what a heavy responsibility was thrown upon me. At the same time it was so entirely unsought on my part, and so unexpected, that I felt I might confidently look to the Lord for the strength and grace which I should certainly need. Moreover it comforted me not a little to have on the part of the Brethren here, the ready assurance of their sympathy and prayers. For all this I have every reason to say, 'Praise the Lord'.

"I have done my best to carry on the Mission on the lines laid down, which for the most part were not new to me. The only change of importance I have ventured to make on my own responsibility is that of bringing down dear Fitch to the coast, for a much needed change. He arrived a few days ago, and received a hearty welcome from all—Europeans and Natives. I am thankful he is here for several reasons—the chief perhaps being that his presence enables me to take the first steps in the formation of a Divinity Class for promising young men, who, with God's blessing, will become the future Evangelists of E. Africa—an object which I have cherished for years, and which I know also was much in the mind of the late Bishop. I think too if I leave by the August Mail as in the ordinary course of events I must be prepared to do, and if no one should arrive before then to supply my place, the Committee will be only too glad to know that Fitch is on the spot to take charge, *pro. tem.*, till a more permanent arrangement can be made.

"Earnestly praying that the Committee may be divinely guided in all, I remain, etc., etc."

To Eugene Stock, Esq.

"MY DEAR FRIEND,—

"Many, many thanks for yours of May 18. It reminds me of old times. How you find time for such correspondence passes my comprehension. Here we are *all*, and *always*, at high pressure, but as a rule it is not so in England.

"I am sorry I shall not be here to welcome the daughter of my old friend Baldey, but I will do all I can to provide for her comfort, and Miss Fitch, who is a jewel, will do all the rest. I rejoice to hear of other ladies offering for the work. There is a splendid field for them here and at Rabai, and not necessarily 'strapping old maids'. . . . . .

"I hope Miss Harvey will stay long enough to get thoroughly set up before returning. When she does come, she will find some outward changes which I hope she will not be sorry for. Some trees, for instance, near her house, which shut out the fresh air and shut in malaria, have been ruthlessly cut down by the hand that planted them. She will find, I hope, a nice little upper-storied bedroom all ready for her; and the dear girls whose welfare she has at heart, comfortably housed, where she can have her eye upon them and cast her wing over them night and day ; and better still, she will, I hope, find some on whom she has bestowed prayerful pains giving proof that her labour and pains have not been in vain ; and I am sure she may reckon upon a hearty welcome from a band of fellow-workers, with whom it is a real pleasure and privilege to be associated. Give her my Christian love, and tell her how sorry I am not to be here to take my part in that welcome.

"How the time flies ! Four of my six months are gone. They have been busy months, and I would fain hope, through God's blessing, not altogether unproductive; and what solemn events have taken place ! 'Verily, it is as a dream when one awaketh.'

"I am sending on Taylor's MS. of his itinerating tour in Giriama. I have read it through with great interest. It is too long to print *in extenso*, but I hope you will find room somewhere for a few selected extracts. It is the narrative of a man of God, thoroughly in earnest, and whose one aim is to evangelize the heathen. It shows too what an opening there is for the preaching of the Gospel to the poor ignorant natives of E. Africa.

" A few days after you get this, unless something unforeseen occurs, I shall be on my way home. Between now and then I have enough to do, if it please God to give me strength to do it.

" I remain, etc., etc."

Wednesday, July, 4. The " Baghdad " came and took off our letters. We breathe again, and make a fresh start !

CHAPTER VI.

TRIPS TO ZANZIBAR AND SHIMBA.

Thursday, July 5. Invited all the Mission party to tea and supper, to meet and give a welcome to Brother Fitch. We were eleven altogether, viz.: Rev. A. G. Smith, Mr. and Mrs. Burness, Mr. and Miss Fitch, Capt. Wilson, Dr. Ardagh, Mr. England, Messrs. Reid and Pratley, and myself. For the domestic arrangements I was much indebted to Mr. and Mrs. Burness; indeed what I should have done without them I really don't know. Before sitting down, my boy Gilbert came to me and asked very gravely, "*Bwana*, which of the *Bibis* shall I give food to *first?*" Poor lad! the question of precedence has puzzled wiser heads than yours before now. After supper, Fitch gave an interesting account of his life in Chaga, and altogether we spent a very pleasant evening.

Friday, July 6. A red letter day in the history of the East Africa Mission! At 10.30 a.m. Messrs. Fitch, Smith and England met at my house, and after invoking the blessing of Almighty God, we took the first steps in the formation of a training class for young men. I quote from the account I gave of it to Mr. Lang :—

"I have taken advantage of Fitch being here to set on foot a Divinity Class for the special training of young men as teachers, catechists, etc. I have long felt that this was the great want of our E. A. Mission, and am very thankful to have had some hand in supplying it. The question may occur to you, 'What will happen when Fitch returns to Chaga?' Well, I can't say, but I earnestly hope the Committee will feel the great importance of making the best provision they can for this most necessary branch of their work, and that once fairly started, it will not be allowed to fall through. We begin modestly and in a small way, taking only those who are already Teachers or wish to become such, and who by their intelligence and Christian character give promise of future usefulness. I hope this new departure will be especially remembered in prayer by all who take an interest in this Mission."

Saturday, July 7. Looking out for the "Oriental" with our English Mails. As there is rather a strong adverse wind she will probably be late. Devoutly hope she will not come in to-morrow. Am making preparations to go in her to Zanzibar.

The Mails for Chaga and Teita must however be first despatched. To Mr. Taylor I wrote :

"Frere Town, July 7, 1888.

" My dear Taylor,—

"Your two letters of June 22 reached me in due course. I thank you for them, and for your very interesting and valuable Report on the Teita Mission, which I have forwarded, together with one, in most respects agreeing with it, from Fitch, to Mr. Lang. . . .

" I am sorry you found Paul D. (Native Catechist) so intractable. I do not wonder at his wishing to follow his old master to the coast, and being rather disgusted at being left behind, but he ought to have acted more like a man in the matter. I hope he is a good fellow at heart, though like all of us he has his faults and failings. It is well however that you are independent of him, in your dealings with that peculiar individual, Mandara. I earnestly pray God to give you a powerful influence for good over that man.

"I am glad on the whole that the R. Catholics are going into the pleasant pastures of Arusha. Why? because I feel sure if it had not been, in some way, for the good of our cause, they would not have been permitted to 'steal a march upon us'. The Lord reigneth!

"Fitch came down in twelve days, including the time spent at Teita. He came on the wings of love. It is very touching to see the joy of brother and sister, at their happy re-union after a separation of four years; and it must be as gratifying to you as it is to me, to have had a hand in bringing it about.

"Pratley says he sent by last 'safari' fourteen pages of proofs—all he had type for—so I hope you received them after you wrote.

"Give my best 'salams' to King Mandara, and tell him that after having spent the best part of forty years in India and Africa, I have a strong desire to make his acquaintance. I do not know if I shall have this pleasure; but whether so or not I earnestly hope he may be led to accept the message of God's love, so that we may meet 'in the better land'. May the Lord, dear Taylor, make you a blessing to him. . . .

"Praying God to prosper your visit to Chaga, and with sincere Christian love,

"Yours, etc., etc."

A large number of freed-slave children were made over to us in 1876, who are now of course grown up men and women. Of these not a few, after receiving a fairly-good school education, have been left to themselves; and it is scarcely to be wondered at that they have run wild, and become a source of trouble in the Mission. One of these is Harry Milford : a fine young fellow in some respects, bright and clever, and well-instructed in the Scriptures; but he turned out badly —was for ever getting into scrapes—and everybody had come to regard him as an incorrigible scapegrace. I have no doubt he well deserved his bad name; but for all that I felt drawn to him, and was anxious to give him another chance. At my request dear Taylor consented to take him with him as his servant—to have a kind eye over him—and to give him a fair opportunity of redeeming his character. So far Taylor reports well of him, and I have a nice letter from himself which inclines me to hope that he is not ungrateful for the kindness shown him, and that he is trying to mend. To this I replied :—

"*July* 8, 1888.

"Dear Harry,—

"I was very pleased to receive your letter, giving me an account of your journey; and we thank God that they who have gone to Chaga, and they who came here from thence, have been brought on their way in safety. It seems that one of the hardest trials the African traveller has to meet with is want of water. What a good thing it would be, if some one would sink wells and build tanks here and there along the road, and right away through the wilderness, where thirsty travellers might refresh themselves. I think everyone would sing the praises of the kind man who should do this, and he would deserve it. But if this be so, as regards the water we need for our bodies, how much more so as regards that which we need for our souls. And yet whilst nobody seems inclined to supply the one the Lord Jesus has made rich provision for the other, so that no one need die of *soul* thirst. He gives the water of life to those who earnestly ask Him for it. Look out in your Bible and read Isaiah lv. 1, etc. I pray God, dear Harry, you may seek for yourself that ' living water '.

"I shall be glad to hear from you again. Meanwhile I hope you will do your best, seeking God's help, to be a faithful servant to your dear master, and to live a good Christian life before the poor dark heathen of Chaga.

" May God help and bless you.

"Your friend and well-wisher, etc."

Monday, July 9. Up goes the signal! off goes the gun! the "Oriental" has anchored; so, snatching a hasty breakfast, Smith and I are soon on board looking for our bag of letters. This is always a thrilling time. What may not have happened in a month? Thank God for good news from my dear wife! A glance through my official letters—no time for more just now —leaves me rather perplexed. There seems to be nothing definite about my own movements. The wish is expressed on the part of the Committee that I may be able to stay on a little longer, and they add that they will approach the Bishop of Norwich on the subject, and also write to my wife. This means for me another month of suspense. It is just a little trying; but there is too much to think about and do to allow time for moping; and, after all, another month will soon be gone.

Nothing but pressing business would take me away to Zanzibar. It has no attractions for me, barring of course the warm welcome I can always count upon at the Agency, and from other friends. Three urgent matters make it necessary for me to go there just now :—

First. I have received a letter from the Parent Committee addressed to the new Sultan, Said Khalifa, congratulating him on his accession to the Throne, and I am particularly requested to present it to His Highness in person.

Second. I am charged to effect the legal transfer of all Property—houses, land, etc., belonging to the C. M. S. in its various Mission Stations, to the " Church Missionary Trust Association ".

Third. In view of troublous times which begin to loom in the near future, there are certain points affecting our Mission, about which it is most desirable for me to confer with the Consul-General.

Left in the " Oriental " on July 10 : and after a fairly good passage made Zanzibar at 11 a.m. the following day. My fellow-passengers were Capt. Berkeley on a visit to his brother, one of the Vice-Consuls, and Mr. and Mrs. Swan of the L. M. S. proceeding to Lake Tanganyika. I found my nest all ready for me at the Agency, and having taken possession I was free to set to work at once on the business for which I had come. The first thing was to find a lawyer who would undertake the conveyance of the Society's property. Judge Cracknell recommended to me Mr. Beyzonji, a Parsi and the principal Barrister in the Judge's Court, and to him I went. I found him most gentlemanly and obliging, and he readily undertook to do what I wanted. I had brought with me all Deeds of sale relating to C. M. S. properties in Frere Town and Mombasa, some of which were in Arabic and had to be translated. Mr. Beyzonji took great pains with the business, and furnished me with the required Deed of transfer, which was duly stamped and registered in the Consular office. Considering the amount of trouble he had taken in the matter, and his position, I was quite prepared to have to pay rather heavily. When, however, I asked Mr. Beyzonji to name his fee, he promptly declined, saying: " It is for a good Society, and it gives me great pleasure to do it for nothing " !

Friday (13th) was fixed for our visit to the Sultan and at 10 a.m. we set out from the Agency for the new Palace. Our party consisted of the Consul General, Capt. Pullen and one or two other Naval Officers—all in full dress uniform —and myself. It was a grand state occasion. The whole of the Sultan's army—regular and irregular—were in attendance, and being drawn up on either side of the line of route. to keep a clear path for us, saluted as we passed along. Behind them were crowds of people—it seemed as if half the population had flocked together, eager to catch a glimpse of the unwonted sight of half a dozen Englishmen walking together under a broiling sun towards the Palace. It is anything but pleasant to have so many eyes focussed on one, and I don't think any of us felt very much at ease or were sorry when this part of the programme was over. The band I must say did their best to keep up our courage by playing " God save the Queen," all the way. At the bottom of the flight of steps of the new Palace, we were met by the Sultan, to whom the Consul General introduced me and the other visitors. His Highness then led the way to the grand reception room up-stairs, where a hundred or more of the principal Arab notables, the Aristocracy—in full dress—were assembled to do honour to H. M. Representative. I noticed a distinct family likeness in the Sultan to his late brother, Said Bargash ; but the expression of his face was very different. The late Sultan had a beaming countenance which was generally lighted up with a smile ; whilst his successor has a somewhat dejected look, which gives the idea of one who has suffered adversity, and has not yet become accustomed to great-ness. He motioned us to our seats on his right, and then took his own on the Throne. After a short con-versation between H. H. and the Consul General, carried on in a friendly way, the opportunity was given me of presenting the Committee's letter, which I did with as much grace as I could command, accompanying it with some remarks in harmony therewith. H. H. received it graciously and promised to furnish me with a reply. I ventured to say a word, which I thought was deserved, in praise of the present Wali of Mombasa. He happened to be in the room, and was so well pleased, that he paid me a special visit afterwards to thank me for it. All passed off well, and it was certainly a very striking function, and one suggestive of many thoughts in connexion with our position as a Missionary Society in this Mahommedan country.

I may add here, that His Highness, at the instance no doubt of Col. Euan Smith, will in future remit to the C. M. S. Mission Custom duties up to Rs. 500 per annum, *i.e.*, up to that amount we have nothing to pay on imported goods, which practically means, I suppose, total exemption. We may look on it as an Ann. Sub. of H. H. the Sultan of Zanzibar to the C. M. S.

In the afternoon took a drive to Mbweni, with the Colonel, Capt. Berkeley and Capt. Pullen, to pay a visit to the Universities' Mission. Saw Archdeacon and Mrs. Hodgson, Miss Berkeley, Miss Bennett, a bright young lady just out, whose fresh English colour made all the rest look very wan. Alas! these roses soon fade in East Africa. Driving through the narrow streets of Zanzibar in a carriage and pair is a ticklish business— a feat of coachman-ship, which requires a quick eye and a steady hand.

At night there was a select party to dinner at the Agency to do honour to Lt. Palmer, who has just received promotion as a reward for his plucky capture of a slave dhow.

Sunday, July 15. Gave a Service this morning on board H.M.S. " Penguin," to an attentive congregation of " blue-jackets ". In the afternoon preached in the Cathedral. I took the notes of an old Wingfield sermon from " Lovest thou me? " I am not aware that anybody cared for it at Wingfield, but two of my hearers to-day cordially thanked me for it. It is one of the " weak things," which may God own and bless.

It seems to me a pity this fine Church was ever placed where it is. As far as concerns the English community it is almost inaccessible, especially to any who may be in delicate health. It occupies a site in the very heart of the native town, and the roads leading to it lie through some of the most filthy and noisy streets of the place ; it is at times positively sickening to pass through them. There is something no doubt in the sentiment of a Christian church on the very site of the old slave market, but other considerations far outweigh this in my estimation.

Being the guest of the Consul General, I have had good opportunities of freely conversing with him on Mission topics. Amongst other things he told me that he had written to the Home authorities, strongly recommending the withdrawal of *all* our Missionaries from the interior, until the clouds which now threaten shall have passed away. This is all right from his point of view, *i.e.*, as H.M. Consul General, having a certain amount of responsibility for protecting the lives and property of Englishmen. I can quite understand this. It simply means that, under circumstances which may any day happen, he would not be able to afford protection or guarantee the safety of our Missionaries in the interior ; but I assured him that I did not think it at all likely that the C. M. S. Committee would take the drastic course of abandoning their Stations even for a season, except under sheer compulsion—that I as their representative could not take any such step without express orders from Home ; and that our Brethren at the Lake and elsewhere knew perfectly well that their lives were in some danger, but for the love of Christ they accepted the situation, and asked for no " arm of flesh " to protect them.

Monday, July 16. *Return to Frere Town.* Left in the " Henry Wright " at noon. We have on board 23 freed slaves, men and women—a recent capture. One of the poor women was so terrified, not knowing what was going to be done to her, that she had to be put on board by force. The sepoys did their work brutally, dragging the poor creature by her legs, whilst her head and body were dashed against the rough stony ground. It was a cruel sight, but I was powerless to interfere. How I would have liked to give those cowardly ruffians a good cudgelling.

Tuesday, July 17. We have had a roughish passage, getting in at 6 a.m. Our little boat showed what she can do in the way of rolling. She shipped seas freely, till there was no dry place anywhere, and we were all tolerably wretched. Thank God, I have accomplished the objects I had in view in going to Zanzibar, and am once more away from that awful place. Had a hearty welcome from all here on my return.

Disquieting tidings come to me from Shimba, which make it necessary that I should pay an early visit to that Station. I purpose going there, D. V., on Friday next, and am asking W. Jones to accompany me. He will be very helpful to me in dealing with the matter in hand. The following account of my visit is from a letter to my wife :—

To Shimba.

"*Sunday, July* 22. We—Jones and I—set out on Friday afternoon for this place, and thinking it a good opportunity of prospecting for a new and better route, we made for Mtongwi, where we landed about 6 p.m. As it was too late to proceed, I had my tent pitched in the midst of a forest of palm-trees. Heavy rain came on in the night, but did not find its way through my canvas double roof. My poor 'wa-pagazi' (about twenty) who were in the open, croodled round the camp fires, and watched for the morning. We were up in good time, and off at 6.30. After three and a half hours' walk—ten miles—we halted a couple of hours for break-fast and rest. Hitherto the sun had very kindly hidden himself behind a bank of clouds; but we had no sooner started again than the storm which had been threatening all morning came down upon us, and from there to the end of our journey—another ten miles which took us four and a half hours—we had to make our way over a rugged and difficult road, through a continuous downpour of rain. Owing to the strong wind, progress was difficult, and we were soon all thoroughly soaked. To add to our troubles we discovered that our guide, Asahel, had actually led us some three or four miles out of our way. Jones proposed we should seek refuge in some hamlet, but I would not hear of it. Here we were, with not a dry rag left; tent, clothes, bedding, all drenched, to say nothing of our poor fellows, who had little indeed besides their own black skins to get wetted; and only about four miles remained to be done; so pointing to the top of Shimba heights, I shouted ' Haya,

haya,' and the men responding with a will, took up their loads and forged ahead. Right glad I was that I had my own way for once. We got in at 4 30, taking everybody by surprise, and, of course, finding no preparations; but Carus, good fellow! extemporized a hot bath for me—a novel contrivance—and to my joy I found a flannel coat and trousers which had escaped the ducking, in my iron box. We were, as you may imagine, completely tired out; so after a hasty supper, I spread a piece of old mat on a native 'kitanda,' and had the soundest sleep I have known for many a day, awaking this morning thoroughly refreshed, and with thankful feelings to Almighty God for His goodness. I am *so* glad we came on, to enjoy the rest after the six days' toil is over. The air too is delicious. It is just about six years ago, that Shaw, Jones and I were running away from this place, to avoid falling into the hands of Mbaruk the rebel chieftain: to-day we are assembled in the House of Prayer, together with a congregation of some eighty souls, whilst many of the poor heathen Wa-Digo are at the door and windows listening to the Word of God!

"Jones gave two good stirring sermons to-day, and in the evening we had a Prayer Meeting in my room for the 'fundis' and others."

Monday, July 23. Held an inquiry into the matter which had been reported to me. When gone into it was not nearly so serious as it seemed at first sight. Carus it appears had rather indiscreetly given a sound beating to one of the bigger boys, for disobedience of orders, whereupon about twelve of his mates took his part, and arming themselves with sticks, surrounded Carus, and dared him to beat any one again. There were as usual faults on both sides, but it was essential to uphold Carus's authority; so picking out the ring-leaders, I told them as this was the first offence, I was ready to forgive them, on their humbly asking Carus's pardon for their conduct, which they readily did. I then privately intimated to Carus that for the future he is not to enforce obedience with the stick. Everything was easily arranged, but such an occurrence shows how desirable it is, that this new and, in many respects, promising Mission should be under the immediate supervision and control of a competent head.

In the afternoon had a walk of four miles along the ridge of the hill, to the end, in a northerly direction. My object was to ascertain if there is any way of descending to the Djimbo road. We found a path steep and rugged indeed, but not very long, and which will save four miles of very bad travelling along the base of the hill.

Wednesday, July 25. The few days here have done me good. I had a nice quiet time for letters yesterday; and to day at 9 a.m. we set out to return home by the new route explored on Monday. An hour and fifty minutes brought us to an oasis—quite a pretty spot with grassy slopes, and shady trees, and a spring of good water. This is a convenient half-way resting place, to which I gave the name Bawakondi, which being interpreted is "Wingfield". It would be well to put up a small rest-house here, for the convenience of persons journeying to or from Shimba and for Missionaries itinerating in Wadigo land.

Monday, July 30. Much occupied the last few days getting ready for the Mail to England, due to leave this on Wednesday next. A few extracts from the following letter, written at this time, will bring information as to the condition of affairs in the Mission up to date :—

To the Rev. R. Lang, Sec. C. M. S.

"Your letter of June 15 came to hand July 10. We rejoice to hear of the Cambridge volunteers, and hope ere long this Mission, among others, will share the blessing.

"We shall look out for Miss Wardlaw Ramsay about August 29. She will have about three days in Zanzibar, and Mrs. Euan Smith has kindly promised to look after her comfort there. She will of course be heartily welcomed here, and Miss Fitch will be delighted to have her society and help. She much needs them, although I am happy to say, since the advent of her brother, she is quite another woman. It has done her— and him too—a world of good.

"I hope Beverley will come up with Miss Ramsay. It costs nothing, as the fare is the same to Zanzibar and Mombasa, and he can return in the 'Henry Wright'. I would suggest that any new Missionary coming out for the inland stations should pay a short visit to Frere Town. As I said it costs nothing either in money or time, and for many reasons is most desirable.

"Smith is delighted at the prospect of being relieved

from secular work. I cherish the hope that the new Assistant Secretary may be already on his way.

" Taylor writes cheerfully of his position and prospects at Chaga. He seems so far to be a *persona grata* with Mandara ; and we may be sure he will make the best use of whatever influence he may obtain over him. The arrangement with Taylor is, that he occupies the post for three months, to give Fitch the benefit of a change to the coast for that time. If the Committee wish to modify this in any way, you should send directions by return Mail, as the three months expire with September.

" The situation at Teita remains unchanged. There is nothing new to communicate. The letters and reports forwarded by last Mail, will, I think, enable the Committee to form a judgment as to what is best to be done. We must await their decision. If I were remaining on, I would gladly go and carry out their wishes, but as I am not, it will be one of the first things to occupy the attention of the new Bishop, or whoever comes out as Director of the Mission.

" Now, one word about myself. I asked only for six months' leave from the Bishop of Norwich, and according to that, I should be leaving by the Mail which takes this letter. In your last you say ' we will approach the Bishop of Norwich, etc.' Relying upon that, and hoping for the best, and being most unwilling to leave the Mission in the lurch, I have decided to stay on, at any rate another month. So now, unless I hear something from you to change my plans, by the Mail we are expecting three days after this leaves, I must take my passage by the Steamer of August 25, due in London Sept. 24. Possibly you may be expecting me by this Mail. I do not wish to consider myself, but if it can be avoided without detriment to the Mission, I should prefer not to leap at once out of an East African summer, into the depth of an English winter.

"I am sorry to say Mr. Smith and Dr. Ardagh are both ill in bed with fever. Dr. Corcorran of H. M. S. "Mariner," now in harbour, is kindly attending to them.

"With kindest Christian regards,

"Yours, etc., etc."

As the departure of the Mail steamer was delayed for a day I was able to add a supplement to the above letter of yesterday to Mr. Lang :—

"*August* 2.

"I have the opportunity of adding a few lines to my letter of yesterday, and I regret the necessity. Dr. Corcorran gives it as his opinion that Dr. Ardagh ought not to remain longer in E. Africa, and recommends his going home as soon as possible. You will be partly prepared for this by what I have said in former letters. It is scarcely possible for him to get away by this Steamer, which leaves a few hours hence, but you may look for him by the next boat, leaving Aug. 29. It is inconvenient for this Station to be left without medical aid just now. Mrs. B. is expecting her confinement early in November. Perhaps Dr. Baxter may be here by then, or he may have gone on to Mpwapwa, setting Dr. Pruen free to come here. Failing both of these strings I have another, which is, to invite Miss Smith, a certificated lady of the Universities' Mission, to come here for a few weeks; or, if it comes to the worst, to send Mrs. B. to Zanzibar for her confinement. We trust the Lord will guide us; but it is only right to let you know the state of things. Smith, I am glad to say, is convalescent. He has suffered from bronchial affection, not fever. I have a long letter from Dr. Pruen, but no doubt he has written fully to you also as to all matters at Mpwapwa. The Mails from the Lake seem to be mysteriously slow!

" Yours, etc."

After all, we got Dr. Ardagh off by the "Oriental" to-day. Having ascertained that there would be a delay of five hours in the Steamer's departure, I summoned " all hands 'bout ship " and we set to work, to pack his boxes, books, clothes, etc. This done we had a short farewell meeting, to commend our sick Brother to the care and protection of our Heavenly Father. An hour before the Steamer left he was safely on board. It is sharp work, but in his case it may be a matter of life or death ; anyway, since he *must* go, it is better now than a month hence. This is the first break in our little party since I came out!

CHAPTER VII.

ANOTHER SIX MONTHS.—A FRESH START.

THE three or four days between the outgoing and
incoming Mails is our slackest time. For one thing we
have been working at high pressure, and having sent off
our letters there is a disposition to open the valve and
let off steam ; and there a feeling of uncertainty as to
what the letters we are expecting may bring us. It is
hard to settle down to steady work, and to make plans
for the future. Under these circumstances we gladly
responded to Capt. Arbuthnot's kind invitation to join
him and his Officers, on Saturday, Aug. 4, in a pic-nic to
Mtongwi in Port Reitz. We all went except Smith,
who after his recent illness was afraid to venture. We
were conveyed in the " Mariner's " steam pinnace, and
a whaler. On landing we found a nice open space under
the shade of a fine old mango tree, and the Captain's
steward, assisted by three or four sailors, set to work to
prepare for lunch. First, a clearing was made, and a
large table-cloth spread out on the grass, and then
several hampers, full of all sorts of good things, were
brought up from the boat, unpacked, and their contents
tastefully arranged. When all was ready, we sat down
—no that is not the word, but rather we assumed every
kind of attitude possible to us under the circumstances
—each to his own fancy—some kneeling—some sitting
tailor fashion—and the rest lounging ; but whatever the

position, we were all in excellent trim for the business in hand and did full justice to the sumptuous repast spread out before us. And what a feast it was in an African jungle! It is no joke to cater for such a party —about thirty in all—in East Africa; but the good Captain's thoughtfulness had extended to every detail— nothing was forgotten. Happily he had taken for granted we should all be as hungry as hawks, and made ample provision, so that not we only, but our friends the "blue-jackets" had enough and to spare.

After lunch we divided into groups, and roamed in various directions about four miles inland, exploring the country—looking into the "shambas" of the natives, who seemed both surprised and pleased to see so many Englishmen and ladies—and generally enjoying a ramble. Returned about 5 p.m. refreshed ourselves with tea and "mdafu," and finished off by rounding the island. It was rough outside, and we had a good tossing about, but came in all safe and sound, after a most enjoyable day, at 7 p.m.

Sunday, August 5. Sorry to hear the "Mariner" is ordered away. She leaves here for Pemba, and it is not likely we shall see her in these waters again. We shall very much miss her occasional visits. The genial, cheery, kind-hearted Captain is a favourite with us all —Dr. Corcorran has been most kind in attending our invalids—all the officers are fine gentlemanly fellows, whom it is a pleasure to know—whilst the crew are a well-behaved set of men, whom we are always glad to meet with in their strolls through our Settlement. I sent a parting word to the Captain, as follows :—

"FRERE TOWN, *August* 5, 1888.

" MY DEAR CAPTAIN ARBUTHNOT,—

"We all thank you much for the great treat you gave us yesterday, including the finish, which was a new experience to some of our party. We are very sorry to hear that we are 'not likely to see the " Mariner " again in these parts'. It is a changeful world! I hope however, wherever you go, God's blessing may be with you—giving you prosperous voyages, and a happy re-union with the dear ones at home at the end of them. It will be a great pleasure to meet you in England and have a talk over our 'yambo' days. Failing that, we will hope to meet on 'a happier shore' when 'travelling days are done'. Adieu!

" Yours very sincerely, etc."

The Rev. Mr. Carthew of the Methodist Mission attended our Service this morning and dined with me afterwards. Smith rather worse.

Monday, August 6. The " Java " with our English Mail is in this morning. What news? Well, much and very important, but the item which concerns me most just now is that the Committee ask me to stay on another six months, and inform me that the Bishop of Norwich has kindly given his consent. It is the unexpected that happens. I had scarcely realized the likelihood of this, and I read the announcement with mixed feelings. What they were will best be told in the words addressed to my wife, when my heart was full :—

" Frere Town, *August* 8.

" The Mail came in yesterday with your letter of July 11, and one from Mr. Lang, asking me to stay on for another six months. Much as I love this work, I confess this came upon me as a shock. I had been making all my plans for leaving by the Steamer of the 29th inst. I had even indulged in pleasant dreams of the happy meeting on Dover Pier, and of visits to Canterbury, Cavendish, etc., and of the return to our old home at Wingfield ; and now it is all cruelly knocked on the head, and I have to look forward to another six months of this lonely life, with the hot season before me. I had—shall I confess it ?—a sleepless night and somehow felt very faint-hearted. Your brave letter has set me up, and I hope I may be able to say, ' not grudgingly or of necessity,' the Lord's will be done. Of course there are many things which would naturally reconcile me to a longer stay—my intense interest in the work itself—the desire to see the development of plans, in the conception of which I have had a hand—and not least the warm expressions of gladness on the part of all my colleagues, European and Native, when they heard the news. Nor do I count it a small blessing to be permitted to bring forth, as I trust I may, a little more fruit in old age. If in the Lord's goodness we are spared to meet again, the joy will be none the less for its having been deferred. The Committee say six months, but if they succeed in finding a young Bishop to their mind earlier, there will be no need for me to remain, so now as at the first, we must just try to do the work of to-day, and leave the rest to Him who ordereth all things for them that wait upon Him.

"Dear Begbie, how good and kind of him ! I wish I could write and thank him and his people for their loving and prayerful remembrance of me, but my pen has as much as it can do. Mails of the interior : Uganda—Nasa—Usambiro—Mpwapwa—Mamboia—Chaga—and Teita, are always coming and going ; and be it night or day, they must be attended to. I am now in touch with nearly all the distant Stations, and correspondence with the Brethren occupying these outposts entails a large amount of thought and work. But write you to Begbie and tell him how much I value the kind thoughts and prayers of him and his people.

"Mr. Lang says the Committee would be quite willing to send you out to me, if we wish it ; but much as I should like it for several reasons—and they not altogether selfish ones—I bow to your judgment, that it would not be right to put the Society to so much expense. After this, will you be surprised to hear that I went on board the Mail Steamer half hoping that I might see your dear face among the passengers, and that for a moment I was most unreasonably disappointed?

"You ask about our old Sharanpur friends. Well, Jones and Ishmael, as you know, are the Pastors respectively of Rabai and Frere Town—both good, useful men. They have had hard times of it, but this Mission would have been badly off without them. Dora Bai is better in health than she was, but not equal to much work. Priscilla Bai is usefully employed as a Bible-woman. All their children are nicely brought up, and the elder ones are decided Christians. They were very pleased to get your kind messages, and are always wondering why you do not come to see your African children once more. How the bells would ring out if you did !

" I wish it were possible for me to get a few *green* things from Wingfield. I *do* miss the vegetables so much, for though I consume the juice of several limes a day, it is a poor substitute for the luxuries of the kitchen garden.

" It is pleasant to find that the Bishop of Norwich is so satisfied with the arrangement for Wingfield, and also that the Parish is so well off under Pickford's ministry. I do not feel a bit jealous, I shall only rejoice if by God's help he succeeds where I have failed.

" Dear A. has of course been much in my thoughts and prayers during the last month. I hope, ere this, she has been brought safely through her trial, and that next Mail may bring me cheering news of her and ' mtoto '.

" You will see from my letters that I am a good deal on the move, from Station to Station, as I feel it my duty to be ; although I always thought it a mistake in the two Bishops going so far from their base. There is no English Missionary at any of these Stations except Frere Town, so it is very desirable that the Director of the Mission should pay the Native Brethren occasional fatherly visits, ' to see how they do,' and to encourage them in their work."

On the arrival of the English Mail I wrote to the Brethren in the interior, from whom we have had no ir ect communications, since that announcing the death of Bishop Parker. There is reason to fear that the unsettled state of feeling on the Coast, owing to the German operations, has spread into the interior, and rendered the roads unsafe for native messengers in European employ. To Mr. Mackay I wrote :—

"*August* 7, 1888.

" My Dear Mackay,—

"Though we have never met, I seem to know you so well, that I may drop the 'Mr.' You have heard no doubt of my coming out, and that since the lamented death of the Bishop I am *pro tem.* in charge of this Mission. I am anxious to convey to you, and to the other Brethren at the Lake, the assurance of my warmest sympathy with you and them in all your trials and difficulties and sorrows. We often remember you all in our prayers.

"In the absence of news from you or any of the Brethren since May, it is impossible for us to realize your present position, or to write anything to the point. I would earnestly hope that 'no news is good news'; and that your next letters will bring us cheering tidings of you all, and of your work.

"You are of course well informed as to the late Bishop's plans, and will endeavour as far as may be to carry them out, until a new Bishop or other Director of the Mission is appointed. Though entrusted with 'full powers,' I should not dream of dictating to you in any way; yet at the same time I have a certain amount of responsibility, and shall therefore be glad if you will freely communicate with me as to your affairs, and particularly if you will always let me know if there is any matter in which I can be helpful to you.

.   .   .   .   .   .

"The Mails at your end of the line seem to be unaccountably delayed. We have nothing from you since May. Cannot you organize a better system between you and Unyanyembe? It is a matter of first importance. There are difficulties no doubt, but you if anyone will know how to circumvent them.

"With Christian love to you, and any of the Brethren who may be with you. Yours, etc."

Thursday, August 9. *To Rabai.* Have come up here in the hope of getting a few days' rest, which I much need ; and a quiet time for reflection on the altered condition of affairs, and for considering how I can best lay myself out, with God's help, to promote the interests of the Mission during the next six months. It is well to have a plan and a policy, even though it may be impossible rigidly to adhere to it—the more so as there is every reason to apprehend that we are on the eve of stirring, if not trying times. It is very important that I should be thoroughly informed from personal inspection, as to the condition of things in each Mission Station under my charge. I regret that I have not hitherto found opportunity of paying a visit to the outlying station of Mwaiba. This must be done without further delay.

Sunday, August 12. A grand day ! It does one good to come here and see what God is doing. The Church was full, as indeed it always is. Jones gave a rousing sermon in the morning, and Jonah (Evangelist) in the afternoon. I adminstered Holy Communion to upwards of one hundred Natives. "It is a field that the Lord hath blessed." Much refreshed by my few days sojourn here. To-morrow (D.V.) I set out for Mwaiba.

To Mwaiba.

By referring to the chart, it will be seen that this Station lies almost due north from Frere Town, at a distance by road of about 50 miles. It occupies an elevated spot—some 800 or 900 feet above sea-level. As a Mission Station it has much to recommend it. It is central for evangelistic work among the Wa-Giriama, a race closely resembling, yet quite distinct from, the Wa-Nika—and the air is pure and bracing, free from malarious taint. It has however one great drawback : like Jericho, "the situation is pleasant, but the water is nought, and the ground barren". Unless the water difficulty can be got over, it is not a place for permanent occupation by a European. The day is coming, I hope, when there will be many outposts up and down the country manned by earnest Native Evangelists, under European supervision. The Mission was started in 1882, when I placed there George David, Native Catechist ; and since his death, four years ago, Robert Keating has carried on the work.·

On *Monday, Aug.* 13, I set out, with W. Jones as my companion, purposing to spend the night at the Methodist Station of Ribe ; distant from Rabai about eight miles. We had great difficulty in getting my donkey over the river. There were some huge boulders, which were very slippery, and donkey-like she would persist in taking an unnecessary leap, whereby she cut her leg rather badly. Got to Ribe at 5 p.m. Alas! how the place has changed since I was last here, six years ago, on a farewell visit to Mr. and Mrs. Wakefield! I felt sad to see it; it had such a dilapidated appearance— some of the buildings have tumbled down, and heaps of *dèbris* are lying about—the garden is overgrown with weeds and jungle—and everything about the place bespeaks neglect. Mr. Heroe, a West African, who is as much a foreigner here as a European would be, is in charge. There are no Wa-Galla here now—some went to Golbanti with Mr. and Mrs. Houghton, and were killed. In their place there are a good many Wa-Nika and "watoro". Several devoted Missionaries, and many fond hopes lie buried here!

Tuesday, Aug. 14. Left Ribe at 6. 30 a.m. It was showery and the grass very wet. After three hours' march, which I did partly on foot and partly on my donkey's back, we stopped to get breakfast, and then as it was cloudy we pushed on for another three hours, when we halted for a good hour's rest. The men cooked their dinner and Jones and I dined off tinned haddock; a dish I cannot strongly recommend; it is portable, but not particularly palatable! Off again, for we have still some miles before us, and our way becomes more difficult. It lies mostly through a dense forest, with here and there a pretty glade. After another three hours we emerged from the forest and came to a place named Memgongo. It is only three or four miles from Mwaiba, which now lay before us, but we had been actually on the tramp nine hours, and had covered a good 27 miles from Ribe; so I said: "'Bus'—pitch the tent and here let us remain for the night". The people of the place were as usual very curious, and flocked to see us. Said one: "Come, come, see Mzungu, he's a giant!" The unwonted apparition of an Englishman, with a white beard, sitting on a white donkey no doubt suggested the idea. However they soon got over their alarm, and we became good friends. One old man took a great fancy to my beard, and privately asked Jones if it actually grew there or was artificial. We were both well tired, so, after a supper of boiled rice—rather meagre fare after such a hard day's work—and after Prayer with our porters, we turned in and slept. I pitied the poor men with their loads; they are a much enduring race. I much doubt if one of Pickford's stalwart porters would carry a 60 lb. load on head or back for nine hours in the day under any circumstances—to say nothing of an African sun, and African roads. A striking feature in Giriama scenery is large masses of climbers, completely hiding the great trees which give them support, and looking for all the world like ruined castles covered with ivy.

Wednesday, August 15. Up at 6. An hour's walk, mostly through wild jungle, brought us to the foot of the hill. We were quite unexpected, but our guns soon brought Robert Keating and all his people running to meet us. Our coming was a glad surprise, and they welcomed us in true African fashion. Our larder, which was in an exhausted condition, was soon replenished, as almost immediately after our arrival one and another brought me a present of a fowl. It was about the only thing they had to give, for as regards food it is a poor place—no cattle, sheep or goats and no water within 4 or 5 miles, and that of the colour and consistency of pea soup. There are no vegetables of any kind, Indian corn, which grows freely, being the staple food of the natives.

At noon, assembled all the people of the Settlement —men and women—to the number of fifty. I called over their names, and found that the little community is variously made up. Some are pure Wa-Giriama— others from one cause or other have migrated here from Frere Town or Rabai—whilst there are a few whom I could not well make out: they may possibly be " watoro," who prefer living here to Fulladoyo. They listened attentively to our addresses, after which we sang a hymn, and Jones concluded with prayer. We had then several difficult cases to deal with, which took up most of the day. I also arranged with Robert about his duties ; directing him to give his chief attention to this little community—instruction of catechumens—a school for the children—and ministering to the Christians. To do this well will occupy nearly all his time and strength. He ought to have his wife with him, who could be useful among the women. His house must be put in order—re-thatched, etc.—and he needs a supply of school materials, to enable him to carry on his work efficiently. I was glad to learn that the Prayer-house had been built entirely by the people themselves. It is not a grand building but it is the best in the Settlement, and quite sufficient for the present needs. Some people are always complaining that Native Christians want everything done *for* them ; it is most unjust ; I should like to see an agricultural Parish in England cheerfully doing what these poor people have done.

Br. Taylor's heart's desire is, on his return from Chaga, to go on with translation work, and at the same time evangelize the Wa-Giriama. In that case he will find Mwaiba a useful centre, although not, I think, the best place for his head-quarters.

The old man from whom we purchased land for the Settlement is rather a troublesome customer : having received hard dollars for his supposed rights in the property on the hill, he is for repudiating the agreement, and claiming back what he has disposed of. Unfortunately the Deed of sale was most loosely drawn out, and the witnesses to it are either dead or far to seek. I have gone thoroughly into the matter, and with the help of Paulus and Petrus—two of the converts who have been here from the first—have determined the boundaries, and I hope there may be no further trouble.

Thursday, August 16. After a final Meeting with the people, we set out at 10.45 on our return, and at 1.15 reached the river, where we rested an hour for lunch. Started again, and pushed on till sunset. We were overtaken by a shower, and got to our camping-ground pretty well soaked. A down-pour of rain makes things very miserable on a journey, and very foolishly I have brought no change of warm clothing. *Mem.* Always have one or two changes of woollen clothes when travelling at this season. Pitched my tent in a small hamlet, consisting of three grass huts, belonging to Abe Ka

Nazi. He and his women seemed very pleased to give us a place for the night, and watched our proceedings with the utmost curiosity. When I drew off my wet shoes and socks, they were all on tiptoe to see my white feet, which called forth an exclamation of surprise. They all gathered round Jones and me to see us at our evening meal : a black and a white " Mzungu " eating together ! It was as good as a show to them. I gave Abe Ka Nazi a digestive biscuit which he nibbled cautiously ; suspicious of " medicine " I rather think ; but when I gave him a Rupee as a present for his kind hospitality, he was moved to his centre, and called his chief wife to receive it from the hand of " Mzungu " himself. A little present goes a long way with these simple people, and when they receive us kindly it should always be given ; it paves the way for those who come after us. Notwithstanding the heavy rain, we were badly off for water ; " water, water everywhere, and not a drop to drink ". Every traveller should see to this himself, and not leave it to his followers.

How impossible to convey to friends in England any true idea of my present life. I have journeyed to-day, for instance, for $6\frac{1}{2}$ hours under an African sun —through forest and swamp in sunshine and shower— and now find myself encamped for the night, in a wild, outlandish place, where man and beast are in perpetual struggle for supremacy. " I lay me down in peace, and take my rest: for it is Thou, Lord, only that makest me dwell in safety."

Friday, August 17. Another downpour during the night. I felt half ashamed of myself to be lying so dry

and snug in my little tent, whilst my poor fellows were
shivering outside in their wet rags. But what could I
do? If I had turned out to share my lot with them, it
would not have done them a particle of good—it would
most likely have done me most serious harm. There
are some things we cannot remedy, and this occasional
experience of African travel is one of them. We were
up at 6, and had all packed up and got off at 6.30.
Immediately the rain came down again, and in a few
minutes we were like a lot of drowned rats. No in-
equality this time! It would have been much the
same if it had not rained, for the long grass—often
eight or ten feet high—through which we had to grope
our way, was all dank and dripping from last night's
showers. This long grass is a serious impediment at
this season. The "siafu" were particularly troublesome this morning. One lot were in great force, and
on hearing the warning cry "siafu, siafu," I put my
donkey to the gallop; but all of no use. In a moment
she and I were covered with those little furies—up my
legs and arms, in my hair and beard, in short, in every
available place they made their attack. Once or twice
as they dug their teeth into the tender flesh, I literally
shrieked with pain; and the poor donkey, who didn't
know how to shriek, relieved her feelings by kicking.
They had me too at a great disadvantage, as I had to
steer my way through grass and brambles, and it required all my wits to escape scratches and falls. However, in three hours we were glad to find ourselves
once more at Ribe, and able to change our wet clothes;
and when water was obtained, which was in about two

hours, to get our breakfast. Jones who knows most of the people here, has been making a house to house visitation, and giving them a word of exhortation. This evening messengers arrived on their way to Mwaiba, bringing me a budget of letters, which have come up from Zanzibar by the "Henry Wright"; some of them on important business, and one from dear Mac, bearing Sierra Leone postmark of June 14. As I was sitting in the verandah of the Mission House, I, all at once, began to experience very uncomfortable sensations, and on looking about for the cause, found myself covered with fleas!—they were big ones, with no doubt "little ones on their backs to bite them"— and not one or two, but hosts. Oh! these insects! to an Englishman this plague is one of the most serious drawbacks to life in Africa.

Saturday, August 18. Left Ribe at 7 for Make-rungi, a village on the creek, about six miles distant, where we found a boat awaiting us which brought us to Frere Town at 1 p.m. There is so much in the circumstances connected with journeying in East Africa to remind us how entirely we depend for safety on the protecting arm of the Almighty; that the successful conclusion of even a little tour like this calls for special acknowledgment of His goodness.

To my wife I wrote :—

" I have just returned from a little tour in the Giriama country. . . .

" It is wonderful how God gives me strength for this hard life. I am sometimes amazed, and I hope thankful too. Jones said to me a day or two ago, ' Bwana, this African climate and life are telling upon you '. I asked ' How so ? ' ' Why,' he said, ' you are not nearly so stout as you were six months ago.' ' Indeed,' I replied, ' if that is so, and I think it is, I am rather glad, as it only shows I am getting into better " form " for this kind of work.' Certainly I do here what I should never dream of doing in England. On getting in I had the luxury of a cold bath, which I missed on the journey, and a warm greeting from all the dear Brethren. Of course I am awfully sunburnt—as brown as a gipsy —and good Mrs. Burness naïvely remarked : ' Why, Bwana, you put us all to shame by your good looks '. When last in Zanzibar I bought a pith hat, an inch thick, and as big as a coal-scuttle, and it is the best investment but one I ever made. *That* one I leave you to guess : it was made some thirty-nine years ago ! This hat has been a real friend to me, not only protecting me from the sun, but serving as a shield to my poor head from thorns and brambles.

"The S.S. ' Madura ' has come in direct from England. She picked up Mails at Aden which left London, July 27. I wonder you did not hear of it. ' Bwana mkubwa ' felt rather small to see his colleagues gloating over letters from home, and he not one ! You might have sent me latest news from Rose Cottage. Well, there is this to be said, that I have *my* cake in reserve."

From now till Mail day I remained at Frere Town, writing letters, and occupying myself with some important matters which claimed attention. How things were with us at this time may be gathered from the following extracts from my letter to the Rev. R. Lang :—

" Frere Town, *August* 28, 1888.

" My Dear Mr. Lang,—

"Yours of July 13 came to hand on the 6th inst. I was of course not wholly unprepared for the request that I would stay on another six months, yet (must I confess it?) I felt at first rather cast down at the prospect of another half year of this homeless life. But my dear wife's letter made me feel ashamed of my faint-heartness, and set me thinking more of the great privilege which is given me of serving the Lord a little longer in this, to me, most deeply interesting part of His vineyard. I thank the Committee for the expression of their willingness to send out my wife. As regards this *she* writes, ' If I had the means I would come at once, but I scarcely think we should be justified in putting the Society to this expense for so short a time '; and much as I should like her to join me, I have no doubt she has decided rightly in the matter.

" Mr. C. Fraser arrived by the Mail, and as I saw from your letter that you wished him and Beverley to go up to the Lake together, I judged it best to detain him here until the arrival of the latter. Three or four weeks in Zanzibar for a young man with nothing to do, would have been anything but a good preparation for his future work. So he has been here, making himself generally useful, and getting stirred up and quickened, I trust, by intercourse with Christian Brethren and fellow-workers. He is ready to start as soon as may be after Beverley's arrival.

" But about this, I am sorry to say, there is some uncertainty. Mr. Maxworthy's letter, which I enclose, explains the difficulty. It is in answer to one from me, which I wrote immediately I knew that a caravan would be required. You lay great stress on the necessity for an escort, and I feel this most strongly myself. It is all the more necessary owing to the general feeling of uneasiness and apprehension which just now exists in the country. Stokes with his 1200 men has already left, or will have done so before Beverley arrives, he has only been waiting for the 'Madura' which arrived some days ago. It will be bad for any small caravan following in his wake; he will 'leave behind him a desolate wilderness'. There is little chance I fear, at this season, of obtaining any other escort for our two Brethren.

" As regards ' wa-pagazi,' I hope we may be able to get over the difficulty, by giving a hundred men from here and Rabai ; I am calling for volunteers. There are very grave objections to sending away our men on these long expeditions, and this is a question to be seriously gone into ; but in the present emergency we will do our best. I shall send with the caravan a Christian young man, who will act as interpreter—muster the porters for Morning and Evening Prayer—and look after their spiritual interests. He will, I hope, be a comfort and help to our two Brethren.

" Fitch has gone to Zanzibar for a few days, partly on his own account, but mainly to confer with our Agents, and to see that everything is done that can be done to carry out the wishes of the Committee.

"I am glad to hear we may expect Mr. Robson in October.   As soon after his arrival as possible our dear Brother England should go home.   We shall be sorry

MR. ENGLAND.

to part with him, but he sadly needs a change, and he is worth preserving.

"Dr. Ardagh's sudden collapse, and return home makes it unnecessary to enter now upon the question of the Mombasa Medical Mission.   I will only say that I am as keen upon it as the Committee can possibly be ; it was my own proposal years ago ; but what I very strongly feel is, that to be of any use at all, it should be carried out with thorough efficiency in *both* departments. It is just a question of Agents ; and these of the right stamp it is not easy to find.

" I am hoping your next letter will tell me that Dr. Baxter is on his way out to relieve Dr. Pruen from Mpwapwa, and what your wishes are in regard to the latter. You already know of Mrs. B's expected confinement in November; and independently of that, the Committee will, I am sure, feel that it is, to say the least, very undesirable to leave this comparatively large Mission without Medical aid a day longer than necessary. If Pruen can be spared to come here, I shall be very glad to confer with him as to the work in Mombasa.

.   .   .   .

" The Chaga Mail is in, and brings me a deeply interesting letter from Taylor, and as he says he cannot write to you by this opportunity, and as the letter deals with several matters of importance, I send it on to you just as it is, having made from it such extracts as I may require.

" Taylor kindly offers to hold on at Chaga another two or three months, and for the sake of the Divinity Class I shall gladly accept his offer. I may hear something from you by the next Mail which may decide the matter. Anyway Fitch is ready to return at a moment's notice if the Committee wish it. His influence here is good, and I shall be sorry to lose him. I earnestly hope you may be able to send someone out to take up the work he has begun here; though I fear by this time you must be almost case-hardened against the perpetual cry for ' more men '.

" *Latest.* A Steamer just in from Zanzibar, bringing a letter from Col. Euan Smith which I enclose. In the face of it I cannot of course send on the two Brethren to the Lake. Shall await your orders, unless some favourable opportunity turns up.

" A nice letter from Mackay dated ' Kwa Makolo, July 17,' but he has no doubt written to you.

" Miss Wardlaw Ramsay and Mr. Beverley just arrived : all safe and well.

" With kindest regards, etc., etc."

In the letter I received from Col. Euan Smith, referred to above, he urged me most strongly not to allow Messrs. Beverley and Fraser to go up to the Lake at present. What could I do? He must have good reasons for the advice he gives, and I dare not take the responsibility of acting contrary to his judgment. I had already come myself to the conclusion that there would be considerable risk in these Brethren going forward just now; the letter of the Consul-General places this beyond doubt, and I cannot disregard his warning, so I replied :—

" FRERE TOWN, *September* 1.

" MY DEAR COLONEL,—

" Thanks many for your letter of Aug. 27. It takes a load of responsibility off my shoulders. I had almost made up my mind not to send these two young men up country at present, but I might have been blamed. Your letter makes it all right. It is a pity the Committee did not let me know three months ago that a caravan would be required; then we would have secured porters, escort, and everything else. I am very sorry on Mackay's account, from whom I have just heard. The non-arrival of Mr. Fraser for several months will be a sore disappointment; but he is a brave fellow!

"I have just returned from Rabai with our exuberant friend Ehlers, and the Hervey hunting party, who, after a few days are going on to the Tana.

"I am sorry to hear you are rather out of sorts. You will have to come up here for a change. By the way, Mr. Carthow of the Methodist Mission, and Mr. Vanderlein of the Bavarian Mission, who had both suffered badly from fever, availed themselves of my offer to occupy a little house I have put up at Shimba, and after a fortnight's stay there, have returned quite set up. You know I am hopeful that Shimba will prove a valuable sanatorium, and be a means of saving money and lives; so I am glad of these two cases to support my theory.

"Thank you for your nice present of oranges, they were a great treat to me and my friends.

"I hope your letter to Mwanga will have a good effect, if only he gets it read to him without gloss, or note, or comment, and when he is not in his cups!

"One of the two men for the Lake—Mr. Carlile Fraser, mechanical Engineer--is going to Zanzibar in the 'Henry Wright'. He is to enquire and find out if there is any possibility of obtaining a caravan escort. I gather from my letters that the Committee are quite counting on these two men going forward at once.

"Dr. Baxter and wife are coming *viâ* the Cape in three weeks time, to go up to Mpwapwa.

"From all I hear, I suppose we are on the eve of stirring events in East Africa. May God give us all the wisdom needed for the times.

"Yours very sincerely, etc."

After carefully considering the matter in all its bearings, I wrote again, three days later, to the Consul-General, as follows :—

"*September* 3, 1888.

"My dear Colonel,—

"I am anxious nothing should be left undone that can be done to carry out the Committee's wishes in regard to these two young men going up to the Lake. It has occurred to me that if Dr. Baxter, who is an old traveller, determines to go with his wife to Mpwapwa, and can make up a caravan, it may be feasible for them to go with him so far ; and there, with his advice and aid, to arrange for the journey on. It is very probable Dr. Pruen, now at Mpwapwa, will go forward as soon as Baxter relieves him. That would make the matter easier. Messrs. Beverley and Fraser are both going down to Zanzibar : I think it better for them to do so, and on the spot get all the information they can ; and I shall be most thankful if you will advise them, under the circumstances I have mentioned, what is best to be done. Please bear in mind that they are *not* for Uganda, but for the Station of Usambiro at the south end of the Lake. Yours, etc."

To A. Mackay, Esq., Usambiro.

"*August* 30, 1888.

" MY DEAR MACKAY,—

"Many thanks for your kind letter just received. I came out simply to take charge of the Mission for six months, or until Bishop Parker should return to the coast. His lamented death of course put everything out, and at the request of the Committee I have consented to stay on, if the Lord will, another six months. It is, for some reasons, rather inconvenient, but my heart is in the work, so I gladly 'gird up my loins' afresh.

"Now about Reid. The Committee at one time entertained the thought of sending him to you, and under certain conditions, he was prepared to go. But for some reason they came to the conclusion that he was not the right man, and they have sent out Mr. Carlile Fraser, a man of varied experience, to assist you in building the boat, and in any other way, on an agreement for two years. I think from what I have seen of him, that he might be very useful to you. The Rev. J. E. Beverley has also just arrived *viâ* the Cape, and the two were to travel up together. The Committee give very stringent instructions as to their going with Stokes or some other suitable escort. Immediately I got Mr. Lang's letter, I wrote to B. R. & Co. to collect porters, prepare caravan, and look out for escort. They wrote back to say that Stokes had carried off all the porters for his caravan of 1200 men—that he had already left—and no prospect of any other escort at this late period of the season. I was perplexed, but set to work at once and collected about 75 porters at Frere Town and Rabai, hoping that Messrs. B. R. & Co. might at least be able to find 25 or 30 more in Zanzibar. To-day however comes a letter from Col. Euan Smith, urging me on no account to send these two Brethren up country, at the present time, without an escort. In the face of this, I dare not take the responsibility of allowing them to proceed. I am sorely vexed, because I know what a disappointment it must be to you, though you are a brave man, and, during the last twelve years of your life, have had to face disappointments even greater than this. Still I regret it exceedingly. Would I had known three months ago that a caravan would be required. I have written to the Committee about it, and they may cable, but even then I fear it may be too late to do anything, and some months of precious time will be lost. I hear that Dr. Meyer has just left Pangani for Chaga, and that after spending three months there, he intends to go on to your Lake. I shall get from Taylor, all information about this. It may possibly afford us an opportunity of sending on your reinforcements earlier than we might otherwise be able to do. I can at present only say we will do our level best to hasten them on to you.

"Dr. Ardagh went home by last Mail. He had had repeated attacks of fever. The rest of our party are all well. I have had excellent health, thank God, and feel almost as equal to hard work as ever I did. The supervision of these Coast Stations finds plenty of work for one man, if it is to be done efficiently.

"I am sorry we get no late news of Gordon and Walker. We often remember you all in prayer. I wonder if Ashe is still with you; I should be glad to hear he had withdrawn his resignation.

"With best Christian love to you and any of the Brethren who may be with you.

"Yours very faithfully, etc."

To the Rev. W. E. Taylor, Chaga.

"*September* 1, 1888.

"MY DEAR TAYLOR,—

"I have to thank you for your deeply interesting letter of Aug. 17. It is refreshing to hear from one whose heart is in his work, and who has so many opportunities for good. There is so much important information in your letter, that, as you say you have no time to write home by this Mail, and as I have too much on hand to allow of my making as full extracts as I could wish, I shall send it on as it is. There is nothing 'Private'; and I am sure the Secretaries will be glad to see it.

"Before I give you our news, just a word or two on some points referred to in your letter.

"1. I will enquire about type at Jomvu. Thanks for the Kisuaheli Hymns; we have just printed a small selection to go on with, but shall be glad to add what you have sent.

"2. On my visit to Mwaiba I heard, here and there, of the 'Mzungu with four eyes'!* The people would be glad to see and hear him again.

* In allusion to Mr. Taylor's spectacles.

" 3. Poor Mandara! when will he take it in that we are men of peace? I was thinking of getting for him a nice edition of my wind-resisting lamp, but am afraid he still ' loves darkness,' and would despise it. Whatever *his* intentions, God has given him a great opportunity, ' He has sent His servants to call him'. May it please Him to open his heart to receive the Gospel message!

" 4. I have carefully considered what you say about Mr. Braun's suggestion. Whatever may be said in favour of it, it is too serious a matter for us to take action in, without the Parent Committee's sanction ; unless Mandara should become—as he was some while ago—decidedly hostile. The best thing would be, I think, not to relinquish ' Mochi,' but, if possible, to send another Missionary specially fitted for the post in connexion with the new German Settlement. The Parent Committee will see and, no doubt, give prayerful consideration to what you have said.

" 5. I am sorry to hear of your illness. At the same time it is satisfactory to learn that you survived such heroic treatment. I think we must say, ' God gave His Angels charge over you '. It gave you an opportunity of seeing more of the country, and of taking observations which may hereafter be turned to account. It is well always to keep that clearly in view, and to make notes of everything which may be of use to those who come after us ; and this I feel sure you will do.

" 6. I will bear in mind what you say of M., poor fellow. He did, I have no doubt, go wrong when I was last out, as alas! did others who had not his excuse. I am not one however to judge or treat him harshly ; I will do all I can for him. If only he might be led to give his heart to the Lord, what a useful man he might be!

"7. I am most thankful for your kind offer to give Fitch a few months longer spell here; for, much as I should like to see you established in your chosen field among the Wa-Giriama, I do, as you rightly judge, attach great importance to the new Divinity Class; and for the present, or till we hear if the Committee can send out a special man for it, he is the right man for the post.

"8. I am thankful to report that in the absence of a 'mganga,' we are all in good health, 'no more pills or any other medicine!' There is just a chance of Pruen coming here, if Baxter arrives in time to relieve him.

"9. I have had a 'shauri' with 'Mwalimu,' and given him particular directions as to what you wish him to do; and he promises to have some MS. ready to go with this. He asked me something for 'chakula,' and certainly he looked as if he needed it. I gave him $6 on account. Please let me know what your agreement with him is. I hope Pratley will let me have some proofs to send you.

"10. Sir R. Hervey and party arrived to-day and have been spending the evening with me. I pumped them all I could for news from the interior. Mr. E., a German gentleman of independent means, is my guest. He is going to Chaga in a few weeks to relieve Braun —just for the fun of the thing. He is a nice, gentlemanly fellow—kind-hearted towards the natives, etc. You will see a good deal of him, and I earnestly hope your influence over him may be for good.   He is *natur-ally* an amiable man.   May God give you all wisdom !

"11. I hear that Dr. Meyer has just left Pangani for Chaga, and that he purposes, after spending three months there, to go on to the Victoria.   Kindly get from him all information as to his movements, espe-cially as to the length of his stay at Chaga.   Perhaps this may afford an opportunity of sending on Messrs. Beverley and Fraser to the Lake.

" Must close.   Mail men clamouring to be off.

" With warmest Christian love,

" Yours affectionately, etc."

CHAPTER VIII.

THE BEGINNING OF TROUBLES.

Sunday, Sept. 2. The 'Baghdad' with our English letters came in this morning. Good news from dear ones at home. My letters from C. M. S. very perplexing. Pruen and Robson to go forward to the Lake, and Baxter to Mpwapwa, without delay, and Frere Town left in the lurch, without either a doctor or a school-master! However willing to carry out orders, the thing is impossible, but our friends at Salisbury Square have evidently no idea yet of our present difficulties. Our rest to-day sadly broken in upon.

Monday, Sept. 3. Messrs. Beverley and Fraser left for Zanzibar in the 'H. W.' Stormy weather.

Tuesday, Sept. 4. Taken ill in the night with inflammation. Fitch and Smith came and sat up with me—fomented and mustard-poulticed me. Had no sleep all night, and feeling very unwell to-day.

Wednesday, Sept. 5. A little better, but feeling very weak and low. Bibi Fitch came to see me this afternoon, and apologizing for not having come before, said: " We are not used to think of our Bwana as sick ". It is no doubt good for me to be laid aside, that I may learn " how frail I am," and that I am not made of wrought iron. My illness is owing, I imagine, partly to a chill I got on my way from Rabai a day or two ago, and not a little to worry and anxiety. May He who knows all give me needful strength and guide me in these difficult times !

Friday, Sept. 7.   To my surprise the " H. W.' turns up.   The Consul General has sent her up with Last and a lot of men.   He is going about fifty miles inland to prospect for a depòt for the new Company.   Beverley and Fraser return empty handed—no caravan—no escort !

Col. Euan Smith asks for the use of the ' H. W.' for a month—wants her now to return to Zanzibar immediately.   The captain and engineer say " no—impossible ".   They yielded however to my persuasion, and consented to start to-morrow.   I arranged for Fraser to go with them, and assist with the engine.

Saturday, Sept. 8.   The ' H. W.' left at noon.   To Col. Euan Smith I replied :—

" Frere Town, *Sept.* 7, 1888.

" My Dear Colonel,—

" I was startled on seeing the ' H. W.' coming in this morning, as I was not expecting her before next Tuesday.   You did quite right in sending her as you did ; and although it balks me of a trip I was purposing to Kilifi and Melindi next week, I gladly place the boat at your service, as far as practicable, for the next month.   Mind I do this for *you*, and the Company will no doubt pay ' the damage ' whatever it may be.   I say as far as practicable, because she is undermanned for continuous sea work.   The trip, either way, means a trying, sleepless night for the engineer, and in a lesser degree for the captain. One journey to Zanzibar and back per week, especially during this unsettled weather, is quite enough for her to do. You would probably not require more frequent communication than that. Heavy cargo can of course easily come up now by dhow. You may depend upon my doing all I can for our friend Ehlers.

"I have a nice letter from Sir John K. He seems not a little disappointed at the turn things have taken ; but it is pleasant to see that he rejoices in your popularity; and that you are holding British influence as high as under the circumstances is possible. It was certainly no fault of his that affairs have come to the pass they have. Considerations, in other parts of the world, have, no doubt, had much to do with it. After all, it remains for each and all of us to do our best, according to our lights and opportunities, and not to forget that ' the Lord reigneth '.

"With kindest regards. Yours, etc."

After sending off our little steamer, held a meeting of the Finance Committee, to consider Mr. Lang's letter, and to confer together as to what action to take under the circumstances. The extract given below from my letter to the Secretary, will throw light on this and some other matters :—

"*September* 8, 1888.

"I thank you for your letter of August 8, with enclosures, which came to hand on the 2nd inst.

"I am glad the Plan for the girls' Dormitory, and

]adies' accommodation commends itself to Miss Harvey and Mr. Shaw, and has been approved by the Committee. I am persuaded it is the best and most economical arrangement. Mr. Burness has already begun operations, and I hope, in three months from this time —which will be sharp work for East Africa—to see the girls and ladies comfortably housed in their new quarters. We quite feel the importance of having the girls' supply of water near at hand, and I have fixed upon a spot in the compound for a well, for their exclusive use. It is difficult beforehand to estimate the cost of a *well;* but, judging from past experience, I should think these two works, (1) the fencing in of girls' compound, and (2) sinking a well, may be done for £20 or £25.

" At the same time, I must say that Miss Harvey's remarks about the water supply are very misleading. They would give the impression that Frere Town is a particularly unhealthy place for Europeans, and *that,* owing to the want of good water. There is not the slightest ground for either of these assumptions. As a matter of fact, there is no more healthy Station for Europeans on the east coast of Africa; and the water supply, so far as *they* are concerned, is first rate. Each Mission house is furnished with one or two good cemented cisterns, for storing water from the iron or cemented roof, which, when filtered, is about the purest form in which water can be obtained in this country. So far as Miss H. was concerned, it is very easy to account for her fever. She was living in what was tantamount to a mangrove swamp; her house was literally buried in trees, so that it would have been a marvel if she and Miss Fitch had not suffered from fever. I am glad to say these obstructions to fresh, pure air have been swept away. In nearly every case of a European suffering from fever at Frere Town, it would be easy to show that it was not due so much to the climate, or to bad water, as to undue exposure, or to some neglect of ordinary sanitary conditions. Dr. Ardagh, for instance, was living in Mombasa, where he had too good reason to complain of the water, and various other nuisances ; and it was to this, and to his frequent journeys to and fro in a little open boat – often in the hottest part of the day—that he attributed his oft-recurring attacks of fever His last attack was the immediate result of a long walk of eight hours, in the sun, from Shimba to Rabai—an excursion which could only be undertaken with impunity by a man in good health and training. It is most important the Committee should be under no misapprehension as to this matter. Doubtless, the African climate is trying under any circumstances, but you may rely upon it there is no Station in Eastern Intertropical Africa, where that climate is met with under more favourable circumstances, on the whole, than in your Station of Frere Town.

"I entirely agree with your general proposal as to the location of the ladies, when the whole staff of five are available—at present we have only two ! Three are not too many for Frere Town and Mombasa, and two good earnest women will find ample scope for most useful and happy work at Rabai. Shimba, for some time to come, must be content with a Native Christian woman, with an occasional visit from one or other of the English ladies. It would be a great advantage if the lady for Mombasa were a trained nurse, or had medical knowledge. Her sphere would be much the same as that of a Zenana lady in India. It will be a grand day when all this comes to pass.

"I come now to what you rightly term, 'a difficult question,' viz., the reinforcements for the Lake Missions, etc.—difficult for you, but much more so for us, who have a knowledge of adverse circumstances which you had not when you wrote. You did not know, for instance, (1) that Dr. Ardagh was on his way home, (2) that Mr. T. (accountant) would at the last moment withdraw, and (3) that the two brethren, Beverley and Fraser, instead of being well on their way to Usambiro, would be detained here by circumstances, and by the almost express veto of the Consul General.

"I read and re-read this portion of your letter, and must confess I felt not a little perplexed. I invited Fitch, England and Smith to confer with me upon it; and after prayer for divine guidance, I laid the matter before them.

"Your proposal involved a sore disappointment to two of our number. Brother Smith has been eagerly looking forward to release from his present post, that he might give himself to the language, and to spiritual work. You did not of course foresee the failure of Mr. T., but he having failed, it will take time to supply his place, and till that is done Smith cannot be spared. The accounts are very varied and complicated, and these together with formal correspondence are quite enough to occupy the full time and energies of one man. There is no one here competent to take it in hand, even if willing to do so. So here you have a young ardent Missionary who is longing to go forth to the work for which he has been solemnly set apart, tied down to the routine duties of an office, which could be performed equally well, if not better, by any properly qualified accountant.

"Then there is dear England; everyone feels that he ought to have gone home six months ago; but he has patiently held on, in the hope of someone being appointed to take up and carry on his most useful and important work. Mr. Robson—a trained schoolmaster like himself—was to take his place. Now suddenly all that is changed; Mr. Robson is to go forward with Dr. Pruen to occupy a new Station, and not a hint is given of anyone coming out to take charge of the School at Frere Town. We are now on the eve of the hot season, and in any and every case, England will have to leave not later than October 24. It would be at great risk if he remained longer.

"Shall I be excused if I write plainly and strongly, as I feel on this point? Frere Town is your educational and training centre. If this had been duly recognized and acted upon in the past, we should now have had a goodly band of well qualified Native Agents, available as Teachers and Evangelists in all our E. African Mission stations. Instead of that, youths have had an education given them up to a certain point—many of them in English—and then been converted into cooks and donkey-boys! It is simply deplorable, and almost makes one weep. A grand opportunity has been thrown away; but the past should suffice. I am by no means insensible to the desirableness of sending reinforcements to the Lake Brethren; but I am thoroughly convinced that if it is a question of *that* or *this*, your best policy is, *to let nothing interfere with the education and training of a Native Agency at Frere Town.* Only give us a fair chance, and in two or three years, with God's blessing, we shall be able to supply you with men—'axes,' as dear old Lenpolt used to say, 'from the tree itself'— for all your Stations in the interior. I don't know, but I cannot help feeling that even the Committee are not fully alive to the fact that the evangelization of Africa *is to be done by Africans.* You will pardon an old Missionary, if he has expressed himself too strongly on a point which he deems of vital importance.

" So far I have written on receipt of your letter; but at the same time I am doing all I can to expedite the departure of Messrs. Beverley and Fraser. I have sent them to Zanzibar with a letter to the Consul General, requesting him to aid them in every possible way, in getting on to their destination. In regard to other points in your letter, you may be sure it would have given us the greatest satisfaction to have been able to say in reply 'we not only entirely agree with your proposals, but will set to work at once to carry them out'. I much regret that with all the facts and circumstances before us, it was impossible to do this.

"I enclose a copy of the Finance Committee's Resolution, which will show you the action we have taken and the reasons for it. I also enclose copies of correspondence which will help to explain the situation, and in some measure account for our proceedings."

The decisions of the Finance Committee were—

1. To keep Mr. Robson at Frere Town, as originally designed, to take charge of the School from Mr. England.
2. To arrange for Dr. Pruen to come to Frere Town as soon as possible.
3. To do our utmost to send Messrs. Beverley and Fraser, with Dr. Baxter, on their way to the Lake.

This is sadly in contravention of the P. Committee's direction; but they wrote entirely in the dark as to the present condition of affairs. Hope we have done right; if not, must bear the blame. May God direct!

Acting on the above decisions, I wrote at once to Dr. Pruen:

"FRERE TOWN, *September* 8, 1888.

"DEAR DR. PRUEN,—

"Many thanks for your welcome letter of August 23. It helps to remove a difficulty. You no doubt heard by last Mail of the Committee's wish, that on Dr. Baxter's arrival, you should go on, with a new man now on his way out—Mr. Robson—and select a site for a new Station, in place of Uyui. I had a long letter from Mr. Lang on the subject, but whilst we would of course desire to carry out the expressed wishes of the Committee, we have to take into account facts and circumstances which were not known to them, and to act according to the best of our own judgment; taking the responsibility. In the present instance, after prayerfully considering the matter in all its bearings, we have no doubt that the right thing for you to do is to come here—as you express your readiness to do—at as early a date as you consider it safe to do so—say, about the first week in October. I am writing to B. R. & Co. to send you up 50 or 60 porters; there is just now a great scarcity and an unusual demand for them. I shall put on the screw, and hope they will not fail to collect so many and send them on in good time.

"You and your dear wife may count on a warm welcome here, and we shall do our best to put you up comfortably. We are glad to hear that Mrs. Pruen and infant are doing so well. With kindest Christian regards.—Yours, etc."

Sunday, September 9. Very thankful for a nice quiet day, no Mail interruptions!

Monday, September 10. Heard that Mr. Last, now in the employ of the B. E. A. Co., is, in opposition to my wishes, taking on porters from here and Rabai, for his "safari". If so, it is a very poor return for all the kindness I have shown him.

Went over to Mombasa, and discovered that about 25 of our people had been engaged. Mr. Edmunds, the officer in charge, promised to strike them off the list. Mr. Last had already gone to Rabai. It will be necessary before long to come to an understanding with the Company's Agents, in regard to the employment of men belonging to our Mission.

Conducted the S.S. reading to-night.—Phil. ii. 12-18.

Tuesday, September 11. Determined, in view of another lady—Miss Scott—soon coming out, and of our needing accommodation, for a time at least, for three or

UP THE CREEK TO RABAL.

four extra Europeans, to put up a row of three huts, for bachelors, each hut 16 ft. × 11 ft., with bath and cooking accommodation. Chose a good site in the present girls' compound, to the west of Wright House.

Wednesday, September 12. Set people to work clearing away jungle from the site of the new bachelors' quarters. No sign of the " H.W."—very annoying and inconvenient. Hinders me in various ways.

Thursday, September 13. This afternoon eleven boys, who had been carefully prepared by Mr. England, were baptized. One of them was my boy, Salama, an Abyssinian, who received the name of Stephano. I was his god-father. It was a solemn Service; and the devout behaviour of all the candidates was most striking.

No sign yet of the " H.W."—provoking.

In a letter received a few days back from the Consul General, he cautions us not to get mixed up in any way with the Germans. I have no idea what he alludes to or is driving at. There is not the slightest ground to fear our getting mixed up with the Germans—our danger lies in another direction, and about this I wrote as follows :—

To Col. Euan Smith.

" FRERE TOWN, *September*, 15*th*, 1888.

" MY DEAR COLONEL,—

" I quite agree with what you say in your letter of the 6th instant, about the undesirableness of our getting in any way mixed up with the Germans and their schemes ; so much so, that, on the principle of avoiding the appearance of evil, although privately I

have a great regard for Ehlers—and would do anything
I could to help and oblige him—he would not have got
a single man from here for his 'safari,' but for you ; not
that I think there is much cause to fear anything on
that score.   The ways of the Germans and ours are so
far apart; and the natives have already learnt to distinguish between the English and 'Wa Daitch '.

"But unless my instinct is at fault there is more
real cause for anxiety lest we should become too much
identified and mixed up with the affairs of the British
E. A. Company.   Don't misunderstand me.   We hail
with joy the advent of the new Company, and quite
hope that, under God, it will, in one way and another,
do much to remove many existing obstacles to Missionary progress.   We shall not be insensible to these
benefits, nor slow to find opportunities of showing our
gratitude ; but I feel sure you will see with me how
important it is for us to avoid any action or co-operation which would be calculated to give the idea to the
natives that the 'I. B. E. A. C.' and 'C. M. S.' are only
different names for the same thing.   Our relation to
the Co. will be very much the same as our relation to
the Government in India ; and as there, so here, we
shall, I doubt not, be very good friends, and, working
side by side, be mutually helpful ; but, in order to that,
it is essential that *we*, at least, keep strictly to our own
line of things.   Our object is the very simple one of
bringing the Gospel of Christ to bear in every lawful
way upon all sorts and conditions of men, to whom we
can gain access ; and everything which would obscure
that object, or give us a different character in the eyes of
the natives, would be a serious, if not fatal, hindrance to

our success. Besides, although we have every confidence in the Board of Directors, as at present constituted, and are thankful to have in H. M.'s Representative an old and warm friend of the Society; it may not always be so. Time brings changes, so that we cannot count upon the continuance of these happy conditions. It is therefore the part of wisdom for us, to have a policy and to let it be clearly understood, which will survive all possible vicissitudes in the administration of the Company.

"The necessity for my writing to you just now on this subject is forced upon me by Mr. L.'s recent extraordinary proceedings at Rabai. Without saying a word to me, he goes and takes up his quarters in one of our Mission houses there, and converts our Settlement into his Depôt and base of operations. Amongst other things, he invites a lot of Mbaruk's men—armed roughs, amenable to no discipline or restraint—to meet him there, and, for the time being, they roam at will over our Christian Colony. It is easy to see that the control of a population like that of Rabai, made up of some 2000 people of many tribes and in various stages of enlightenment, is no light matter in itself; but with these elements of disturbance, it would become almost impossible. So far perhaps no great harm is done, but we are only at the threshold of what may likely prove a very trying crisis; and it is right at once to have it clearly understood that, in future, all requisitions for help of any kind, should be made through *me*, or whoever may be for the time being the responsible head of the Mission.

"I do not write officially. There is no need, as I

feel sure, with the facts before you, you will see at once the reasonableness of what I have said, and of the position which I deem it right on behalf of the C. M. S. to take up, and because just one word from you will set all right.

" I am yours, etc., etc."

I submitted the above to my colleagues, Messrs. Fitch, Smith and England, who all approved of it, feeling as strongly as I do, the necessity for clearly defining our position at the outset.

Saturday, September 15. The " H. W." in at last. Glad to hear the Consul General has no further need of her.   Mr. Ehlers came with his loads, went up with him to Rabai.   Not feeling well.   Called in at Jomvu, where I found Mr. Last ill in bed.   He returned to Rabai yesterday from the interior, and in the night was taken seriously ill.   Jones did all he could for him, and this morning sent him on in a hammock to Mr. Carthew at Jomvu.   From the symptoms I judge it to be a case of sunstroke.   He was for going on to Mombasa, but I recommended him to stay where he was till fairly recovered.

Sunday, September 16. Church full as usual this morning.   Ehlers to whom it was a new and strange sight, was delighted.   Had a nice quiet day, but feeling rather out of sorts, and a little anxious.   Twelve of Mbaruk's men came to take up loads for Mr. Last—a noisy lot !

Monday, September 17.   Gave Ehlers all the porters he needed for his " safari " and started him on his way to Chaga.   I am afraid he will have much trouble by

the way. He is badly equipped, does not know a word
of the language, and has had no experience of travelling
in Africa. One thing in his favour is that he is kindly
disposed towards natives.

A., one of our young men, came to me to-night, saying he was very unhappy in his mind in consequence of
his sin ; he could not sleep at night, and if he did fall
asleep he was troubled with horrid dreams ; he felt that
Christ was judging him. I have noticed for some time
a strangeness in him, as of a man whose mind was ill
at ease ; and although for certain reasons I had as yet
not said a word to him of the grievous matter to which
he refers, I was only waiting for an opportunity. It is
well he comes of himself, and makes a clean breast of it
—with no prevarication or excuse—and I pray God to
give him " true repentance ". Still it is a case for
Church discipline, and must be dealt with.

To Col. Euan Smith.

" RABAI, *September* 17, 1888.

" MY DEAR COLONEL,—

" I came up here on Saturday with dear old
Ehlers, and to-day have sent him off with fifty porters
—all Rabai men—and two good headmen. I hope he
may reach Chaga safely in about fourteen days, but he
will meet with enough to try his courage and patience
by the way. It is a bad time for travelling, and I'm
afraid he was very poorly equipped for such a journey.
His tent was a miserable affair, and he hadn't a single
peg with it ! The cloth he brought from Zanzibar for
' posho ' was useless, and it was with difficulty we sup-

plied him with enough of the current kind to enable him to pay his way. Besides he had no proper cook or decent servant of any kind. I am sure he will have a very trying fortnight, and I shall anxiously look for news of his safe arrival at Chaga. He will meet our Mail runners on their way to the Coast about four days hence and will let me know by them how he is getting on; I should be very sorry if any harm came to him. You will be pleased to hear that he gave me a cq. for $200 as a donation to the C. M. S. It was quite spontaneous. I am glad of it for his sake, more than for the Society's. At another time I would have gone with him at least as far as Teita, where we have a Station which sadly needs over-hauling; but just now, and till the air clears, my place is on the Coast or within easy call.

"On my way here on Saturday I called in at Jomvu and found Mr. Last there, ill in bed with sun-stroke. Carthew will take care of him; and I will do anything I can for him.

"The news you send me from the coast S. of Mombasa is rather disturbing. I confess to a little anxiety as to what may happen, when the B. E. A. Co. begin to take possession—they must not expect a quiet 'walk over'. There is always a turbulent element in Mombasa ready to break forth on the slightest provocation; and there can be little doubt that one of the first objects of attack in such a case would be the Freed-slave Settlement of Frere Town. Humanly speaking we are defenceless. We already number thirteen English, of whom four are ladies!

"A man named Khamis Khombo is the ring-leader of the malcontents—he hates the English and has an

old grudge against them. It would be well quietly to
get hold of this man, and to treat him kindly till the
business is settled. It is curious that I heard nothing
of what has taken place to the South, till I got it from
you and Ehlers. No doubt they know all about it in
Mombasa; it will be well if they come to learn also that
resistance is in vain.

"In haste, Yours, etc., etc."

Tuesday, September 18. Writing Home letters—just
now rather trying work—gave me a headache. Went
with Jones a walk through the Settlement, calling in
here and there. Met Mark, son of old Abe Ngoa, in the
garb of an ordinary M-Nika—a dirty rag saturated with
oil. He was one of three youths sent by Rebmann
some years ago to Zanzibar, to be instructed for baptism by Bishop Tozer, and he has relapsed into heathen-
ism. It was strange to hear this man, to all appearance
a M-Nika of the Wa-Nika, speaking to me in very good
English. I spoke to him of his great sin in forsaking
the true way, and he admitted it. I could not say all I
would in presence of his heathen companions; but will
try to see him again by himself.

Wednesday, September 19. A messenger came in from
Frere Town. He had been stopped on the way by some
Wa-Suaheli at Jomvu, who, he says, wanted to kill him;
but whilst they were calling others to their help, he
managed to escape. Hear from Smith that Burness is
unwell; we are all suffering more or less just now from
the heat. A characteristic note from Herr Ehlers,
thanking me for my "phenominal kindness". He had
reached Gora—his first stage, about twenty-five miles

—without mishap, and wrote in good spirits. Beverley came up this Evening.

Thursday, September 20.   Jones wrote on thirty-six men for Beverley's " safari " ; but where the rest are to come from it is not easy to see, at this season when men are occupied in their " shambas ".   Beverly much gratified with his visit to Rabai.   Had a meeting of " Fundis " in my house this Evening, for a few parting words and prayer.

A hundred men of Mr. Last's caravan passed through Rabai, on their way to his newly selected Station of the B. E. A. Co. at Gulu Gulu.

Friday, Sept. 21.   *Return to F. Town.*   Left Rabai at 6.30 and landed at F. Town at 11.   A messenger came over from the Wali of Mombasa to inform me that he is going to-morrow to Melindi.   It is a strange time for him to be thinking of going away, just when H.M. Consul General is expected here on a visit, and I returned a polite message to that effect.

Bishop Hannington had a dog, " Tom "—a mongrel, with a good deal of English blood in him—that accompanied him on his last fatal tour.   Since then the dog has been a member of Jones's family, and seems to have been well taken care of.   On each occasion of my visiting Rabai, " Tom " has been one of the first to welcome me, and has attached himself to me during my stay, although I have never reciprocated his affection, beyond giving him an occasional pat on the head.   This morning, however, the poor dog followed me to the " banderini," and swam off to my boat, so that I could do no less than take him in.   He has installed himself as my body-guard, and sticks to me night and day.   He is a famous animal, who is said to have killed a leopard, and who carries some honourable scars—one unfortunately near his tail—of wounds received in his conflict with the savage beast. I cannot account for his strange preference for myself, as there is no personal resemblance between me and his late master, except in the colour of the skin.

Saturday, Sept. 22. The Wali sends word that he will postpone his trip to Melindi, till after the arrival of the Mail steamer from Zanzibar. Weather getting perceptibly warmer, but, thank God, I am feeling better to-day than I have done the last week or two, and in better spirits, although the outlook is not very cheering.

Sunday, Sept. 23. On the whole a peaceful and refreshing day. Attended Morning and Afternoon Services in Kisuaheli. In the afternoon through some misunderstanding there was no Preacher. Ishmael came to the rescue, and gave an earnest practical sermon.

Monday, Sept. 24. Disquieting rumours come from Mombasa. The Arabs and Wa-Suaheli are angry with the Sultan for having " sold them," as they say, " to the English Co." Their great fear is, that *Slave Traffic* is doomed. There are threats of an attack upon F. Town, as they naturally enough conclude that we must have a hand in any movement directed against their cherished Institution. As a matter of fact we have nothing in the world to do with it.

To Rev. A. Lang.

"*September* 24.

" The ' H. W.' arrived from Zanzibar a few days ago bringing me a letter from Col. Euan Smith, which tells me that the Germans are meeting with much opposition in establishing themselves at Pangani, and other places on the Coast. There has been severe fighting and loss of life. In a fortnight hence, the British E. A. Co. will be hoisting their flag at Mombasa and other places on the Coast, and it is impossible to say what may happen. Knowing what I do of the people—Arabs and Wa-Suaheli—of Mombasa, I think it not at all unlikely that F. Town may be exposed to the danger of an attack. I telegraphed to you, asking the lowest price for the ' H. W.' but in view of possible contingencies, I shall not, in any case, part with her for the present. She may be worth her weight in gold to us at a pinch. It is an anxious time for us, and you will, I am sure, remember us in prayer, that we may ' abide under the shadow of the Almighty, till these calamities be overpast '.

"You will be pleased to hear that Herr Ehlers, the German gentleman referred to in Col. Euan Smith's letter, who has just gone up to Chaga, has handed me a donation of 200 dollars for our Mission.   If this is the first money contribution to the C.M.S. in this country —and as far as I know it is—it is singular that it should come from a German !   I think of appropriating it to the Church Fund, in the hope that others may be led to follow Mr. E.'s example. We may surely expect that amongst the large number of Englishmen now flocking to this country—many of them moneyed men—some will be only too glad to help on our work, when they see that we need their help.

" Thanks for your answer to my Telegram. Glad to hear the Accountant is on his way."

To the same (three days later).

"*September* 27.

"All our plans are set aside for the present. Dr. Baxter has arrived with wife and child, and all his goods. Messengers have been sent to stop Pruen from attempting to come to the coast. All the country is in a ferment—war is in the air—we know not what a day may bring forth. You have probably heard by cable of the state of things, and will not forget us. I am wiring to you not to send out any more Missionaries—men or women—till these troubles are over! ' Delay reinforcements, country disturbed.' We are now nineteen English, all told, at Frere Town—including four ladies and a baby !—and quite full up. I am putting up a row of three Bachelors' rooms, but they cannot be ready for another fortnight or so. I enclose a copy of Mrs. Euan Smith's letter to me, which will throw some light on our position. All kinds of strange rumours are coming in. In view of the possibility of a sudden outbreak and attack from Mombasa, I have warned Captain Wilson to be ready to get up steam on the shortest notice. The ' H. W.' may at least afford us a refuge for the ladies. Whatever comes, God help us to glorify Him in our lives or by our deaths, as He may see good, and overrule all to the furtherance of the Gospel in E. Africa.

" Of course, for the present, Fitch remains here, and Taylor at Chaga. The former was preparing to start a week hence. He would go and take all risks, even now, if I would let him ; but in face of the Consul General's expressed wishes, it would not be right. As soon as the veto is taken off he will go forward.

" Beverley and Fraser are both here. The former is going at once to Rabai. It will be good for him in various ways; he will come in contact with Missionary work on a large scale, and in a most interesting field. He will find some branches of work in which he can at once take his part, and will get a good opportunity— which every Missionary ought to have—of studying the language. Fraser finding his way to the Lake blocked, was for returning home forthwith ; but I showed him that according to the terms of his agreement he could not do this. I have come to a comfortable arrangement with him. He consents to take the post of acting engineer of the ' H. W.' and to do any work for which he is competent, and which I may require of him, until we can learn the Committee's wishes in regard to him, under altered circumstances. It is quite impossible to say when the road to the Lake will be re-opened. If you agree to this arrangement please cable the one word ' white '—if you wish F. to return home, say ' black '.

" Reid is much wanted on shore; there are many things to be done—sanctioned work—which he can do well, nobody better.

" Robson will take England's place, in charge of the School, and England will leave by next Mail Steamer.

" Smith, as soon as he has inducted the new Accountant into the ' in's and out's ' of his department, will be free for Shimba, Mwaiba, Teita, or wherever else his services may be required.

" I should have been glad to have had Dr. Pruen here in view of the Mombas Medical Mission, and of the work of training a class of young men and women as assistant doctors and nurses ; but I am afraid it may

be some months before this can be. The Lord knows
what is best. . . ."

Wednesday, September 26. The 'Baghdad' from Zanzibar came in, bringing worse and worse news from the
coast. The Germans are meeting with determined
opposition everywhere. Two have been murdered at
Kilwa, and there has been severe fighting at Bagomoyo,
Pangani and Tanga. It is nothing to be wondered at
that the Arabs and others should resist the assumption
by any Foreign Power of sovereign authority over them,
and over Territory hitherto under the sway of the Mohammedan Sultan of Zanzibar, in which they have so long
carried on their nefarious traffic in slaves, without let
or hindrance. All the more is it to be regretted that
the delicate business of taking possession was not entrusted to officers, who would have had some regard for
the natural susceptibilities of a proud and sensitive
people. These in any case could scarcely be expected
tamely to submit to changes, which involved so much
humiliation and possible loss to themselves. It was
evidently a case for wise, considerate and firm dealing
on the part of the newcomers. Their action appears to
have been the opposite of this. If it be true, as stated,
that two agents of the German Company entered a
Mohammedan Mosque with their lighted cigars, and
having a dog with them, nothing more is required to
account for the recent outrages and murders.

CHAPTER IX.

A DIFFICULT BUSINESS HAPPILY ARRANGED.

Friday, September 28. The " Oriental " in this afternoon with our precious Home letters. I have again to praise God for good tidings of dear ones. Dr. Edwards and Mr. Robson arrived : both intended for the Lake ; but here they must stop. Our friends at Salisbury Square, when they left, had evidently not realized the state of things here at the present time. We are more than full up, and put to it to stow all away. Who can tell what God's will may be in bringing so many of us together here at this time ?

Make the best arrangements we can to accommodate the newly arrived Brethren. England gives up his house to the Baxters, and comes to live with me—Smith also joins my mess—Messrs. Edwards and Beverley will move on to Rabai on Monday. This as a make-shift for the present.

Sunday, September 30. Services as usual—very hot and oppressive in Church. In the evening held a special Service at my house to welcome the newcomers, and to commend them to the blessing of Almighty God. Said a few words on Nehemiah iv.

Monday, October 1. Sent off Chaga and Teita Mails. Beverley and Edwards left in " dhow " for Rabai. Much occupied in providing accommodation for the new Brethren, and in drawing up a plan giving " to every man his work to do ". Happily they are all most willing and anxious to be doing something.

Wednesday, October 3. Smith and I went over to Mombasa and called on Mr. Buchanan, the Agent of the Company. He promised to take on no more of our men as porters, without a note from us, and, in the case of any married men employed by them, to make a monthly payment of Rs. 3 to each wife left behind.

I hope some settled form of Government will soon be set up beyond the ten miles' limit ; at present all is anarchy. The road between this place and Rabai lies through Jomvu, where there is a colony of Wa-Suaheli, who are making our communications difficult and dangerous. Two of our messengers have narrowly escaped with their lives, and there is no authority to appeal to, whereas formerly we could invoke the Wali's interference. I am afraid, unless something is done soon, things will go from bad to worse.

Thursday, October 4. A new Steamer, the " Kistna," came in, bringing Mr. G. S. Mackenzie, Director of the B. E. A. Co., and a staff of eight Englishmen. We (Fitch and I) dined with them on board, and were much pleased with what we saw of them. None of them are novices ; they have all had experience in India or elsewhere. So far, good ; but in the life and work before them in East Africa they have many hard lessons to learn !

Had another letter from the Consul General giving a deplorable account of the state of things all along the coast S. of Mombasa, and expressing himself strongly against Fitch's return to Chaga, or any of our party going inland. He says the Germans are in great diffi-

culties ; all the peaceable people—Hindis and others—
of Bagomoyo, have gone over to Zanzibar. The latter
place is in a state of commotion, and an attack on the
German Consulate is threatened. Under the circumstances, he does not consider it safe for any Englishman to go inland. I replied :—

"Frere Town, *October* 5, 1888.

" My Dear Colonel,—

"This morning a special messenger from
Kilifi brings me your letter of the 1st inst., for which
many thanks.

" I am very sorry for the tidings of the coast. The
Germans appear to have gone about a very delicate
business in the rudest fashion. As far as one can judge
from the accounts that come to us, the massacre at
Bagamoyo was a cruel act of atrocity, and wholly inde-
fensible. They will not get over that in a hurry. The
worst of it is, that it stirs up bad blood between *blacks*
and *whites*—between Mohammedans and Christians—so
that we, who wish to deal fairly and considerately
towards all, may come in for a share of the ill-feeling
and hostility, which the Germans, by their insane proceedings, have evoked.

" I dined last night on board the ' Kistna,' and was
most gratified to find myself in the company of English
gentlemen, some of whom, at least, seem to be Christian
men, in full sympathy with our Missionary objects. If
they are a fair sample of the sort of men the Company
are sending out, we shall pull together most harmoniously ; and there is every reason to hope for their ulti-

mate success in an enterprise which is not without its difficulties. Mr. M., the chief, will, we may trust, act warily—feeling his way—and doing everything that is honourable and right. Will you please tell him that our Mission house at Mombasa is at his service, until he can make better arrangements for himself.

" After what you say, I shall, of course, not sanction Fitch's return to Chaga at present. Personally, I am rather glad of so good an excuse for keeping him here a while longer. The blame, if any there be, of his detention, will rest on you, not on me ; and your shoulders are broader than mine.

" I am pleased to learn from Mr. Mackenzie that there is no immediate intention of hoisting the Company's flag ; ' polè-polè ' is the rule with these people, and ' everything is possible to those who can wait '.

" It is impossible to say what effect may be produced by the news from the coast on the turbulent spirits of Mombasa, but I am sure it is a wise precaution to keep K. K. out of the way.

" All our party are well, with the exception of Mr. England, who has quite run down, and will leave by next Mail Steamer.

" With kindest regards, etc., etc."

Saturday, October 6. Gave a note to eighteen men (eleven married), permitting them to join the Company's " safari ". That makes 23 in all from Frere Town, and there we must stop. It is not good these men should go at all, at this juncture. It is bad for the Mission— bad for the men—and bad for their wives. Mr. C., a gentleman who came out in the " Kistna," and who is bound for Melindi, on a hunting excursion, applied to me for porters from Frere Town. I was obliged to tell him I could not give him a single man. I feel it necessary to make a stand at once against the practice of furnishing any Englishman who may turn up with porters for his caravan. They are not always well treated, and even when they are, they return to us more or less demoralized.

Sunday, October 7. Early Communion—good attendance—also at both M. and A. Services. " Welcome sweet day of rest," and all the more welcome by reason of " the storms that round us rise ".

Monday, October 8. Much rain during the night, which has continued through the day, so that we could not gather as usual for Morning Prayer, nor the children for school, all our houses leaking like sieves.

Engaged most of the day on the Finance Committee making bye-laws for Frere Town.

Commenced my monthly letter to my wife. As it touches upon matters of pressing interest at this critical and anxious time, I give some extracts from it here.

" FRERE TOWN, October 8th, 1888.

" MY DEAREST WIFE,—

" Yours of September 7 came to hand on the 28th, just three weeks, but it referred to matters, many of which are ancient history. Poor Hall ! I had no idea he was so ill. I had heard only that he was out of sorts. I am very sorry, but sincerely hope Pickford's ministry may be blest to him, and that in his extremity he may find ' peace with God, through Jesus Christ '. Every one has his proper gift of God, and mine, I have often felt, is not in personal dealing with individuals. I don't think it is so much from want of courage, as from want of tact. I am so afraid that by rough or unskilful handling I may "quench the smoking flax". My only comfort in this case is, that poor Hall has heard many a time the Gospel of Christ from my lips, and in the hope that though he gave no sign, he may not have been so insensible as he seemed to the word spoken.

"I am sorry A. will be gone when I return. Poor old Flo gone! and now A. gone! the old place will scarcely look itself; but as an old lady—a heathen—said to me the other day: 'We must take what God sends and make the best of it'. I only hope A. will find a good husband in E. She has been a faithful servant to us, and I should be very sorry to see her badly mated.

"I had, as you know, nothing from dear Mac by this Mail. I bear in mind that this is the trying season on the West coast, and earnestly pray God to 'keep' him.

"So far, I have indeed much reason to be thankful for the opportunity given me of revisiting the scene of former labours in East Africa, and I hope, through God's help and blessing, it has not been altogether in vain. Dear England, an earnest fellow, who has completely broken down in health, and who is going home by this Mail, said to me, 'The last seven months have been the happiest I have spent in Africa,' and there is more in that than appears at first sight. I should so like you to meet him. He is a native of Guernsey, and will not stay long in England, but I will give him your address at Richmond, and ask him to call, and tell you all about us and our goings on at Frere Town.   The Steads will like to see him ; and he is worthy of all the kindness and hospitality they can show him.

"Jerusalem! oh yes!   I should dearly like to make a pilgrimage to the sacred city on my way home ; but as *you* cannot meet me there, I do not know if I shall carry out my plan.   It would indeed be a grand treat —a sublime finish to our earthly wanderings—if we could spend a week or two together in those 'holy places'; but I suppose we must postpone our pleasure, till we walk together, as, through God's mercy we may hope to do, in the streets of 'the New Jerusalem'.

"I hope your visit to C. will not be in vain, of course it has been a great comfort to dear A. and your words to the old women will bear fruit.   'In all labour there is profit.'

"How kind and noble of dear Clowes! and how strange that not he only, but many others seem determined to take and make me a Bishop.   Their idea seems to be that I have been badly treated by the Committee.   I am sure I have never said anything to originate such a notion.   Indeed if the offer were made to me, which is not at all likely, I should be 'in a great strait'.   My intense love for the work here would incline me to say 'yes' – whilst a profound sense of my unworthiness would incline me to say 'no'. The thought does not trouble *me*.   If the Lord knew it would be good for me and for His cause, the way would be made plain, and obstacles removed.   As it is, I am more than content to be counted worthy to fill a gap, and to give the best I have of mind and body to the furtherance of the Gospel in East Africa. I do not know what I should do as a Bishop; but I do know that with Him with whom we have to do 'a man is accepted according to that he hath, and not according to that he hath not'.

"You will see from the papers that the country south of Mombasa is in a disturbed state. The Germans by high-handed proceedings have provoked hostility and opposition. There has been a good deal of fighting— many lives lost on both sides—and it is very doubtful what will be the end of it. As a rule the Natives distinguish between the Germans, whom they call Wa-Daitch, and us, in our favour; but when once their passions are aroused against foreigners and Christians, it is to be feared they will not be so discriminating. For the present, all the routes into the interior are stopped, whereby four Missionaries and one lady, sent out in post-haste by the Committee to go forward to the Lake are detained here, certainly for several months. So I have a staff of eighteen all told! It has taxed my ingenuity to house them all, though I had no difficulty in finding them work to do. Of course the Committee's plans are all upset, and, what is worse, our Brethren at the Lake will be sorely disappointed. It is very sad, yet we may be sure God would not have permitted it but for some good and wise purpose.

"Yesterday morning in bed, between awake and asleep, I saw you reading a letter, when suddenly looking up you said: 'H. is very ill'. I don't think I am particularly superstitious, but the thought somehow took hold of me, and I could only find relief by commending him in prayer to our Heavenly Father. May he and all our dear children be numbered amongst the people of God, for Christ's sake."

Tuesday, October 9.   A deluge of rain all through the night, and this morning tanks all running over, whereof we are glad ; and not a dry spot anywhere, which is very miserable !   Pratley, whilst playing football with the boys, met with a nasty fall, dislocating something in his knee.   Smith at my request left for Shimba. Some matters there require looking into, and I cannot get away from here just now.   Questions are continually cropping up, which must be met and dealt with at once.

Thursday, October 11.   The Sultan's S.S. " Swordsman " came in, having on board the new Wali of Melindi.   She also brings letters from His Highness to all the Walis north of Mombasa, giving them notice of the coming of the B. E. A. Co.   Burness and I went over to Mombasa and removed all the Mission furniture to F. Town.

Friday, October 12.   At midnight I was roused up by Robson.   Mr. Edmunds, one of the Company's agents, had come over from Mombasa to ask for Dr. Baxter to attend some of the Company's porters, who had been savagely attacked and badly wounded by some Wa-Suaheli in the town.   Robson and Baxter were ready to go, so I immediately slipped on my clothes and joined them.   On our way to call Ishmael, we missed the path in the dark, and walked right into the midst of an army of " siafu " on thé march.   Oh ! the torments ! we were entirely at their mercy, and they almost drove us wild.   We rowed quickly across the harbour to Mombasa, and landing, wended our

way cautiously through a number of dismal streets—
narrow, and reeking with filthy odours—not knowing
but any moment we might encounter a band of cut-

STREET IN MOMBASA.

throats, till we came to an unfinished house near
Buchanan's, in which the wounded men were lying.
A ghastly sight met our eyes on entering. There lay a

strongly built man, stark naked, who had been fearfully hacked and cut on the head and in various parts of the body ; the large gaping wounds must have bled profusely, and the poor fellow was in a semi-comatose state, and there were several other cases nearly as bad. The Doctor set to work at once, stitching up the worst of the gashes. After a while, leaving him and Robson engaged in this work, I took Ishmael with me to call on the Wali. The old gentleman had often assured me he was at my service night or day, so now I must put him to the test. We got to his house about 2 a.m., and on learning who it was that wanted to see him he came down at once, looking awfully scared. He said he was greatly concerned at what had happened and that although he had gone to bed, he could not sleep, but lay thinking what could be done. He said there was a strong feeling on the part of many in Mombasa against " Wazungu," whilst there was also a party in their favour. He knew that Khamis Khombo, who is now in the town, was one of the principal fomenters of strife. He added : " I am quite perplexed ; if I go into this case to-morrow, I shall most likely find that some of the leading men of Mombasa are at the bottom of the mischief, and if I take them prisoners all the town will be up in arms ; I want force to back me up ". We agreed that if either of us should hear of any plotting he should at once let the other know. He as usual professed eternal friendship for me, and I would fain believe him to be sincere ; but he is an Arab ! The Dr. was only able to dress the worst of the wounds, and we recrossed the water, very tired, at 4·30 a.m. I do not think I could stand many repetitions of last night's experiences.

This afternoon the "Kistna" came in from Zanzibar bringing some seventy porters, and all the Mackenzie party, except the Chief himself. He, Col. Euan Smith, and General Matthews are coming on Sunday in the Flagship " Boadicea ".

Saturday, October 13. Lt. Erskine, an officer of the " Boadicea," died on board the " Kistna," of remittent fever, and was buried at F. Town this afternoon.

The following extract from my letter to the Rev. R. Lang, of this date, will show what was the condition of affairs with us at this time :—

"FRERE TOWN, *October* 13, 1888.

"DEAR MR. LANG,—

" Your letter of 5th September came to hand on the 28th. Since you wrote, the aspect of things has entirely changed, and events have taken place which for the present set aside all our plans, and by the time you get this God only knows what may happen still further to disarrange our calculations. We must not complain. God answers our prayers and leads us by a way we know not ; but it is ' the right way'. We walk by Faith. It is not your fault, and it certainly is not mine that Messrs. Baxter, Beverley, Fraser, and Robson are detained here, but here they are, and it is all uncertain when the way will be open for them to go forward.

" My telegram would, I fear, be too late to stop Miss Scott. I was most anxious to prevent her or any other lady coming out just now whilst all is so uncertain and unsettled. It may be that, in spite of murmurings and threats which reach us, all will pass off quietly. God grant it may be so ; but anyway, till things settle down, it would be well to keep back any more ladies who may be coming out. The Accountant we shall, of course, be glad to see.

" There is no doubt, I think, that the Company will proceed with caution, and with every desire not to do needless violence to the feelings of Arabs, etc. ; but it will be a bitter pill, however much it may be gilded. The crisis will be when the Company begin to put down slave traffic, as by the terms of their charter they are required to do.

"It may be well for you to know how our present staff are located and utilized.

" (1) Mr. Beverley and Dr. Edwards are at Rabai. The first chief work of each is to learn the language. Beverley will in addition give an hour or two daily to the instruction of the Schoolmaster and his assistants ; in short, conduct a Divinity class on a small scale. As he acquires the language he will find plenty of opportunities of turning his new talent to account—the openings are limitless.

" Dr. Edwards will have ample scope for the exercise of his medical knowledge and skill among the 2000, more or less, inhabitants of Rabai, to say nothing of the poor Wa-Nika, who will gladly avail themselves of the English 'mganga'. A medical Mission here is just now much more feasible than at Mombasa.

" (2) Reid is, *pro tem.*, overseer of works at F. Town— fully occupied and in his element. Burness is most thankful to be relieved of secular work and to be able to give more time to the language.

"(3) Fraser is acting engineer on the 'H. W.,' and as just now she has not much to do, he is, at my request, engaged on a careful survey of the Frere Town Settlement, and in making a Chart which will supersede the rather rough and ready one made by Mr. Biddlecome in '81. This will be a useful work.

"(4) Dr. Baxter has his hands full. He has not been able as yet to begin work in Mombasa, but a number of sick folk from Mombasa and other places come here for advice and treatment. We are just now considering how best to give a Missionary character to his work.

"(5) Our two ladies—Miss Fitch and Miss Ramsay —are, as usual, fully occupied. Miss R. enters most heartily into her new life and work. She is a great help and comfort to Miss Fitch, about whose health I am extremely anxious. I am afraid it will go hard with her during the hot season now coming on.

"(6) Fitch is chiefly occupied with the Divinity Class, which is now in full swing. He also takes part in the Sunday Services, which is good for himself as well as for the people : and besides he is a willing helper to me in various ways.

"(7) Pratley has his own work. His new house, with printing office attached, has been finished and occupied for some time past.

"(8) Smith is still at his desk. I shall be glad both for his and the work's sake when he is free. Our out-stations at Shimba and Mwaiba need more regular supervision than I can possibly give to them under present circumstances.

"(9) Robson enters *con amore* into the School work. It is in some respects not easy to succeed England, but he is fond of boys and will I hope make his way.

"Really it looks on paper as if we had quite a formidable staff—there are five more than were assigned to us—yet there are no supernumeraries, and it would be quite easy to find posts of usefulness for as many more. You will regret, as do I, the great disappointment to our Lake Brethren, but it is some satisfaction to know that these reinforcements, though delayed, are not debarred from active work. It may be in God's good purpose thus to fit and prepare them for their future spheres of labour.

"Dear England leaves by next Steamer. He has been living with me the last month, and the more I see of him the more I love and value him. You will, I feel sure, give him a warm welcome, and let him see that faithful, conscientious service, such as his has been, is gratefully appreciated by the Committee. I regret very much the necessity for his going, and earnestly pray he may soon recover health and strength, and return to his post."

.   .   .   .

Sunday, October 14.   Services as usual, Fitch preaching in the Morning, and James D. in the Afternoon. A little incident this afternoon during the Prayers may serve to show the state of tension which exists just now amongst our people. The report of a gun was heard twice—not an unusual thing—and immediately all were

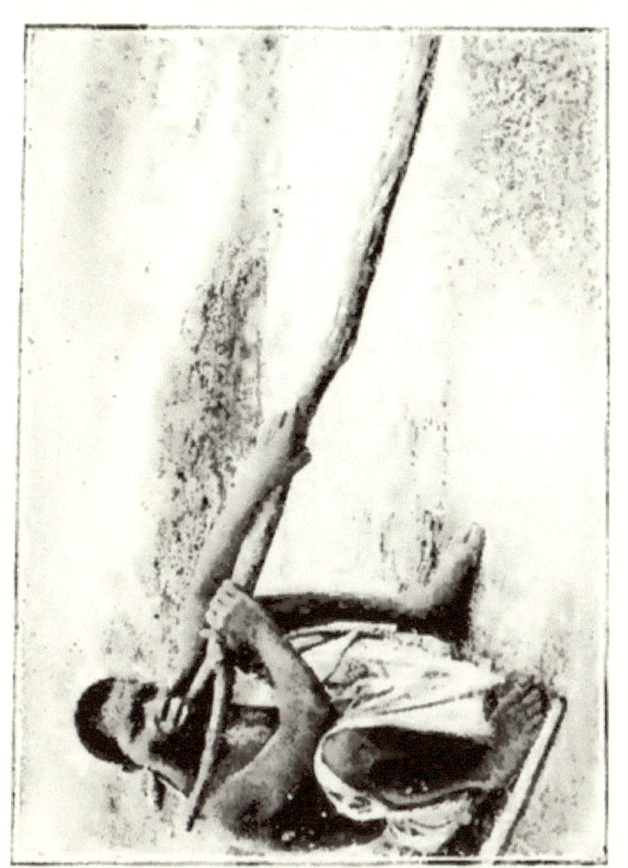

RESCUED FROM SLAVE GANG.

getting up and anxiously looking through the windows. If anyone with a gun had happened to be passing, there would, I fear, have been a panic and a stampede. Happily we were spared this, and on coming out we found that all that had occurred was the shooting of a leopard, which has lately been giving us a good deal of trouble. All the Brethren met at my house in the evening for singing and prayer.

Monday, October 15. The Sultan's S.S. "Kilwa" arrived, bringing Mr. Mackenzie and General Matthews; also for me a long letter from the Consul General, about the "watoro" at Rabai; and asking for the use of the "H.W." for the new Company. To this I replied as follows :—

"FRERE TOWN, October 16, 1889.

"MY DEAR COLONEL,—

"The 'Kilwa' arrived at 9 a.m., and your letter of the 14th was not delivered to me till 6 p.m. Not receiving any word from you as I was expecting, I had arranged for the 'H.W.' to leave for Zanzibar to-day, and it is important she should do so, and return here with as little delay as possible. She should leave Zanzibar not later than Friday. I could not send he away at the usual time, as, in the event of an attack upon us from Mombasa—a very possible contingency —she afforded us the only refuge for our ladies (four in number). I had reason, as you know, to expect the 'Mariner' or some other boat would be here at the critical moment.

"The murderous attack made last week on some

porters of the Company, shows plainly enough what is the state of feeling on the part of some at least of the Mombasa people. . . .

"Now as to the 'H.W.'; after this trip I accept the responsibility of placing her at *your* disposal for the purposes of the Company during the present emergency for one trip to Zanzibar and back per month, the details I will arrange with Mr. Mackenzie, who is coming to see me to-day.

"As regards Rabai, I regret exceedingly you cannot come yourself and see into the matter, and the more so that you have deputed for this work one who, though he professes friendship for me personally, has not the character of being very friendly to Missions or Missionaries.

"That, in spite of our wishes and stringent rules, some 'watoro' have found refuge in our Settlement is exceedingly probable, but in every case in which application has been made to me by Arabs or Wa-Suaheli owners, I have offered to go with them myself and secure them every opportunity of ascertaining if their slaves were with us, and see that they had fair play. That being so, I cannot see that these people have any real ground of complaint. I shall go up with Mr. Mackenzie, and see that every facility is given him in his investigation. . . .

"Yours sincerely, etc., etc."

Tuesday, October 16. Smith returns from Shimba, having set things in order. "H.W." left for Zanzibar. A letter from Mr. Mackenzie asking for a hundred porters! He does not understand our position, and is

evidently under the impression that the employment of our people by the Co. must in some way or
other be a benefit to the Mission. As it was necessary
to undeceive him as to this, I replied as follows :—

"*October* 16, 1888.

"DEAR MR. MACKENZIE,—

"I am anxious to meet your wishes in regard
to porters, though it is most difficult and inconvenient
to do so, especially at the present time.

"In the first place we want fifty men almost immediately for a 'safari' to Chaga; these I *must* retain.
Then, twenty-five or more are already engaged with the
Company. If I give you 80 or 100 more, that will
pretty well clear us out of all our young able-bodied
men, leaving us with any number of helpless women
and children on our hands, at a time when from day to
day it is impossible to say what may happen. You will
not fail, I think, to take in the difficulty of the situation.

"Then too, it is no advantage either to our men or
to the Mission, for them to be employed in this manner;
quite the contrary. They may, it is true, earn more
money just for the time ; but it is 'easy come easy go'
—they get into loose, improvident habits, and are ruined
for anything like steady, industrial work. There can
be no doubt it would be seriously detrimental, from
almost every point of view, to the objects of the
Mission.

"I think it only right to put all this clearly before
you ; whilst, at the same time, knowing your present
emergency, and anxious to help all I can, I have called
for volunteers, both here and at Rabai, ' to carry loads,'

as you say 'to your first encampment and to return,' and I will let you know as soon as possible how many turn up.

"I hope you will have every reason to be satisfied with your 'shauri,' with the Wali and grandees of Mombasa, and shall be glad to see you and the General when you find time to honour me with a visit.

"Yours, etc., etc."

Mr. Mackenzie is just now engaged in a difficult business—holding conferences with the Arab Sheiks and others, with the view of reconciling them to the new order of things. The difficulty is greatly aggravated by the unwise action of the Germans, who have met with determined, and, here and there, to some extent, successful resistance. Mr. M. will at least avoid their mistakes, and try a policy of conciliation. These Sheiks possess a good deal of power for mischief, and have to be reckoned with ; and Mr. M. has begun, I hear, by making presents of large sums of money to all the principal men. How far this will go in satisfying them, remains to be seen.

I gather from Col. Euan Smith's letter, that it is intended shortly to send an officer to Rabai, to make an inquiry on the spot as to how many "watoro" may be there, to search them out, and to hand them over to their "owners". I do not know—indeed have no means of knowing—how many of these poor runaways there may be in our Mission Settlement. I have always set my face against allowing them—as far as we had power to prevent it—to find shelter within our borders. Feeling strongly that, however much it may go against the grain to turn our backs on these people, it was our duty under the circumstances to take every precaution to exclude them—I have, over and over again, earnestly urged this policy on my Missionary Brethren, and have no reason to suppose that they have acted contrary to it. It is not surprising if, in spite of their vigilance, some refugees have, from time to time, crept in unobserved, and become absorbed in the community. It is one thing however to discourage, as far as possible, the reception of fugitive slaves, and quite another to allow our Mission Station to be converted into a trap, whereby these unfortunate men and women may be caught and handed over again to the cruel bondage from which they have escaped. I can have no hand in that, so on receipt of the letter above referred to, I wrote at once to Mr. Jones :—

" F. Town, October 16, 1888.

" My Dear Jones,—

" The Consul General cannot come for the present, but he writes to me that serious complaints are made by the Sheiks of Mombasa of their slaves being harboured at Rabai, and that General Matthews is going up to investigate the matter, and to hand over any 'watoro' he may find there, to their 'owners'. You had better give a general order all round, for every man, woman and child of this description to clear out of our Settlement with the least possible delay. They may go wherever they please, but it is woe to them if

they are found at Rabai; the General will not spare.
Send messenger at once to let me know if the ' coast
is clear '.

" Yours, etc."

Wednesday, October 17.   Juma bin Raschid, an Arab,
called to give me the "khabari".   He says Khamis
Khombo is doing all he can to stir up opposition to
" Wazungu," but he (Juma) and others refuse to join.
We in F. Town are closely watched.   I had two letters
on Monday, one from Colonel Euan Smith, and one
from Mackenzie ; and when this was reported to the
" Wazee," they at once concluded that these letters
must contain secret information as to the designs of
the Company. This morning, Mr. Mackenzie had a meeting with the Wali and the Sheiks.   He explained to them
the objects of the Company, their desire to respect all
rights, to redress all grievances, etc. ; but the Sheiks
postponed their reply till they had conferred amongst
themselves.   They have decided to put to him the
question : " Will you interfere with our Slave Traffic ? "
So far Juma bin Raschid.   What answer will Mr. M.
give to the Sheiks, with the Company's charter staring
him in the face, I do not know ; *they* of course know
what it says.   There is a good deal of shouting and
gun-firing in Mombasa to-night ; but what it is all
about we do not know.

Thursday, October 18.   Messrs. Mackenzie and Matthews had promised to come over and see me to-day.
I waited in all day, but they did not turn up.   They
are still occupied with the Sheiks.

Friday, October 19.   The " H. W." came in from

Zanzibar, at 7 a.m., rather sharp work! She brings me a long letter from the Colonel, which is painful reading. He makes a great to-do about the "watoro" at Rabai. Evidently many misrepresentations have been made to him, and he thinks matters are a great deal worse than they are. About 9 a.m. arrived the Sultan's steamer "Glasgow," bringing Hamid bin Sulieman and a hundred soldiers. In the afternoon came in the Flag-ship "Boadicea," with Admiral Fremantle, who came at once on shore and called upon me, with another letter from the Consul-General! What a day of worry! Dined with the Admiral, and met Mr. Mackenzie, who told me he had at last settled matters comfortably with the Arabs.

Replied to Col. Euan Smith :—

"FRERE TOWN, *October* 19, 1888.

" MY DEAR COLONEL,—

"The 'H. W.' came in at 7 a.m. this morning bringing me your letter of the 17th. Thanks for this, and for the excellent arrangement you have made for our protection. The 'Stork' is a capital idea!

"Now as to Rabai and the runaways, after reading and re-reading what you have written on this subject, I feel sure that the case as against this Mission has been greatly exaggerated.

What I meant by saying that the Arabs have no real cause of complaint was, that I have always shown my willingness to assist them to the utmost of my power in finding out any of their slaves, should they have taken refuge either here or at Rabai. I do not know what more I could do. We cannot, of course, prevent their slaves running away; that they will do, and more and more so as time goes on, whether they find refuge with us or not.

Rabai is a large Settlement, and very variously peopled; there are *freed* slaves, Wa-Nika, Wa-Khamba, Wa-Masai, and many others. As I said, it is quite possible that, now and then, a runaway or two may steal in and find shelter; but it is quite contrary to our Rules, and I have over and over again strictly charged Mr. Jones to keep a sharp look-out, and to expel at once any suspicious interlopers. It is not only against our Rules, but altogether contrary to our wishes to have anything to do, under existing circumstances, with these poor people; they constitute a troublesome and dangerous element. I shall, as I said, afford every facility for a searching inquiry, as I am as anxious as you can be to give no just cause of offence to our Arab and Suaheli neighbours.

" You know, I suppose, that in this matter, Mbaruk is the chief offender. His following is made up mainly of runaways; and that was one reason why I was so annoyed at Last for bringing these people into our Settlement.

" Fulladoyo is a purely 'watoro' colony, with which we have absolutely no connexion. I hear that several hundreds of them are there, and, as *they* are certainly not under the protection of the British flag, their owners need have no scruple in dealing with them. It is most important you should clearly understand that neither the C. M. S., nor, as far as I know, any other Missionary

Society, has any sort of responsibility in connexion with the ' watoro' colony of Fulladoyo.

"I am still expecting a visit from Mr. Mackenzie and the General, but they have probably their hands full just now. It is an anxious time for you and for all of us. May God give us all the wisdom we need for the emergency.

" Yours, etc., etc."

Saturday, October 20. This morning Mr. Mackenzie and General Matthews came over for breakfast, and afterwards to a long "shauri"; at which Smith and Esa, Buchanan's man, were present. Mr. M. gave me an account of his negotiations with the Sheiks, and read from a Paper the stipulations they had made to him as representative of the B. E. A. Co. These were six in number. The only one which concerned us was " that the Company should assist them in obtaining their slaves who had found refuge in any of the Mission Stations," which Mr. M. had, of course, undertaken to do. To this I said that I had always shown my willingness to assist them as far as lay in my power, and that I was prepared to do so still ; and that the harbouring of runaways was entirely against our Rules, and against our wishes. I made no objection to a proposal to appoint a Commission to investigate the matter at Rabai and to make such arrangements as may appear necessary to prevent any "watoro "in future from settling there. This seemed to give satisfaction, and I promised to meet the Sheiks in "baraza " on Monday next, to talk the matter over with them.

The " Boadicea " left at 3 p.m. for Zanzibar, and the " Kilwa" later on.

Sunday, October 21.   Our Day of Rest sadly marred by the accounts brought by Mackenzie and Buchanan of the bad feeling against the Company in Mombasa. There was a great disturbance in the town last night. It appears that the younger men are not at all satisfied with the agreement come to by their seniors with Mr. Mackenzie, and are for rebellion.   The trouble is evidently not yet over.

Dr. Baxter and James, at the request of Mr. M., went over to Mombasa to attend to five wounded men.

Monday, October 22.   By appointment, accompanied by Fitch, Smith, and Ishmael, attended a grand " baraza " at the Wali's palace.   Said Hamid bin Sulieman, uncle of the Sultan, was the great man, and he gave me the seat of honour.   Mr. Mackenzie and Gen. Matthews came next.   A large number—all in fact—of the principal Sheiks were in attendance.   After formal preliminaries I read my address on the subject of runaway slaves, which appeared to give general satisfaction. Khamis Khombo put several questions, which I had no difficulty in answering, and I hope the Sheiks will feel that they have now no further cause of complaint.

It was proposed that a number of Arabs and other slave owners, who suppose their slaves to be in hiding at Rabai, should go up accompanied by Mr. Mackenzie and Gen. Matthews on Monday next to claim and take possession of them.   If the latter have an inkling of what is going to happen and possess the instinct of self-preservation, the expedition will find an empty cage !

I am deeply grieved for these poor hunted creatures; but our duty is plain. We cannot, if we would, shelter them; they must look out for themselves. May God help them, and make them a way of escape!

Tuesday, October 23. Startling news reaches me from Rabai. The " watoro " there—numbering to my intense astonishment some four hundred—refuse to leave. They are determined to make a stand. They are desperate, and will fight for their homes and liberty, and many freed slaves and others will join them. If the Arab party go up on Monday, as proposed, there will be war and bloodshed, and what that may lead to, who shall predict? It will be bad for all concerned; I must do all I can to avert this calamity.

This afternoon, Said Hamid bin Sulieman, the Wali, and a number of grandees came over to pay me a ceremonial visit. At their request I showed them over the Settlement, and they expressed themselves much pleased with all they saw. They were very agreeable, and, it goes without saying, profuse in their compliments. Little they suspected how my heart was aching for the poor people at Rabai!

Had, this evening, Holy Communion with dear England, who is leaving us to-morrow.

As Post time is drawing near, finished off my letters for Home, giving latest intelligence.

To the Rev. R. Lang.

" *October* 23.

" We are just now in a whirl of excitement. It is *the* crisis we have been looking forward to. Problems are continually cropping up which call for quick decision. It is quite easy to make mistakes, yet we trust that He who rules over all, will give us a right judgment, and keep us from doing or saying anything that would place us in the wrong. So far all is well. I am enclosing a budget of Letters, etc., as I deem it important the Committee should be fully informed as to how matters stand between us—the new Company —and the Consul General. All Mombasa is in a ferment. General Matthews is there with a hundred sepoys.

"You will see that I have done all I could to avert trouble at Rabai. You may perhaps think I have gone too far in the way of concession, but the matter is not to be so easily settled. I hear this morning that the runaways are in much more considerable numbers than any of us had any idea of: some four hundred—and that they refuse to go. Many of them have been there for several years ; have been baptized and confirmed ; have their own houses and 'shambas,' wives and children ! They are in hot blood and determined to fight for their liberty. I am afraid they are beyond all control, even of Jones, for whom they have the greatest respect. It is a matter of life and death to them. I will do my utmost, God being my helper, to prevent a collision ; for if once blood be shed on either side, there will be a terrible catastrophe. Should it come, you will hear of it by cable before you get this. May God, in His great mercy, bring us all safely out of this trouble. I am writing in great sorrow of heart — 'cast down but not in despair'—I need scarcely say again, ' Brethren, pray for us '.

" With Christian love to you and all your brother Secretaries, and to the Committee.

"Yours very affectionately,

"W. Salter Price.

" P.S.—Please tell General Hutchinson I am sending by T. E. England the Plans of Mission houses he asked for."

To my Wife.

" *Sunday, October* 21, 1888.

" It is a time of trouble and perplexity, and I feel sure you are praying for us. It wants only three days to the Mail, and I shall be sorely taxed to get through all I have to do 'twixt now and then ; so I finish my letter to you, dearest, to-day, leaving it open till the last, in the hope I may be able to report some change for the better in our situation. I cannot enter into details now. If anything serious happens you will get it in the Telegrams. 'God is our Refuge and Strength.' Love to all the dear children—much refreshed by their letters— sorry I cannot send a line to each. Fond love, etc."

Wednesday, October 24. At 8 a.m. as the " Oriental " was coming in, she went on the rocks near the Point and stuck fast. Smith and I pulled out to her and got our letters (from the south). At 3 p.m. after many ineffectual attempts to get the steamer afloat, at Mr. Mackenzie's request the " H. W." steamed out to her help, I and two others of our party going in her. We got a strong hawser on her quarter, and put on full speed. There was a tremendous strain, which threatened to snap the cable, thick as it was. Suddenly there was a loud crash ; the aft bulwark of the " H. W." was carried

away, and we had to let go.   After a while we picked
up the hawser again, and were just going ahead, when
a welcome shout came from the "Oriental".   "Let go
—she's off!"   We were glad enough to obey the order,
for it was getting rather risky work.

A telegram, presumably from Salisbury Square is
forwarded to me by our Zanzibar agents:

"Tell Price,—complaints of harbouring runaways—
report."   What next!

Thursday, October 25.   A grand red letter day!
Went over to Mombasa, and had a long talk with Mr.
Mackenzie.   I pointed out the extreme danger of a
collision between the "watoro" and their Arab owners,
if the plan is persisted in of allowing the latter to go to
Rabai, to claim and carry off their slaves.   It may be
the beginning of a servile war, the consequences of
which would be disastrous to all concerned.   I found
Mr. M. very reasonable, and we came to an understanding that the affair should be settled, not by the forcible
handing over of the slaves to their owners, but in the
way of *compensation.*   We agreed to a commission
to enquire on the spot as to the actual number of
"watoro" at Rabai—how long there?—their owners?
etc., etc.   We are to go up next Monday—he, Gen.
Matthews and I—to look into the matter.   Having
ascertained how many are really claimable by the
Arabs, a fair amount by way of ransom is to be offered
to them, and the slaves to be set Free!   God be praised!
What a load is lifted off my mind!

Went on board the "Oriental" to say farewell to
dear England, and to send off our Mail.

In order to present a connected account of the

settlement of the runaway slave question, I insert here a short correspondence I had with the Rev. W. H. Jones, Native Pastor of Rabai.

In reply to my letter of the 16th inst. (see p. 185) Mr. Jones wrote :

RABAI, *October* 20, 1888.

" MY DEAR SIR,—

"No peace! On receiving your letter I made the so-called 'watoro' understand the sorrowful subject of it. They first of all proposed to go to the 'banderini' and meet General Matthews on his arrival, and tell him their grievances, so that the Mission here should have less to do in the matter. On Friday, I called them together and told them how strongly you have written that they should leave the place and go elsewhere. To-day they have gone on the way to Jimba for further consideration of this bitter state of things. They resolve that, as Mbaruk, who has slain thousands of the Sultan's subjects, has been allowed to throw himself into the hands of the B.E.A. Co. and is now safe, they would do the same. Hence they have now proclaimed themselves the subjects of the Company. This Mission was the first to suggest this plan to Mbaruk, why should it not answer now? For this they want very much to see the Chief of the Company, and to throw themselves— men, women and children—at his feet, and implore his protection. I earnestly pray the merciful Lord will look down upon them, and grant their request.

" You may depend upon it, Sir, I am doing all I can to carry out your instructions. Our people sleep out of their houses—many of them in the jungle—it is a fearful state of things. I trust that strength will be given you in these trying times. I enclose the people's determination for life or death. May God help them.

"To-day the representatives of the 'watoro' are going to Jimba to surrender themselves to Lt. Swayne (one of the Co.'s officers).

"I remain, etc."

To this I replied :—

"FRERE TOWN, *October* 21, 1888.

"MY DEAR JONES,—

"My heart bleeds for those poor people, and I am very sorry for *you*, but there is no choice left us—only one way for us, as far as I can see, out of this difficulty. It is, that they all flee from Rabai ; it is no longer a safe place for them, and their remaining there will be the break-up of our Mission. They will get nothing by going to Lt. Swayne ; he has no authority to protect them. It is indeed a time of trouble for us all. There was a great row in Mombasa last night, and some of the ring-leaders are, I hear, in prison. There is a tremendous noise of shouting and drumming going on now as I am writing. May God, in His great mercy, shield us all from the evils which threaten, and give us Peace, for Christ's sake. In haste,—

"Yours affectionately,

"W. SALTER PRICE."

After my conference with the Arabs on the 22nd, I wrote to Jones informing him of the project of Mr. Mackenzie, General Matthews, and a number of Arabs, going up to Rabai on a certain day, to search for and carry off their slaves, and to this I received the following touching reply :—

"RABAI, *October* 24, 1888.

" MY DEAR SIR,—

" Mnubi has come with your letter last night. We are glad to hear you are well, and doing all you can for our people. Allow me to write as follows :—

" 1. When Mr. Mackenzie, General Matthews, and the Arabs come to pick out their slaves, I shall prove myself a useless servant. I will not, and I cannot, hand these poor souls to their cruel and unmerciful masters, after I have been preaching to them the sweet liberty of my Lord and Saviour, Jesus Christ, and of His Gospel. Somebody else will have to do that wicked work.

" 2. Be it understood that such people as those whom their masters are coming to pick out, will not be found in the Mission Station, but two miles off ; so that after they have picked them out, they will take them to the coast by some other way, and not through our Station. How could I bear to see these poor baptized Christians, and communicants, pass by me, with their hands fastened—beaten—abused—and dragged through the village where they have lived and sung praises to the God of heaven ?

" 3. If Mr. M. and Gen. M. come with no other object but to gratify the wishes of the Suaheli population, then, alas ! for the healing of the ' open sore ' of East Africa. . . .

" I remain, dear Sir,

" Your obedient Servant,

" W. H. JONES."

" After my interview with Mr. Mackenzie on the 25th, at which we had agreed to the principle of compensation and ransom, I sat down with a thankful heart to communicate the good news to Mr. Jones, and sent off my letter by a special messenger.

"Frere Town, *October 25, 1888.*

" MY DEAR JONES,—

"God has heard our prayers! All is peace! I had a long 'shauri' with Mr. Mackenzie this morning, and I rejoice to tell you he is ready to do all he can for your poor people. They have nothing to fear! We shall come up on Monday, all being well—Mr M., the General, and I. The object of our visit is *simply* to ascertain, as far as can be done, the real state of affairs as regards the runaways. *Our* policy is, to throw no obstacle in the way of this investigation, but to assist it to the utmost of our power; and let me add, it is *your own* best policy too. Now I want you to do three things :—

"1. Praise God, who has heard our prayers, and brought good out of evil.

"2. Pacify the minds of our poor people ; make them clearly to understand that they have now nothing to fear. I cannot tell you all just now, but for the present this is enough—they are Free ! Free !! Free !!! Mr. M. is their friend and deliverer, and I want them to meet us at the top of Buni and give him a warm reception, such as they gave me, or, if possible, warmer. Tell them not to shake hands, that is a troublesome business when there are so many, and, under the circumstances, our friends might not like it. If there is any gun-firing see that it is only in 'furaha,' and with *blank* cartridges. It would be a bad thing if anyone were shot, even by accident. If they want to shoot anyone let them shoot me. I hope the women will muster strong.

"Lastly, let Ribe and Fulladoyo keep aloof. I assured the Sheiks and Mr. Mackenzie that we had no connexion with Jomvu, Ribe, or Fulladoyo.

"Have the iron house—Krapf Cottage—thoroughly cleaned—compound also—and everything in trim order.

KRAPF COTTAGE.

"Now write back and let me know if you fully understand everything and can ensure the proper carrying out of my wishes. If you cannot keep out the Ribe and

Fulladoyo people, better have no ' furaha '. That would
spoil everything.   God prosper you !

" Yours affectionately,

" W. Salter Price."

Next day brought me the following reply :—

" Rabai, *October* 26, 1888.

" My Dear Sir,—

"Our prayers are indeed answered.   Your joyful
letter, which has brought peace to our village, arrived
here last night—at midnight—and since that hour to
this my eyes have not winked in sleep.   What shall I
say?   Glory be to God, let the name of our God be
exalted for His mercies to us, His unworthy creatures.
The whole village is out to rejoice at the peace which
has crowned our once terrified homes.   That word
' FREE ' has made my heart light : so now all is peace,
for Jesus lives.   We shall turn up on Monday at the
Buni hill, and others below the hill with our guns.
No Ribe or Fulladoyo men will be allowed to come
near our free Settlement on that day.   I thank the Lord
for the success He has granted you in this great battle
of healing the big ' open sore '.   All honour, too, to Mr.
M. for his good work of giving our countrymen their
liberty.   God be praised !   I hope soon to see you on
Monday.

" With my great respects to you, Sir,

" Yours most obediently,

" W. H. Jones."

CHAPTER X.

THE BLOCKADE—ROUTES CHANGED.

Friday, October 26.   Busy writing to up-country Brethren, Hooper, Roscoe, and Dr. Pruen.   The latter, with wife and infant, has already left Mpwapwa for the coast.   I am afraid they will encounter much difficulty. To him I wrote :—

" Frere Town, October 26, 1888.

" My Dear Dr. Pruen,—

" Your letter from Mlale of 10th inst. to hand yesterday.   At Saadani your messengers were put in prison and your letters taken from them.   Our Agents, B. R. & Co., got the Sultan to interfere and obtain their release.

" I am afraid the Consul General will not sanction your coming down, though it will be very inconvenient for you and Mrs. Pruen to be left houseless at Mamboia.

" Perhaps you may find some opportunity of making your way to the coast without incurring any extra-ordinary risk, in which case you will no doubt avail yourself of it, and we shall all be glad to see you, for although we are already not badly off for Doctors, yet these two are here only *pro tem.*   This is now *your* Station.

"We have had a trying time of it the last few weeks— endless 'shauris' and 'manenos'.   I am almost distracted.   I have had a troublesome business in connexion with the 'watoro' of Rabai. The crisis is not quite over, but the clouds are dispersing, and God, I trust, is bringing good out of evil, so that without war or bloodshed this long-standing cause of offence will be removed, and the poor runaways of Rabai made free. This matter is occupying much of my time and thoughts, which must be my excuse for this shabby little note.

" May the Lord have you in His safe keeping, and prosper your way to us.

" Whilst at Mamboia, you can go fully into Mr. Roscoe's building plans.

" Give my love to Ashe ; I am glad to hear he is recovering, and hope by the time he gets here it will be ' eyes right '.

" With kindest Christian regards to you both and to any of the Brethren you may meet,

" Yours very faithfully, etc."

I wrote also to Col. Euan Smith :

"Frere Town, *October* 26, 1888.

" My Dear Colonel,—

" I can only send a hurried line. We are in the thick of the fight, mind and body on the stretch. There are more runaways at Rabai than I had dreamt of. If it came to it they would fight for their freedom, and if left to deal with their Arab ' owners,' there is little doubt which would gain the day. But fighting and bloodshed must be avoided at all cost.

" Mackenzie and I had a long conference yesterday,

and we are quite agreed as to the line of action to be pursued, so, as regards this matter, I think you may leave it in our hands, and have an easy mind. God has heard our prayer, and will make us a way out of our difficulties.

"I received a strange Telegram through our Agents, from Salisbury Square, I suppose. 'Tell Price—complaints of harbouring runaways, report.' I wonder who can have sent such an absurd report of me! I have always done all I could to discourage the practice, and shall be greatly surprised if any have been knowingly received since I came out.

"At my first interview with the Wali, I told him that I heard some of the people of Mombasa were complaining about their slaves, and said I should like an opportunity of meeting them in 'baraza,' to hear what they had to say, and to see what could be done to satisfy them. He put me off—from what motive I cannot tell—saying there was no necessity for anything of the kind. What more could I do? I tell *you* this, that you may see that I, at least, have acted straightforwardly in the matter. I do not ask you to mention it, as it might go against the Wali. It may be that he was only anxious to stave off a troublesome business. We—Mr. M., the General, and I—are going to Rabai on Monday, and I am in good hopes this difficulty will be amicably arranged.

"The 'Stork' came in this morning, and Captain Pullen is at it, placing out his flags, here, there, and everywhere. I advised him to give good notice to the people of Mombasa that he was not going to 'eat them up'.

" God help us all to do what is right in His sight, and then, come what may, all will be well for us and for His cause.

" Many thanks for the oranges—what a treat !

" God bless you and yours !

" With kindest regards, etc., etc."

Saturday, October 27. The " Java" with our English Mails in this morning at 9. She brings an addition of three to our Mission band. Miss Scott, Miss Holmes, and Mr. Ward, the latter to act as Accountant and Assistant to the Secretary.

Greatly disappointed at not getting a letter from my dear wife, and although I heard from three of the children, they none of them tell me anything about her. If she is alive and well she would not fail to write. Possibly by mistake her letter has gone on to Zanzibar.

Saw Captain Pullen, and arranged to hold an English Service on board the " Stork " to-morrow.

Only a very short letter from Mr. Lang. The " recess" seems to put things very much out of gear.

Monday, October 29. A note from Mr. Mackenzie postponing our visit to Rabai till to-morrow ; as the " Glasgow" and " Kilwa " are both leaving to-day. I am glad *he* postpones it, and not I, though not sorry for the postponement. As there is an opportunity of sending letters by a French Steamer, I availed myself of it to write to Mr. Lang.

"FRERE TOWN, *October* 29, 1888.

"MY DEAR MR. LANG,—

"Your short letter of the 5th inst. came to hand two days ago, and I have just time for a few words in reply by the French Mail.

"Miss Scott, Miss Holmes, and Mr. Ward have arrived safe and well. Having done all I could to stop them (the ladies) I cannot doubt that it is for some good and wise purpose they are here. Indeed this thwarting of our plans, by which several Brethren, whom we wished to push forward to the Lake, are congregated here, is, we may feel sure, wisely ordered for the best. 'They assayed to go into Bithynia, but the Spirit suffered them not'."

After describing the plan I had agreed upon with Mr. Mackenzie for the settlement of the runaway slave question, I added :—

"Of course we shall have to take very effective measures for preventing a recurrence of the difficulty in future. The time is coming, no doubt, when the slaves on a large scale will make a stand for freedom, and they will get it; but it will be a hard struggle, and our safe policy is to keep clear of it, whatever our wishes and sympathies may be.

"You may depend on my sending on Fraser and the others the moment the way opens up.

"Fitch is leaving this week for Chaga, to relieve Taylor. I think it not well, in the present state of the country, that he should go alone; so Reid will accompany him and return with Taylor. It will be useful for Reid to get some experience of caravan travelling, especially in the prospect of this route being opened up to the Lake, as it must be before long.

"Yours, in great haste, etc., etc."

Tuesday, October 30. *Rabai.* There is plenty of variety in our present life. In the midst of many pressing anxieties, what a day of joyful excitement this has been ! The dark cloud which has been hanging over us has burst, and dissolved itself in showers of blessing. As proposed, Mr. Mackenzie, General Matthews, Smith and I, came up here this morning. Midway between the "banderini" and Rabai, is Buni hill, a steep ascent of six or seven hundred feet ; as we neared the summit, sounds caught our ear, which under other circumstances would have been ominous and alarming —the blast of the war-horn, accompanied with shouting and firing of guns—echoing and re-echoing among the hills. To anyone unused to African life, there was something intensely weird, if not threatening, in this demonstration. Mr. M. asked, " Is it war ? " " No," I said, " it is peace—' furaha ' (joy)—and all in your honour, because I have told them you are their friend." At the top of the hill, we were met by a large number of Rabai men—" watoro " and others—all armed with guns, bows and arrows, or other weapons ; but preceded by a white flag as a token of peace. They were in excellent order, and lined each side of the road through which we passed. Then at a signal they broke up and dispersed on all sides, firing, singing, shouting and dancing, in the wildest fashion. There were several hundreds of them, and not one without his weapon.

At the entrance to the Settlement, there was a grand display of flags of all colours and designs, and a triumphal arch with "WELCOME" in large letters; and here some hundreds of women, all in their gayest and best, joined our procession, and dancing, clapping hands, and *trilling*, as only African women can, they led the way into the Church Square. We were all too much tired with excitement to settle down to business to-day.

Wednesday, October 31. At early Service, the Church was crowded to overflowing: a grand sight! What must our visitors have thought of it!

At 10 a.m., all the runaway *women* slaves belonging to Mombasa were assembled, numbering to my astonishment 276. Each was questioned as to (1) Her own name? (2) Her tribe? (3) If married, her husband's name? (4) How many children? (5) Owner's name? and lastly, How long here? It took six hours to get through them. General Matthews, who is thoroughly at home in the language, put the questions; Messrs. Mackenzie and Smith recorded the answers. Some interesting facts were brought to light: (1) A large proportion came four or five years ago, at the time of the great famine. With starvation staring them in the face, they came here just to save life, and, when the famine was over, stayed on. (2) Very few came when I was last out, in 1881-2, and very few during the last eight months. (3) A considerable number of them have already been declared free by a former Consul General.

Friday, November 2. Yesterday and to-day we have been hard at work from morning to night, and are thankful the investigation is now complete. The result goes to show, that over a period of twelve years, about 650 slaves, men and women in nearly equal proportions, belonging to Mombasa and other Coast towns, have found refuge in the Mission Station of Rabai; whilst about 300 more have similarly been sheltered at the Stations of other Missionary Societies.

They were all distinctly given to understand by Mr. M. and myself that they would be made free; and on the strength of that promise, they readily came forward and made a clean breast of it. Having ascertained these particulars, the next great point is, to come to terms with the Arabs, as to the price of redemption.

Saturday, November 3. Making all arrangements for Fitch and Reid to start for Chaga on Monday, Beverley to go with them, and remain with Fitch till the way opens for him to go on to the Lake. But alas! these are shifting times, and our wisest plans are easily set aside. This afternoon "a special" comes from Frere Town, with a packet of letters from Zanzibar, brought up by the "H. W." There is a Telegram from Salisbury Square which runs: "Can men be sent now to Mackay by *parcels* route—wire Lang". For "parcels" I read "Parker's"; but I cannot send reply till I hear from Colonel Euan Smith. After consultation with Fitch and Smith, decided to detain Fitch's caravan till we can get an answer from the Consul General, as in the event of his giving permission, Beverley and Fraser, at least, must go forward. But I very much doubt his doing so, and even if he does, the season is not good for travelling, and there will still be the difficulty of porters. The Committee, I surmise, have a number of offers in response to Mackay's appeal;

and are naturally anxious to send on a contingent. They do not quite take in the difficulties we, on the spot, have to face. Still we must do all we possibly can to further their wishes.

I insert here a letter written to me by Herr Ehlers on his arrival at Chaga. It is important as an unsolicited testimony to the good behaviour of our native Christian porters: a class of men whom it is the custom with some travellers first to maltreat and then to run down.

"Chaga, *October* 25, 1888.

" Dear Mr. Price,—

" Yesterday I arrived here in good health, and lose no time to thank you most sincerely for all your kindness and friendship. I am very glad to be able to write you that I had the best ' safari ' as any possible, and that I was very satisfied with all my people. I never believed that the black men would be such good companions. Robin will tell you all details.

" Please pay to him and Peter (two headmen) 5 dollars each, gratification.

" In great haste I end with my best compliments for you and your staff. I remain,

" Yours very truly,

" Otto Ehlers."

Sunday, November 4. Thankful to God, after a week's work, bustle and excitement, for a quiet Sunday at Rabai. Had a pleasant stroll and chat with Smith after evening Service; and another afterwards with Fitch. I find the latter not over keen upon going again to Chaga.   He said the post requires a good linguist, which he does not profess to be.   Then, although he has lived down Mandara's hostility, and is now on easier relations with him, he sees no sign of fruit, or of openings for direct Evangelistic work, and is discouraged.   I suggested that he should take with him about six promising lads from Frere Town, to train as Teachers or Evangelists.   It would give him useful and hopeful occupation; and whilst patiently waiting God's time for more active Missionary work among the "Wa-Chaga," he would be preparing men for the opportunity.

Monday, November 5.   To Frere Town.   Smith and I left Rabai at 8 a.m.   Coming to the "banderini," we found the tide out ; it was spring tide, and the water was very low.   We had hard work to find a passage, and were five hours on the water, doing ten miles !   What that means, our good friends at Salisbury Square can have no conception, or they would spare no effort to supply us with the long-promised steam launch, which would bring Frere Town and Rabai within a couple of hours of each other.

Wrote to-day to Col. Euan Smith.   After giving him a report of our proceedings in connexion with the runaway slaves, I added :—

" Now for another and a very urgent matter.   The Committee are most anxious to reinforce the Lake Mission ; and appear to have many offers for service, in answer to Mackay's appeal.   I have a Telegram asking if it is ' possible to send up men by Parker's route '.   If I acted simply on my own responsibility, knowing what I do, I should reply decidedly ' No '.   Parker's route passes through the part of the country where Dr. Meyer came to grief. But at such a time it is to you we must look. May I ask you kindly to hand a Telegram to our Agents, to be forwarded to the Society, in reply to the Committee's question. I should be glad to know its purport, and if at the same time you can give me any idea as to how long it may be before the way will be again open. Unless there is some change for the better before long, our Missionaries at the Lake will be placed in a situation of extreme difficulty and danger; the only way of getting at them will be through Masai-land.

"Mr. Taylor is, I fear, very ill at Chaga, and all alone. Mr. Fitch is going to relieve him.

"I much want to see you, and have a good talk with you on many matters; but it is hard to get away. I am expecting to leave by the Messageries boat of Jan. 2, in which case I shall hope to see you then; but we are living from hand to mouth, and know not what any day may bring forth.

"No word yet about my successor. I am fully expecting to hear by the next Mail. Perhaps the Bishop himself may turn up. If so, I hope he may be a man for the times. With kindest regards,

"Yours very faithfully,

"W. SALTER PRICE."

Tuesday, November 6. The "Kilwa" in from Zanzibar. Letter from Agents to say that Ashe, 90 miles from the coast, sent on two porters with letters, etc. They were robbed by Wa-Seguha and the letters destroyed.

Had a quiet interview with Ward. He does not profess to be a regular Accountant, such as we ought to have, but he seems to think he can manage the work, and I hope he may. If the accounts get into a muddle the Committee must not blame me.

Mail from Chaga. A letter from Taylor which causes me some anxiety. He is ill, and seems alarmed about himself. Determined to ask Fitch to go at once to his relief, and with him Dr. Edwards to look after Taylor and bring him down. Sent off messenger to Rabai to call Dr. Edwards to confer with me on the matter.

Feeling quite out of sorts: heat, work, and worry!

Thursday, November 8. Dr. E. came in time for breakfast. He consented to go with Fitch to Chaga, and returned to Rabai to prepare for the journey.

Commenced my monthly letter to the Rev. R. Lang, a few extracts from which are here given :—

" You will see from memo. enclosed what has been done in the matter of the runaway slaves at Rabai.

. . . . . .

" Your telegram, despatched at 4 p.m. on Thursday, November 1, was brought up from Zanzibar by the ' H. W.' (20 hours)—forwarded from F. Town by foot messenger (6 hours)—and reached me at Rabai at 3 p.m. on Saturday, November 3, which gives the whole distance from Ludgate Circus to Rabai in less than 44 hours !

" If I could have replied I should simply have wired ' No,' but as that was out of the question I have asked the Consul General to reply. Parker's route lies through the country where Dr. Meyer was only a short time ago savagely handled, and only barely escaped with his life on payment of Rs. 12,000. I am afraid from all I hear that our communications with our dear Brethren at the Lake are cut off for an indefinite period. It may be that our only way to them will be through Masai-land, and why not? This *is* our route, as I have been contending for the last ten years. Fraser would start to-morrow if I gave him leave, but this I dare not do without your permission.

"You must make up your minds, I think, to give up Mamboia and Mpwapwa. Strategically they are untenable by us, except at great risk and expense. Why not hand them over if possible to some good German Protestant Society?

"Then you will be able to concentrate your efforts on a line of Stations right away through Ukambani to Uganda, and Dr. Krapf's inspired dream will be realized. It must come to this, and the sooner the better. With your two Bishops—as Mackay suggests—one at Frere Town and one at Nasa or in Uganda, you would have a complete supervision of all the links in the chain— which under present circumstances is simply impossible —and every link would be an element of strength.

"The new Company are starting operations, and, as was to be expected, are meeting with a good deal of opposition on the part of the Arabs and others. It is too soon to predict what may happen, but Mr. Mackenzie and his staff are men of experience, who may be expected to act cautiously and with due regard for the natural susceptibilities of the people. In that case we may hope they will in time obtain a firm footing.

"They are already surveying for a road suitable for

wheel and camel traffic, through Ukambani to the Victoria. This, when completed, will be a great help to us in many ways, in keeping up our connexion with the interior Stations. We must keep our eyes open and make all the use we can of this road. Before deciding on a new site for a Station in place of Sagalla, for instance, we shall do well to see what line the road takes. Other things being equal, or nearly so, accessibility is a matter of very great importance.

"I have a letter from dear Taylor. He is ill at Chaga, and thinks he has started an aneurism in his chest, which would, of course, be a very serious matter. I am hopeful, however, that he may be out in his diagnosis. Still, he must not be left alone, and I have arranged for his relief, and for his being brought here if the Dr. considers it safe for him to be moved. I trust it may please God to heal our dear Brother, and bring him to us in safety.

"Miss Holmes and Miss Scott are working hard at the language and making good progress. They seem to be full of zeal and eager for work. Some kind friends had filled up Miss S. with strange notions of what she had to expect in East Africa ; in less than a week she would be on her back with fever, etc. We have done our best to laugh her out of these notions, and she is glad to find that, instead of a dreary howling wilderness, her lot is cast in 'pleasant places'.

"Burness is, as you know, very desirous of having definite spiritual work, so I have promised to post him at Rabai as soon as he can conveniently go. We want a man there who can worthily represent the Society in all dealings with the I. B. E. A. Co., and who will relieve Mr. Jones of many cares and responsibilities now resting upon him, and set him free for his pastorate duties, which are quite sufficient to occupy all his time and thoughts. Mr. B. will find ample opportunities at Rabai for spiritual work, and I hope he will be there the right man in the right place. Then, too, it is contemplated to transfer two of the ladies—Miss Ramsay and Miss Holmes—to Rabai, and they will probably find it convenient, for a time at least, to board with the Burnesses."

Saturday, November 10. Finished and sent off letters to Teita and Chaga. To Rev. W. E. Taylor I wrote :—

"FRERE TOWN, *November* 10, 1888.

" MY DEAR TAYLOR,—

" Yours of October 24 to hand, and I am very sorry for the poor account it brings of yourself. I hope you may be out in your diagnosis. However it seems desirable that Fitch should return to Chaga without further delay, and I am sending along with him Dr. Edwards and Reid, so that if you are able to be moved, they may take care of you to the coast. I send also a ' dandy,' in which you may make the journey comfortably without much fatigue. It will require eight men, four at a time, taking turn and turn about. I shall not bother you with any 'Proof' this time ; you must take things easy till you are better. Earnestly commending you to the loving care of Him who is able to ' keep ' you ; and hoping to see you here, D.V., about this time next month.

" Yours very affectionately, etc."

Took the ladies for a row up the creek to Port Reitz; they enjoyed it immensely.

Dear L.'s birthday. Had much freedom in interceding for her. Praise God for all His goodness to us both all these years.

Sunday, November 11. Attended morning and afternoon Service. Heat very oppressive.

After afternoon Service, had a nice quiet walk and talk with Jas. Deimler (licensed Reader). What an intelligent fellow he is! May God raise up many such, and fit them by His grace for the work of the ministry!

Monday, November 12. *To Rabai.* Left at 5.30 a.m., and with tide in our favour, reached the " banderini," in 2½ hours. Another 1½ hour's walk under a grilling sun brought us in.

Had a parting prayer with our dear Brethren—Fitch, Dr. Edwards, and Reid—and started them off at 4 p.m. They will suffer, I fear, from want of water, though they have taken with them as much as they can conveniently carry. May the Lord supply all their needs, and bring them on their way.

Tuesday, November 13. Returned with Miss Fitch and Miss Ramsay to Frere Town.

Received a long letter from Mr. Mackenzie on several matters of importance. Amongst other things, he invites us to take up Gulu-gulu as a Mission Station, and to go on planting Stations at convenient stages along the new route.

Wednesday, November 14. Wrote to Buchanan declining all responsibility on the part of any of our Mission Agents, in connexion with money transactions of the Company ; payment of porters, etc.

Replied to Mr. Mackenzie's letter of yesterday :—

November 14, 1888.

"DEAR MR. MACKENZIE,—

"I have to thank you for your letter of yester-terday, which I received on my return from Rabai last night. I am pleased to hear your negotiations with the slave owners are progressing so favourably, and shall be very glad if I am able to report to my Committee the definite settlement of this vexed question by next Mail.

"I enclose a memo. which I have drawn up, partly to explain my own position, and that of my colleagues, in regard to the large number of runaways found at Rabai, and partly to state my views as to the best way of dealing with the situation. Personally, or rather as representing the C. M. S., I should prefer that *we*, and not the Company, should make all square with the so-called 'owners'. A special appeal for an object like this—giving Freedom to 700 slaves !—would soon produce the necessary funds. One of my colleagues, directly he heard that compensation was talked about, said, 'You may put me down for £1000 !'

"But I can see that it would be greatly to the advantage of the B. E. A. Co. to settle the business, even at the very large figure you mention, which I hope will be considerably reduced. It would place them well with the good people at home, and ought to remove some difficulties, in their dealing with the Arabs, etc. For this and for no other reason I am content to leave the matter for *you* to deal with.

"As to the value—$50 per head—which they put on

their slaves, it is out of all reason. In settling the value, several circumstances should be borne in mind.

" 1. Of the 700, more or less, found in Rabai, there are two or three women who, for certain purposes, would probably fetch a good price in the market, but many of them are old and infirm, who would count for little or nothing.

" (2) One hundred and six of them have been more than six years in the Settlement, and being unclaimed were, I am informed, declared free (informally) by Sir John Kirk a few years ago. About 200 more came in the famine years, and most of them cost their masters just nothing but a little food to keep them from starvation. $5 each for such would be ample compensation.

" (3) The slave-owners should be made clearly to understand that *we* do not derive a particle of profit from any of these people. In the case of many of them —the sick and infirm—they are a burden upon us ; and as for the rest, they simply occupy land and cultivate, and are independent of us.

" (4) I must repudiate on behalf of myself and colleagues, the charge of ' *harbouring* runaways '. We have done nothing of the kind. The most that can be said is that, in the years of war and famine, many in their extremity sought refuge in our Mission Stations. It was not a time to inquire particularly into their antecedents. Men and women were perishing, and cast themselves upon the charity and hospitality of the Missionaries. That a considerable number of these were ' watoro ' there were no means of telling. They were simply allowed to settle, and support themselves by their own industry.

"If the 'owners' say $50 per head, they don't, of course, expect to get it. They should be well satisfied if they get all round $20. Regarding them from a commercial point of view, they are a damaged article. Having run away once and tasted the sweets of liberty, they would most likely seize the first opportunity to run away again!

"I now gladly turn to the, to me, much more engrossing topic of your letter; the planting of a chain of Mission Stations along the Ukambani route, which you are intent upon opening up. Your proposal entirely coincides with my own views. It is rather singular that, before receiving your letter, I had written to our Home Committee, suggesting to them, for strategic reasons, to hand over the Usagara Stations of Mamboia and Mpwapwa to some German Protestant Society, and to concentrate their efforts on a series of well-selected Stations, along the new line of route from Mombasa to the Victoria; and your letter, a copy of which I am forwarding to them, will just clinch my recommendation.

"As a proof to you how heartily I enter into the scheme, I willingly give up my best available man, and the one I can least spare, to commence operations at Gulu-gulu: the Rev. A. G. Smith. As soon as we are free of the English Mails, I propose going with Mr. Smith to Gulu-gulu to prospect for a site, and to give him a start. I hope to see you, and talk over the matter before then.

.   .   .   .

"Yours very sincerely, etc."

The "Kilwa," from Zanzibar, brings the startling news that the coast from Tanga to Rovuma is to be blockaded by the English and German Fleets, from the 19th inst.; no firearms to be landed, and no slaves exported!

Thursday, November 15. Received a kind letter from Colonel Euan Smith, telling me all about the blockade—the perilous situation of the Pruens, and the measures he had taken for their safe conduct to the coast, and other matters of interest. Yes, it was a very kind letter, but there was one paragraph in it, which I read with profound amazement; it cut me to the quick. After expressing himself very strongly (needlessly so I could not but think) as to the difficulty of dealing with the Arab slave-owners, he went on to suggest *whether it would not be wise to give up Rabai as a C. M. Station!* The very thought of such a thing was so shocking to me, I could scarcely believe my own eyes. As it was, with very painful feelings I sat down to reply to that letter; and those feelings found expression in what may perhaps appear to be rather strong language; yet, not stronger, I think, than the occasion justified. For, be it remembered that this suggestion came not from 'an enemy'—in that case it would not have cost me a thought—but from one for whom I entertain the highest regard as a warm friend of Missions. My reply was as follows:—

"Frere Town, *November* 16, 1888.

"My Dear Colonel,—

"Many thanks for your kind letter. The first

part of it almost takes my breath away. The bare suggestion of the possibility of giving up Rabai as a Mission Station is overwhelming. Give up Rabai! Why, my dear friend, I would rather die than do it. It would be a sin in the sight of God and man! In nearly forty years of Missionary experience, and having visited some of the most flourishing Missions in different parts of India, I confess I have never seen any Mission Station which presented more manifest tokens of the presence and power of Almighty God, than are to be found at Rabai. Only come and see for yourself, and I am quite sure you will never entertain the idea of giving it up.

"The 'watoro' affair is a mere accident; and much as I regret it in some respects—in so far at least as it might have been in any way preventable by us, or may appear to have been so—I do not think we shall be greatly blamed, when all is said that may be said on our side. I reserve our defence till circumstances call for it, if they ever do; but before then I hope we shall have the opportunity of a quiet talk over this and several other matters. Anyway, there ought to be no great difficulty in settling this 'watoro' business amicably, unless the slave-owners are put up to making unreasonable demands. Mr. Mackenzie informs me that negotiations are progressing favourably, only Khamis Kombo remains to be reckoned with.

"Many thanks for Pruen's letter, which I return; and for notices of the blockade, which I have handed on as you desired.

"If Abdallah bin Heri carries out your orders faithfully, the Pruens may perhaps arrive in time to come up by the 'Java' on the 20th. I do hope they will come to no harm.

"I sent off a 'special' to Chaga to-day with your despatches for friend Ehlers, etc.

"What effect the blockade of the southern ports will have on Mombasa it is impossible to say. No doubt there will be all sorts of exaggerated reports, and an immense amount of irritation and of hostile feeling against Europeans. How it may show itself no one can tell. Whatever comes our hope is in the Lord our God, that in some way or other He will make for us a safe path.

"With kindest regards, etc., etc."

Saturday, November 17. Went over to Mombasa at 6 a.m. to see Mackenzie on important business, but he had not come to the Mission house and I thought it better not to go to him in the town for fear of exciting suspicion. All our movements are watched and reported and discussed.

Tuesday, November 20. The Chaga Mail in. Thankful to hear Taylor is better.

Very busy the last few days with English letters.

The following extracts will bring my narrative of events up to date :—

To my Wife.

" *November* 20.

Referring to the circumstance of so many runaway slaves being found at Rabai :

" Many influences have worked together under Providence to bring all these poor people of many tribes, and speaking many languages, under Gospel teaching. May we not hope that in some way or other it will be brought about that not a few of them shall become Christ's messengers and witnesses to their own people! Why not? The Lord reigneth!

   .   .   .   .   .   .

" I am just now so fully occupied, have so much to think about and plan in connexion with this Mission that I can scarcely realize that in less than two months hence, if my life is spared, I shall be taking my last look of East Africa, and leaving to another to build on the foundation I have been privileged to lay. Still, as the boys say, I have had 'a good innings,' and I am permitted to hope that through God's good hand upon me, I have been enabled to set some things in order and to put in a plant here and there which will bear fruit when I am gone.

" I am a long time without news from, or of, dear Mac. If all's well with him, or ill, we ought to be turning up about the same time. If so, how we shall enjoy comparing notes. We ought to have a grand Missionary meeting at Wingfield between us."

To my Son in Sierra Leone.

" Frere Town, *November* 20, 1888.

" My Dearest Mac,—

" Your last letter is dated June 14—5 months ago— and since then I have had very little news of you. I did not get your dear mother's usual letter by the last Mail. I fear it may have gone to 'Free' instead of 'Frere' Town. It would most certainly have told me something about you. I hope by this time you are well through your bad season, as I imagine November, December, and January are your three best months; your winter is our summer. I suppose you heard what troublous times we have had, and still have on this side. How the blockade may affect us and our Brethren in the interior we cannot say; for the present our communications with them are entirely cut off; it is not safe for Europeans to travel in any direction. It is, of course, an anxious time for us all; still we trust that He who has graciously watched over us hitherto, will bring us safely through. How I long to hear how you are and how getting on. My time here is rapidly drawing to a close; I am expecting to leave by the French steamer on January 2. So if all goes well I shall be home early in February, and I am indulging the hope that you will be taking your furlough about the same time. We shall have much to talk about of interest to both. How little we saw what was before us when we waved our last adieus in the Mersey two years ago, and how good God has been to us both!

"My kind regards to the Bishop and to Nevill if they have returned. With much love, and wishing you a happy Xmas, and all blessings for the new year,

"Your affectionate Father."

To the Rev. R. Lang.

"Events are following thickly one upon another. I have had a 'special' from the Consul General informing me of the blockade, and confirming my worst fears as to the closing of the Usagara route, and the consequent isolation of our Brethren at Mamboia, Mpwapwa and the Lake. He enclosed also a short letter from Dr. Pruen to him, in which Dr. P. states that he, his wife, and child, together with Ashe, are at a village—Mto ya Mawe—5 miles march this side Mamboia, short of cloth and provisions. The current report was that Abdalla bin Heri of Saadani had sent orders for all European travellers and their servants to be murdered. Pruen sent a secret messenger to the Consul General, giving this information and asking help. The Sultan, at Col. Euan Smith's request, has charged the very man, Abdalla, to go and escort the party safely to the coast, so if all goes well with them they will be here a few days hence.

"Mr. Mackenzie's invitation to C. M. S. to occupy Stations along the new route singularly dovetails with the views I have already expressed. I rejoice to think that God, in His Providence, is opening up to us a highway into the centre of Africa. It lies through Rabai, and the first Station is Gulu-gulu, about 20 miles forward. It will go through Ukambani and Ulu—a populous and splendid country—to lake Baringo; thence striking South to Kavirondo, and North to Wadelai. I cannot doubt that the Committee will fall in with the general idea; but it is important to enter upon our inheritance at once; so fully anticipating their sanction, I have asked dear Smith to go and commence work at Gulu-gulu.

"I see a Telegram to the effect that Thompson is going to lead a relief expedition to Wadelai. If so, it is almost certain he will come this way ; in which case, would it not be well to send Fraser, Beverley, and Edwards under his escort, as far as their paths lie together, leaving them to make their own way from that point to Mackay ? I am only afraid there will be great difficulty in getting porters, owing to the coast disturbances. We must depend mainly on our poor ' watoro '. As I shall probably leave on January 2, I cannot, of course, expect an answer to this letter *here ;* but I should esteem it a great favour if I find a line from you at Aden, letting me know briefly what dispositions you have made. Three days after this leaves the English Mail Steamer is due, and I shall not be surprised if she brings either a Bishop, or some one to take charge of the Mission from me. This is a critical time, and it is of the utmost importance you should have some one at the helm in whom you have entire confidence, and to whom, in exigencies, you can give a considerable amount of freedom of action.

" I feel so identified with everything and everybody in this Mission that it is hard to realize that, in six weeks hence, I shall be tearing myself away from it all. The thought is almost heartbreaking, and yet I have strong home-longings, and I know that God can carry on His work quite as well without me, as with me : it would be sheer vanity to think otherwise.

" The Chaga Mail is in, and I am glad to learn that Taylor *was* wrong in his diagnosis. There is no aneurism, but anyway it is just as well he should return to the coast. He has collected materials for a ki-Chaga Vocabulary and Grammar, and a quiet month or two here will allow of his putting them into ship-shape for the press. He reports several earnest inquirers. His influence on Mandara has been good, and Fitch's position will be bettered by the change. By the time you get this, Fitch will be again at Chaga, and Taylor here."

Wednesday, November 21. The "Java" came in for our English Mail. No better news from the coast: "wars and rumours of wars"! The blockade delayed—the proclamation awaits the Sultan's signature, and he is, or pretends to be, sick.

A Telegram from Salisbury Square, which sorely puzzled us all:—"White anxious keep post open if closed try parkers". The difficulty was "White," who is "White"? and why is he "anxious"? Is he the new Bishop? and the first intimation we have of him that he is "anxious"? And what "post" is he anxious to keep open? I have already closed my Post for this Mail, and if not, why keep it open? We laid our heads together to solve the riddle. Somebody suggested "wife" for "white". That may be true—my wife may well be a little anxious if she sees the Zanzibar Telegrams; but even so, she would not make a fuss about it; and then "trying parkers" would scarcely relieve her anxiety. Miss Fitch suggested "wait," with a full stop after it; but it was hard to make sense of the rest of the message; it left "anxious" without a subject. At last it dawned upon me: for "white" read "while," and then filling in ellipses, it will run:—
" While (we are most) anxious (if possible to) keep open (the old) route (?) if (you on the spot consider that to be quite) closed, try (to get men to go by) Parker's

(route to Mamboia)". I wonder if I am right. Anyway, I will try what can be done.

Note.—I was not very far out, but the mystery was not quite cleared up till some time after, when, in a letter from Mr. Lang, I came across the words: "On Nov. 19, we wired to you 'white'". How absurd! My own cipher, and I did not know it! Two months before, I had written to Mr. Lang in regard to a certain proposal, "If you agree, wire the single word 'white,' if not, 'black'". But, alas! in two months, what changes have taken place! what was possible *then* is utterly out of the question *now*. Still I ought not to have been puzzled by "white"; nor should I, had it stood alone, or been fenced off by a full stop from the complicated sentence which followed. "White anxious, etc.," that was the puzzle!

CHAPTER XI

FIRST LINK IN KRAPF'S CHAIN.

Friday, November 23. The " Baghdad " arrived with Home letters. Brings good news of all, thank God! Not a word from Salisbury Square about my successor, or about my leaving! They do not seem to have realized that my time is so nearly up. The Committee are very anxious about opening up communications with the up-country Brethren. So am I, intensely so; I am looking this way and that : it is always in my thoughts. Sent to Jones entreating him to do his best to get four men to go to Mamboia by Parker's route—promising them a good reward.

Saturday, November 24. Jones replies—" All say impossible—the risks too great—no amount of money would induce men to go !"

Sunday, November 25. Early Communion in English. Address on Rom. viii. 15, " The spirit of adoption ".

Gave a Service on board the " Stork "—" Sirs, what must I do to be saved ? "

Mr. Mackenzie is purposing to make Xmas day the day for giving freedom to the runaways. He is inviting Mrs. Euan Smith to give them their Papers. If this is carried out, it will be such a Xmas day as Rabai has never witnessed before.

Monday, November 26.   Over to Mombasa this morning to see Mackenzie paying off the Arabs.   What a sight!   In a stuffy little room these gentlemen were crowded together—some of the biggest swells of Mombasa—all eager to clutch the blood-money which was being so lavishly dealt out! no sense of shame at being found mixed up in the villainous business held anyone back from putting in his claim.

This afternoon a messenger came to say that Mbaruk, the rebel Chief, was on his way to see me, and would be glad if I would put him up for the night.   I sallied forth to meet him, wondering what I should do. Presently a rapid firing of guns, which woke up our Settlement, signalled his approach.   He was preceded by a hundred or more of his roughs—all armed with guns and swords—who came along shouting, blowing war horns and firing, with all their might, as if they were going to attack us; and here comes Mbaruk— the man who for years has defied the Sultan, and been a scourge to the whole country.   Six years ago I just escaped falling into his hands, and to-day he comes and claims my hospitality!   What queer times we are living in!   It appears he has been invited by Mr. Mackenzie to come in; but he evidently has a strong objection to going into Mombasa—fears treachery— and feels himself more safe in the Settlement of Frere Town.   He is about sixty years of age, with an aristocratic face, and fine physique, although possessing a worn-out and battered look—the result no doubt of the rough life he has led for so many years. I put him and his attendant Arabs up in an iron cottage in my compound, and made them as comfortable as I could; whilst his 150 or more dusky warriors lay thick on the ground under the trees. The ladies had very cautiously to thread their way among them to get to the evening Prayer Meeting in my house. I learn that the Consul General has made peace between Mbaruk and the Sultan, and the new Company find it to their advantage to make friends with him.

Tuesday, November 27. To-day Mbaruk was visited by the Wali, and many of the principal Arabs of Mombasa. It has been a day of constant coming and going, and as each fresh arrival was made the occasion for a salute, we have been under fire all day! Among the Arabs, strange to say, was Khamis Kombo, between whom and Mbaruk there has been a deadly feud these many years. How remarkable that these two men should come together and shake hands under my roof! General Matthews succeeded in persuading Mbaruk to go over to Mombasa, and he left in grand state, crossing over in the Mission boat, under the British flag, at 4 p.m.

Wrote to the Rev. E. A. Fitch.

"Frere Town, *November* 27 1890.

" My Dear Fitch,—

" I hope this will find you and your party safely landed at Chaga. I have much to say, and little time to say it in, so must compress.

" I have pressing letters and telegrams from the Committee about opening up communications with our Lake brethren, also with Mamboia and Mpwapwa. I have tried to get men to go with letters by Parker's route—offering them double pay and a good present if they succeed, but they all say ' no '—who can wonder?

" But this is an urgent business ; the lives of our Brethren may depend on it.   Would it be possible through Mandara or otherwise to send men from Chaga to the south end of the Lake ?   If so let me know at once, and I will send up a ' special ' with letters to be forwarded.   It will be a grand achievement if you can open up a tolerably safe route between Chaga and Nasa. The men must, of course, be *liberally* paid.   The ordinary channels from the coast are completely closed, and there is no prospect of their being opened again for some time to come.   Do, my dear Fitch, your very best to accomplish this good work, and may God bless your efforts !

" All the ordinary news of these parts you will be sure to get from your dear sister, so with Christian love and all good wishes, and prayers that you may have much to comfort and encourage you in your work, I remain,

" Yours affectionately,

" W. Salter Price."

Wednesday, November 28.   Had a pressing request from Admiral Fremantle to allow the Admiralty to charter the " Henry Wright " as a despatch boat, to keep up communication between the flagship and the other ships engaged in the blockade.   I replied, saying I was sorry I could not comply with his request. It would never do for the " H. W.," well known as she is up and down the Coast as belonging to our Mission, to be employed in connexion with the blockade. Apart from this, there are other reasons which make it impossible for me to take the responsibility of letting her go on this service.

My correspondence just now very heavy, and takes up most of my time. I am in frequent communication with the Consul General, the Director of the new Company, and other officials, and with all the Brethren in the interior who are accessible—to say nothing of my regular epistles to the Secretaries at Home, and to my wife. In order to give as true an account as possible of our circumstances—our difficulties, joys, and sorrows— I must needs draw largely on this correspondence.

To the Rev. J. Roscoe, Mamboia.

"FRERE TOWN, *November* 28, 1888.

" MY DEAR ROSCOE,—

" Have received your two letters of October 22 and November 11. Let me first express my sympathy with you and your dear wife under the trying circumstances of your late illness, and at the same time my thankfulness at hearing that you are both in the way of recovery. I quite understand your wish to have the services of Dr. Pruen in April next, and as far as it rests with me everything shall be done to meet it, even though I may not be here. I would advise you to write again on the subject about January.

"As regards Mr. Wood, if the way were open for him to go forward to reinforce the Lake brethren I would say at once, "Go, and the Lord prosper you"; and I am sure the Committee would approve. But whilst the Consul General declares 'all routes unsafe' I dare not give the word. I am afraid he must wait; but tell Mr. Wood, with my love, that I shall be glad if he will hold himself ready to go forward as soon as it may be prudent to do so.

"General Matthews promises to do his best to forward this letter to you, if possible, by the ordinary route; and to make more sure I am trying to send a duplicate by a variation of Parker's route. Kindly, if you can, let your answer also travel by both lines.

"And now, I want to enlist your best services in a most urgent business. The Company are most anxious to send reinforcements to the Lake, and three men—Beverley, Fraser, and Dr. Edwards—have been waiting here for some time, ready to move as soon as the way opens. Meanwhile the position of the Brethren inland is a matter for gravest anxiety. When distorted reports of what is going on upon the coast spread, as they will, they will be placed, humanly speaking, in great peril. Clearly, we must leave no stone unturned to open communication with them—to ascertain their real position—and to convey to them supplies and succour. I want you at Mamboia, and Price at Mpwapwa to help all you can in this. The first thing is for you to organize good communication between you and Mpwapwa—and then Price from thence to the Lake. You will require to employ more men and to give them higher pay; don't stick at that. It is a matter of life and death, and the thing must be done if it is possible to do it, cost what it may!

" Kindly copy this paragraph, and send on to Price with my love and earnest solicitations for his co-operation. Then let me hear from you as quickly as possible, giving full information—(1) as to the state of the country about you and on ahead—what reports from the coast—the temper of the people—your own position, etc.; (2) any news or rumours concerning the Lake brethren; (3) any suggestions you can make in furtherance of the object in view.

" We do not cease to remember you in our prayers. May the Almighty have you, your dear wife, and all the Brethren, under His gracious protection, and give to you and us 'a happy issue'. I am sorry I missed getting your dear wife's letter. With best love to you both.

" Yours affectionately, etc., etc."

To the Rev. R. Lang, Sec., C.M.S.

" FRERE TOWN, *November* 28, 1888.

" MY DEAR MR. LANG,—

" Just a line to catch the French boat.

" 1. All here are annoyed at the Anglo-German blockade. It is expected to extend to Mombasa and north in a few days. The ' H. W.' applied for (see above).

" 2. The runaway slave question is, I hope, finally

disposed of. Mr. Mackenzie has agreed with the Arabs to ransom all found in the Mission Stations of Rabai, Ribe, and Jomvu, at \$25 per head. In all, at present, 450 have been claimed and paid for. Mr. M. proposes giving them all Freedom papers, at Rabai, on Xmas day, and has invited Mrs. Euan Smith to do it. I only hope the Consul General will consent, and that he will come and see Rabai for himself.

"3. I am going (D.V.) to-morrow with Smith to Gulu-gulu. There are a considerable number of our people of Rabai, in the Company's employ at that place as porters and otherwise, who need to be cared for spiritually. Then, too, there are several Europeans of the Company's staff, constantly passing to and fro, who will be glad of the opportunity of attending an English Service occasionally ; and last, not least, there are the Wa-Kamba to be evangelized—Missionary work pure and simple to any extent ! I cannot doubt the Committee will see the importance of our occupying this Station *at once*, and permanently ; still I make now only a provisional arrangement, awaiting their formal sanction. If *we* do not take up this work, Mr. M. will, doubtless, pass on his invitation to another Society. The French Priests of Bagamoyo are already on the alert. Several of them are coming to Mombasa in a few days to prospect for new openings. They actually applied to me for the ' H. W.' to bring them here !

" 4. The Pruens, you will be glad to hear, have safely reached Zanzibar. We expect them here next week. Dr. Baxter will then take charge of Shimba, till he can find his way to Mpwapwa.

" No time for more. My letter to Roscoe will explain itself. I am doing all I can to get in touch with our Brethren in the interior. With kindest regards, etc., etc."

To Mrs. Euan Smith, Zanzibar.

"Frere Town, *November* 28, 1888.

"Dear Mrs. Euan Smith,—

"It seems long since I had a line from you; but I am delighted to hear from one and all, that you are keeping up wonderfully. It is well it is so, for the last few months must have been a time of intense worry and anxiety to your dear husband, and he must many a time have 'blessed his stars,' that he had you at his side to cheer him up, and divert him from the pressing cares of office. Of course, he has the satisfaction of knowing that he is 'making History'; but making History in these troublous times is risky work. It is all very well if all turns out right, for, as dear old Dizzy says, 'nothing succeeds like success'. I earnestly hope your husband's efforts in a good cause, in face of many difficulties, will be crowned with success, and meet with just acknowledgment, and an appropriate reward.

"Mr. Mackenzie has been paying off all the slave-owners for their slaves found at Rabai, etc. If he had not done it, I should have done it myself; but *patriotically* I left it to him and the Company. Anyway the thing is done, and the sore healed, and now Mr. M.'s heart is set upon a grand function on Xmas Day, in which I most heartily sympathize. He would have you, as the wife of the Consul General, to distribute the Freedom papers to these poor people, who have been redeemed. It is a grand idea, and I sincerely hope you will find it possible to fall in with it, and that the Colonel will not object. We will do all we can to make it comfortable and pleasant for you. It will form an episode in your life in East Africa, to look back upon with pleasure in the days to come. I promise you, you will be delighted with what you will see and hear, and you will never repent your visit to Rabai. So, do say 'Yes'.

"I hope you have good news of your dear Hilda. May God's richest blessings rest on you all.

"Yours very sincerely,

"W. SALTER PRICE."

Friday, Nov. 30. Started at 6 a.m. with Smith and Burness for Rabai. Got in at 11; heat very trying. Found a special Mail from Chaga just arrived. Ehlers had reached the highest point yet accomplished on Kilima-Njaro. A nice letter from Taylor, who hopes shortly to be here.

Saturday, December 1. It is a very wholesome rule, pretty generally observed by Protestant Societies, that one Society should not intrude into a sphere already occupied by another. Unhappily this rule was set aside a few years ago by the Bavarian Missionary Society planting a Station at Jimba, a couple of miles or so from Rabai. This was a mistake, but as the Missionaries themselves were excellent men and good neighbours, and as their operations were on a very

limited scale, the intrusion, although objected to by
Mr. Binns, on the part of the C.M.S., did not meet
with any formal protest. Now, however, it appears,
that from Jimba as their base, they have gone forward
and planted a new Station among the Wakamba, at
Gulu-gulu or rather Mbungu—the very place we are
now invited to occupy—on the threshold of Ukambani,
which from Dr. Krapf's time has been regarded as the
proper sphere for the development of our Mission from
our base at Rabai; and which becomes all the more
necessary to us now, as it is through this territory our
main line of route will pass to our Stations on Lake
Victoria. Under these circumstances we cannot be
accused of any breach of etiquette in going to Mbungu;
nevertheless, to prevent misunderstandings, I wrote to
the Rev. J. Hoffman, Senior Missionary of the Bavarian
Society, as follows :—

"Rabai, *December,* 1888.

"Dear Mr. Hoffman,—

"You have probably heard that the British
E. A. Co. have invited the C.M.S. to establish a chain
of Missions corresponding with their own Stations on
the new line of route into the interior. The first of
these is Gulu-gulu, and there in response to their
invitation we are about to form a Mission Station at
once. It is unfortunate that you should have fixed
upon the same place, and under ordinary circumstances
I should not have thought of planting a Mission where
another Society was already in possession. But the
circumstances are not ordinary, and I venture to hope

that you will see that we could not reasonably decline this opening for—1. We have been here now more than forty years, and have always been looking forward to the time when we should be able to extend our operations in the direction now opening up.

"2. Without any disparagement of you and your respected colleagues, the Company are naturally desirous, for the sake of the Englishmen in their employ, that the Missionaries with whom they come in contact should be Englishmen, and Ministers of their own Church.

"3. We have for some years had Missions in Uganda, and on the shores of the Nyanza, and it is of vital importance for us to establish communications with them by this route. The old route lies through Usagara—is now under German influence—and owing to the doings on the coast, it is, and is likely to be, closed; in consequence of which our Brethren in those distant Stations are isolated, and placed in a position of great peril.

"4. Many of our people from Rabai are, and will be, employed in various ways by the Company, and it is most desirable that we should make provision for their instruction and spiritual oversight.

"There are other points, but these are, I think, sufficient to show you that it is in no spirit of rivalry, and certainly not out of any want of courtesy to yourselves, that we have decided to commence a Mission at Gulu-gulu. What under the circumstances you may wish to do, I do not know, and I do not now suggest. I would prefer to talk the matter over quietly with you and your colleagues; and as Mr. Smith and I are coming to Gulu-gulu (D.V.) on Monday, we shall have an opportunity of doing this.

"I can assure you, dear Hoffman, whatever the result may be, that we esteem you as fellow-labourers of the same Blessed Master, and that we heartily wish you 'God speed' in all your labours in His cause. With kindest regards to you and your colleagues,

"I remain,

"Yours very sincerely,

"W. SALTER PRICE."

Sunday, December 2. Administered Holy Communion to about 100. Quiet day—but getting very hot.

Monday, December 3. Started with Smith for Gulu-gulu. We were too late, ought to have left at 5; did not get off till 9 a.m. Nothing very striking in the country through which we passed; some pretty patches of park-like land, with here and there stretches of forest, composed mainly of prickly acacia. It was excessively hot travelling to-day, and being the first day neither we nor our men were in best "form". At 4 p.m. came to a good camping place on the bank of a river, to which our people gave the name of "Mto-ya-chuma" (the river of iron). It was thickly covered with a lily, having a profusion of very pretty pink flowers. We were not sorry to pitch our tents, and rest here for the night.

Tuesday, December 4. Up at 4 a.m., and got well under way by 5. At 7 came to Dindini—a good sized village, where a crowd of Wa-Kamba assembled round us, to gratify their curiosity. Every movement was watched with intense interest. The climax of wonders was when I took off my huge pith helmet, which almost sent them into fits. They jumped to the conclusion that Smith was my son. My beard seemed to puzzle them most, and they wanted to know how I made it so long. Poor simple people! How I wish I could speak to them in their own tongue. But the time is coming, even now is, when they shall hear from the lips of Englishmen, " the wonderful words of Life". We came to Gulu-gulu about 8, and here I saw for the first time the Flag of the new Company—on a blue and white ground, a crown, a Union Jack, and the rising sun, with the motto " Light and Liberty". This Station occupies rather a dreary and, I should fear, swampy situation, and consists at present of a number of very temporary buildings, for the accommodation of two or three Europeans, and about 400 natives. Messrs. Crauford and Gedge gave us a hearty welcome. They are living here in great discomfort. They do it " for a corruptible crown ". Shall we do less ?

After breakfast moved on to Mbungu, two miles distant and some 300 feet higher, where the Bavarian Missionaries are located. The situation, vastly superior to Gulu-gulu—removed from malarious influences—and commanding an extensive view of the surrounding country. There is, in the dry season, a scarcity of water, but that may be remedied. There are three Wa-Kamba villages on the plateau, within easy distance. The natives cultivate cereals sufficient for their own consumption and for the purchase of " tembo " from Rabai. They have also flocks and herds, which thrive on the extensive pasture land of the district ; but as one of them assured me it was against their principles to sell cows, any Missionary living here will have to trust to himself for meat supply of every kind. The prices asked by the natives are exorbitant—a fowl 1s. 6d., an egg ¾d., a bottle of milk 7½d. Probably they will learn better by and bye—as yet they scarcely know the value of money.

All day long the Wa-Kamba—men, women, and children—came swarming in to feast their eyes on the new comers. They expressed great delight when they heard we were coming to settle among them—not that they had any fault to find with the " Wa-Daitch," but for some inscrutable reason they preferred the English. Had a long conversation with Mr. Hoffman, who hospitably entertained us. He showed me copies of a correspondence which passed between his Society and the C. M. S. a few years ago, when they first came out. Of this I was entirely ignorant; all I did know was that when they first came to Jimba, Mr. Binns, then in charge at Rabai, disapproved, and that, regardless of his disapproval, the Mission was commenced. We discussed the question amicably, and I explained more fully the views I had expressed in my letter. It now remains for each of us to refer the matter for final decision to the authorities of our respective Societies at home.

In the evening Smith and I took a ramble to prospect a good site for the new Station. Mbungu is an extensive plateau, about 600 feet above sea level. There is abundance of good pasturage, but, as far as we could see, very little cultivation. We selected a spot about a quarter of a mile from the Germans, from the highest point of which a good view is obtained of Rabai, Giriama, Shimba, and even the Teita Mountains.

Wednesday, December 5. Crauford came up early to confer with us about the site. He showed us another, but after looking at all the *pros* and *cons*, it was finally agreed that the spot we had fixed upon was the best ; and there Smith is at once going to work to put up for himself a cottage of wattle and daub.

After a final word of prayer with dear Smith took leave of him and our German friends, and at 10 a.m. set out to return to Rabai. Called at Gulu-gulu and spent half-an-hour with Gedge. What a piggery they are living in ! a great mistake I venture to think. A few miles further on, in the middle of a dense thorny forest, we were overtaken by a violent thunderstorm ; in two minutes I had not a dry thread on my body, and my poor men were in wretched plight. When we came to the resting place near the river, where I was intending to encamp for the night, I saw the safest plan was to move on, so I told the men, "I shall give you only half a 'posho' of rice here, and the rest at Rabai—we must push on—I give you one hour to cook and eat". In an hour and a half we were off. It was very hard riding a donkey owing to the slippery ground and thorny jungle, so I took to my feet ; but, again, the heat was very trying, and by the time we got to the German Mission at Jimba I was fairly done up, and very thankful for a rest and for a glass of wine which my good friend there kindly gave me. Only three miles remained, so in half-an-hour we were off again in good spirits, and went along merrily, getting into Rabai a little after sunset.

The distance from Mbungu to Rabai, Crauford reckons at 24 miles, which we had covered in 7 hours, allowing for stoppages—not bad travelling under the circumstances. Jones was surprised to see me, as he was not expecting me till to-morrow evening.

Before going to bed wrote a short letter to Smith, to cheer him in his loneliness :—

" RABAI, *December* 5, 1888.

" MY DEAR SMITH,—

" I am rather tired, but must drop you a line before turning in. I am very glad I came on ; I can now go to bed without thinking of 4 o'clock to-morrow morning !

" We met a lot of fine cattle—cows and bullocks— on their way to Gulu-gulu. They are a superior breed to the Wa-Kamba animals. You might see if you cannot secure one or two.

" You will, of course, keep up the most friendly relations with Hoffman, whilst, at the same time, taking your own line.

" One of your first cares is to make spiritual provision for all our Native people in the Company's employ. Let them see that they are not uncared for. This is a very important point, in its bearing on the whole question.

" God bless you, my dear brother, and give you all the grace and wisdom you need for the post you are called to fill. I feel that I am taking upon myself a grave responsibility in this arrangement, although I have confidence that the Committee, in view of all the circumstances, will ratify the course we have taken.

"I do not like to think that I may never see you again; it was this thought that over-mastered me in our last prayer together. But if it be so, I shall not cease to pray that your path may be 'as the morning light, which shineth,' etc.

"Yours very affectionately,

"W. S. P."

Thursday, December 6. Left Rabai at 2 p.m., and landed at Frere Town at 7.30. Mrs. Pruen recovering from fever—the rest of the Brethren fairly well; though all more or less feeling the excessive heat.

Friday, December 7. Three men-of-war hanging about in the offing, and the "Penguin" is expected; so I conclude the blockade has commenced. Heard the rumbling of heavy guns this morning.

Called on the Pruens. They have had a terribly trying journey to the coast; but God has most graciously heard our prayers, and "saved them from the lion's mouth". No wonder they suffer from fever after all they have gone through!

The "Boadicea" came in. Admiral Fremantle called, and pressed me about the "H. W." Very sorry to seem grumpy and disobliging, but I could not give consent. Went with him in his steam Pinnace up the creek about ten miles, acting as Pilot! rather a risky thing: piloting an Admiral!!

Saturday, December 8. Flag-ship left. The blockade now established; what will come of it?

Monday, December 10. Dr. Baxter goes to Shimba to make ready. The Chaga party—Taylor, Dr. Edwards, and Reid—safely arrived at Rabai, all well. Thank God !—

Last night very oppressive, little sleep.

Wrote to Mr. Eugene Stock :—

" FRERE TOWN, *December* 10.

" MY DEAR FRIEND,—

" Many thanks for your kind letter of sympathy of November 2. We have passed through strange experiences, and the crisis is not yet over, though things look more peaceful than they did a little while ago. The new Company have been paving their way with dollars —better, no doubt, than bullets—but whether the effect will be permanent or not remains to be seen. This ill-starred Anglo-German blockade will, doubtless, act as an irritant. At such a time the wildest reports are easily fabricated—spread about—and eagerly accepted as true. Thus, at Mamboia, it was fully believed that we at Frere Town were all murdered ; and the news which had reached Chaga was equally alarming and unfounded. This is just the danger, so far as the interior is concerned. No doubt, the clouds have, at times, been dark and threatening, but we can still raise our ' Ebenezer,' and rejoice in the thought that, in the midst of strife and confusion, ' the valleys are exalted, and the mountains and hills brought low,' and the way is being prepared for the revelation of the glory of God, in the darkest corners of this ' dark Continent '. ' It is the Lord's doing, and marvellous in our eyes '—' Be still, and know that I am God : I will be exalted in the earth '—only let us hang more on the word—' Lo ! I am with you '—let us follow as He leads, and we shall ' see greater things than these '.

" I feel that I am leaving East Africa at a time of thrilling interest. The Lord's will be done ; I only pray that some Joshua may be forthcoming ' in whom the spirit of the Lord is,' whose high privilege it shall be to carry on the work which has been but too feebly begun.

" I enclose a letter from Taylor, just received, which is, as his letters always are, deeply interesting. You may perhaps like to take some notice of what he says about Herr Ehler's ascent of Kilima-Njaro, even though it may inspire some enterprising Englishman to come out and try to ' beat the record '. Ehlers himself writes to me : ' When I came down my face was burned, my hands frozen, my lips and eyes very bad, but I was glad and happy that I reached more than other men. Excelsior ! '

" In two months hence, if all goes well, I shall be looking in upon you in your snug little office at Salisbury Square, and then going down to my quiet Parish in Suffolk ! Can you form an idea of the change from my present life and surroundings ? Will you kindly forward Taylor's letter, when read, to my dear wife.

" With best love, etc., etc."

Wednesday, December 12. Mr. Mackenzie and Capt. Pullen came over. The former informs me that Mrs. Euan Smith promises to come and give out Freedom papers at Rabai, on New Year's Day. They ask me to allow a Flag-staff to be erected near the Mission House, which will be the leading mark for ships entering Mombasa harbour. I agreed, provided it was done by them, not by me. I don't want to fight the battle of the flag over again.

A telegram from Salisbury Square. "Leave extended May, if cannot remain beyond January telegraph." What can I say or do? It of course puts out my plans, and is in some sense a disappointment; but what of that if so the Lord wills? I must suppose that the Bishop of Norwich and my dear wife have given consent, so I make up my mind to stay on.

Wrote a few words of counsel, with hints and suggestions to Brother Smith :—

"FRERE TOWN, *December* 12, 1888.

" MY DEAR SMITH,—

" Let me first congratulate you on being set free from those secular duties which, however important and necessary in their bearing on the welfare of the Mission, were yet not such as you might naturally have been led to expect to be occupied in, when you came out as an ordained Missionary to the Heathen. I feel sure the Committee will highly appreciate—as I do— the self-abnegation with which you threw yourself into the work of the moment, asking no question, and the thorough efficiency with which you performed the duties required of you. You have now your reward.

" It is a great honour to be called to break up new ground, and to occupy the first of what—there is good reason to hope—will be a chain of Mission centres, leading right on into the very heart of Africa. This honour is yours. May God Himself supply all your need, and furnish you in every way for the very important post you are now called to fill.

"You know, of course, that the arrangement is provisional, and awaits the approval and sanction of the Parent Committee; I think there is no doubt that will be cordially given.

"The fatherly interest I take in you, and my concern for the success of the undertaking, embolden me to offer a few hints, which I feel sure you will take in good part; and, if I put them in didactic form, you will understand that I do so simply for clearness' sake.

"1. You will come in contact with Englishmen, especially those of the Company's staff. As far as one has seen of them, they are gentlemanly fellows, and some of them not indifferent to spiritual things. But they are exposed to many and great temptations, and it will be for you to set before them a true standard of Christian life and consistency—to be 'an example to believers'.

"Carefully avoid getting mixed up with their disputes and quarrels, which, sooner or later, are almost sure to occur; don't take sides. If you become the confidant of one, you forfeit the confidence of the other, and lose influence. Let one and all feel that in you they have one they can freely come to for Christian sympathy, counsel, and comfort in all their times of sickness or trouble—in short, let them know that there is a Prophet in Mbungu.

"And in this connexion I would say, do all you can by word and example to uphold the *due observance* of the Lord's day.

"Should, unhappily, any dispute arise between you and any of these good gentlemen, be careful not to commit yourself to any hasty expressions ; keep the fires low. First pray—'wait on the Lord,' and then, as a rule, don't write but *go* and talk over the matter, never forgetting the rule 'Be courteous'.

"2. But after all, nay rather, before all, you will remember that you are *a Missionary to the Heathen.* The evangelization of the Wa-Kamba is your first concern— your life work ! This being so, you will naturally long for the time when you shall be able to preach among them, in their own tongue, ' the unsearchable riches of Christ ' ; and to this end you will give all the time you possibly can to the study of the language. You will need two strings to your bow : Kisuaheli and Kikamba. That means a good deal of hard work ; but how happy you will be when you are able to speak to every poor Mkamba you meet of ' Jesus Christ, who came to save sinners '.

"3. As you know, many of our native Christians from Rabai—some who are only catechumens—have found employment with the Company, and this will probably be still more so as time goes on. There will often be some of them in or near Gulu-gulu, and I am so glad to think that although away from the influences and instructions of the Settlement, they will not be left as ' sheep without a shepherd'. You will no doubt do your best to get touch of them, to provide regular

Services for them, and in every way 'to care for their souls'.

" 4. If I allude to two apparently lesser matters, it is not that I have any reason to think that you are in any particular danger yourself, but because I feel that we ought all, as far as possible, to discountenance in others the things I refer to.   I would say then :—

" (1) Guard against the tendency—to which, in our circumstances, we are all more or less exposed—to become 'washensi'.   Live as *simply* as you like, but be neat and clean in person, and insist on cleanliness in those around you, especially in *food* arrangements. There is no virtue in putting up with a table-cloth covered with grease spots, or in wearing a coat dirty and out at elbows, or in making a tumbler do duty, first at the toilet and then at the dinner table, without an intermediate rinsing out !   This is not self-denial, but laziness, and it may easily degenerate into something worse.

" (2) Guard against the *curio* mania.   I see nothing wrong in collecting a few things of this kind when they come in your way, or when going Home ; but you know as well as I, that this hobby may be indulged in till it becomes a snare in more ways than one, especially to a Missionary.

" 5. You will find it well often to call to mind that you are one of a great army, scattered over the world— all under the orders of the same Captain—all working to the same end, and all on the winning side ! 'The Lord reigneth,' so don't be discouraged if you do not see *immediate* results.   'In all labour there is profit.'

Ours is a work of Faith, and 'bread cast on the waters' is often found 'after *many* days'. It is not given to *all* now, to reap where they have sown; but nothing is lost, and if not now 'the Day will declare it,' and when 'He who is our Life shall appear,' the faithful servant will not fail of his reward. The most successful Missionaries doubtless are they who most honour the Holy Spirit, whose alone it is 'to give the increase' and to 'turn men from darkness to light, etc.'

"I have very imperfectly expressed what I would say. Forgive me if I seem to write to you with a semblance of authority. I have none but such as a father might have in writing to a son. I write to you just as I would to my own son on the other side of Africa; and I have warned you against certain things, not because you do not know, but because you do— simply by way of stirring you up, by putting you in remembrance.

"And now, in conclusion, let me say how thankful I am for the happy Christian intercourse I have had with you, and how hard I find it to say 'good-bye' to you and to others whom I have learned to love and esteem for their own and for their work's sake.

"May God endue you with all grace, and make you a workman of whom 'He will not need be ashamed,' and grant us a happy meeting in the great day of 'the manifestation of the sons of God,' for Christ's sake.

"Yours very affectionately,

"W. SALTER PRICE."

Thursday, December 13. Again hard up for accommodation. Taylor comes to live with me. I am glad to have him, only it adds to my housekeeping cares. Busy with letters for Home.

To my Wife.

"*December* 9.

" Preparing to leave on 2nd of next month. My good friends here don't believe in my going away, or else cling to the idea that I shall soon come back. It makes it all the harder to say 'good-bye' to them, much as I long to see again you and our children. I have been away a week about forty miles inland, opening up a new Station, and on my return last night, what a welcome I received from one and all !

" It is rather a serious step, forming a new Station on one's own responsibility ; but the opening was too good to let go, so I hope the Committee will not be *rery* angry. It is on the direct road to Kilima-Njaro and the Nyanza. It is (not Bungay, but) Mbungu, and beyond Rabai is the first link in dear old Krapf's chain !

" *December* 12. Just received another Telegram : ' Leave extended, etc.' I conclude that means that both the Bishop and you have been consulted and given your consent, so though I was actually packing up and looking forward to a happy meeting a few weeks hence, and although I am ignorant of the real cause of the delay, I accept it as an indication of God's will, and trust that ' all will be well'. It certainly affords me the opportunity of giving the finishing touch to one or two matters. True they are the three hottest and most trying months here, but then I escape the three coldest in England! As I prepared for only *six* months, I am getting badly off for clothes, especially Jaeger articles. I am reduced to my last pair of socks, and they will have to do duty till the English Steamer arrives, when I hope to get a dozen pairs, ordered four months ago from D. & S. They have been lying at Aden a month, and I shall not be greatly surprised if they remain there till doomsday—in which case I must get what rubbish I can from Zanzibar.

" I wonder if the Mail will throw any light on the Telegram. Of course *you* know all about it and have arranged with Pickford to stay on.

" Sorry you are still shut out from your own quiet home. I shall think of you spending Xmas at C. I hope to spend it at Rabai, where now are Mr. and Mrs. Burness, Miss Holmes, and Miss Scott. Rabai was never so well manned, or rather *womanned*, as now."

Sunday, December 16. Early Communion—very few natives present. Several officers from the " Stork " came to the Afternoon Service. There were present in all sixteen Europeans. Tormented with prickly heat.

Wednesday, December 19. The Mail S. " Baghdad " from Zanzibar. She brings strange and shocking news. The Sultan is in a blood-thirsty mood. There are some 35 men who from Said Bargash's time have been in prison, with or without just cause. The mild and gentle Said Khalifa has suddenly decreed their death. Four are brought out every day, and hacked to pieces in the public market! This ghastly sight is not likely to have a soothing effect on the minds of the turbulent natives of Zanzibar.   Happily, after eight poor fellows had been thus cruelly slaughtered, Col. Euan Smith interfered, and insisted on the Sultan's putting an end to the horrible butchery.   The state of native feeling in Zanzibar is as bad as it can well be.   The Germans have had more fighting at Bagomoyo.   Being attacked by Bushiri, they landed men and guns, and killed over a hundred natives.   It is reported, and generally accepted as true, that Emin and Stanley have been handed over in fetters, by their own men, to the Mahdi.   *I* don't believe it.

Posted letter to Mr. Lang :—

" December 11, 1888.

" DEAR MR. LANG,—

"Already replied, *viâ* Marseilles, to yours of November 2.   Since then we have been enjoying a season of tranquillity, and we seem to be settling down to the more normal condition of things.   The last has been a busy month, and there are certain matters which require to be explained.

"A special feature is the commencement of the new Station of Mbungu : *see above*.   A copy of my letter to Herr Hoffman, and of a memo. I have drawn up on the subject will put the whole matter fully before the Committee.   It is still open to them if they disapprove my action to repudiate it ; but if I had let the opportunity slip it would have been past recall.

" In view of my expected return Home by the Steamer of January 2, I have been anxious to locate all the members of the staff, according to my knowledge of them and of the needs of the Mission, so as to leave things in ship-shape for my successor. It has been a rather difficult business, but I hope the dispositions made will meet with the Committee's approval. What they are you will gather from enclosures.

"The absorbing question just now is, how to open up communications with the Lake brethren, and with Mamboia and Mpwapwa. It haunts me night and day. Matthews has promised to send on my letter to Roscoe; but I have utterly failed to bribe men to venture by Parker's route! You may rest assured that as far as it lies with me, nothing shall be left undone which can be done to bring succours to our Brethren.

"I begin to realize that I shall have to postpone my departure another month.

"*December* 13. I had written so far when I got your Telegram : 'Leave extended, etc.' I take it for granted you have communicated with the Bishop of Norwich, and with my wife ; so though I had begun to pack up, and to set my face homeward, I accept it as God's will that I should hold on another three months or so, and if so I am content. I hope Pickford is staying on at Wingfield. The change has been good for him and his wife ; and his Ministry, I am thankful to hear, has been very acceptable in the Parish.

"You will be glad to hear that the Consul General is coming to Rabai on New Year's day, and that Mrs. Euan Smith is going to distribute Freedom papers to the ransomed runaways! It will be a happy finale to what has been a very troublesome business. I shall be especially pleased for Col. Euan Smith to see Rabai and the work there, for himself.

" Yours, etc."

Memo. on Mbungu as a new Mission Station.

The Wa-Kamba are a most important tribe, and occupy a wide extent of country. Altogether they offer a splendid field for missionary effort, yet, with the exception of Dr. Krapf's attempts forty years ago, no direct and systematic endeavours have been made to evangelize them. It is virgin soil.

There are special reasons why the C.M.S. should occupy this field.

1. Our direct, and, probably, for a long time to come, only route to the Lake district lies right through it. The old way, which, for obvious reasons, we clung to, is blocked, and just as it is so, a new way, in the providence of God, is opened up to us.

2. If there is to be a chain of Missions into the heart of Africa, and if the C.M.S. is to be the honoured instrument of carrying out the grand design, there can be little doubt that this is the line it must take.

3. Our position as a Missionary Society is unique. We have a capital base at Frere Town and Rabai, and vital interests in Uganda and on the Lake. For strategic reasons, and for economy's sake, it is incumbent on us to bring these two extremes as nearly together as possible.

4. In addition to all this, comes the distinct and cordial invitation of the Director of the British East

Africa Company to take up the work, and to establish a series of Missions at convenient distances along the route they are opening up into the interior. I am very sensible of the grave responsibility I am taking upon myself in accepting, in the name of the Society, this invitation. I may have done wrong, and if so, must take the blame. All I can say is, that, earnestly seeking Divine guidance, I have done what, to the best of my judgment, seemed to be right ; and I am inclined to think that I should have incurred greater responsibility by declining than by accepting the invitation. Of course, I could have said : " I will refer the matter to the Parent Committee," but that would have meant a delay of two or three months before giving a decided answer. It was necessary to decide one way or the other at once. I saw that if I hesitated the opportunity would be lost. I now learn from Mr. Mackenzie, who has just returned from a short visit to Zanzibar, that the French Roman Catholics had expressed their desire to enter on this promising field, and that he replied that he had invited the C.M.S. to take up this work—that Mr. Price had already commenced operations—and that the Company thought it every way desirable that the Mission Stations which might be planted along the new line should all belong to one Society.

So far as to the main question. We now come to the lesser, yet still not unimportant one, as to the occupation of Mbungu.

There can be no doubt that, if we are to take up the work at all, this spot has everything to recommend it as our frontier Station. The only thing that can be said against it is that the Bavarian Mission is, to some extent, already in possession, *i.e.*, they have built a small wattle-and-mud house, in which two Missionaries have just recently taken up their abode, with the view, doubtless, of carrying on missionary work among the Wa-Kamba as soon as they have learnt the language, and are prepared, in other respects, to begin. . . .

To me it seems that for us to decline to take up this Ukambani route would be a suicidal policy. It would be to turn away from "an open door," which God, in answer to many prayers, is placing before us, and to forget some of the most cherished traditions of the past. It is forty years ago that Krapf wrote, "I planned to-day a journey to Ukambani, so that the north-west, too, might be explored, and preparation made for the erection of future Missionary Stations; for the Missionaries in Rabai must be the pioneers of Eastern Africa". It reads like a prophecy, the fulfilment of which is near at hand.

A year later, Krapf was advocating before the Committee of the C.M.S. his grand scheme for an "African chain of Missions through the whole breadth of the land," and the Committee so far fell in with the idea, that they appointed a young ardent Missionary, Pfefferle, to go out under Krapf's direction, and found a Station in Ukambani. The time was not yet come. The early death of Pfefferle postponed for a season the founding of the new Station, but the idea was by no means abandoned. The brave, good man, disappointed, but not daunted, took up his staff again, and traversed once more, all alone, the tract of country which he longed to bring under the dominion of Christ ; and on his return, after many perils, hair-breadth escapes and privations, he recorded his matured conviction in these words : " This Mission, so long as there are not more Missionaries at Rabai, ought to be postponed, but not given up ; since the Wa-Kamba are connected with very many tribes in the interior, who are only to be come at through Ukambani ".

Can we—shall we forget all this ? Shall we not rather recognise that God's time has come ; and that " the bread cast on the waters " forty years ago—the heroic labours of Krapf, and the death of the first Missionary to the Wa-Kamba on the very threshold of his work—is now coming to the surface ?

I will only add that from all I hear, the heart of Bishop Parker was much set upon a line of Stations on this route.

Friday, December 21. The " Mecca " brings our English Mail. Very kind letters from Wigram and Lang ; they refreshed and comforted me not a little. My leave is extended to May 31, but Shaw, who is appointed to take my place, is ready to leave at a moment's notice, so that if it should be necessary for me to leave earlier, I have only to telegraph to that effect. After full consideration of the matter, I have come to the conclusion to stay on another three months from now, *i.e.*, to leave, if God will, by the first Mail in April, supposing no fresh troubles should arise to make it desirable to stop on another month. So, trusting in the Strong One for strength, I gird up my loins once more.

Dr. and Mrs. Baxter left for Shimba. Miss Holmes reported to be suffering from fever—the result no doubt of exposure and toil in the journey to Rabai.

To Col. Euan Smith.

"FRERE TOWN, *December* 12, 1890.

" MY DEAR COLONEL,—

" I am very sorry to hear from one and another, that you are ailing. I don't wonder at it, considering all the worries you must have at this time, from day to day and from hour to hour. Any sensible doctor would tell you that the best, and almost, only remedy is, cessation from official work, and an entire change. Cannot you arrange for this—for a fortnight or at least a week or ten days? Of course it is very difficult in the present crisis, when events are rapidly developing; but you need not be out of call in any sudden emergency. 1 am quite persuaded you ought to do this; and what could be better than for you and your good wife to come up here, as I understand from Mackenzie *she* has already promised to do, to take part in the grand fête at Rabai on New Year's Day? It will give me infinite pleasure to place my house here, and another at Rabai, at your entire disposal, as some little return for all your kindness to me and my Brother Missionaries. Of course, I do not dream of *entertaining* you—poor grass widower as I am—I provide shelter, you supply the provender !

" Just a word about Mrs. Roscoe. She expects to

be confined in April. It would be hard to leave her without medical aid on the occasion ; but to secure this either they should come to the coast *not later than January;* or Dr. Edwards should go to Mamboia towards the end of March. Pruen recommends the

MISSION HOUSE. FRERE TOWN.

former plan, if feasible, and I too think it the better of the two. Besides, it may be easier to procure for them a safe conduct *to* the coast, than for the doctor later on *from* the coast inland.

"If they are to come down, arrangements should

be made at once, but I cannot move without your consent.

"With all good wishes of the season for you and yours, here and elsewhere,

"Yours very sincerely, etc."

Monday, December 24. *To Rabai.* Admiral Fremantle also came up for the day.

Began my monthly letter to my wife:—

"It is Christmas Eve, and for reasons which I cannot explain, I have come here for Christmas Day, instead of spending it at Frere Town. Before leaving this afternoon, I went to see the decorations in the temporary Church. They were gorgeous, yet in good taste—quite a fairy scene. The palm fronds are very effective, and just now the 'gold-mohurs' which I planted twelve years ago furnish any amount of the gayest of gay flowers.

"I had by last Mail a most kind letter from Mr. Wigram, in which he said: 'I cannot resist giving you an extract from a letter received from your brave and loyal wife'. I leave you to guess what it was.

"Many were the expressions of joy on the part of the brethren and *sisterēn*, when they heard I was staying on another four months. My own feelings are mixed. Of course it cannot be otherwise than gratifying to find that my conduct of the Mission, under difficult circumstances, is appreciated by our good friends at Home; and don't for a moment suppose I am getting tired of the work, etc."

Christmas Day, 1888. Had early Communion in

English with an address. Only twelve, including Crauford and Smith from Mbungu, present; but it was a refreshing season: "a table in the wilderness," and that too "in the presence of our enemies"! A Kisuaheli Service at 11 for the Native Church.

Mrs. Burness prepared a big dinner, expecting a party of Officers from the "Stork"; but they did not turn up. Had long talk with Smith; he is delighted with his work and prospects at Mbungu.

Wednesday, December 26. On my way to Frere Town this morning, accompanied by Hoffman and his two colleagues, looked in on Auburn—one of the Company's officers, who has been stationed at Buni for several weeks. On going into his little tent, we were shocked to see the poor fellow, stretched in his cot, apparently in a dying state—no colour, no perceptible pulse—his life just ebbing away, with not a soul near to care for him, except two or three native boys, who did not know in the least what to do. It was a pitiable sight, and argues carelessness or mismanagement somewhere. We knelt by his cot—unconscious though he seemed to be—and offered up a prayer, at the close of which I was glad to see his lips open, and to hear a faint "Amen". After giving him a little stimulant, I arranged for his being carefully carried to Rabai, and then hastened to Frere Town to send up a doctor to his aid. There can be little doubt, if we had not dropped in just as we did, poor Auburn would have died of sheer exhaustion in a few hours. Even now his recovery is very doubtful, but he will have kind friends to tend him. Hoffman and his two friends came and asked me to put them up for the night; they don't quite like the idea of sleeping in Mombasa. With mats and mattresses I made them as comfortable as I could in the verandah, and they were quite happy. They had of course to reckon with ants and mosquitoes! Dr. Edwards to Rabai, to attend to Auburn and Miss Holmes.

Saw Mackenzie. He is well pleased with the result of his visit to Melindi, Lamu, etc.—everywhere well received.

Thursday, December 27.   Having posted Mr. Burness to Rabai, it was important, without loss of time, to define his position and duties.   Sent to him a letter of instructions, as follows :—

"December 27, 1888.

"My Dear Burness,—

"I heartily congratulate you on your appointment to a post in which you will find full scope for direct Missionary work, and at the same time be able to turn other talents you possess to good account in the Mission.   I can only briefly indicate what your new position and duties are.

"Your position is that of Lay Missionary in charge of the very important Station of Rabai; and in that capacity you will have the general supervision and control of the whole Settlement.

"(1) There are four 'askari' newly appointed—one for each quarter. These are under your orders, and their duty is to keep order in their respective quarters—to report to you any unusual occurrences, breaches of bye-laws, etc.—and especially to bring to your notice all who come and go, so that it may be practically impossible for any 'watoro' to creep in unawares. However much we may sympathize with these poor people, who are longing to throw off the yoke of slavery, so long as the law is what it is, we must conform to it. We have only just escaped a great catastrophe, and I must urge upon you to be very much on your guard in this matter, lest a worse thing happen to us.

" (2) There are two other 'askari'. The one strikes the hour, tolls for Church, keeps order during Divine Service, etc. He is under Mr. Jones's orders. The other is under yours for general Mission purposes.

"(3) I have requested Mr. Buchanan to advise all the Company's Agents, that, for the future all business transactions between the Co. and Rabai, are to be carried on through *you* ; and I have given him clearly to understand that we absolutely decline all money responsibilities. This will be a welcome relief to Mr. Jones, and will place our relations with the Co. on a better footing.

" (4) Please consider yourself responsible for all C. M. S. property - houses—furniture—cocoanut trees, etc. I would advise you to keep a book, which you may call ' Rabai C. M. S. Station Memoranda,' in which to enter these, and any other particulars, which may be useful to you or to any one who may succeed you.

" (5) Make an order that no one is to settle at Rabai, and that no cottage is to be erected, without your sanction ; and please see to it that all cottages are built with due regard to sanitary principles, and to the general symmetry of the Settlement.

" (6) A code of regulations will shortly be drawn up, and it will be for you, with Mr. Jones, and one or two members of the Church, to deal with any infringements of the same. In some cases they may have to be dealt with subsequently by the Church Council.

" (7) Two ladies—young and to some extent inexperienced—are now connected with the Rabai Mission: Miss Holmes to work amongst the women, and Miss Scott amongst the girls. You will be a father to them, and help them in any way you can.

" II. *Spiritual Work.* In a Station like Rabai, the opportunities are practically limitless—one may say ' where there's a will, there's a way '; so I have only one or two remarks to make.

" (1) As regards the Settlement itself, Mr. Jones is Native Pastor, and very able and painstaking in that capacity ; and I feel sure you will do all you can to recognise his position, and to honour him before the people. At the same time, I have no doubt, he will be glad of any hints and suggestions and help you can give him.

" (2) There are two Out Stations—Fimboni and Kisimani—carried on by two Native Evangelists— Jonah Mitchell and Lewis Bren. It will be well if you can pay them an occasional visit to encourage them and stir them up.

" (3) There are other villages within a radius of five miles or so, where you will find many people willing to hear the Gospel.

" (4) Much—I had almost said everything—depends on your ability to speak to the people in their own tongue ; so, of course, the study of the language will be your first concern.

" You are at liberty to read to Mr. Jones any part of this letter you may think fit.

" God bless you, dear Brother, and make you a chosen vessel to the people among whom your lot is cast, for Christ's sake.

" Yours very affectionately, etc."

Saturday, December 29. At 6 a.m. to Rabai, getting in at 10. Burness very grateful for " Instructions ". He and Jones have prayed and talked over the matter and come to a good understanding as to their respective duties. I trust they will work happily together, and be mutually helpful. Smith and Cranford arrived from Mbungu ; Robson and Ward from Frere Town.

Sunday, December 30. This morning, half-an-hour before the bell, the people in their Christmas best were flocking to Church. When I went in all the seats were filled, and the aisles and porch. I had difficulty in picking my way to the vestry. Tears of joy and thankfulness—I could not help it—trickled down my face. Oh ! what a sight, as I called to mind our experience thirteen years ago ! At Holy Communion there were 140, of whom eight were English, and the rest Natives. All praise to God !

Headache all day—the effect of heat and excitement. Hoffman writes asking for Dr. Edwards to go over to Jimba to see Venderlein, who is ill with fever. Mrs. Jones too is very bad. Sorrows and joys strangely mixed together ! A party met in my house and finished the day with singing and prayer.

Monday, December 31. All day engaged with Smith giving tickets to " watoro " ; to save time to-morrow in distributing Papers of Freedom—a big job ! Mackenzie and Matthews came to be ready for to-morrow. Sorry Mrs. Euan Smith cannot be with us after all.

1889.

New Year's Day. A never-to-be-forgotten day in the history of the Mission Station of Rabai ; such as it has never seen before, and is not likely ever to see again. From early dawn the place was all astir ; the main roads were gay with flags and triumphal arches ; Europeans and Natives streamed in from various quarters, and everything betokened that something very unusual was about to occur. Mr. Mackenzie, General Matthews, I, and several others, were engaged all day long in the delightful occupation of distributing Papers of Freedom to * 900 runaways who had been ransomed by the British E. A. Company. Each Paper contained the name of the reputed owner, and of the slave in question, with a renouncement by the former of all claim over the latter, which Paper having been signed, was duly stamped with the official seal of H.M. Consul General. Truly, it was a heart-moving occasion, and one worth coming 6000 miles to see and take part in !

In the evening I gave a dinner in the verandah of the old Mission house to twenty guests—all English except W. Jones and Heroe, a West African of the

---

* Of these 640 were of Rabai, and the rest of Stations belonging to other Missionary Societies.

Methodist Mission. What would dear old Rebmann have thought of it all? After dinner all the Settlement flocked to the Church square, where Mr. Mackenzie let off a number of splendid rockets which he had brought for the occasion, and which must have greatly astonished the natives of the surrounding country.

REBMANN LODGE. RABAI.

Wednesday, January 2. Held a special Thanksgiving Service at 6·30 a.m. Looking out of my window in the early morning, long before the time for Service, I saw a crowd of men and women squatting on the ground around the Church ; and on going out to ascertain what it meant, I found it was just the overflow from the Church, already as full as it would hold, and fresh streams were still pouring in from all quarters of the Settlement.   At the appointed hour all the English visitors—twenty in all, including Miss Holmes from her sick couch—were assembled, and as the body of the Church was closely packed from end to end, they had to be accommodated within the Communion rails. After special Prayers and Thanksgivings, I gave a short address.   I do not envy the man who could look down, as I did, on that sea of upturned faces—black indeed, but beaming with joy at the thought of recent deliverance from bondage—without his spirit being stirred within him.   What a congregation !   What a grand occasion !   What strange surroundings !

My subject was *Ransom*, and I had not far to go for a Text—" If the Son make you *Free*, ye shall be *Free* indeed "—John viii., 36.

"Yesterday was the greatest day in your lives. Before that, what was your condition ?   You were SLAVES ! RUNAWAYS ! haunted day and night with the fear of being carried away again into cruel bondage !

" And what is your condition now? You are FREE —men, women and children, all of you—as FREE as the air you breathe !   No man—Arab or Suaheli—may lay his hand on anyone of you and say : ' Come along, you are my slave '.   If he do, show him the *paper* you received yesterday.   That is your *charter*—keep it safe —as long as you have that to show you have nothing to fear—you are *Free* men and *Free* women !   (' Ashant,

ashant '—thanks, thanks—was the glad and hearty response.)

"How has it all come about? Why, one you never saw or heard of before has come thousands of miles across the sea to be your friend and deliverer; and, at great cost, has paid down the full price for every one of you! The price *has been* paid, and therefore you are *Free!* We all rejoice with you, and praise God for what has been done.

"And now it remains for you to show by your lives that you are not unworthy of the Freedom which has been given to you. Many of you will no doubt find employment with the new Company—not as slaves— you will be paid for your labour. Let all see that you are all the better for having been freed—more diligent, more trustworthy—better men and better women!

"But our Text has its lesson for *all* of us—whites as well as blacks—English and African alike!

"We are all *born* slaves—bond slaves of sin!

"And only ONE can deliver from this bondage— 'There is none other name, etc.,' and 'If the *Son* make you *Free*, etc.,' and 'God so loved the world, etc.'

"And only *one way*—by paying the price for each and all. That price *has been* paid! Jesus, our mighty friend, *has* paid it; and what a price!—not, as in this case, 'silver and gold'—but His own most precious blood!

"It is *sufficient for all!* and the proclamation is to all —'Ho! every one that thirsteth, etc.,' and 'Whosoever will let him come, etc.'

"As only those of you who came forward and con- fessed yourselves to be slaves are rejoicing in your liberty to-day, so only those of us who come to Jesus, the Great Deliverer, confessing their sin and helplessness, will share in His glorious Redemption.

" God help us all to embrace this offer—to claim our Freedom, before the books are closed and the door shut."

After Service sent off a Telegram to Sir W. Mackinnon, President of the I. British E. A. Company :—

" Grand New Year's Day at Rabai. Nine hundred slaves made free by Mackenzie. Great rejoicings. All send best thanks to Board of Directors, and pray God to prosper Company's work in East Africa."

Returned to Frere Town this evening.

Thursday, January 3. Writing letters for French Mail Steamer. I give a few extracts from one to the Rev. R. Lang :—

" I quite agree with what you say as to the respective needs of the various Missions. I put Frere Town *first*, because it is the base, and its Institutions properly maintained ought to furnish a supply of all kinds of Agents to all the other Stations ; but I don't want to keep a man here, who was not meant for us. I would much rather speed them on their way.

" The blockade is established, but hitherto it has not affected us ; as far as the English part of the coast is concerned it is a very mild affair, and ' nobody seems one penny the worse '. It is different down South. The Germans are everywhere cordially hated, and seem to make no progress. They have occasional fights, and lives are lost on both sides ; but with no tangible result, save that the old routes into the interior are rendered

GIVING FREEDOM PAPERS TO 1000 RUNAWAY SLAVES AT RABAI ON NEW YEAR'S DAY, 1889.

unsafe. Of course all this tends to increase the importance of Mombasa, and to divert travellers and traffic to this new channel.

"Just now I am in difficulty about Roscoe's wife. I am in correspondence with Colonel Euan Smith about bringing them to the coast, if it is possible. I begin to think that in the present state of things in East Africa, young wives are a mistake. The time will come, but it is not now.

"I am almost ashamed to say another word about myself; but it is important the Parent Committee should know definitely when I am leaving that they may arrange to have some one here to take my place. Under present circumstances anything like an interregnum is to be avoided. My intention is, unless anything unforeseen occurs, to leave on April 2. That gives me just three months from this time; and many things may happen between now and then. We seem to be living 'from hand to mouth'; but have confidence that all is working together for the furtherance of the Gospel.

"I grieve that as yet there is no break in the clouds as regards our dear Brethren at the Lake, etc. I am casting about in every direction for some means of getting at them. We must earnestly pray God to remove the barriers and open up the way."

Friday, January 4. Gave treat to the children—200 boys and girls—in the "Shamba" opposite Mombasa, in which Mrs. Krapf's grave is. Mr. Mackenzie kindly lent his steam-launch, to convey the children across the harbour.

Chaga and Teita Mail arrived. All well.

Saturday, January 5. The "Kilwa" from Zanzibar, bringing the Hon. Guy Dawney and Mr. Buckley, who are going up country on a hunting excursion. The latter is ill with fever. Dr. Pruen went over to see and prescribe for him.

Sunday, January 6. Preached this morning from John viii. 39. There was a full church. Heat overpowering.

Mail in from Mbungu. R. Livingstone has struck for wages! He was Bishop Parker's favourite boy: was with him when he died. Smith is, and so am I, greatly disappointed.

Monday, January 7. Dr. Pruen commenced a Medical Mission in Mombasa. I hope it may be well sustained, and prove, with God's blessing, a valuable means of access to all classes in that benighted town.

Conducted Evening Prayer meeting; three sailors of the "Boadicea" came in during my address.

Tuesday, January 8. Had a very exhausting night— no breeze—tossing about tormented with prickly heat. This morning feeling quite out of sorts; headache; no appetite! Had a talk with R. Livingstone; but he was proof against my persuasions and arguments. He finished off by saying: "I am not fit for this work; I must give it up". Maybe the poor boy is conscious of some special unfitness, which he does not like to confess. Alas! who indeed is fit? I am exceedingly sorry and disappointed, both on his own account and on Smith's.

At 11 p.m. Pruen roused me up to tell me that the "Penguin" had come in, with Colonel Euan Smith on

board.   As he wished to see me, and might not be able
to come on shore, he invited me to breakfast.

Wednesday, January 9.   Another bad night, but feeling better this morning.   Went off to the " Penguin "
for breakfast.   Mackenzie and Buchanan there.   Had
a long, pleasant chat with the Colonel.   Had the opportunity of correcting some misapprehensions on his part.
He begged me to tell him how, in any way, he could
be helpful to our Mission.   Afterwards he came on
shore with me to call on the ladies, and was intending
to go on to Kilifi, and, after a cruise of two or three
days, to return to Zanzibar.   But he had scarcely
landed when the Despatch-boat steamed in, with a
" special," calling him back at once to Zanzibar.
The Germans, taking advantage of his absence, are
manœuvring the Sultan.   What a wicked, scheming
world it is !   What they want, I hear, is to get Lamu
conceded to them, and they take the first opportunity
of the Consul General's back being turned to frighten
the Sultan into compliance with their wishes.   England will surely never consent to that ; or, if she does,
there must be a very good *quid pro quo* somewhere.

The Colonel tells me that Bushiri has now declared
war against the white man—English as well as German ; and that Bagomoyo is in ruins !

Five men-of-war are in the harbour to-day : " Boadicea," " Algerine," " Stork," " Penguin " and " Woodcock ".   What must the Natives think of it all !

Admiral Fremantle came over and invited me to
dinner, but I am so covered with prickly-heat that I
dread putting on a black coat ; so beg to be excused.

Friday, January 11. Taylor still ill; an abscess has formed on his side. A messenger comes from Mbungu with the sad news that Smith is very bad with fever. Ask Dr. Edwards to go to his aid, and, if necessary, bring him to Rabai. I go there (D.V.) early to-morrow morning.

Saturday, January 12. Started at 5.30 a.m., and reached Rabai at 10.30! The doctor had returned last night, bringing a more favourable report of Smith. Miss Holmes quite recovered, and beginning her work among the women. Auburn is better, but dreadfully run down. I don't think he will ever again be fit for work in East Africa.

Towards evening I got sore throat, headache, and other unpleasant symptoms; felt like fever, but fought shy of the Thermometer and went to bed early. After midnight I was roused by a great uproar—loud talking, dogs barking, etc.—close to my tent. On inquiry, found that a man had been brought in on a stretcher from Gulu-Gulu very ill. The doctor gave him a dose of brandy and milk to fortify him for the journey on to Mombasa—eight or nine hours! He afterwards came to me with a similar potion, and, as it seemed to me, in the identical four-ounce measure; but my soul loathed the dirty glass and its contents, so I sent it away.

Sunday, January 13. Feeling generally unwell. Could not attend Church this morning. The Lord knows our weaknesses, and will allow for them. All are crying out about the heat. This is really our hot season; and it will last till I go! Glad to see Burness so happy in his work. He and Jones hit it off most pleasantly. Already things begin to look all the brighter for his presence. In a few months, under his care, there will be a great change for the better.

Monday, January 14. Better to-day. Wrote an official to the Consul General on the " watoro" question :—

" *To Col. Euan Smith, H.M. Consul General.*

" RABAI, *January* 14, 1889.

" SIR,—

" I beg to state, for your information, what arrangements I have made to prevent, in future, any 'watoro' finding shelter in our Mission Station of Rabai.

" In the first place, I have placed Mr. Burness—an energetic and thorough business man—in the position of Lay Missionary in charge of the Station, and four 'askari' under his orders, whose almost sole duty it is to see that our Rules in this matter are strictly carried out.

" In addition, I have had the following notice translated, and put up in all our Mission Stations :—

" NOTICE.

" 1. The 'askaris' are strictly enjoined to report at once all fresh arrivals in the Settlement, and not to allow any one to stay the night, without the sanction of the Superintendent.

" 2. Any 'mtoro' found in the Settlement after this notice, who has not received a Paper of Freedom or a Permit, will be liable, at any moment, to be handed over to his or her master.

" 3. Any one living here, who shall secretly give shelter to an 'mtoro,' will himself be expelled from the Settlement, and forfeit all claims for compensation.

" 4. This notice is to be posted up in a conspicuous place, and to be read out publicly on the first and third Monday in every month, until further notice.

" I will only add that, if any Arab or Suaheli has reason to suspect that any of his slaves are at Rabai, and will apply to Mr. Burness, he will be courteously treated, and have every facility given him to ascertain if they are there or not, and if there, in obtaining possession of them.

" These provisions will, I trust, be found in every way satisfactory, and remove all cause of suspicion or complaint on the part of slave-owners.

" I have the honour to remain,

" Sir,

" Your most obedient Servant,

" W. SALTER PRICE."

Tuesday, January 15.   Left at 7 a.m. with Auburn, for Frere Town.   Called on C., and spent the day. He was very kind and hospitable—plenty to eat and drink—but his dirty boys took away my relish.   I was very dainty, but Auburn, who is making up for lost time, had the appetite of a horse, and atoned for my shortcomings. Reached Frere Town at 6 p.m. Taylor still confined to his couch, very weak, but on the mending tack, I hope.

Wednesday, January 16. Busy all day preparing for the Mail. She ought to be in to-day, but, for some unaccountable reason, is delayed.

Two men brought up by the "askari". They say they were with the "wazungu" at Kilwa. When their German masters were murdered, they were seized by a Suaheli, who sent them to Pemba. On the way they escaped, and made for Mombasa. Trying to cross over to Frere Town at night, they were arrested and handed over to Khamis Kombo, who took them to his place at Mtwapa. Thence they escaped and made their way to Frere Town. Their story may be true or false, but it is impossible to ascertain; so I gave strict orders to the "askari," that they must clear out to-morrow morning. It looks to me like a "plant" to entrap us.

Finished off letter to my wife :—

"It comforts me much to know that I am upheld by the prayers of so many kind friends. Your and their intercessions have not been in vain; many dangers have been averted, and we have been permitted, in comparative peace and quietness, to enter upon another year.

"Yes, dearest, I have often thought of that morning more than a year ago, when on reading Mr. Lang's letter I said: 'Here is a call for me to go to East Africa'. It came upon me so suddenly, it was like an inspiration. Something seemed to say to me: 'You must go'. I am so glad to know that you now feel that it was all right.

It has, of course, been a trial in some ways, but I don't think we shall either of us have cause to regret it.

"Every day brings its work and cares; and in the midst of it all I have to carry on a difficult correspondence with the Government and Company officials—more diplomatic than pleasant. Just now this is a very arduous post, and though, thank God, I am wonderfully sustained, the wear and tear is great, and you must not be surprised to see me looking a good deal whiter than I did a year ago. I shall be very thankful if God gives me strength to hold on another two months, etc.'

Thursday, January 17. What a day this has been! The "Mecca" came in from Zanzibar at 7 a.m., and I went off to her at once. She brings heavy tidings :—

1. There have been a succession of revolutions in Uganda. Our Brethren have been robbed of everything, and expelled almost in a state of nudity! But, thank God, they escaped with their lives, and had found shelter with Mackay at Usambiro. Deeply interesting letters from Walker and Mackay.

2. The German Mission at Fugu has been attacked—one Brother and two Sisters killed—the rest fugitives or prisoners with the Arabs!

3. A letter from Col. Euan Smith, urging me to call Fitch and Wray to the coast *at once!*

4. He has utterly failed to get an escort for the Roscoes. They are probably in imminent peril, and apparently left to their fate. I must do my best to get help to them one way or another.

Had a long talk with Herr Vohsen, Director of the German Company, now on his way home. Gathered from him that the Company is defunct—nothing for it but either to abandon the enterprise or for the Imperial Government to take it in hand.

Crossed the bay six times to-day under a blazing sun !

I give here a few extracts from two letters received from Mr. Mackay by this Mail, bearing date respectively October 25 and November 27, 1888, and both in reply to two letters from myself to him :—

"USAMBIRO KWA MAKOLO, *October* 25.

" MY DEAR MR. PRICE,—

"On the 6th inst. I received your welcome letter of August 6.

"Next to the satisfaction I have in knowing that you are in Frere Town, where your experience will be invaluable in the present state of the Mission there, is the pleasure of hearing directly from yourself.

"Some time ago I wrote to our Home Committee proposing a division of this Diocese into Eastern *and* Equatorial Africa. Considering the distances and mode of travelling, it is to my mind worse than ridiculous to expect a Bishop located on the coast to be of any real value in this Lake district, and *vice versâ*. The very fact of your having come out to East Africa while Bishop Parker was delayed inland, confirms my belief in this matter. Fever and other ills make no respect of persons, and under the present arrangement we shall need a new Bishop every few years.

" It is the unexpected which always happens.   Who would have thought that at this moment Mwanga would be a fugitive at Magu, while a brother of his named Kayondo would be made Kabaka ! From all I can hear our Brethren were safe during the revolution. Mwanga implores me to go to Magu and take him to the coast.

" Here we have had a serious war, Msalala having been attacked by old Makolo. The fighting lasted three days, but, thank God, our chief was victorious. Had it been otherwise, I fear we should have been plundered, if not murdered also. But the gracious protection of our loving Father was over us, and we suffered nothing except days and nights of watching and anxiety. I have been alone for the last three months ; but look for companionship sometime."

" *November* 27. I have received your welcome letter of September 1, and thank you much for writing me so fully, as well as for all your trouble in trying to forward our new men. I hear from Ashe that he is prepared to show them the way up country, and, although I consider he runs considerable risk in doing so, yet he might get up as far as Usongo without harm. Here he had too many fevers to warrant his return to Usambiro.

" Mr. Lang tells me that Dr. Edwards and Mr. Robson are under orders for the interior. It would be well, therefore, for the whole party to travel together, even should Beverley and Fraser have to wait at the coast for some time. Hurry has been the bane of our Mission ; nothing is ever gained by it.

.   .   .   .

" Walker and Gordon are both here, as also Deekes ;

the latter will soon (D.V.) return to Nasa. The last
news from Buganda reports the removal of the new
king, Kiwewa, while a brother of his, Kalema, is in
possession of the throne. Practically there are now two
kings, each followed by a strong party. Kiwewa has
most of the old expelled chiefs with him, while Kalema
has the Arabs and the Mohammedan party. There will
thus be, or more probably has been already, much
fighting and bloodshed. The issue is in God's hands,
and we must patiently await the result.

" With affectionate regards,

" Believe me, yours faithfully,

"A. M. MACKAY."

CHAPTER XII.

STARTLING NEWS FROM UGANDA—WARS AND RUMOURS OF WARS.

Friday, January 18. The " Java," with our English Mail in, brings me a good budget of letters—comforting and refreshing, like springs of water in a dry and thirsty land!

Hear that the B. E. A. Company having taken to themselves all the glory of freeing the runaway slaves, have asked the C. M. S. to bear a share of the cost. This is really too bad !

Monday, January 21. There is some anxiety for the safety of Bishop Smythies and the Missionary party at Magila.

Sent off Chaga Mail. In view of my intended departure two months hence, and of there being no prospect of any Missionary of experience being on the spot to take my place, I have been anxiously considering what is the best provision to make. This is not a time to leave the Mission without a competent head. I have come to the conclusion that if Brother Fitch is willing to come, and if suitable provision can be made for Chaga, he is the best man to leave in temporary charge. On the 16th instant I wrote to sound him on the subject, suggesting a plan :—

"It occurs to me the best thing would be to send Beverley and Dr. Edwards to 'hold the Fort' at Chaga *pro tem*—till the way opens for them to go forward. Will you tell me without reserve what you think of this, *with the least possible delay.* I am anxious to settle this business before I leave !

"Give my most profound 'yambos' to King Mandara, and tell him I am still hopeful of making his personal acquaintance. It is very much a question of rain ! Should I not be able to come, tell him that I thank him much for his kind present of a spear, which is a splendid specimen of workmanship, and which I shall show with great pleasure to my friends in England as a sample of what the 'Wa-Chaga' can do. There is nothing to be had here worth sending him in return, but he may depend upon it, I will forward him something from England with which he will be pleased, etc."

To-day it became necessary to add the following P.S. to my letter :—

"So far I had written, when a steamer arrives from Zanzibar, and lo! 'a change comes o'er the spirit of the dream'. A good deal of the above is now out of date; still it may interest you to see what my hopes and plans were. *Now,* the Consul General urgently requests me to send for you and Wray at once to the coast, and with such a mandate—whatever my own judgment may be—I dare not trifle. You will get all the startling news of Uganda and the coast from your sister; so all I need say is, that I am sending up twenty men to bring your goods. If they are too few leave what they cannot carry in the custody of some trust-worthy person, with promise of reward, if handed over in safety to you or your successor.

"Now, dear Fitch, commending you to the loving care and protection of our Heavenly Father, and hoping soon to welcome you here,

"Yours, etc."

I wrote of course to the same effect to Mr. Wray at Teita.

Tuesday, January 22. Sent medicines to Shimba. Dhow with lime, Miss Scott's boxes, etc., to Rabai. Prayer and S.S. Meeting in the evening.   Ep. i. 15 to end.

Wednesday, January 23. Accompanied Miss Scott to Rabai, getting in at 6 p.m.

Friday, January 25. More bad news reaches me from Zanzibar; another "official" from the Consul General, telling me of the murder of Missionaries on the coast, and putting me on my guard against the Arabs of Mombasa.

To the Rev. W. E. Taylor, Frere Town.

"RABAI, *January* 25.

"MY DEAR TAYLOR,—

"My news from Zanzibar is very bad. A 'rising' in Zanzibar and Pemba is imminent, to depose Seyed Khalifa, in favour of his brother Seyed Abdul Aziz. The Consul General warns me that 'the Arabs of Mombasa should be carefully watched'; but

how am *I* to watch them ? and if they become warlike
what am I to do ? I trust it may please God to give
us peace ; but the outlook is not encouraging.

"Thanks for the loaf! I hope to return (D.V.) early
on Monday morning.

"Ever yours, etc."

Saturday, January 26. Pigott in from Jimba. Finds
a letter from Mackenzie transferring him to the Tana
river expedition. We are all sorry to lose him from
this district.

Sunday, January 26. A peaceful and refreshing Sabbath at Rabai! It was the monthly Collection day. Some
time before Service begins, men and women are seen
trooping in from all quarters towards the Church, each
carrying a little basket on the head, containing a contribution to the collection. A quaint, but very pleasing
picture !

Monday, January 28. Left Rabai with Pigott at 5
a.m., but having tide against us, did not get to F. Town
till 10. At the " banderini," " Tom," Bishop Hannington's old dog, again put in an appearance, and pitifully
whined to be taken on board ; but this time I had made
up my mind not to take him, so ordering one of the
Rabai men to hold him back we pushed off. We had
no sooner done so, than " Tom " broke loose, and dash-
ing into the water swam after us. It was hard work
against the tide, but he soon came up with us. We
kept him at bay, however, till the poor brute, almost
exhausted, had to make for the nearest shore. Then
running along the bank, through mud and brambles,
till within measurable distance of the boat, in he

plunged again and swam alongside, only again to be warned off. This was repeated several times, till at last both Pigott and I felt it would be positively cruel to refuse shelter any longer to the " runaway". Why this dog so clings to me I do not know ; perhaps he has a mission to take charge of me !

Tuesday, January 29. The " Adowa " coming in this morning ran on the rocks, and stuck for several hours. She brought me an official letter from Mr. Mackenzie, which distressed me not a little. It is only one of many such which I received much too frequently about this time. I would most gladly draw a veil over this irritating and needless correspondence—the more so as in spite of it, the most amicable relations existed between the writer and myself up to the last—but the sketch which I am drawing of my missionary life at this time would be very imperfect if it left out of account the constant worry and annoyance which for several months I had to endure from this source. The nature of the correspondence may be gathered from my answer in reply, which I give simply as a sample, and with no intention of referring to the matter again.

To G. S. Mackenzie, Esq.,

" FRERE TOWN, *January* 29, 1889.

" DEAR SIR,—

" I beg to acknowledge your letter of the 24th inst. There is one point in it which I cannot pass over, because on it the whole question in dispute between us turns. You have over and over again brought a most grave and unjust charge, not against me, but against my Missionary brethren, who are not here to defend themselves, of ' harbouring and secreting runaways and of knowingly breaking the law '. As you reiterate the charge in even stronger terms in this letter, I must again, as I have done before, protest against this calumny, which I am prepared to show is utterly without foundation.

" For the rest your rather long letter touches upon many debatable points, and contains many inaccurate statements—resulting no doubt from the defective and one-sided information on which you have relied—and alas ! the paragraphs are not numbered for convenience of reference. Under these circumstances I cannot undertake the task of replying seriatim to your letter ; and indeed it seems to me worse than useless to continue a correspondence which is calculated to engender strife, and cannot possibly lead to any good practical result.

" I am quite sure we have, both of us, at this time quite enough on hand to engage all our wits ; and it is to the interest of all concerned that the good feeling which has hitherto subsisted between us should continue.

" It is quite true, as you say, ' that our stand-points of viewing this question are very wide apart '—that is not surprising. Yet, even so, we have each of us the opportunity of taking a principal part in a noble work, and I see no reason why we may not go on, working harmoniously together, on our separate yet parallel lines, and being mutually helpful to one another.

"*Our* opportunity is rapidly coming to a close, and those who succeed us will have difficulties of no ordinary kind to cope with. Let us, at least, leave to them our legacy of peace and good-will.

"I remain,

"Yours faithfully,

"W. Salter Price."

On the same day I wrote to Colonel Euan Smith:—

"My Dear Colonel,—

"Allow me to introduce to you Dr. Edwards. He, personally, is quite ready to attempt the journey to Mamboia by a new route which he will explain to you, if he has your sanction for doing so. I thought it better for him to go to Zanzibar and see you, and also get all the information he can from Maxworthy and others. I shall be guided entirely by what you say. It would, of course, be a grand thing if he could get to Mamboia in time to help poor Mrs. Roscoe in her confinement, and at the same time discover a way of getting into touch with Mackay and the others, without coming into collision with the cut-throats at Saadani. It is worth running *some* risk, but what the risk *is*, you are best able to judge.

"We are much in the dark here as to what is going on to the south of us. The news of the murder of poor Brooks comes to us from England ! in a Reuter's Telegram ! I fancy the intelligence department in Mombasa is more complete than ours.

"The 'Adowa' in entering the harbour missed the

channel and went on the rocks. I saw the whole thing from my verandah, and I don't think the captain was in the least to blame. She was too lightly laden, and did not, owing to the strong spring tide, answer to her helm. She stuck hard and fast for some twelve hours, but got off at last, apparently not much the worse.

"I have to acknowledge and thank you for your 'official' of January 17 ; and, although I do not think our friends at Chaga and Teita are in any particular danger, I have acted promptly on your advice and sent up men to bring down Fitch, Ehlers, and Wray to the coast. I warned them to be particularly careful to blind Mandara's one eye, with your presents, and in any other way they may see best, so as not to give *him* the idea that they were running away. They will have a bad journey for want of water, but I hope they will come safely through, etc., etc."

It will illustrate the diversified character of my correspondence at this time if I add here another letter written on the same date as the above :—

To Miss Scott, Rabai.

" My Dear Miss Scott,—

"It has been a great pleasure to me to see you entering upon your new sphere of work at Rabai, and I earnestly pray God to give you health and every needful grace for the discharge of its important duties.

"Your special mission is to the girls of Rabai, and I am very hopeful that many who are now neglected, will be brought under your instruction and influence.

As soon as arrangements can be made, the younger girls now in the dormitory at F. Town will probably be transferred to Rabai, and come under your immediate charge.

" I wish you to understand that you have a free hand as regards plans and arrangements in your own department, whilst, at the same time, you will endeavour to make them harmonize, as far as possible, with the general order of things in the Mission.

" In the event of any necessity, you may confidently apply to Mr. Burness or Mr. Jones for any advice or assistance they may have it in their power to render you.

" In Miss Holmes, you will, I trust, have a loving Christian friend and companion, and as your spheres of work are distinct—yet, with a common aim—you will be the better able to sympathize with, and be helpful to one another.

" Much—I had almost said everything—depends on you and she being very good friends. You have a grand opportunity before you—may the Lord be with and prosper you.

" Yours very sincerely, etc."

Thursday, January 31. Again disquieting rumours reach us from Mombasa. " An attack is to be made on Frere Town—Bushiri is on the war path, and threatens to pay us a visit with some hundreds of his braves ! " Two special deputations come to me to-day from the Wali with presents of fruit, etc., and profuse professions of friendship—what does it all mean ? The second deputation consisted of the "Akida," and another Arab, and three children! I gave them tea and biscuits. They said that Mackenzie and I had done a good work in freeing the runaways, but that Mackenzie could have done nothing in it without me; and they expressed great concern that I was contemplating going away, etc. I *do* wish we could have more confidence in the sincerity of these people.

Had a parting meeting with R. Keating, Paulus, and Gona, and dismissed them to Mwaiba. Gave strict injunctions about runaways; and notices to put up.

Saturday, February 2. Began packing for England. Sent Ishmael with presents to the Wali, and a promise to visit him on Monday Adamji (a Hindi merchant) came over this evening to give us warning that something is brewing in Mombasa against the English and Frere Town. Similar rumours come also from other quarters, and there may be something in them. But what can we do?—only keep our eyes open, and "look to the Hills from whence cometh our help".

Wrote letter to Mr. Lang by the French Mail. A few extracts are here given:—

"I send a memo. on the runaway-slave question, which will put you in possession of all the facts, and so enable you to refute calumnies and misrepresentations, and to decide as to your line of action. Whatever may have been in the past, my larger acquaintance with the iniquities and abominations of domestic slavery (as it is called), as it exists in this country, in-

clines me to say, ' Touch not the unclean thing '.   The
time has come for us to take a firm stand, and make it
plain that, whilst under existing circumstances we will
do our best to exclude runaways from our Mission
Stations, we will have nothing to do with catching
them, and handing them over to the—in many cases—
cruel bondage from which they have escaped.   We
may close *our* gates against them, but other refuges
are open to them, and what right have we to stand in
their way ?

" The Consul General has failed to open communications with the Roscoes. or to secure their safe conduct
to the coast.   His own ' Askari ' was beaten, put in
chains, and sent back in disgrace to Zanzibar.   ' Every
inlet,' he says, ' from the coast is closed.'   Mrs. Roscoe,
in addition to her expected confinement, is suffering
from a painful malady, and they are without the proper
remedies.   Dr. Pruen has put up what is needed, and
we have asked Maxworthy to do his best to get it to
them ; but I fear there is little chance of his success.

" Providentially, we may now say, there has been
an accumulation of stores at Usambiro, so that our
Brethren there will be able to hold out for some time
to come.

Sunday, February 3.   Assisted at native Communion
—very few *men* present.   Lieutenant Tippyng and four
sailors at Morning Service.

All day there has been an uneasy feeling in the
Settlement, as if something were going to happen.
Scarcely any men at any of the Services.   The report is
that an attack is to be made on us at 3 a.m. to-morrow

—the object being to kill us, and carry off all our freed slaves again into slavery; as has been done at Fugu! It was no use to pooh-pooh the thing—our people were in a panic, and arming for fight. Happily the "Griffon" came in this afternoon; but hearing that she was leaving again early to-morrow morning Taylor and I went on board at 9 p.m. I saw Captain Blaxland, and told him the state of things. He expressed his willingness to defer his departure, and afford us any protection in his power, if I would request him to do so in writing; and this under the circumstances I felt quite justified in doing. I accordingly wrote to him as follows:—

To Captain Blaxland, H.M.S. "Griffon".

" DEAR SIR,—

" Reports have come to me from various quarters—chiefly from Adamji, one of the principal Hindi merchants of Mombasa—that a plot is hatching to kill the Europeans and carry off all the freed slaves; whilst to-day a more definite rumour reaches us, that an attack is to be made upon Frere Town early to-morrow morning. What foundation there may be for these reports it is impossible to say, but they are disquieting, and our people are in a sort of panic—the more so as many of our able-bodied men are away, and with a large number of women and children on our hands we are practically defenceless.

" I shall be glad therefore if you can kindly afford

us the protection of your presence in the harbour for a
few days, or until some other ship comes in.

"I am, yours truly,

"W. SALTER PRICE."

This is a case in which prevention is better than
cure ; for once blood is shed on either side, the consequences are too fearful to contemplate.   My strict
orders to our people are that whilst they keep their
eyes and ears open, not a shot is to be fired till there
are unmistakable signs of an enemy.   Things are in
such a state of tension that the striking of a lucifer
match might set all in commotion.

Monday, February 4.   At 1.30 a.m. I was knocked
up.   A company of thirty " blue-jackets " under three
officers, kindly sent by Captain Blaxland, had come
over, and were making their dispositions for our protection in case of attack.   We were all up with them
the rest of the night, till 5.30 a.m.   Happily all passed
off quietly, and we thanked God for the light of another
day.

At 11 a.m. called with Taylor and Dr. Pruen on the
Wali.   He quite outdid himself in extravagant compliments.   "Your feet carry a blessing with them; wherever they come there is stability," and so on, *ad
nauseam*.   I asked him if the people of Mombasa had
any cause of complaint against us, and he said : " No,
nothing, but there is much ' fitina ' (plotting) in the
town ".   At 9 p.m. a man was brought to me with the
news that early to-morrow morning we are to be
attacked by some people of Mombasa from the Makupa

side of the island. I have told Captain Blaxland that if he hears two guns fired he is to take it as a signal for help. Instead of the usual Bible reading to-night we had a meeting for Thanksgiving and Prayer; only a few present; most were too tired with last night's watching.

Tuesday, February 5. I slept peacefully, but I heard that all night the Settlement was in a state of alarm. A number of Mbaruk's armed roughs were seen passing through a " shamba" near our place.

At 7 a.m. the "H. W." came in, bringing a good big Mail, which had come by French Steamer to Zanzibar —an unexpected treat in the midst of our troubles! Some time after I had gone to bed, Taylor, who was sleeping in the verandah, shouted "Bwana, Bwana," and opening my eyes I was startled by a tremendous glare, night turned into day. It was consoling to find it was nothing more alarming than a man-of-war coming into harbour, and casting her electric light over Mombasa and Frere Town in every direction. It was a grand sight, and must greatly have astonished the natives! I hope too it may have a good moral effect.

Thursday, February 7. Chaga Mail in. Fitch and Wray both object to retire from their Stations. I cannot blame them, but they must take the responsibility, which I would myself do if I were in their place.

Wrote to Rev. A. G. Smith, Mbungu.

" Your two notes of the 4th and 5th to hand. They bring rather gloomy tidings. The water difficulty is a

serious matter. Dr. Pruen agrees with me that you
and Morris should at once fall back on Rabai till rain
falls ; it may be only a matter of a few weeks. Meanwhile you can leave two trustworthy men in charge,
with promise of extra pay if they look well after
Mission property. This, I have no doubt, is the best
thing for you to do.

"I am sorry to hear of Mr. Kendrick's breakdown,
and of the cruel desertion of his porters, though as regards this we have to hear the other side. If he was
so bad, it seems even more strange that his own countrymen should have left him in the lurch. The conduct
of 'wazungu' to one another does not set a very good
example to the natives."

To Mr. Burness, Rabai.

"I am coming to-morrow with Captain Blaxland
and a party from the 'Griffon'; but they will be *my*
guests. I shall make all food arrangements, only shall
be glad if you will get me a sheep, or even a tender
goat or a kid, and a good supply of water and milk for
the day ; for all of which I will, of course, pay.

"We can put up in the iron house, and if Miss
Scott has gone to her 'watch-tower' we shall put
nobody to inconvenience.

"Please send off things to Mbungu without delay,
not forgetting the 'dandy' for Mr. Kendrick.

"I hope you will join us at our mid-day meal, which
will answer for dinner. Sorry I cannot ask the ladies
for want of accommodation ; and our visitors will pro-

bably not be in a fit state for female eyes to look upon after the hot walk up. I hope to stay over Sunday."

Friday, February 8. Had made all arrangements for an early start to Rabai this morning, but about 1 a.m. one of the officers of the " Griffon " woke me up to give me the sad news that a sailor had fallen overboard and was drowned ; so we must put off our trip. At 7 a.m. went on board and arranged for the funeral.

The " Woodcock " arrived, bringing a long " official " from the Consul General addressed to our Missionaries at Mamboia and Mpwapwa, telling them of the danger they are in, and of the steps he is taking to secure their safe retreat to the coast.

Buried the poor drowned man in our little cemetery at 5 p.m.

Sunday, February 10. Commenced an English Service at 10 a.m., of which I had sent notice to the " Griffon " and to the Company's English staff in Mombasa. Captain Blaxland, his officers, and fifty men, also Mr. Mackenzie and two of his staff, came. We are very short of Hymn Books, and the temporary Church is in a wretched state.

Mackenzie wants to go to Zanzibar on urgent business, and asks for the " H. W."

In the evening Lieutenants Tippyng and Palmer joined us at our singing party.

Monday, February 11. Robson and Ward in bed with fever—Pruen and Taylor also suffering.

The " Penguin " came in, made a few signals which I could not read, and steamed away again South. We ought to have a Code and Flags.

Tuesday, February 12.   Robson and Ward very bad to-day.   They are living together in the same house, and I strongly suspect their fever is owing to inattention to sanitary laws, to bad water, and unwholesome food !

The illness of Ward throws heavy work upon me in connexion with the Mails.

Wednesday, February 13.   The Mail Steamer not in from Zanzibar, but the " Boadicea " and several other ships are here awaiting her arrival.

Mackenzie has been trying to find out all about the Mombasa plotting.   He says he heard of nothing against the Mission—it was all against him and the Company. This is an important item.

Thursday, February 14.   The " Java " arrives from Zanzibar.   Has orders to wait here for the " Baghdad," bringing the English Mail—expected to-morrow.   The news of our late scare comes back to us from Zanzibar, with all kinds of exaggerations.

I give below extracts from letters posted by this Mail, which will fill up any gaps in my narrative of the events of the last month :—

" To the Rev. R. Lang,—

     " You would appear to have had nothing later from me than December 2.   I was then expecting to leave on January 2.   Since then many important events have happened—some of them very seriously affecting our Mission and our Missionary brethren.   It is a comfort to know that much earnest prayer is being put up on our behalf, which prayer has been, and is being, signally answered.   The clouds have been very threatening at times, and I feel sure we owe our immunity from calamity much more to those prayers than to H.M. gunboats, although it is only right and proper they should afford us such protection as they can, especially as the present situation is none of our seeking.

"At Col. Euan Smith's request I forward a copy of his letter addressed to the Missionaries at Mamboia and Mpwapwa. It lays on them a grave responsibility, but if I were in their place I think I should hold on at all risks rather than trust myself to the tender mercies of Nasr bin Sulieman, or any other Arab. May the Lord direct them!

"I sent up porters to convey Fitch and Wray to the coast. I could do no other, in view of the Consul General's mandate. They both refuse to come, and I do not blame them. At best it is only a choice of risks.

"As the Committee have already paid £1200* towards the ransom of the runaways, I need say no more about it. I feel strongly they ought not to have been asked to do so.

"I am rather anxiously looking for your answer to mine of December 19; which referred to some important matters. I hope the Committee will not fail to see how remarkably God is leading us in regard to our line of operations. What a splendid sphere for your new Bishop, if he be a man of organizing power, and can take in the situation!

*It is a satisfaction to me to learn that this sum was not paid out of the Funds of the C.M.S., but by Sir T. Fowell Buxton and other friends.

"Mr. Mackenzie has asked for the 'H.W.' for a special trip to Zanzibar, and I have consented. It is on very urgent business! He has discovered, or thinks he has, the prime mover in all the seditious plottings in Mombasa—a leading Arab of position and influence in Zanzibar—and he wants to lay his information before the authorities, and nip the conspiracy in the bud. I think you will approve of my action. The Company will of course supply coal and defray working expenses.

"You asked for an estimate of the cost of the Freed Slaves. In the case of able-bodied *adults*, they are clothed—fed for a few days—and helped in building huts for themselves, the average cost being about £2 per head. Children come to us of all ages—from infants in arms to twelve or thirteen years. It would be difficult to arrive at a correct estimate; but it would not be far out to reckon them as on the Mission for support on an average for four years, and each child in the Dormitory costs about £4 per year—say for four years, £16. But the children constitute the most hopeful branch of our Mission. It is from them, if properly taught and trained, that, under God's blessing, we are to look for a supply of Teachers and Evangelists, to carry on the great work which is opening up to us. Other Societies, not nearly so well off as ours, are quite ready to receive any number of children, whilst they fight shy of adults—they are *wise* in their generation. Hitherto *we* have taken all sent to us—old and young —and in this respect we, I venture to think, are *wiser*; for who shall say ' whether shall prosper this or that, etc.' As far as one can see the blockade is not likely to bring us more, but fewer than formerly. The Arabs have discovered that under the French flag they can carry on their abominable traffic to their heart's content, with impunity; and French bunting is in great demand.

"I am sorry to say Messrs. Robson and Ward are both ill in bed with fever. Miss Holmes and Mr. Smith are better. The weather is still very oppressive and trying to all, especially new comers. Water is very scarce inland. At Rabai it has to be fetched three or four miles! We are better off here, but *our* supply too is getting low."

To my Wife.

"I must put you off with a short scrap, I am winding up. Your two letters of 4th and 11th January came on by French Steamer and reached me on the 5th inst., and I thank God for all the good news they contain. It is close on twelve months since, on that cold dreary morning, I left you ill in bed, and set out on my lonely way to E. A., and how graciously the Lord has dealt with us since then! It seems, indeed, a long, long time ago; but then three years have been crammed into one, though that would make me 65 instead of 63, or 73 as Mr. Gedge worked it out.

"My intention still is, if the Lord will, to leave on 2nd April, which should bring me to Dover about 26th April. It is just possible that a Bishop may be coming by the Mail next week, in which case I might get away earlier; but, if so, I shall probably accept John Roberts' invitation, and spend a week or two in the Holy Land;

and should still not reach England earlier than April 26. I would fain escape some of the coldest of the cold season.

"I do not anticipate any further Telegrams. The Bishop of Norwich would scarcely agree to any renewal of leave ; and, unless under very pressing circumstances, I should not feel justified in prolonging my stay : although the worst of the hot season will be over, and as time goes on, the work becomes more intensely interesting.

"You will learn from my letter to W. that things are not very comfortable with us as yet. It reminds me of our condition in India, during the Mutiny—now (who would think it?) 32 years ago. East Africa is in the pains of travail ; and what the issue is to be, God only knows."

To my dear old friend, the Rev. Ruttonji Nowroji of
Aurungabad.

"FRERE TOWN, *February* 14, 1889.

"MY DEAR RUTTON,—

"I was glad to receive your kind loving letter of May 16, 1888. At that time I was expecting to be on my way back in August, and so put it by with one or two others to answer from Aden. Then, as perhaps you know, came a request that I would stay on another six months ; to which I could not say ' No '. Before that term had expired, and when I had begun to pack up, came another Telegram, telling me that my Bishop consented to give me another four months' leave of absence from my Parish, and asking me to stay on for that time. I was getting weary of my lonely, homeless life, but again, under the circumstances, how could I refuse? At such a critical time, it would have been most difficult for any stranger, however wise and experienced, to take the helm. There were rocks and shoals on all sides, and, of course, it was easier for me than for any new man to steer a safe course.

"The past twelve months has, as you may suppose, been a very trying time, and you may be sure it has added not a few grey hairs to my head and beard. Sometimes, for days and nights, we were exposed to the danger of an attack. The will of the Arabs and Suahelis was good, but 'the Lord was our Shield and Defence'; and, although, as I write, fresh rumours come to us of their wicked designs, our hope is that He will still deliver us. These troubles are owing to the advent of the new Company. The Arabs are naturally incensed at seeing the country passing out of their hands, and under the Rule of a Foreign Power; and it is not surprising if they lay much of the blame at our door, seeing that we were first in the field. Then, too, negotiations with the Company itself have brought me a good deal of anxious work and correspondence.

"I am getting rather tired and home-sick, and beginning to count the days till April 3, when, if it please God, I shall be setting out once more for old England. I have to praise God, for the wonderful amount of health and energy which He has given me— I have scarcely been laid aside a day from active work.

" Many thanks for all your news. What changes in the Western India Mission ! Few of the old hands left, and they growing old. I should dearly like to pay you a visit on my way home—though sadness would mingle with pleasure. It is scarcely now possible—we must wait till we meet within ' the golden gates,' as, through God's infinite mercy in Christ Jesus, we hope to do. Oh! what a meeting that will be.

" You tell me nothing of your dear children—give them my love—also loving salams to Lucas—his wife Karuna Bai—my old friend M. W., and to any others who have kind recollections of me.

" Some of the Nasik boys and girls have done badly and suffered, but a good number have turned out well, and have been, and still are, most useful in the Mission. With best love,

" Your ever affectionately,

" W. Salter Price."

CHAPTER XIII.

LAST DAYS IN EAST AFRICA.

Friday, February 15. The "Baghdad" comes with
our English letters. Met Sir John Kirk and daughter
on board. He looks much pulled down, owing probably
to his late accident. They came over to Frere Town
in the afternoon. Made the acquaintance of several
noted men, who have come in the same boat. There is
Dr. Wolff, a German, who is specially commissioned by
Bismark—very observant and intelligent—speaks English fluently—a nice fellow in every way. He
lunched with, and gave us all the latest news. Then
there is Stephens—a Yankeeized Englishman, who has
made the " tower " of the world on a Bi-cycle ! He is
now a Reporter of the " New York World," and has
been sent out to hunt up Stanley. He was eager for
every scrap of information he could pick up, but I
was on my guard. And there were others more or less
famous. What a little world it is ! and how it all seems
to turn up at Mombasa! The Company are meeting with
a great deal of opposition just now, and Mr. Mackenzie
is trying to get to the bottom of it —not an easy matter.

I have a large budget of letters from C. M. S., and on
the whole most satisfactory. The new policy of a line

of Stations, *viâ* Ukambani and the commencement of the new Station of Mbungu is approved. I was just a little doubtful of this, and the result is almost a pleasant surprise.

Saturday, February 16. Went on board the " Baghdad " and had a long talk with Sir John. He explained to me the principle on which he formerly dealt with the Giriama slaves at Rabai, " as the country was Pagan, and we had no treaty with its Chiefs, I considered we had no right of interference between so-called owners and their slaves ".

Yesterday we had in the harbour the " Boadicea " and four other ships—to-day all have departed, and not one English vessel is to be seen—this at such a time seems scarcely prudent. Smith and Morris have fallen back on Rabai, both more or less out of sorts—the doctor has gone to look after them.

Sunday, February 17. At the English Service with Holy Communion this morning, a poor attendance— only five English and one Native. Four of our Brethren are ill in bed. Reported that Suliema Kimaynyie has come to Mtwapa—Khamis Kombo's place—with the intention of attacking us or Mackenzie's people.

Monday, February 18. Two of Mackenzie's men taken up by our " askari," caught in the act of offering " serkali " guns for sale. One, if not both, is a runaway slave. Sent word to Buchanan. At 9 p.m. Dr. Edwards, Morris and Kendrick came from Rabai—the latter so changed I could scarcely recognise him.

Tuesday, February 19. In the night two poor slaves managed to cross over from Mombasa in a canoe, and sought our protection. They are both heavily ironed, and say that the fetters have been on since Ramadhan —seven months! That they have been on a long time is evident from the sores they have made They made their escape four days ago, and have been hiding in the bushes without food waiting for an opportunity to cross. Poor fellows! their ghastly appearance corroborated their piteous story; and the brutes who can treat their fellow-creatures so, richly deserve to be flogged. But what can I do for these poor wretches? If I hand them over to the Wali, he will probably send them back to their stony-hearted mistress, and their latter end will be worse than the first. Ishmael and others say: "Knock off their fetters and set them free," and my own feelings quite fall in with this advice; but I have to consider not simply what I *feel*, or what even in the abstract it would be right to do, but what under the circumstances it is possible to do without coming into collision with the law of the land. I concluded to send a note to Ishmael, simply telling him that the poor fellows must leave our Station at once, and giving them 2 Rs. to keep them going in food for a few days. I shall not enquire too particularly *how* my mandate has been carried out. I hope somebody has had sense and humanity enough to strike off their fetters!

Wednesday, February 20. Mr. Mackenzie returns in the " H. W." He is in high feather at his success. The great man in Zanzibar, who is at the bottom of the mischief in Mombasa has been put in irons, and M. brings a letter from the Sultan to Khamis Kombo and other malcontents warning them that if there is any more trouble, they will be held responsible and have to suffer.

Ehlers and Dr. Abbott arrived from Chaga, and are my guests. The *cuisine* department put to the stretch ; but my visitors not hard to please. After their wild jungle life they are "awfully" glad to get a square meal, with a clean tablecloth, etc.

A Telegram from Salisbury Square telling me to leave Dr. Pruen in charge. A few days after its despatch, the Committee would get one from me, "Send no ladies; country unsettled". I am quite sure *that* was right. This is not the time for ladies to come to East Africa, much as we need them. We are living on the edge of a volcano. The Company have been very cautiously feeling their way, but as yet have made little progress. In spite of their lavish distribution of largesses among Arab and Suaheli Sheiks, and the ransom of the runaways, there is no love for the Company on the part of the Mombasa people. There is a strong hostile faction, and any moment something may occur to drive them into open rebellion. The fires have been banked up with dollars ! but they are still aglow.

Thursday, February 21. Ward has a relapse, and is worse. About 20 feet from the surface in the spot I selected for a well in the girls' new compound we have struck a fine spring of water ; good news for Miss Harvey !

Smith comes from Rabai. He is better, and quite willing to tackle the books and keep things going till Ward is able to resume work. He is a kind, good fellow, and I am very grateful to him.

The Chaplain and four Officers of "Agamemnon" (turret ship) paid me a visit. The big ship was afraid to venture into the harbour. She anchored outside last night, and was sporting her electric light. It reminded one of a grand display of the aurora borealis.

Saturday, February 23. Had a talk with Dr. Edwards about his going to Chaga. He does not like to face the journey at this season, owing to the great scarcity of water on the road. It is a valid objection, and I cannot put pressure on him to go. It is, I confess, disappointing, and upsets one's calculations and plans ; but the Lord knows what is *best.* There is absolutely no hope now of getting to Mamboia by Parker's or any other route, and as little of anyone relieving Fitch, so as to enable him to be here before the end of April.

Sunday, February 24. English Service better attended. Preached from Rom. viii. 28. Called on Ward. Poor fellow ! what a shadow he has become. I fear his work in East Africa is done. Had prayer with him.

Monday, February 25. A letter from Wray. He writes that on the 12th they distinctly heard cannon in the direction of Mombasa, and are anxious to know the cause. It was the "Agamemnon" at firing practice a few miles away. Strange to say *we* scarcely heard anything, whilst the sound travelled 100 miles inland, and 4000 feet above sea level !

Wrote to Mr. Fitch.

" My Dear Fitch,—

" I was glad to get yours of the 7th inst., and

made up my mind to send up Morris and Edwards at once to relieve you, but Morris is unfitted for travel by a bad toe—and Abbott and Ehlers give such a fearful account of the drought on the road that the Dr. even does not like to face it. So I am afraid there is now no prospect of my seeing you here before I leave—which I regret. As regards yourself, I think it is every way desirable you should come here as soon as the way opens, and you can be relieved, and take up your work as Principal of the Divinity Class—the most hopeful work in the Mission in its present stage. Robson has been carrying on in your absence, and he likes it, but the school suffers. May I suggest that it would be well if you could arrange with him to take at least one subject—whatever you and he may agree upon—so as not altogether to sever his connexion with the Class.

" Smith will send up his tent for you, and in your reply to this enclose a list of anything else you may want.

" It is quite possible Mr. Steggall may be here a month hence ; in which case, he, Morris, and perhaps Dr. Edwards would be coming up together. I forgot to ask Ehlers, but suppose there would be no objection to occupying his empty house and keeping down the bats.

" I congratulate you on your escape from a conflagration. Through our Heavenly Father's goodness we are always escaping something or other!

" Many thanks for the two eggs—one got a little cracked, but it is easily mended.

" I sincerely hope nothing will interfere to prevent your being here within two months from now ; and that you will be able to throw all your heart and strength into the Divinity Class, until you take your furlough, by which time it ought to be fairly on its legs.

"I am very sorry not to see you, to say 'kwa-heri,' but if our lives are spared, it will not be long before we meet in a more genial clime, either at 'yours' or 'mine'.

"God bless you, dear Fitch, and give you many tokens of His favour on yourself, and on your work for Christ's sake. I am afraid a trying time is before the East African Mission, but 'The Lord of Hosts is with us'.

"Believe me,

"Ever yours affectionately in 'The Truth,'

"W. SALTER PRICE."

Thursday, February 28. Rabai. Came up yesterday. Very close last night; and as I had no curtains, I had to cover myself with my rug—the remedy as bad as the disease. I had a sleepless night. Wrote and sent off letters to go by French Mail. Heard many interesting particulars from Jones of his journey with the late Bp. Hannington to the Victoria Lake. Amongst other things he told me of the tragic end of my old and faithful servant, Pinto. He took service with the lamented Bishop, waited upon him in his captivity, and shared his master's fate.

Friday, March 1. Held a conference with Herr Hofmann on the Mbungu difficulty, Smith and Morris being present. Hofmann was not authorized to negotiate, he could only state the views of his Society, and his own. I gathered from him that they were intending to take their line through Ulu, Kikuyu, etc. In that case, I urged, whilst a large part of Ukambani would be altogether uncared for, we should be treading on each other's toes all along the line. It is most desirable that now, at the outset, we should come to a proper understanding. H. has been instructed by his Committee to sound us as to whether in return for

MY FAITHFUL PINTO.

their giving up Mbungu and adopting another route, we would be willing to hand over Chaga to them. This, I pointed out would mean an entire change of plan on their part; but, in any case, I felt sure the C. M. S. would not be willing to relinquish their hold on Chaga. It has become, and will become more and more, essential to us, not only as a Missionary centre, but as a depôt at the parting of the ways—the one leading direct to the South end of the Lake, and the other to Kavirondo and the North end—a most important link in the chain connecting our head quarters on the coast, with our Missions in the Lake District. I suggested that for several reasons, it would be to their advantage to adhere to their original design, as *we* understood it from their letters to the C. M. S., *i.e.*, that they take as their sphere of action, the portion of Ukambani bounded by Giriama and Galla-land on the East, and by the Ulu route on the West.

REASONS.

1. This is their most direct route to Kenia from this base, and affords a wide field for Evangelistic work among a large section of the Wa-Kamba, who would otherwise be unvisited for a long time.

2. Whilst there would be no danger of our colliding, the Agents of the two Societies would be sufficiently near to be mutually helpful to one another in case of necessity.

3. It is *the* part of the Country within the English zone, where they are least likely to come in contact with or in any way to be interfered with, by the British E. A. Co.—a not unimportant point in the case of a German Society.

Mr. H. was very reasonable. He quite saw the necessity of our coming to a clear understanding *now*, as to our respective spheres. He expressed his general acquiescence in my proposal, and promised to write to his Society to that effect. I told him we would take over their temporary buildings at Mbungu at such valuation as may be agreed upon between himself and whoever may be here to represent the C. M. S.

GROUP OF WA-NIKA WOMEN.

As far as we here on the spot are concerned, the matter is practically settled.

Saturday, March 2. This afternoon made an expedition with several of the Brethren to Rabai Mpia. In spite of the heat, which was overpowering, we all much enjoyed our visit to this beautifully situated and deeply interesting spot, where Krapf and Rebmann spent their first four years together in a native hut, in the midst of the Wa-Nika—collecting information, learning the

GROUP OF WA-NIKA MEN.

language, preaching the Gospel by their lives, and, as they were able, with their lips, and planning schemes for extending "the kingdom" into regions then unknown. Before the war, six years ago, the place was thickly populated—now most of the cottages are deserted and in ruins, and everything presents a wild and unkempt appearance. Still there are a considerable number of people, and among them we saw many women and children. There ought certainly to be a school here. There is the ruin of one which was built by Mr. Shaw several years ago—it suffered when the people were scattered at the time of war. It should be rebuilt, and might easily be superintended from "Kisulitini". To me this is a sacred spot, and I should like to see some simple yet suitable monument erected, with its legend, proclaiming to this and future generations the historical fact that here in a little mud hut, some 40 years ago, the grand project was conceived in the minds of two young ardent Missionaries of opening up the vast East African Continent to the light of civilization and the blessings of the Gospel of Christ. It is a lesson for all time " not to despise the day of small things ".

Sunday, March 3. Services well attended morning and afternoon. Singing much improved with Miss Scott's playing. The Rabai service, with its orderly and attentive congregation, always refreshing ! Assisted Mr. Jones at Holy Communion — a hundred communicants, including six English. I find I have only three Sundays left, of which I propose spending one at Shimba, one at Frere Town, and one at Rabai. These will be precious opportunities. Now that the parting time draws near I shall be thankful to have it all over.

Monday, March 4. Returned with Smith to Frere Town. Pruen consents to take over charge of secretariat from me *pro tem*. It is the best arrangement I can make, though it is to be regretted no one is on the spot who

DIGGING FOR WATER ON THE MARCH.

would be free to give all his time and thought to the work. I felt half inclined to say I would stay on another month; but it would be just the same, and, except for very weighty reasons, I feel I ought not longer to delay my return.

Tuesday, March 5. A fierce attack of " siafu " in the night in overwhelming force—Taylor driven from his bed. I fought them, not very successfully, with carbolic acid powder!

Wednesday, March 6. To Shimba. Got away at 6 a.m., and, towed by Mackenzie's launch, reached the landing stage at Djimbo in two hours. I had given directions for my donkey to meet me here, but someone has blundered : and, alas ! no donkey awaits me. There is no choice but to trudge it, though a tramp of twelve miles—a good deal of it up-hill, under a cloudless sky— at this season is—well, no joke ! Misfortunes seldom come alone. When I asked my boy to give me some breakfast before starting he forthwith produced a very scraggy chicken, but he had forgotten to bring either bread or salt ! or, likely enough, he thought such luxuries out of place on a journey. Happily I had two or three Captain's biscuits, and I munched one of these, without much relish, just to stave off cravings of hunger. For the first seven miles I got on bravely—now and then our way lying through forest, which afforded a grateful shade. This brought us to Bawa Konde (Wingfield), where we rested for two hours. My men were very thirsty, and as not a drop of water was to be had anywhere on the road, I doled out to them all I had. The next stage was much more difficult, involving—

especially the last three miles—a good deal of stiff climbing; the sun was at its fiercest, and the heat so intense that two or three times I felt like fainting. However, by dint of rather frequent rests, we jogged along, and got to the end of our journey in rather sorry plight about 4 p.m. Dr. and Mrs. Baxter gave me a hospitable welcome, but I am afraid I was not in the mood to appreciate it. Glad and thankful I was indeed to find myself under cover and to stretch myself on Baxter's iron cot. " You are in for a fever," says Dr. B. " Well, I can't say. I hope not ; anyway, kindly give me first a good cold douche on my head." This was done, and oh! how delicious ! " And now," I said, " I have fasted all day, and have an empty stomach, and yet no appetite for food." The Doctor kindly met the difficulty by giving me a teaspoonful or two of liquid meat ; and after a sound sleep of an hour or two I awoke feeling wonderfully refreshed, and not much the worse for the adventure.

Thursday, March 7. Had conversation with Baxter on the condition of things in this Station. As far as I can make out, the scheme has proved a complete failure. About twenty-five freed-slave boys were drafted off from Frere Town to be trained here in agricultural industry. Had there been anyone to train them it might have been a useful experiment, but as a matter of fact, there has been no proper oversight or management—the lads have turned work into play—and strong young fellows who ought to be entirely self-supporting, are being expensively fed on rice and other imported food. This Mission has been a source of much anxiety to me—the more so, that owing to the incessant calls upon me in these troublous times, I have been unable to give to it the time and attention it deserves. The sooner the present state of things comes to an end the better.

On the other hand, I attach great importance to the Shimba Mission, both as a health resort for convalescents, and as a centre for Evangelistic work among the Wa-Digo.

Friday, March 8. Slept soundly under my rug – cold tub delightfully refreshing. Am occupying a small cottage built by a native for himself; of which I gladly avail myself in exchange for the " Palace " (?) at Frere Town.

In company with Beverley and Baxter, made some alterations :—

1. Drafted off twelve of the bigger boys from the Dormitory and placed them on their own support.

2. The smaller boys, eleven in number, to attend school.

3. Settled two special cases of runaway slaves.

4. Arranged with Beverley and Baxter as to their respective positions and duties.

Am delighted to find that in this season of extreme drought, the water has not failed; within an hour's distance there is an abundant supply.

Sunday, March 10. The Services better on the whole than I expected to find, but very poor after Frere Town and Rabai. In the afternoon Baxter gave an address. In the evening the Brethren came over to my place, and we spent a pleasant time, and had our parting prayer together.

Monday, March 11. Started at 5.30 a.m. and got to Frere Town exactly at noon. Hands and face bronzed and blistered! Found Pruen in bed with fever; the other patients convalescent. Had our usual Prayer Meeting to-night—fourteen present—at which Smith gave a nice little address.

Thursday, March 14. Very busy—finishing off packing, etc. The "Turquoise" came in, with the report that yesterday she sighted a B.I. Steamer off Pemba making for Zanzibar. No doubt it is the "Mecca" with all our Home letters and packages on board! Dr. Peters and some of his men are supposed to be in her, and in order to prevent their landing at Lamu or Mombasa, the Captain has been ordered not to touch at either of these Ports. So Dr. Peters is check-mated! and we are deprived of our Mails. Most inconvenient and disappointing, especially to me, as there are probably letters containing final directions to be attended to before I leave, and the time is short.

Saturday, March 16. As there is no sign of our Mails from Zanzibar, though several Steamers have called in, despatched "H. W." at 12·30 p.m. She had an unusual number of Hindi passengers—enough to pay for the trip. Robson went in her for a little change.

Poor KHAMIS BIN SAAD died this afternoon. He has been ailing a long time, and lately went to Barava for change of air—but all of no avail. I grieve to think he has passed away without having found peace through Christ. He had often heard the Gospel, but, as far as one knows, he has died a Mohammedan. It was from him I bought the land on which Frere Town now

stands. He was a kind friend to us in many ways—
on one occasion risking his own life for our protection.
For all this he had to suffer bitter persecution at the
hands of his brother Arabs—they never forgave him!
Am I wrong in hoping that he may at least find a
place among those to whom the Lord will say: "Inas-

KHAMIS BIN SAAD.

much as ye did it unto one of these, the least of my
disciples, ye did it unto ME"?

SIAFU.

For more than a week we have been every night in

a state of siege! After night-fall we have been invaded and attacked by an army of these venomous insects—they come in their myriads! The slaying of 10,000 of them is as nothing – they come and come, and still they come! They find their way into your bed, and you soon become painfully aware of their presence. They have a marvellous instinct which leads them to the most tender and vulnerable parts of your body. If, in desperation, you think to make your escape, you are almost bound to put your foot in it, and as sure as you do, they are over you in a trice—from head to foot— in your hair—in your beard—between your toes, etc.; you are entirely at their mercy, and they give no quarter. Last night I took the precaution of barricading my cot with a wall of carbolic acid powder, which certainly afforded me some protection; but on getting up this morning at 5 for my bath, lo! there was the enemy in full force, straggling about in every direction. What shall I do? How shall I make my way through these beleaguering hosts? Well, pluck up courage— make a dash and jump into your tub! Anyway you are safe for five or ten minutes—you can watch their evolutions with equanimity, and quietly make observations of their manners and customs. Oh! luckless boast! they have followed me into my tub—and in anything but a philosophic frame of mind I pluck them from my body. Doubtless this is one of the plagues which has to be reckoned with. I would almost as soon face a lion as an army of "siafu". Yet this is one of the concomitants of life in East Africa!

Sunday, March 17. My last Sunday at Frere Town.

Had Holy Communion in English. Two of the Company's staff—Mr. Simons and Mr. Cranford joined us. Gave an address to the Native congregation from John x. 27.

Tuesday, March 19. At last! the "H. W" bringing our too long delayed precious Mail. I have a long and important letter from Mr. Lang, which I ought to have received six days ago.

Mr. Buckley returns from Taveta with the shocking news of the death of the Hon. Guy Dawney. The deceased, who was a daring hunter, had been gored to death by a buffalo.

Meeting to-night, at which I gave an address, from Peter's words: "Master, we have toiled all the night, etc."

Wednesday, March 20. *To Rabai*, for my farewell visit.

Friday, March 22. The Dormitory children of Frere Town—to the number of 150 boys and girls—came up to-day. I wanted to give them a grand treat—something they will not soon forget—before I go. They came in four dhows and boats, towed by Mr. Mackenzie's launch, as far as the "banderini"—and thence to Rabai—five miles—on foot. I went out about a mile to meet them. It was a charming sight--the like to which Rabai hills have never seen before—as in single file they threaded their way among the trees, and down the sloping pathway. No wonder the Wa-Nika—men, women, and children—came running from their hamlets to feast their eyes on the unwonted spectacle! On reaching the entrance to the Settlement, Robson formed his boys four abreast, and then marched them to the Church square singing, " Onward, Christian soldiers "—amid many demonstrations of welcome on the part of the Rabai people. Miss Fitch, of course, came up with her girls.

And now comes the serious question—How am I to feed so large a multitude? The children from Frere Town, with their teachers, number 160, and on an occasion like this, the Rabai children cannot be left out. I draw the line at those who attend Sunday School, which adds 120 more—in all 280 ! I have purchased two oxen for £3, and I am afraid both will have to be sacrificed to provide one good meal. Be it so, it is an event in the lives of these young folks, which they will remember to their dying day—an epoch ! I hope this visit to Rabai may, through God's blessing, be a good thing for all. One effect will be, I trust, to draw the two Stations closer together.

Saturday, March 23. At 6 a.m., the Church was well filled for Morning Prayer. The Frere Town contingent were accommodated with front seats, and added a striking feature to this always deeply interesting gathering. There were also eleven English members of the Mission. After Prayers, the children, in groups, perambulated the Settlement—roaming about at will—and thoroughly enjoying their liberty and the novelty of the situation. Meanwhile, the two oxen were cut up, and several huge cauldrons, containing meat, rice, etc., were in full swing, and many busy hands were engaged —some bringing water—some bundles of firewood— some cooking—and some clearing a space in the shade of a monster mango-tree, where the feast was to be held. At 1 p.m. all was ready, and 300 children sat down to a sumptuous feed, such as few of them had ever partaken of in their lives before. Their appetites were in excellent order, and the best part of the two oxen, with rice in proportion, was soon disposed of. After dinner all had liberty to spend the rest of the day as they chose—some were for play—most preferred roaming about over the hills—and some, I'm afraid, were more inclined to aid digestion by a quiet sleep! All passed off merrily, without a hitch, except that Ward was bitten on the hand by a snake, which gave us a little anxiety. There was pain and swelling, but they yielded to treatment, and in a few hours he was apparently none the worse.

Sunday, March 24. *My last Lord's Day at Rabai*—a day not soon to be forgotten. In the midst of many cares and anxieties, my spirit has often found refreshment here, and fresh strength and courage for my task. An hour before time for Service this morning the Church was filled, and many sitting outside—these we brought in and packed as best we could in the aisles. I gave the sermon, Jones being my Aaron; after which we once more gathered round the Lord's Table. In the afternoon I had another opportunity—my last—and said my few parting words from the text: " Gather up the fragments, etc."

Invited all the European Brethren, also Mr. Jones and his wife—17 in all—to supper. We sung some of our favourite Hymns, and after a few last words from myself, to which Burness replied, we had our parting Prayer together !

Monday, March 25.   Left Rabai with the children at 8 a.m.   It was fearfully hot, but we got to the "banderini" all right, and off by about 10.   There were two dhows and three boats—filled as closely as they could pack—towed by the steam launch, again kindly lent by Mr. Mackenzie.   It was a pretty picture as the boats, sometimes in a straight line, and sometimes, through bad steering, in serpentine fashion, wound along the lake-like broads of the charming creek.   Happily the water was smooth, and the sun every now and then hidden behind clouds.   The children kept up a continuous singing of Hymns, and at noon we safely landed our little party on the beach at Frere Town, where warm greetings met us from crowds of people who had assembled to welcome our return.

Tuesday, March 26.   Heavy rain in the night.   It is a great boon, and we are thankful, but it starts into life myriads of insects, which are a torment.   Taylor has hit upon a grand invention—let every one make a note of it : a large wash-hand basin, nearly filled with water, placed near the lamp.   Thousands of insects of every kind—ants, moths, flying-bugs, etc., all dazzled by the light, fall in, and pass away quietly, without noise or smell !

Wednesday, March 27.   Called on the Admiral, who kindly offered me a passage in the flag-ship to Zanzibar ; and also invited me to dinner to-night ; but my hours with my dear friends on shore are fast running out, so I must make the most of them.   Strange to say, Col. and Mrs. Euan Smith are to be my fellow-passengers, and probably Mackenzie from Aden !   It will be "odd" if we three—chiefs in our own departments—should go home together in the same boat—an " undesigned coincidence ! " I can only hope that, in some way, it may be for good. We have had, as might be expected, some diplomatic tussles, but I have great regard for both, highly appreciate the work they have done, and know no reason why we should not continue to be very good friends.

Thursday, March 28. Paid my farewell visit to the Wali. He was as usual lavish of good words. " It was well at such a critical time, that there had been a wise man at the head of the Mission, etc., etc." It would not be fair to take him too literally ; but if there is any honesty and truth in what he says, neither he nor the people of Mombasa have any ground of complaint against us. He had written a letter in Arabic, which he asked me to accept—a testimonial of good character, I suppose ; and no doubt he expects me to return the favour. Certainly I can say that my intercourse with him has always been most cordial, and I have invariably found him courteous and obliging. He made me a present of two silver coffee cup holders—native work of Lamu—and we parted the best of friends.

This evening there was a farewell Meeting, attended by all the European and (English-speaking) Native Brethren. Taylor was appointed to address a few words to me in the name of all. Needless to say they were very kind and to the point, and went to my heart. I replied as best I could ; it is hard to say what one would or ought to say on such an occasion. Still it was a happy gathering, and one that cannot easily be

forgotten.   It takes not a little from the pain of parting
to hear from one and all the expression of the hope—
however unlikely it may be—that they shall soon welcome me back again.

Friday, March 29.   At 2 p.m. the beech presented a
lively scene.   The children were of course there in full
force, under Robson's charge, and there were groups of
men and women—old friends and new—all waiting
to say "kwa heri" to "Bwana Mkubwa," who was
leaving them for the third, and probably last, time.
From all who knew her there were loving messages
for "mama".   One and another expressed their gratitude for what I had been permitted to accomplish
during the past year, and their hope to see me again in
their midst.   I found it very hard to say "good bye" to
all these dear friends—black and white—especially as
there is too much reason to fear that severe trials are
still in store for the East African Mission.   Present or
absent, it will always have a warm place in my heart,
and if by counsel or otherwise I can serve it, I shall
rejoice.

Punctually at 2.30 p.m. the anchor was hauled in ;
and as the last "farewells" were wafted to us from the
shore, the little "Henry Wright" steamed at full speed
out of the lovely harbour of Mombasa.   A little incident
occurred worth mentioning.   As the anchor was being
wound up a boat came alongside, in which was my old
friend, Sudi Mahomed, one of the leading Arabs of
Mombasa.   In the hurry of my departure I had not
found time to pay him a farewell visit ; so having heard
that I was leaving to-day, he had come off in all haste

to say "good bye". He was only just in the nick of time—indeed scarcely that, for whilst he was pouring forth his expressions of kind regard for me, and of his regret at my going away, the screw began to revolve—we were off! The Captain who was at the wheel, had given the order, not being aware that any stranger was on board. I rushed forward at once and requested him to stop and set down my friend. He replied, " I can't do it, sir; he will have to go on to Zanzibar". I was greatly vexed, but could only protest, which I did as vigorously as I could. I don't know how it would have ended, but luckily before getting outside the harbour we came across a canoe, in which we deposited Sudi. I gave the canoe-man a rupee, and had the satisfaction of seeing my Arab friend on his way to the shore.

Three of my colleagues—Taylor, Burness, and Smith—are coming along to see the last of me. We are rather thick on the ground, and the sanitary arrangements on board are very insufficient for so large a party ; bathing quite out of the question, but it is not for long.

Saturday, March 30. Had a fair passage through the night, only Taylor and one or two others being rather upset, and anchored at Zanzibar at 10 a.m. The Flag-ship's light was in view all night, and she got in only half an hour before us. I did not go on shore to call at the Agency till afternoon, when I met as usual with a cordial reception from Colonel and Mrs. Euan Smith. They insisted on my being their guest ; but as I did not like deserting my good friends on the "H. W.," I could only promise to avail myself of their kindness on Monday.

Sunday, March 31. Last night dear Captain Arbuthnot came over in his boat and asked me to give a Service on board the "Mariner" this morning, which I gladly consented to do. Several of the Brethren accompanied me, and a very hearty Service we had. The First Lieutenant, Mr. Stileman, had made excellent arrangements. He appears to be an earnest Christian, and his brother, I hear, has just been accepted by the C.M.S. Most of the Brethren attended afternoon Service in the Cathedral. I felt too tired and was glad of the opportunity of getting a quiet hour to myself on board. What a pity the Cathedral is so badly placed! only to be got at by a depressing walk through noisy bazaars and filthy slums.

Monday, April 1. Removed to my old quarters at the Agency. The place wonderfully improved—an oriental Palace! The Colonel and his good wife will find it hard to leave this beautiful and luxurious home, which they have created, and where they have reigned supreme.

In the afternoon took a carriage, and drove with Smith and Burness to the Universities' Mission Stations of Kinngani and Mbweni. At the former found Miss Bartlett, Archdeacon Jones Bateman and Bishop Smythies. The latter was confined to his room with slight fever. Had a long and interesting talk with him, and was pleased to find we are in full accord on several important matters of Mission policy.

Tuesday, April 2. Mosquitoes in force—drove me from my bed. I took refuge on the roof, in the open, and slept fairly well. Commander Pretyman most kindly sent his galley at eleven to take me and my friends on board the "Agamemnon". He took us all over the big ship, showing and explaining the working of the guns, and the other wonderful machinery. Very interesting and instructive! The French Steamer, "Rio Grande," came in at noon, and I lost no time in boarding her. She is a large ship, but alas! crowded with passengers, so that it was with difficulty I secured a berth—the last in the saloon, just over the screw—the Colonel and Mrs. Euan Smith having the corresponding one on the opposite side. From all I can see, as regards cleanliness and good order, it is an age behind the P. and O.

This morning Captain Weissman came to breakfast. He seems a nice gentlemanly fellow. Speaks English well. Has twice crossed Africa from West to East, and now comes out accredited by the German Government as a Chief Commissioner.

There was a farewell dinner at the Agency—a select party of old friends, who met together under this hospitable roof for the last time.

Wednesday, April 3. Took leave of Zanzibar and all my dear friends there. We had our last Prayer together on the deck of the "H.W.," after which, I went on board the "Rio Grande". Presently the Consul General arrived under a Royal salute from the Sultan's "Glasgow". The German Admiral, General Matthews, Captain Weissman, and others, together with a good number of Hindis, came to see the Consul General off; but I could not help noticing, amongst the latter, a great lack of enthusiasm—the leave-taking was a sombre affair ! It was very different with me and my dear Missionary brethren. They were all on board, and it was, I believe, with mutual feelings of loving regret we pressed each other's hands for the last time, and exchanged our parting adieus !

Admiral Fremantle led the way, in his Flag-ship, out of the harbour, and having drawn aside for us to pass, the ships saluted, and the band struck up the old familiar strains of " Auld Lang Syne " and " Home, Sweet Home ".

So ends another chapter of my Missionary life. Ebenezer ! Praised be God for all His mercies and loving kindnesses ! May He graciously pardon all my unworthiness and shortcomings, and accept and prosper anything said or done according to His will ! May His richest blessings rest on all my dear fellow-labourers, whom I love in the Lord, and on all the Native converts ! And may He grant us a happy re-union—if not before—then in the grand day of " the manifestation of the sons of God," for the Redeemer's sake !

GLOSSARY.

A.

Akida, an officer, second in command.
Askari, a soldier, policeman.

B.

Baba lók, children.
Banderini, a landing place.
Baraza, durbar, council.
Bibi, a lady.
Bas, enough.
Bwana, master.
Bwana mkubwa, great master, chief.

C.

Chakula, food.

D.

Dhobi, a washerman.
Dhow, a native vessel.

F.

Fitina, plotting.
Fundi, a workman, teacher.
Furaha, joy.

H.

Haya-haya, come along! quick!

J.

Jembe, a hoe.

K.

Khabari, news.
Kitanda, a native cot.
Kwa heri, good bye.

M.

Mdafu, an immature cocoa-nut, the juice of which (*dafu*) forms a
     cooling and delicious drink.
Mganga, a doctor.
Mtoro, a runaway slave ; pl. *watoro.*
Mtoto, a child ; pl. *watoto.*
Mwalimu, a teacher.
Mzungu, a European ; pl. *wazungu.*

N.

Nimechoka, I am tired.

P.

Pagazi, a porter : pl. *wapagazi.*
Pojo, a kind of bean.
Pole-pole, slowly, slowly.
Posho, rations.
Punda, a donkey.

S.

Safari, a journey, caravan.
Serkali, the government.
Shamba, a garden, field.
Shauri, a consultation.
Siafu, a reddish brown ant.

T.

Tembo, palm wine.
Topes, groves.

W.

Wa-Daitch, the Germans.
Wa-shensi, uncivilized.
Wazee, elders.

Y.

Yambo, the common salutation, " Hope you are well".

Z.

Zoli, a kind of litter.

TWO HINTS.

1. *Pronunciation.* In the case of Proper names of more than one syllable, it will be a safe rule to place the accent on the last syllable but one as—

    Lámu, Ugánda, Mombása, Tanganyíka, Kisulútini.

The exceptions are very few.

2. The reader will do well to note the force of the *Prefixes* U-, M-, Wa- and Ki-, when applied to Proper names. It is as follows :

U signifies a country, as, *U-ganda, U-nika.*
M   ,,   one individual of that country, as, *M-ganda, M-nika.*
Wa   ,,   two or more individuals, as, *Wa-ganda, Wa-nika.*
Ki   ,,   anything belonging to that country, especially the
           language, as, *Ki-ganda, Ki-nika.*

LONDON: WILLIAM HUNT AND COMPANY,

12 PATERNOSTER ROW.